What the Scarecrow Said

What the Scarecrow Said

A NOVEL

Stewart David Ikeda

ReganBooks
An Imprint of HarperCollins*Publishers*

Grateful acknowledgment is made for the use of an excerpt from "Imagined Life," by Maxine Hong Kingston, which appeared in *Speaking of Writing: Selected Hopwood Lectures,* Nicholas Delbanco, editor. Copyright © 1990 by the University of Michigan. Used by permission.

HarperCollins books may be purchased for educational, business, or sales promotional use. For information please write: Special Markets Department, HarperCollins Publishers, Inc., 10 East 53rd Street, New York, NY 10022.

FIRST EDITION

Designed by Caitlin Daniels

Library of Congress Cataloging-in-Publication Data

Ikeda, Stewart David, 1966–
What the scarecrow said : a novel / Stewart David Ikeda. — 1st ed.
p. cm.
ISBN 0-06-039164-2
1. World War, 1939–1945—United States—Fiction. 2. Japanese Americans—Massachusetts—Fiction. 3. Japanese American families—Fiction. 4. Friendship—Massachusetts—Fiction. I. Title.
PS3559.I W
813' .54—dc20 96-2244

---

96 97 98 99 00 ❖/HC 10 9 8 7 6 5 4 3 2 1

This book is dedicated to the more than 120,000 Japanese Americans uprooted during World War II, in loving memory of Carol Kazuo Ikeda

Contents/Mokuji

Yes, the imagined life is so exhilarating that householders go in quest of new lands—the Gold Mountain . . . a land of gold-cobbled streets . . . a country with no war and no taxes; it is governed by women. Most of us are here in America today because someone in our families imagined the Gold Mountain vividly enough to come looking for it. I guess most people think they've found it. . . . But we aren't peaceful; taxes are due the day after tomorrow; and women aren't in charge. You see how much work we have ahead of us—we still have that country to find, and we still have its stories to tell.

Maxine Hong Kingston
Hopwood Lecture, University of Michigan
April 1983

Nations, like individuals, make mistakes.
We must be big enough to acknowledge our mistakes
of the past and correct them.

Franklin D. Roosevelt
Public Papers, 1943

Acknowledgments

I wish to gratefully acknowledge the institutional support of the University of Michigan: the Rackham School of Graduate Studies, Minority Affairs Office, Department of English, MFA creative writing workshops, and especially the Avery & Jule Hopwood Awards Committee, who encouraged the embryonic novel with a much-needed Major Fiction Award. At the University of Wisconsin–Madison, my thanks also go to the Asian American Studies and Creative Writing Programs, my students, and Dr. Amy Ling.

I am indebted to Professors Stephen Sumida and Gail Nomura, for their inspiration and guidance, and for sharing their extensive knowledge of Japanese-American history and literature.

My appreciation also goes to the family of Herbert and Madeline Nicholson, Haru Kuromiya, and my new friends at Pasadena's Lincoln Avenue Nursery and Altadena's First Presbyterian Church.

To Hank and Mary Takemura, Ted and Kaz Ikeda, Sue Tong, and Ted Tajima, I offer my loving gratitude for returning with me to the scene of the crime in memory and body.

Thanks go to my grandfather Dr. Charles W. Fox for his vivid war stories, and to my grandmother Sally Fox for the research assistance. Drs. Ahuva and Arie Oren, and my friends from the Radiology Department, have all generously and patiently provided expert guidance in my medical research. Further thanks go to David Mura and Garrett Hongo for their pep talks and their groundbreaking, honest writings; to artist Alfred Duca, of Annisquam, Massachusetts, for being a point of light; to Sarah Zevin for her sharp, hard reading; to Jennifer Gates Hayes, Kristin Kiser, and others I know have supported the novel at ReganBooks but were bustling around too fast to see; to David Rakoff, for the lovely poem translation, *arígato*; and to the extended, ever-supportive Fox and Ikeda clans.

I owe a considerable debt of thanks to Warren Frazier, David Groff, Mitchell Ivers, and Judith Regan for their unflagging faith and professional guidance.

I remain especially and forever grateful for the encouragement, (repeated) readings, criticism, hugs, and beatings of Tasha Oren, Pamela Fox, Frank DeSanto, Charles Baxter, Nicholas Delbanco, and Al Young—all have sustained me above and beyond the calls of love or duty.

Above all, my efforts on this novel cannot begin to express my indebtedness to my grandparents Carol K. and Ruth S. Ikeda.

PROLOGUE

To the City of Angels

William Hiroshi Fujita was born to Japanese immigrant parents on January 2, 1897, on the mainland United States of America. Barely. He might have emerged before the three-thousand-ton American steamer *Pacific Angel,* sailing east from Japan to California, had even passed Hawaii, except for the foresight of his mother, Tamie, née Asakawa. If he were as restless as his mother—and as disdainful of enclosed spaces—he might have tried to jump ship prematurely before they ever left port at Yokohama. But he would rarely be able to leap headfirst into anything: not love, not marriage, not business, and certainly not his first breath. In this, as in so many important life events, his steps were choreographed by his mother—that nineteen-year-old pioneer herself so determined to be Issei, "The First," the original Japanese American.

Aching and nauseous in her cramped berth on that New Year's Eve voyage, when her water finally broke, Tamie demanded that her husband, Ichiro, get hold of himself long enough to bind her legs together. Although the fetus was what she called "overripe" at almost ten months, she felt confident he would bide the time patiently enough.

"I knew all along," she would tell her son, "that you'd be in no hurry. What were you *brooding* about in there?"

But she wanted to be certain; with some twenty-four hours to go before reaching California, she commanded Ichiro to tie her tighter, then tried to will herself into a breathing rock for the duration of her voyage.

"Does this . . . help with your pain?" asked Ichiro, who knew nothing of childbirth or any women's matters, and who would certainly have disapproved of her intentions.

In fact, he would have wished his family to see his child's birth, but the agencies at Yokohama were waging another week-long price war and the fare Ichiro had socked away for his own return trip to Los Angeles would now serve to transport them both. Fearing that the rates might shoot back up, and realizing that further delay would require him to pay out *three* fares, he had finally surrendered to Tamie's insistence that they sail for America as soon as possible.

"Can you hear me?" He shuddered when she did not answer. Placing his scaly hands on her ankles as if handling the stems of crystal goblets, he tugged at the knot and turned away, pale with helplessness and worry.

Ichiro Fujita was a deceptively strong man, his upper body powerful as a bull's above his bandy legs. As a teenager in Tokyo, he had once killed a ruffian twice his size when the drunken man and two smaller friends followed him into an alley and challenged him to a boxing match. Ichiro lost a front tooth but won the fight and sent the other two into fearful retreat. He hadn't been sorry about pounding the life out of the man, but he hadn't meant to do it, either. Ichiro well knew—and took pride in—his hidden strength, but he always touched Tamie as if his mere sneeze could break her in two. Her comfort was important to him, and he could not bear to imagine the agony childbirth might inflict on her fragile frame.

He was himself immune, he often said, to the exhaustion of hard work and to pain, though he was intimately familiar with both. He worked on a fishing wharf in Los Angeles, emptying ships of their smelly cargoes. For six dollars a week he tiptoed among the great nets, discarded the seaweed and sludge, removed the fish to smaller mesh shoulder sacks, and hauled them into a dockside warehouse where the women cleaned them. Ten hours a day of hidden hooks, dorsal spikes, scale armor, and slipping on the slimy deck had ruined his hands, so callous and bloated they seemed less hands than paws.

As Ichiro fumbled with the knots in the stockings he used to bind her, Tamie groaned, "Yes, yes, that is better, that eases my pain," and Ichiro readily believed her. The coming son would prove, like the father, to be uncomfortable, almost formal, with most women. And gullible, too. After these nine months, Ichiro was still fond of his new wife, but the woman his uncle had arranged for him to marry was bright, vibrant, educated, and therefore bore some watching. Tamie ranked as the top graduate of Nippon Joshidai, the women's university in Tokyo—an achievement conspicuous enough that for her graduation the mayor of the city bestowed upon her the gift of a not-inexpensive wall hanging from his own home.

At Tamie's request, that scroll hung now over the cabin's only porthole. In its foreground, three fat men in scarlet robes squatted over a chart marked with colored spots; whether they were planning a building, devising a military strategy, or playing at some game of chance, the artist left unclear. To either side and behind the sturdy gray lean-to above them rose a wall of spiky orange-brown splashes like flames—wind-tossed rows of grain. Above this to the right unfurled two narrow tree branches, misty with white flowers, showering blue-black seeds upon the roof. Far into the horizon beyond these loomed an ash-colored mountain, silhouetted against the crimson and purple streamers of approaching dawn or falling dusk, encircled by a halo of clouds and a train of wheeling herons.

Tamie did not know the artist; she supposed that his unusual, somewhat European style made him unpopular. In Japan, paintings so shadowy, so busy and hectic, so determinedly off-balance were uncommon. Ichiro said the artist painted with no control, painted like diarrhea. It made his head hurt, he could focus on nothing; he suggested that the Tokyo mayor pawned it off on her because he knew it was an inferior work.

In the throes of her labor, it comforted Tamie to focus as

always on one particular spot, a minute figure visible only after studying the work up close. A bell-shaped shadow, capped by a round dot, sat atop the mountain crest—a ceremonial bell, or a temple, perhaps a disproportionately large person sitting cross-legged. Since she had first discovered the nearly invisible detail, her glance flew to it whenever she passed the artwork.

"That's a mountain of gold," she told Ichiro once, just before they had been married. "That's where I want to go."

"But it's *gray*," Ichiro had corrected her.

But this is not what she meant. In Tokyo, a missionary's wife once told her that "Gold Mountain" was, in the language of Chinese emigrants, synonymous with America.

"How stupid the Chinese are!" Ichiro had grumbled. And from that moment on, he knew he must watch his new wife carefully.

And now, staring into this hopeful vision, its landscape rocked by the earthquake of her contractions and the ocean tides, Tamie whispered, "We are going to the mountain of gold."

"There is no mountain of gold," Ichiro replied, not wishing to upset her but irritated. He knew; he had lived in Los Angeles. In that city, he had learned, there was only a mountain of fish to be unloaded.

"And that is my son sitting up there on top of the mountain."

"No," Ichiro said. "That is a mistake. That is the work of a sloppy artist."

Yet the image eased Tamie in her delirium. *That is where we are going.* She mouthed the voiceless words to her quavering belly. *We are going to the gold mountain!*

So, even if William would have preferred to be a son of Japan, Tamie intended, on her peril, for her child to be born on the U.S. mainland—a Nisei, The Second. She could easily have delivered in Hawaii, but despite earnest American agitation, the island chain was yet a year or so away from annexation. At university Tamie had heard about and studied the situation. For all she knew, Hawaii could have been taken as a territory during their voyage; so it appeared, passing Oahu and the new naval base at Pearl Harbor, where the view beyond the scroll was spotted with American flags. Nonetheless, it was surely better to be born in a state than a territory. The distance of extra travel was short compared with the distance already behind her.

Ichiro would have balked, had he understood her intention. Although he had already lived and worked in California for three and a half years, he did not expect to remain there forever. His trip back to Japan to collect his bride—arranged through a series of photographs and letters from his uncle—had convinced him. Family and old friends had been enraptured by his clothing, and the relative fortune and exotic stories he brought home with him. Oh, they thought, he had it made.

As with so many young male immigrants—of all nationalities—Ichiro had been pushed and pulled toward America by financial considerations and more than a bit of wanderlust. At that time, the still-minute Japanese population in Los Angeles enjoyed some popularity, not because that city had any particular fondness for Japanese nationals, but because Ichiro's countrymen provided cheap labor preferable to the generally disliked Chinese. Nonetheless, Ichiro counted himself among those men known to U.S. immigration officials as "birds of passage," young adventure seekers and fortune hunters who had no intention of staying.

That he was prohibited from becoming an American posed no problem for Ichiro. That the City of Angels should segregate yellows from whites in its daily affairs seemed only natural to him: A tourist must not expect to impose himself on the lives of the natives. That coloreds had only limited access to recreational areas, for example, affected him as no more than a petty annoyance—his hard work allowed little enough time for soft diversions. That he could not, by law, love or wed a *hakujin* woman only codified the laws of common sense. Ichiro had his adventure and found his temporary country as hospitable as could reasonably be expected. Still, Ichiro had assured his family, he looked forward to enjoying a leisurely, civilized, Japanese life when he'd finished in California. America was no place to be an old man. To slave and drink and slave and drink through ten-hour days took a hard toll on the body and spirit. This was, he concluded, a young man's pursuit.

Like most of the wharf crew, Ichiro was an immoderate after-work drinker, and at the dock's bar he often challenged coworkers to test his hardiness. For the price of a drink, all comers were invited to throw him their best, punching him squarely in the chest. To elicit a grunt—or better, to knock down Ichiro Fujita—was a feat always talked up the next day around the wharf. Most often, the tit-for-tat contest ended with Ichiro slamming the wind out of his opponent. He would call to the barkeep to mix up "the usual," reach over the prone and breathless man, slip the wallet from a back pocket, and extract from its folds the cost of the powerful concoction known locally as the Ichi-Bomb.

As a matter of principle, Ichiro never drank anything that was drinkable (except sake, which was expensive and not easy to come by). He wanted to invent a drink so terrible—a brew to be named after him, like a Tom Collins or Rob Roy—that only the manliest of men could stomach it. Perhaps the foul cigars he smoked had deadened his taste buds—as the calluses of his bear-paw hands deadened his touch, as his ever-present cologne of fishiness deadened his sense of smell. For he daily adjusted the Ichi-Bomb's proportions to increase its potency. At base, the drink consisted of rye, vodka, a syrupy cherry liqueur, peppermint schnapps, and a shot of beer for the lightest carbonated tingle. In consolation to the fellow he just pounded, Ichiro sometimes sprang for an extra glass (with the defeated man's money), claiming the Ichi-Bomb could restore breath to a corpse.

Yet there were two things that could unman the Little Bull. First, despite his vocation, Ichiro was no seaman; he was a poor swimmer, and all his fortitude melted away when he actually sailed. The second, more fearful thing was women—their minds, their fragile bodies, their genitalia in particular—and his wife most of all. Ichiro had visited—and would continue to visit his whole short life—many paid women, but these were less daunting, for Ichiro was comforted by the professional detachment of these encounters. Often the kind of woman who would lower herself to sleep with him for payment was also, like him, no stranger to dank smells, strong drink, and the facts of brute strength.

The discovery that Tamie shared the same qualities, equipment, and appetites as those women unsettled the newlywed Ichiro. To his vague but powerful sensibilities regarding women, no connection could be made between a wife and a lover. Visiting a paid woman was like admiring a ferocious animal at the zoo, one he never dreamed could appear in his home. Pregnancy, menstruation, soapy clots of hair in the bathtub—these would forever lay ruin to the otherwise invulnerable stomach of the Ichi-Bomb's inventor.

For twenty-four hours Ichiro wiped the perspiration from Tamie's forehead. Wet and pale, she gasped and heaved like a fish. A nauseating panic arose in him. He thought to call someone, perhaps the ship's doctor, but Tamie carried no passport, and Ichiro did not trust the American officials. A ship's officer had assured him before embarking that paying the fare would preclude the need for a passport; even the U.S. Customs man who had boarded briefly that morning asked only to examine his luggage. Still, Ichiro was not stupid; he opted for caution and patience.

Tamie's tremors grew increasingly violent until Ichiro became quite frightened. As the ship's steam whistle sounded, he ran to the window to shove aside the Tokyo mayor's wall hanging and saw the gray wharf buildings approaching. The docks sparkled with strewn confetti and streamers and empties from the New Year's celebrations. Announcing their arrival, he turned to see Tamie tearing weakly at her bonds.

He ran to his wife and fumbled with the knots, cursing his clumsiness. She gripped his hair and pulled him to his knees so he began tearing at the bindings with his teeth. First her ankles popped apart, then her knees, then her thighs. He ran to the door and called for the captain, a doctor, anybody. Now, as the ship slipped into its berth, the crew was busy preparing the gangplank and the decks began to fill with celebrating passengers.

Little William's spectacular birth—dry and bloody—was assisted only by the most unlikely and unprepared of midwives. Squatting between her knees like a baseball catcher, Ichiro stared at the opening. It seemed to gasp, breathe, and finally gape, like a tear in her young downy skin, like the angry cleft of a peach. The ship pounded against the wood and steel walls of the dock.

On the deck above them, someone ignited a cluster of firecrackers and the passengers erupted into cheering. William wrenched Tamie with the severity of quintuplets as she squeezed him out into his swooning father's rough palms. Catching hold of the slippery child, Ichiro gasped against an upsurge of bile, swallowing at the air like a man drowning. Fearing that nausea would overwhelm him, he could not force open his tight-sealed lips to call out when the purser knocked at the door. Tamie cried out, however, and the purser burst in to see her howling, her body arched back taut like a bowed saw blade, and to see Ichiro crouched below her, drenched purplish brown down to the elbows, his cheeks puffed out like a chipmunk's.

The purser gagged in horror, mistaking the miracle of life beginning for the atrocity of a brutal, cannibalistic murder. The mountainous young man's terror propelled him across the cabin, where he noticed the squirming infant only as he smashed the father's face with a fist as bricklike as Ichiro's own. The first connection was adequate to break Ichiro's left jaw, but he managed to pull his second punch as the new father toppled backward, his body reflexively curling around his child.

A boy? Ichiro thought as his head pounded into the floorboards. In the panic and swirl of the moment, his last conscious sensation was one of awe. The round yellowish mass, squirming, draped in the fuzzlike vernix—he had a vision of the legendary Momotaro, the warrior boy miraculously born of a huge peach, fulfillment of his parents' dreams, savior of his people.

"Please," Ichiro prayed, drowning into black, "be a boy."

When he came to some time later, the purser stood hovering above him, just as Ichiro himself had to the many dockworkers he'd vanquished.

"Stay there," the man ordered, though Ichiro had no intentions of trying to rise yet. Another man had joined them and stood hunched over Tamie, grumbling, gingerly removing from between her legs what looked to Ichiro like a blood-soaked, deflated party balloon. A shrill whine sounded. Ichiro tried to speak, but his jaw allowed for only a clipped, unintelligible moan.

The purser frowned, then asked loudly, "Speakie no English?" Tamie groaned.

Bakatare! Ichiro wanted to say, but he could only blink at the idiotic purser.

"Jesus H. Christ, Ed, keep it down!" the other man hissed without turning from his patient. "He's Japanese, not *deaf*, you fool!" He wrapped a small bag of ice in a towel, laid it across Tamie's abdomen, whispered, "You'll be just fine, ma'am," and then stepped across the cabin with his doctor's bag to examine her husband, placing a hand on the jaw. "It's broke, all right."

Ichiro glared up at the purser, who, although averting his eyes as if shamed, seemed impressed with himself. "Wit hab ta be da face?" Ichiro tried. "I tink wu hoe me a trink."

"Yeah, Japanese," the purser said, nodding.

"Don't try to talk," the doctor warned Ichiro, leaning close to add, "Papa."

Ichiro sighed and remained quiet as the doctor began to wrap his jaw closed with gauze. Before he could tie the knot, however, Ichiro pulled the doctor to him and tried a last time: "Pweenish?"

"Yes, you saw it." The doctor chuckled. "It's a boy."

This was the story Billy Fujita heard his whole young life—the only version his parents would admit to—usually wielded against him whenever Ichiro complained of the boy's complacency, sensitivity, or thoughtfulness—his *boring*ness. "It's not my fault," Ichiro would say. "I started you out right—with a bang bang bang!" And always the story ended in the same thrilling way: with the celebrations and firecrackers sounding above for the bawling new Fujita below. "And that," his father would conclude, beaming, "is the story of how we had you." But Billy, the Nisei, the American, always giggled to his mother, because he knew how his Pop was had, too.

ONE

Mischief Night, 1944

The statue of the Union soldier pointed a thick finger up the hill called Widow's Peak, his head slightly skyward and back—yearning, sniffing for traces of the eastern sea breeze spilling over the cliffs of Cape Ann, but forever facing the wrong way. It seemed the green-rusted soldier, like many in his hometown of Juggeston, dreamed of a life along the more affluent coast a few miles behind him—in Annisquam and Rockport, buzzing places where rugged fishing skiffs berthed, where a band shell stood in the town's center, where sophisticates from Boston and New York en route to the Canadian provinces docked their yachts. At Cape Ann, a jetty wrought of discarded slabs from a century's quarrying thrust so far into the Atlantic some claimed it was the easternmost point in America—farther even than the curly, pig-tailed tip of Cape Cod. Cape Ann's proximity to England, its so-called New British accents and old British blood, were widely coveted by many of its Anglophiliac inland neighbors. The war, on which the soldier boy had turned his back, was fought in those waters.

Those salty towns, however, set on the cold granite skirt of the Atlantic, were not for farmers like the Juggestonians; the rivulets and arteries trickling in from the ocean were too briny, too rocky. Founded as a haven for martyred Quakers back when their presence in colonial Boston was punishable by disfigurement or death, Juggeston remained in many ways a Friends' town and liked to think of itself as the Heart of the North Shore.

The model for the Civil War soldier was a local boy of old Juggeston stock. His outstretched arm, muscular from chopping, digging and hoeing, pointed toward Widow's Peak, which rose like a crown from the surrounding valley carpeted with family farms. From anywhere in the valley, townspeople could make out the shadowy cross formed by the newly erected scarecrow on Margaret Kelly's land up top, which Juggeston liked to consider the heart of the Heart. Dressed now as a physician, now as a debutante, that singular straw woman had recently surprised a few of the locals, climbing up the Peak for civil patrol duty. It was on Nurse Kelly's lofty property that they sat in folding chairs, huddled around tin coffee cups, scanning the sky for Axis planes and regarding the watchtower on Cape Ann's Halibut Point, where their neighbors sat vigilant for U-boats.

On the evening the widow Margaret Kelly herself descended from the Peak on her secret errand, old Harrold Doe and Pete Pedicott sat down by the Union soldier's feet considering the scarecrow she had so freshly set out. After a day in the field or market, townsfolk often congregated on the public benches there to smoke, laze, speculate, and dream. Hours ran long in Juggeston, and people relied on their imaginations to keep things lively, swapping variations on unoriginal stories. Something more than small talk, their gossip usually began, "It's none of my business, but . . ."

"Not that it's my business," old Harrold Doe muttered, "but a woman scarecrow? Isn't that sort of irregular, Pete?"

"No," Pete yawned, shifting on the hard bench. A stork-necked, flush-faced man, the farmer Pedicott was father of four hyperactive children, soon to be five, and his body was all tired angles and knobs and bends, like a well-worn tree house. "But a woman *doctor* scarecrow—that's a new one to me. Well," he sighed, shaking his head, "that's Margaret Kelly all over."

Like the rest of Juggeston, they were tickled, baffled, and mostly concerned when they first awoke one morning last August, 1944, to view the straw woman. Had they been fighting men or war brides, they might have imagined they witnessed a reunion—the scarecrow a grass widow on her elevated walk, awaiting her soldier's safe return to the homestead. But to Doe and Pedicott, farmer and bureaucrat, it looked like a changing of the guard. Though a scarecrow was a more fitting guardian for an agricultural town, changes worried them. Like the silhouettes of Axis planes they so dreaded seeing in the night sky, changes seemed to hover above them, invisible, everywhere.

Lil Wellington appeared to sense it, too. Stepping up from behind the men, out on break from Wellington's general store just as the sun set on Mischief Night, she glared severely westward and sniffed, as if she already intuited trouble brewing on the Peak. "Good evening, boys," she said, nodding, driving her long, thin rump like a wedge between them and drawing a cigarette from her apron. Harrold and Pete looked shyly down to their shoes, as if Juggeston's fiercest gossip had caught them in some compromising act and mumbled their greetings. Lil Wellington had this effect on Juggeston's men. She grinned.

"How's Paulette's . . . condition, Pete?" she asked.

"She's in the pink, Lil. She's big, but okay. Thanks for asking."

"That's fine, fine," she said, her unlit cigarette bobbing like a demand on her lips. Begging her pardon, Harrold frisked himself for a match and lit her up. "It's not my business, of course," Lil began, wolfing in the smoke, her face narrowed to a painful point. "But I heard the sheriff's office expects Margaret Kelly's Jap to show tonight."

"Oh, that's what you heard?" Harrold shook the match out.

"I heard he's related to the emperor," Lil said. "You know, a sort of bastard, black sheep of the family, but they think he might be manageable."

"That's what they think?" A gray, nervous man, Harrold required much verification.

Lil shrugged. "Well, what they do on Widow's Peak is none of our business."

"For sure it's not," Harrold muttered, startled by the edge in her voice. Still, the tragedy-wracked Peak was *the* topic these days, and he couldn't help asking, "What else did you hear?"

"Hah!" Her laugh emerged in a fist of smoke. Mimicking the soldier-boy statue, she raised a pointed finger to the west as if aiming a throwing dagger. "Why don't you ask her?"

Even before they could discern the lines of the black Dodge slaloming jerkily down Ellsworth Place, they knew the driver. Margaret Kelly always made her entrances known. They cringed as her truck, which had doubled as the town ambulance in less tragic days, screeched to a halt at Childs's Filling Station across the street. The widow engaged in some forced banter with the young Frank Childs for a moment. The second round of gas rationing had been ratified, and everyone was tolerating the moody garage owner's behavior because everyone relied on him to get around. Sighing, he sullenly did Margaret the favor of filling her tank. She rolled her eyes and sat back to wait, straightening her gloves, hat, shoulders. Distractedly, she flipped open a compact mirror, only to immediately snap it shut again. Harrold traded glances with Pete, then cleared his throat and called out, "Looks like you're getting the hang of driving!" He tipped his hat.

"Liar!" Margaret called back, laughing. She pointed to the road. "Really, Harrold. You town-hall types might have those lines painted straight next go-around!"

"What a pleasant surprise to see you down here again!" Lil said, teeth clenched, working her cigarette like a dog chews on rawhide. "And where are you off to this fine Mischief Night?"

"Oh," Margaret said, her musical voice hardening with a tinge of County Kerry Irish. "Just running an errand," she said.

"Errand?" asked Lil.

"Yes, errand." Margaret turned away to face the attendant, who was about to start swabbing the windshield, and blasted him with the horn. "For goodness' sake, Frank!" She thrust her head outside the car. "I told you not to bother with that. Now here." Sheepishly, the fellow accepted the payment and coupon. Margaret tortured the ignition, frowned toward Lil and the men, and lurched away again down Ellsworth Place.

"Bitch," Frank Childs grunted.

"You little worm, Frankie!" Harrold shouted, shaking a fist.

Less than half Harrold's age, Childs only grinned and cracked his knuckles. "Margaret better not try to bring the son of a bitch *here*, I'll tell you that." He returned to the garage office to do, as usual, nothing.

Lil Wellington *tsked* but smiled. "Poor Margaret!" she sighed, subtle enough not to sound overly sincere.

Poor Margaret. Last New Year's Eve, 1943, Juggeston looked up to that solitary hill called only the Peak and renamed it Widow's Peak. Up there, Margaret—with neighbors Livvie Tufteller and her little Garvin—would have been conducting a lonely holiday dinner, poor souls. Up there, they must have set out an extra chair at the table for Sorrow, who had been haunting that unlucky hill since the war broke out. Livvie's husband, Sig Tufteller, had been shipped to Burma, a corporal in the motorcycle corps. He died of malaria just after Christmas. No neighbor would ever wish to pain Livvie and Garvin, but many who knew the abusive, tomcatting Sig figured in their hearts that they—and poor Livvie—had not lost a wholly irreplaceable man. However, their grief over the loss of Jack Kelly, the town's only physician, was profound. After years fighting a losing battle with his deteriorating lungs, he finally fell last October to emphysema-related bacterial pneumonia, as common in Massachusetts as malaria was in Burma. Also the town's worst patient, Dr. Kelly would have thought his relatively swift end Irish-lucky. "I'll be out of your hair soon enough, Maggie," he'd cough to his nurse wife in those last days, and to his constant company of friends and well-wishers, he'd give a weak grin. "And you'll get the big party you deserve after putting up with me."

No wake was held, though. With only a handful of Irish in the town, and Margaret only half-Irish herself ("the living half," Jack would say), Juggeston buried its shaman in the cemetery behind the meetinghouse in a whisper of a funeral that Margaret declared "would have bored Jack even stiffer." After the funeral, the widow seemed to stop everything: socializing, nursing, attending meeting, *living*. To Juggeston, it had felt like they'd buried their captain at sea and that his widow had dived in right after him. Until a few months ago.

"I browsed through his dossier this summer," said Pete Pedicott, returning to what was on all their minds.

"Hmm?" Lil asked sweetly. "Who's that?"

"Um, the Jap's. The Philly Friends Service Committee sent it up. They had some kind of debate at Town Hall—missed that one, though." With four boys, Pete missed just about everything. "Said he's Californian. Ag-school degree, business minor—like that's going to help them grow anything on that hill. Then at meeting, Margaret said—"

"*Margaret* came to meeting?" asked Lil, smoking, smoking.

"Did she ever! With a vengeance, as they say. This man was in one of those camps for Japs they have out west, you know." Pete paused. "I mean, Japs, sure, but some of them are Americans." Harrold shook his head and Lil shrugged. "So, she marches in with her usual gusto and produces all these articles and letters and things from some West Coast church groups. Went loony, really. She's yelling, 'This is barbaric!' waving the papers over her head. Her voice, well, you know, she's booming like an opera singer, and the meetinghouse is tiny—things echo."

"They sure do, Pete." This time the spite rang clear in her tone, and Pete shut up.

Harrold filled in the pause. "She met him in Boston," he said significantly, as if that explained everything. As if only in a big city like Boston could such complicated gears be set in motion: how a man might be brought from California to Arizona to Chicago to the East, where the Service Committee helped him get into a garden-supply job in Boston's North End, where Nurse Kelly met him. Unlike Pete Pedicott, Harrold missed no public function or any opportunity to get out of Dolly's house. He didn't want to add fuel to Lil's fire, but he had been at both meeting and Town Hall when Margaret pleaded her case that summer. After sitting in silent worship for an hour, the nurse rose and began talking—sort of too philosophically for Harrold—about farming, this community, making things grow. "Grow physically," she had said. "Grow spiritually." As a nurse, she said, her life's work had been an act of preservation, not creation. And now, in wartime, this time of destruction, she decided she would start a farm, too, and hire a Japanese man to work it.

There were a few chuckles, more gasps. Proposals made to the Juggeston Meeting at large required cautious consideration toward the unanimous consensus that Quakers call a "sense of meeting." Margaret always loudly complained that the process, though sound and democratic, was "agonizingly" slow. She had never sought to become a full-fledged member—a Convinced Friend. As all had heard Jack fondly put it, "That's my Maggie; she's a doer, not a thinker. She's got horsepower." Harrold admired Margaret's energy and altruism but wondered about her horse *sense*.

The Kellys were like royalty—it never mattered before if they couldn't grow more than a bit of basil and a few recreational perennials up on that hill. The Tuftellers had tried—so young and poor when they moved there in 1935 that a lousy little plot on the Peak's north face was all they could afford. Strong and willing as they were, the enterprise failed. But Margaret had money, didn't need to work that way; she was, Harrold thought, looking at his own paper-cut, bureaucrat's hands, made for better things.

He'd meant to take her aside after meeting, but then, standing tall and alone above the congregation, she said, "I've found a man . . ." He had experience in cultivation and distribution, she argued, and owned his own nursery out west. Then she had doled out instructions to various members, depending upon their station on the committee, to make arrangements with the War Relocation Authority or whoever for him to move up here before winter. Unfortunately, many listeners never got beyond "I've found a man . . ."

That's what got Harrold and everybody else about "Mrs. Kelly's charity case," as some referred to Fujita. "Not that I know anything about it," he told Pete and Lil, lighting up his own cigarette, "but I have to wonder about the fellow's intentions."

Pete nodded. "She's as attractive a woman as this town's seen." Noticing Lil's scowl, his face boiled even redder. "One of them, anyway."

"And well-off," Lil added. "Let's not forget *well-off*. There are certain wolves out there who might try to take advantage of her." She dropped her cigarette and ground it with her heel into the gravel. "And she is, at this time, particularly vulnerable, after all." She grabbed Harrold's wrist and twisted it to check his watch. "Probably not thinking right at all, I'm sure. Ah, such intrigue!" Heading back into the shop, Lil left the men nodding in dour agreement. Yet they could bet that whatever Lil thought on any subject, Mrs. Kelly would think differently.

Margaret had her way at meeting, of course. A free spirit and a powerful convincer, she had as Jack's nurse seen almost the entire town without their clothes on. The general wisdom about her was that no one could gainsay her when she'd made up her mind; that she read a horrible amount of books and could talk like a lawyer. Some neighbors sneered when she painstakingly erected the scarecrow in anticipation of the Jap's arrival. She stuffed the silhouette of her old wire sewing dummy with straw, fashioned arms and a head with eyes made of broken knobs of real Irish leaded crystal; for clothing, she patched together one of her old dresses—bright green with sparkling fringe and a plunging neckline, twenties-style. A black wig adorned the head, and costume-jewelry earrings; its lips she made of a thick plumbing O-ring, painted a sassy red. She added a pair of cracked spectacles, fastened around the neck by a fillet of aluminum, which caught the sunlight at certain times of day so that one could see them winking even down at Wellington's shop. Wetting the straw, she had molded into the face a high, rounded forehead, cheekbones, and a thin nose. Finally, she hung one of Jack's old stethoscopes about its neck and topped it off with a plumed woman's bonnet. The straw woman had an eerily knowing expression. But the more care Margaret had put into animating that scarecrow, the more some people whispered.

Staring up at it, the farmer Pedicott sighed, "Well, they say Japs have rock gardens and trees a foot high. Good thing, too, because that's *all* you'll ever grow on that hill."

Harrold nodded. Rising heavily to his feet, he cracked his stiff back, *pop, crick*, and checked his watch. "Sheesh. I gotta get home, or Dolly will have my head."

"Me too," Pete said, unbending his branchlike limbs into a stretch, "or the boys are gonna be trouble tonight."

They both turned and glanced one last time up at the scarecrow, distrustfully, as though it were her fault, as though she were some freeloader there, putting bad ideas into good people's heads. It wasn't their business, but they believed it should be *someone's* business. Those grim neighbors didn't know then that angels can sometimes live in scarecrows; that if the inanimate protectors can't walk and talk, they have their own inner light and can know the prayers in your heart and mind; that they see and hear and know more about you than you suspect.

Choking back his terrified sobs before she could detect him, eight-and-one-quarter-year-old Garvin Tufteller watched the witch's reflection in the pocket mirror he used to fry insects. As the last strands of scarlet receded from the evening sky, the old woman made her way past the gate hemming the Kelly property, pausing to wipe her forehead with a palmful of water from the birdbath. The dried twigs and leaves crackled like a fireplace beneath her boots as she trampled what remained of Margaret Kelly's sparse flower garden. Garvin did not dare leave his perch in the elm: Who would disturb the Annisquam Witch on her semiannual, cross-county trek in search of stray children? Every October 30—for more than two hundred years, went the schoolyard rumors—she left her shack just as dusk settled on Mischief Night. Passing under the shadow of the old fort at Cape Ann—a squadron of hungry bats pouring from its crannies, wheeling skyward on their own night hunt—she disappeared down through the thorny bowels of the abandoned quarry, seeking small people to carry home to her husband to mince up for winter fishing bait. Then, exactly six months later on Walpurgisnacht—Witches' Night—she traced the same route, this time transforming her prey into summer squash to plant in her garden. Carrying a great wicker basket (to take the squash-children home in), she hobbled right through people's yards and paid no mind to dogs or fences or KEEP OUT signs. A big man might scare her away by shouting and running at her with a stick, but big men were scarce in Juggeston in 1944, and the witch had grown especially bold since the war broke out. For a boy as young as Garvin, even to look at her was perilous.

In the hours before the new man was to arrive, Garvin spent all afternoon in the elm hiding from his mother; he wanted to avoid letting her see his raccoon-eye shiners from the recess brawl at school. The teacher, Miss Hardy, had been momentarily preoccupied soothing crybaby Mary Barker, who got so frightened during the air-raid drill that she refused to come out from beneath her desk for recess. Two boys jumped at this opportunity to tease Garvin in the playground. Badgering him had become almost routine—since rumors of his grandparents' connections to the German-American Bund had spread—so he held back at first, as his mother had instructed him to do. He ignored them when they claimed that the Japs were moving in next-door to him any day now—that his mother and Nurse Kelly were harboring *the enemy*. He counted to ten when they called him "Jerry" Tufteller. Even when they called his father a no-good Kraut, he only rose in the face of this lie and began walking to the other side of the playground.

"Hey, Tufteller!" the fat one named Byron whined behind him. "Cryin' shame you won't get to go out for Halloween tomorrow, seeing as how you don't have that Nazi dad of yours to go around with you no more."

"Yeah," the also fat Franklin Bunkinson sneered, "but I guess you can stay home with your *mommy* and learn how to *sew*."

Garvin got in a solid roundhouse for Pop that bloodied Byron's freckled snout, but he was overcome before he could connect for his mom. Franklin yanked his head back by the hair, and Byron avenged himself twice on both eyes before Miss Hardy hurried in. As she dragged them toward the headmaster's office, Byron vowed to give Garvin worse at the first possible chance. His revenge, he swore, his great red cheeks puffing like a blowfish, would be "swift and merciless!"

"Nothing about you is *swift*," Garvin had fired back. "You're too rubbery-blubbery-tubbolard-fat!" But he was humiliated, and a swelling heat had wrung drops from his eyes.

Careful not to rustle the branch he now sat on, he silently and politely as possible willed the Annisquam Witch to please, pretty please take Byron and Franklin this year. They were enough bait to last all season.

Get them! he thought. Skin them alive, then boil them, and *then* kill them!

The old woman suddenly froze, and Garvin feared that she'd actually heard his thoughts. In the approaching dark, he could almost feel her glance sweep in an arc around the yard, brush the tree where he sat camouflaged, pass on—and alight warily on the woman scarecrow. "What?" she croaked at it; and again, "What's that?" She dropped her head back, sniffing, as Garvin believed, his blood's scent carried by a treacherous breeze. A rain of brown and gold and copper leaves tumbled past him, and he dropped the pocket mirror to cling to the quaking branch. As it shattered on the root below, the witch wheeled around toward him, hissing like a cornered animal, "Is someone there?"

Yesss, the wind whispered, *yessss.* The scarecrow's flowing dress clapped like a flag. Garvin surrendered and began to sob again. The witch took a few halting steps in his direction, and he swallowed back his breath and waited to be transformed into something horrible. Just then, two shafts of light snaked around the corner of the house and the boy braced himself to be engulfed by the evil eye, the dragon's breath. He heard the old woman mutter in some strange tongue some witches' incantation, a curse. But nothing happened. Ducking from the lights, the Annisquam Witch scurried out the gate away down the hill. Above the crunch of her footfalls over dead leaves, he thought he heard a raven screech close by.

But it was only the brakes of Margaret Kelly's Dodge. Thank goodness.

Faint with relief, Garvin was about to climb down to greet her when he saw another shadow in the passenger seat. His mother? He remained motionless in the tree. He hadn't meant to be out so late. There came a man's laugh. "Well, we actually *made* it!" The inflection and timbre sounded vaguely Negro, to Garvin, or maybe Indian. The stranger and Margaret seemed to be sharing some joke.

"I'm afraid I don't drive very well," Garvin heard her tell the man. "Especially this monster. It was my husband Jack's truck." The headlights snapped off, and again he could see nothing. "I suppose I confirm the suspicions of those people driving behind me muttering about 'women drivers.' But it's not because I'm a *woman*; I'm a bad driver because I don't concentrate very well. I sightsee and daydream a lot." Doors slammed, feet clumped up the porch steps, and keys tinkled. "So the truck is all yours, mostly. I hope you drive. Do you?"

"I had a truck for the nursery, of course. My car I had to sell during the evacuation," the man replied. "It was a beauty. An old Ford Model A convertible I bought in Los Angeles for twenty dollars and rebuilt myself—whitewalls, new chrome caps, rumble seat, the works."

Garvin heard the key ring clink on wood, then Margaret's "Oh, shoot!" and sounds of scuffling feet. He hopped down from the tree and ran past the stranger up the steps. "Mugsie?" he called. "It's just me. I'll find 'em." He dropped to the porch floor and began groping.

"Oh, Garvin," she replied. "Good, we need a set of sharp young eyes."

Handing her the keys, Garvin squinted at the man's shadowy outline. Margaret opened the door, reached inside, and flipped on the porch floodlight. Garvin and the man blinked at each other, both temporarily blinded.

"Garvin, this is Mister Fujita," Margaret said, and the slow way she pronounced Mister sounded odd to Garvin, like steam. "Mister Fujita, this is Livvie's boy, Master Garvin Tufteller."

As his eyes adjusted, the overexposed face sharpened into focus and Garvin felt a fresh bolt of alarm. Margaret had said the man had moved from Arizona and was coming to the hill to help them start a farm. Garvin, who had never been outside of Massachusetts, had pictured the man to look like a *cowboy*. His mother warned that the man was Japanese, but Garvin had never seen an actual Jap before, either. Confused, he snuck away one recess to study the Armed Forces recruitment poster taped to the wall of the high school gym—a bat-winged, caricature Nip, both monstrous as Satan and silly as Mickey Mouse, carrying a bomb in one hand and a squirming, naked lady in the other. Garvin now sized up the new man in a blink. He could not quite graft that cartoon enemy onto the real face, but the man now extending his hand down to him was definitely no cowboy. The excruciating memory of Byron's taunts flooded back to him.

The Jap's ears were large, thrust forward by a cap of hair that only looked short because it was slicked back with a generous amount of tonic. The deep, true-black sheen of the hair was spangled by a few silver flecks, as was the fabric of his suit—also black, and slightly formal, though too long in the sleeves. Much about the stranger seemed formal: from his stiff, upright posture to the tilt of his chin to the one uplifted eyebrow arching above a heavy-lidded eye, also practically black. Yet, framed in all this darkness, his face seemed to radiate, round and wide as a sandwich plate. Although the man's smile was bright enough, his teeth were stained and gnarled, and they protruded in a way that, together with all his other features, reminded Garvin of Bela Lugosi's Dracula come to life.

"Hey! There he is!"

The shout rang from just outside the perimeter of the floodlight. Garvin and the stranger froze, and an instant later Garvin felt a hard crack against his shoulder, another on his hip—a hail of eggs was pelting them. He barely saw a white bullet whizzing into the man's dark pant leg, and the yolky explosion. There was a blur of motion; Margaret shrieked. Garvin yelped as the man yanked him back onto the porch, then bounded down the steps into the darkness with a bestial yowl.

"Mr. Fujita! Wait!" Margaret called after him, stepping back out of the doorway.

"Cowards!" the man shouted. "Come on, here I am!" There was a child's squeal, pounding footfalls, then Byron's blubbery laughter.

"Ohhh boy!" Garvin whispered. Margaret turned to him, caught her breath.

"*Honey!* What happened to your *eyes*?" She reached out, but he instinctively bolted down the steps and across the yard toward his own house, almost colliding with the Jap, who stepped back into the ring of light with a frown that could sour fresh milk. Garvin gave a cry. The new man forced his scowl into a shrug and lighthearted grin for the boy, but too late. Garvin had seen the killer's face.

As he twisted his way past the fence toward home, he heard Margaret's voice fading behind him. "Please don't take it personally, Mr. Fujita," she was saying. "It's just a child's prank. Don't they have Mischief Night out west?"

There he is! As hordes of teenage goblins swarmed laughing and hooting through the woods of Widow's Peak, Fujita lay awake late that night in his new room above Mrs. Kelly's garage, thinking of the boy who was so afraid of him. He had conjured memories of Fujita's son, as all boys seemed to do those days. Nothing in particular—just Tony's round face, at eight or nine, his dimpled smile full of toothless holes.

"Sleep now," he ordered himself, shaking his head, dodging the memory. "You need to sleep." The evening's "mischief," the travel, new surroundings, and Margaret's hospitality with drinks and cake had exhausted him. Forced to excuse himself during a tour of the main house, he had asked her to point the way to the garage and begged her not to trouble about showing him out. He just needed to be alone, rest, breathe some fresh air. Unable to find a light switch, he crept blindly upstairs, where he brushed against something that clattered like a tree of wooden castanets. The long-unused storm shutters were sealed on the outside, but groping along the windows he found one with a broken lock. The window faced away from the moon, now in its first quarter, so only the meagerest glow helped him locate the cot Margaret had prepared. Throwing himself on it facedown, he wriggled out of his trousers and shirt.

Socializing, he thought. Nice people. People, period. Is this another mistake?

As his eyes adjusted to the dark, he saw by the stairwell a humanoid figure. There: Staring harder, he recognized a skeleton; the clacking sound had come from its free-dangling bones. He gave no start, nor even blinked. "Sleep now," he murmured, closing his eyes. "Sleep."

After his mother scolded him for his shiners and soaked his egg-stained trousers, Garvin watched her drown her aggravation in her usual soporific of brandy with warm milk, then sulkily followed her upstairs. He put himself to bed, scared, sore, and hearing the echo, "There he is!" Garvin guessed that would have been Franklin Bunkinson's older brother, Theo—alone, Franklin and Byron wouldn't have dared ambush him in the presence of adults. They wouldn't have dared, he thought, if Pop were here. But Garvin held no delusions about the fact that his father had died; he knew where his father died, fighting whom. Although his mother never told him the exact circumstances of Sig's last moments, he had constructed a movie epic in his mind. Spliced from films, radio plays, comics, and newspapers, those scenes from the Burma Hump had replayed in his imagination a thousand times. He knew what the enemy in that movie looked liked, those who his father so valiantly repelled. And although Garvin had only caught a fleeting glimpse of his new neighbor, he could not erase the man's enraged expression from his memory.

As he fought off sleep, the image mingled with the pale features of Bela Lugosi, transforming into the yellow-fanged, bat-winged Nip soldier on the recruitment poster. Imagining the stranger sitting up thirsty in the dark across the two hundred yards that separated them, he placed his hands over his throat, checked the window lock, then groped beneath the bed for paper and his colored pencils. His fingertips found them easily, their wood shafts rough with his teeth marks. This was an image he reproduced on the stucco walls of the basement, the floor of his closet, the headboard of his bed, the slates of the rear walkway. He started his picture with what he knew best: He drew Widow's Peak. Just feeling that waxy point skimming on the paper was enough, for the moment, to put his night fears to rest.

A nightmare jolted Fujita awake around six-fifteen, later than he usually arose anyway. He had dreamt he was lost in the barren tundra of the North Pole wearing only a windbreaker, Bermuda shorts, and for some reason, golf shoes. By the dream's end, he came to an igloo, the only one visible for endless miles in any direction. The rounded top issued wisps of wood smoke and cries of an infant within. He had been scratching, clawing with bleeding nails at a domed chunk of ice blocking the port. A stupid dream. Dire as the situation was, Fujita took no stock in dreams, only found them annoying, pointless, wasted effort.

Perturbed, he opened his eyes to find half-decayed wooden rafters above him, the mattress bricklike beneath him. In his groggy, semiconscious state he had the sensation that he had been resuscitated on the autopsy table. For his new room above the garage was the late Dr. Kelly's office, left messy with the business of healing: a leather padded gurney, a chrome instrument tray, pharmaceutical crates, glass medicine cabinets. Smacking his sticky mouth open and shut, he surveyed the space. It was larger than the Los Angeles apartment he had grown up in, squeezed together with his parents; smaller than the master bedroom above his nursery in Pasadena; and about the same size as his "apartment"—his *koya*—in Gila River, Arizona. The wire-jointed skeleton suspended like a doorman by the stairwell looked more cordial than it had the previous night; diffuse morning sun now filled the recesses of its skull, softening the gouges that had made its countenance so stern under the faint lunar glow. Although drafty, the office maintained a sickly aroma of gasoline and ether. Making a note to unlock the storm shutters first thing, he opened all the windows to provide a whisper of autumn air.

He did not unpack; he would not, for he had his plans. Yet he unsnapped, untied, and untaped his long-brutalized suitcase and drew out his shaving gear. The office had no toilet (though it was a cornucopia of lima bean–shaped bedpans), but at one end stood a porcelain basin, its faucets corroded, the stopper missing from its chain. Above it hung a dark green velvety drape attached to a rod, which he drew aside to reveal a mirror. He imagined that in a doctor's office some things were better left unseen. The size of the upper half of a doorway, the mirror had ripples running down its surface, distorting all images, as in a fun house. He slit his chin while shaving, alarmed by the reflection of the skeleton's hand now animated by a breeze pushing through the shutter cracks. Suddenly claustrophobic, he finished his grooming, threw on his heaviest coat—not heavy enough—tramped to the stairs, frowned at the skeleton, and rushed outside.

A wet, Halloween-morning chill ran through him as he padded across the yard from the garage toward Mrs. Kelly's house. The day's first lucid thought announced itself, loud and clear: So this is old New England.

A search of both coat pockets produced no gloves, only a ragged postcard with an illustration of a cactus-covered butte, its colors faded. An early taunt from Yoneko, it was postmarked from Kingman, Arizona. God knows what she was doing around the base, or how—or *if*—she managed to elude the M.P.'s there. She always did have a taste for uniforms, Fujita thought bitterly. The sloppy pencil read:

> I am writing you as I said I would. Said I wouldn't too. Suppose you are wondering what happened, well I changed my mind. I think you're still wicked but for Tony I write. Don't bother looking as I'm leaving today —Y

As always, she addressed it to "Fujita-san," which she knew annoyed him and made him anxious. Her notes had grown less bitter and mocking over the year since he received the first one at camp. They traced her path through the northern states, the upper Midwest, and into New England, until in Boston she vanished into silence. Often mischievous and always carefully aloof, she never betrayed what he really yearned to know as he tried to decipher the pronouns in every postcard—usually singular, but sometimes vaguely first-person plural, such as in one early card, a photo of the Grand Canyon sent from Billings, Montana.

> This is a Tony place: the weather and the landscape we enjoy up here, the wide open roads, I mean. We ride motorcycles or bicycles when it's warm enough. I think, Fujita-san, it could have been a nice place for our whole family to settle in, but that's all nothing. And I leave tomorrow. —Y
>
> P.S. I won't say Thanks! for the money; but I'd like if you'd send the next through same channels & I'll write later.

Our whole family! thought Fujita, who no longer had a family. That vulgar girl—he'd never trusted her. Torturing him still, as she had done when she got her hooks into his son. She'd sucker-punched the boy with her too long eyelashes, too long roller-curled hair, too short dresses, and her pinup-magazine ambitions. Oh, she tried so hard not to look Japanese. He slapped his side and rolled his eyes to the sky. Birds soared in patterns below the darkening clouds, fleeing the sudden and unseasonable chill. Settling himself down cross-legged beside the scarecrow, he pinched his coat closed and named them: He saw Canada geese in a flying V, ravens, starlings, mallards, a hawk.

He couldn't think about Yoneko now; the girl agitated his stomach. Rest first, he thought, then work, then Yoneko. First have a plan. He made a mental note to check the mailbox; perhaps his postal forwarding order had already gone into effect.

The geese honked away toward the warmer coast. The eastward ocean view and lower Juggeston itself was completely obscured in gray mist, but he could see halfway down the wooded slope. How unlike any place he'd ever lived! These low, shaggy evergreens and pines, hundreds of tangled berry bushes. This cold climate. This remote peak, like a desert island, miles from the nearest real city. The thought, *This is where I've ended up?* was unbearable, so he willed himself to think nothing at all. Juggeston was just temporary, he reminded himself, just a place to regroup, re-arm, until he resumed his search for her, recovered what he'd lost. Closing his eyes, he tried to feel the heat rising up from the soil beneath his rump. He determined to consider this morning in Juggeston a pleasant morning of firsts. Adorning the flora on the slope was evidence of the Mischief Night magic that New England boys, armed with rolls of bathroom tissue, could wreak upon a landscape. The eastern slope—the side facing town, where the firs stood lowest to the ground—undulated with windblown white tendrils reaching toward the coast. They reminded him of the dazzling streamers of Little Tokyo streets during festivals, but this East Coast strain, like everything and everybody else in Juggeston, was just white.

A lone snowflake settled on the wide bridge of his nose, and he sneezed. Across the silent hill he heard a rickety door slam and then small voices. Sometime later he heard a thump on the gravel behind the main house and stalked briskly around to find the *Crier* at the top of the driveway. Hesitating a moment, he scanned the hill again; his back felt stiff, made a muffled popping noise as he bent to lift it. On the way to the kitchen entrance, he rolled a loose garden hose into neat hoops beside the tap. Taking care not to let the door slam, he sat himself down with the paper until Margaret awoke, curious to find some news about the army of litterbugs that had stormed the town during the night, as well as the latest news of his nation at war.

He read an article on girls' beauty classes at a local high school, coupled with a longer piece about women's improving status and average incomes during the war. On page 2 he read a column about preserving lingonberries and an AP service item recapping last week's troop movements in France and the Pacific. Page 3 advised how to winterize a house effectively and economically without using materials vital to the war effort. "Don't forget to open the storm shutters," he reminded himself. The conservation ad on page 4 urged, "Use it up, wear it out, make it do or do without!" Fujita nodded approvingly. Beneath, a shushing Uncle Sam warned, "Sshhh! The enemy is listening!" Different enemy here, Fujita reminded himself, searching the eastern morning fog for a glimpse of the Atlantic. "It's not California," he said aloud. Leafing through the remaining *Crier*—just ads, obits, comics, and public announcements—he found it rather quaint, this sheet of small-town odds and ends whose editors apparently found little bad news worth reporting that day. "It's definitely not California," Fujita said, and for the moment, that was just fine with him.

On the other side of Widow's Peak the unholy morning started out badly for the Tuftellers. Anxious about Garvin's two black eyes, still nerve-wracked from last night's vigil waiting for him to come home, and above all angry about the fistfight, Livvie had refused to commit herself to trick-or-treating. Avoiding further discussion of the matter, she pushed Garvin's chair in, pinning him at the breakfast table to interrogate him about the new man. She darted around the kitchen, firing questions at him, trying to rouse him from his slow simmer.

"Well, honey?" she said, dropping a steaming bowl of Quaker oats before him.

"Mom?" he replied, topping his bowl with a heaping mound of brown sugar.

"Garvin, take it easy! One spoon only. So. What's he like?"

"What's who like?" The boy's mouth was more full of sugar than oatmeal.

"The new man," she said. "This Mr. Fujita."

"I don't know," Garvin said nervously. He made a show of yawning and rubbing his tired and battered eyes.

"Well, is he nice? "

"I don't know." His tone grew annoyed, and he wouldn't look at her.

"What does he look like, then?"

"Mom! I don't know!" he huffed. He pointed to his shiners. "I had other things to worry about." After a few slow mouthfuls, he said, "He looks sort of like a Jap, I guess. Black hair. *Really* black—blacker than yours." Shuddering, he resumed his sloppy eating.

Livvie slumped into the chair opposite him and said nothing, as usual, wanting at once to smack him and cradle him in her lap. The boy had been so wretched lately. Not sad, not depressed or grieving—of course she could understand that. Was it some new tone in her voice, something unconscious, that made him feel picked on? Or was he just going through some self-serious, eight-year-old-boy phase? Sig would know, she thought, grimacing.

She removed an apple-honeyed Old Gold cigarette from the oak container on the table, struck a Blue Tip on her chair, and lit up. Sliding her feet in and out of her slippers, she watched him: the pale skin pulling at his temples as he chewed, the sandy hair tumbling over his bruised eyes as he bent to the bowl, and that scowl—a perfect miniature of his father.

What could she do? He wanted desperately to go out tonight; that much was clear. The thought of having to take him made her imagine the sweet, biting taste of brandy. But no—wasn't it too early? From the cabinet she pulled out the monogrammed silver-and-crystal bottle—a wedding present—and put a few drops in her coffee, just for a bit of flavor. Halloween—what a ridiculous holiday. For a rare and fleeting moment she caught herself wishing she were a man, or could be one in a pinch, or at least had one to spare. This made her feel vulnerable; as a female of her species alone, she felt she'd become lost property in the minds of others—a pocket watch waiting to be picked up, reinscribed, and yoked to a new chain of gold. Sure, Frank Childs, the mechanic, would doubtlessly help out, eager as he was to snuggle up next to her, but the too ardent twitch of his measly lip hair put her off. Despite his apparent gallantry, lust dripped off him thick as axle grease. Once he had tried to impress her with his prowess with automobiles by deriding Sig's own, as if he thought the way to a widow's heart was through scorning her dead husband. Besides, a wicked smell followed him, and his fingernails were always lined with sludge. It irked her that Garvin had taken to lingering around the dirty garage after classes. Picturing him in oil-soaked, navy blue overalls, wiping his nose with his sleeve . . . yes, and swearing, playing cards, sweating over a pinup calendar in the back office—it so distracted her that she began to light a second Old Gold while the first lay burning in the ashtray.

"Well, Jesus Christ, Garvin," she grumbled, "does this Fujita man have all his arms and legs at least?" Slamming the matchbox on the table, she spilled her laced coffee on herself.

"Cripes, Mom," he said, staring at her through the oatmeal's column of steam and shaking his head pityingly. "You're *such* a lush."

"What did you say?" Fairly certain she had heard it right, she felt herself rising from the table as if by a puppet string. How smoothly it had rolled off his tongue, how practiced.

"I don't know," he said, honestly. Realizing his awful miscalculation, he stared at his oatmeal as intensely as if contemplating diving into it for refuge.

Livvie had never been the family disciplinarian and in fact had painfully interposed herself between Garvin and Sig many times.

Yet she now felt something long dormant but essential stir in her. In a lightning movement that also seemed practiced, she hauled him up by the arm and sent two resounding blows across his bottom. "Where did you hear that, goddamn it?" she cried. She dragged him from the kitchen to the vestibule, instinctively sensing that she shouldn't spank a child in the room where a family eats. "Where?" she demanded. Garvin only sobbed. She pushed him away, for his sake. "At school?" He started wiping his nose and black eyes on his sleeve, and it dawned on her. "Childs," she said with certainty. "You got that from Childs."

Garvin looked up at her miserably. "At school, too," he admitted, his tears making his already bloodshot eyes glow more fiercely.

"Well, I've got something to show you!" she hissed. Though not without sympathy, Livvie crammed him into his heavy coat as if she were dressing a rag doll. She threw her own long camel-hair overcoat around her nightgown, kicked her slippers down the hallway, and stomped into a pair of leather work boots she drew from the steamer trunk by the entrance. The chilly morning air stung when she hauled the door open; it exhilarated her.

As she dragged Garvin down the drive, he confessed through ebbing tears that he had thought the word meant someone who did funny, absentminded things like lighting two cigarettes. Or someone, for example, such as a "merry widow," as Childs put it—a woman who had once swerved her car into a gas station's sandwich-board placard.

"Merry? Jesus Christ!" Livvie spat, echoed by the dense woods of Widow's Peak.

Garvin thought Childs meant it sympathetically, for he'd said, "I guess she's pretty lonely. Bring her down to see me next time." At school Byron and Franklin had parroted the comment, meaning it unkindly, but they understood it no more than Garvin himself.

"'Lonely!?' Oh boy!" Livvie fumed.

If most Juggestonians found Childs tolerable in those days of gas rationing, Livvie Tufteller made no concessions for his professional status. Feeling her son to be at risk, she had repeatedly asked Childs, please, when in Garvin's company, to avoid the coarse speech and behavior she assumed must be natural to mechanics. Now, not only did Childs continue the boy's foul instruction, but he further responded to her resistance by trying to court her.

Storming across the Peak, Livvie looked around her unkempt yard, the trees broken-limbed, the fence useless, every second post collapsed. She felt not quite lonely or lost. Stranded: That's what it was—liberated but stranded, as a slave who has escaped to a desert island. Since Sig had left, the hill had grown larger, higher each day. The colors whizzed from brown to green to gold to brown in a blink. On the driveway, the gravel beneath her feet felt looser; rains had shoveled the stones downward so that the top was left bare and muddy, the bottom slippery and soft, like sand dunes. Objects seemed heavier, while sounds grew fainter. This must be what it feels like, she thought, to be old.

Livvie had turned thirty earlier that year, a few months after she transformed from a grass widow to a real widow. Only recently had she realized that, like it or not, Garvin's upbringing had been thrust solely upon her shoulders. This was what made her feel old—too old at least to stand for being courted like a dumb schoolgirl when she did not wish to be courted. Yes, she wanted to teach Garvin a moral lesson, but she was also sick of the ogling, the rumor-mongering, the . . . the scrutiny. "I'll show him *merry*," she growled, yanking Garvin up Ellsworth Place, determined to make him watch as she blasted the mechanic.

Unfortunately, Livvie was a woman whom men naturally tended to ogle—especially in her rough husband's absence. Healthy-looking, she walked with solid, surefooted steps. She had glossy, ebony hair and a set of hazel eyes that seemed to flare up red-gold when caught in a certain light. Yet she dressed dowdily for a woman of her age and physique, which the men of Juggeston might call a "bombshell" figure. She knew she had admirable legs from the knees down but felt the roundness of her hips and thighs and breasts made her look like a peasant, and she masked her shape with the skill of a fan dancer. She customarily draped a button sweater like a cape around her shoulders, which she tended to hunch forward to make less of her bust. While wartime skirts crept up and up, Livvie remended her old calf-length dresses, allowing them to flare wider than suited the day's trends. She sewed masterfully and could maintain clothes to look tidy and to last. Many Juggestonians brought her their finest outfits (some commissioned her to make elegant pieces—even dinner gowns—from scratch), and she could perfectly mimic the latest fashions. She owned such treasures herself but since Sig's enlistment kept them hidden at home, in boxes, in lightless corners of her closets. Post-Sig, as she called this period of her life, she no longer kept her wardrobe current.

So the glances she attracted on her candid Halloween-morning descent from Widow's Peak were mostly of pleasant surprise. Sweeping down Ellsworth with her unbuttoned coat revealing a dash of blue cotton underdress, she caught Alf Wellington eyeing her as he hauled Old Glory up by the statue in front of his store. She clasped her coat shut and did not slow down, even when Alf called to Garvin, "Hey there, young fella! Looking forward to trick-or-treating tonight?"

"Yes, I *am*," Garvin called back pointedly, looking over his shoulder, dragging his toes.

"We'll see," said Livvie, marching on. She had spanked her son as if she had been doing it for years. The echo of that shock coursing through her, palm to shoulder, both nauseated and thrilled her. It felt as if she had left her body for a time—a not unpleasant sensation. Still, tugging him across the street, she could not look at him, so she focused herself on the garage just ahead.

Lounging against Juggeston's one gasoline pump, Frank Childs had his face buried in a pinup magazine when the scraping sound of Garvin's toe caps roused him. Brightening, the mechanic smoothed back his hair, wiped his hand across the chest of his jumpsuit, and flashed a browning tooth. He made a half-hearted effort to hide the pinup, flopping the magazine on top of the pump. He made no effort to prevent himself from eyeing Livvie head to work boots.

"Well, look at those fancy new shoes." He chuckled. "Hey, how's your new Jap?"

Livvie planted herself on the other side of the pump and glared, breathing heavily.

Childs only shrugged. "How'ya doing there, Garvin? Those eyes. Ouch. Hate to see the other guy, huh?"

"Yeah," Garvin mumbled, looking at his feet.

Stepping around the pump, Childs asked, "Whats'a matter, champ?" He reached out a grimy hand to tousle the boy's hair—a good-natured enough gesture—but Livvie grasped his wrist with both hands and flung it away. "Don't you touch him."

Childs stepped back, his one eyebrow wrinkling down on both ends, looking hurt. Then Livvie noticed him drop his eyes to her chest. She pulled her coat closed with one hand and grabbed the magazine with the other, flopping its pages open toward him like a police badge.

"Is this what you do with my son?" she demanded, stepping against him. Childs only stammered something unintelligible and looked away. "Well then, boys," she sneered, scrutinizing the pinup, "let's see what's so terrific about these girls."

The model was a movie starlet whose legs had become popular in water-ballet musicals—scissoring open and closed, swaying like breeze-blown pussy willows above a pond. Her sparkling orange hair, usually tucked beneath a flowered rubber cap, was a pleasant surprise, but overall Livvie found her less appealing out of the water. Her usually submerged upper torso—particularly her lungs—was massive, like a football player's. Or a frog's, Livvie thought. The starlet lounged across a muddy Jeep clad in a star-spangled swimming outfit; propped over one shoulder was a white, bayoneted bolt-action rifle. Not a handsome woman, she wore an unsightly grimace, clenching the pin of a hand grenade between her teeth; her startled expression, eyes guiltily toward the camera, was that of Eve caught biting into the forbidden fruit. Livvie pitied the ugly water ballerina. Remembering Sig, she supposed that the boys in the field weren't much concerned with her face. Above the model arced the tacky caption: "Fire in the Hole!"

"Garvin comes around here after school," Livvie said, thrusting the magazine at Childs, "and you show him this . . . smut?"

"No, Livvie! We just talk about cars and stuff, that's all. Isn't that right, kid?"

"You pathetic, grease-monkey *schoolboy*," she hissed, shoving him back against the glass-paned door to the office. "You keep this crap away from my son!"

The gasoline fumes made her feel light-headed, reckless, and while she had to release her coat again in order to roll up the magazine, she did it boldly. Garvin sniffled behind her, Childs sniveled before her. The town-hall bell chimed eight o'clock. Twisting the magazine into a dense, thick club, she swatted at Childs three times: "Lonely! Merry! Lush!" Even as she pummeled his head and shoulders and parrying forearms, the young man's eyes glistened with a sort of miserable ecstasy. When her paper mace caught his nose tip ("Bring her down to see me!"), he only fanned one open hand before his face, still ogling her, as if playing peek-a-boo. Further enraged, Livvie swung as hard as she could. Then there was a snap.

"Livvie!" Childs yelped, grabbing his little finger.

"Mom!" Garvin shouted.

In the second Livvie turned to look at her son, Childs managed to open the glass office door with much jangling of jamb bells, crawl inside, and slam it closed. On his knees within, he fumbled unsuccessfully with the lock, his sprained pinkie jutting back to the right, rigid and useless.

Livvie left him alone. She picked up Garvin, who was too big to pick up, and cradled him in one arm. Hardening herself, she made him face the lovelorn mechanic, who lay panting and smiling, taking it bravely, pressed against the glass like a lizard in a terrarium. Shrugging, she glanced down with mixed surprise and admiration at the magazine, then hurled it at the glass above his face. "Sorry," she muttered, out of breath. "I'm just one of those girls who does *funny*, *absentminded* things sometimes."

She turned and started walking with Garvin in the direction of the Peak, now bright with morning glow. "Let's get you back before the bus comes," she said. "While you're at school, I'll make a costume. Okay?" Garvin nodded against her. "And if people say things, or if they tease you, it's okay to tell me. You know? I'll handle it. Okay?"

"I'll say," agreed Garvin, still disoriented.

Livvie put him down, sorry to do it but unable to hold him any longer. Walking back up Ellsworth Place without speaking, they heard the flag over Wellington's Arcade whipping in the westward breeze, a sea breeze. Approaching the turn for their driveway, they saw a figure, bent at the waist, one hand to his chin, staring into the mailbox. Garvin caught his breath and halted.

"That's him," he whispered, shrinking back. "That's the new man."

Livvie strained to see. Years of sewing in dimly lit dens had taken a toll on her eyes, particularly on the left side. "What's he doing? Garvin? I can't see." She clamped her left eye closed and tried harder to focus. "Is he *bowing* to the mailbox?"

"I think he's looking in it," Garvin said, squinting. "I think he's got the paper." Some sort of tube appeared to jut from the man's armpit.

The new man stood frozen for several seconds, never looking in their direction. "I guess we should maybe go say hi," Livvie said, but with Garvin glued to her hip, she was by no means sure of this. She closed her overcoat. They began to inch forward, but the new man closed the lid, flipped up the flag, and climbed the drive before they came within hailing distance.

Oh boy, thought Livvie, hugging her nervous son. I hope this isn't a big mistake.

During the war, the power of Fujita's writing hand had increased a hundredfold. In maintaining flimsy, V-Mail ties with his son when Tony shipped out for the Pacific, Fujita had established a rigid routine. Every day he fired off letters, scattering them across the country like a cannon's tracers, seeking the whereabouts of family, colleagues, former friends. In relocation projects, farms, hostels, and factories, he sought those he left behind and those who left him; those he was not allowed to see and those who refused to see him; and, most urgently, those who were taken from him.

His chief correspondent, his mother, had been moved so often since Pearl Harbor that she commanded three pages of his address book. She did not demand it, yet he wrote her often to let her know where he was—in the country, in his life, and in his search for Yoneko. He vowed to work unfailingly until he could hire the right lawyer and try to accomplish her release from prison.

"Mind your business," Mrs. Fujita once wrote. "I am sixty-odd years old and can take care of myself, thank you. I'm content where I am, for now. From what I hear of life out there, I wouldn't come out if you paid me. Pull me out of here and it will be the worse for you, I promise. Don't fret so much."

"Dear Mom," he had replied. "The emphasis, I'd say, is on 'odd.' I'll write again when I've contracted a lawyer."

But Fujita did fret. And so, even before he'd finished reading the *Crier*, he dashed off a note and sent it to her most recent address, an FBI detention center in Montana.

> I've arrived in the town of Juggeston. Did you get the package I sent? I've received no word, as mail forwarding hasn't begun yet. I haven't heard from the girl for quite a while. Since she gave me the slip in Boston, I've been floundering—short on energy, funds, not knowing what to do next. Hire a detective? No money. Here, I'll get some thinking time, working cash, get back on my feet, etc. There are many Quakers here, I'm told. Perhaps they will help me. I'll contact all the War Relocation Authority offices, YWCAs, youth hostels, etc. in the region—hopefully, she hasn't left New England yet.
>
> Juggeston is more of a desert island than even Gila, but I hope I can be of some help. My new employer seems to trust me explicitly—a nice change, but it's a responsibility, too. She's dumped her property (there's quite a lot of it) into my hands, and I must admit, it's a relief to have real work again. It's also a challenge. Northern Massachusetts is not Southern California; the climate, the pests, the soil and diseases—it's all different. I'm an amateur here. A beginner.
>
> At home, Mari and I would be staking the lemon trees about now. And my roses—the potter should be getting the greenhouse ready for them soon. I still haven't heard from him, though, and I fear the worst. Some days I think I only want to get back to the nursery.

> Other days, of course, I hope I'll never set foot in that stupid state again. Like yesterday, when I wired the bank just before leaving Boston. Your account is still frozen, but when I can, I'll send you what money Y hasn't already extorted from me. I hope we can have you out of there soon. Tell me if you need anything and I'll do my best.

"It's not much," he admitted to the mailbox. What else could he do? Nothing for the moment. Nothing until he could find and afford an attorney—a good one, a *Caucasian* one, if one would take the case. He had to make things work in Juggeston, then step up his plans before Yoneko's trail got cold. His mother, he figured, would get on fine, happy to give the Bureau a run for its money.

Tucking the *Crier* beneath his arm, he leaned to the box and adjusted the letter's position, further or nearer to the lid where the postman would be sure to notice it. "Stay there if you want, old woman," he chuckled. "It's a free country." He pushed the lid closed, flipped up the red tin flag, and drew a deep, morning breath.

Margaret and Mr. Fujita moved around each other that morning with the deliberate fluidity of figure skaters—readying breakfast, making coffee, sharing sections of the *Crier*. Downstairs around seven, Margaret had found the new man at the kitchen table studying a topographical map of Juggeston. To her embarrassment, he'd already set the coffee brewing and prepared eggs for them. "Oh, an early bird!" she said from the doorway, still in her dressing gown. "I'll be right back down. Don't do another thing! I want you to make yourself absolutely comfortable." Rising politely, Mr. Fujita begged her not to hurry on his account.

"I want you to feel *absolutely* welcome," she insisted, shaking a finger in mock admonishment.

"Oh, yes, I do," he assured her. "Thank you." Unconvinced, she asked if he lacked or desired anything. Did she only imagine that he looked at her queerly? When he answered, "No, not a thing. You've already been so kind, really," she felt she was pestering him, behaving too formally, or that perhaps her hovering might suggest that she did not trust him to be alone in her house. She promptly swept upstairs again. After dressing for breakfast, she hurried back down and paused by the kitchen door.

"Well!" she cried, wafting into the kitchen, opening the curtains, and, despite the gloom of Halloween day, sighing in ostentatious satisfaction. "This is a morning!"

How do people come together from opposite corners of the country, of the world? For Margaret Kelly, it was easy: It was trade. She desired something she could devote herself to wholeheartedly. The war produced it. It sold her Mr. Fujita, in whose stiff company she had already detected or projected something . . . not comfortable, not relaxed or friendly or easy. Familiar? If she decided to take someone in, she accepted him unconditionally as an old friend. In this spirit, the good hostess launched into their breakfast with an overwhelming barrage of good-willed small talk—the town's history and personalities, locations of stores for this and that, interesting sights on the coast, the tradition of Mischief Night. "And what about you?" she prodded, time and again. Had he a favorite popular tune? Had he ever eaten scrod? "I want to hear *all* about you!"

So they breakfasted together, these strangers trying to become something like friends. Both had been long alone. For the longest time, no one had hovered over his shoulder as he cooked; she'd had nobody to expend her nursely fussing on since Jack. As the meal dragged on, she was powerless to restrain her nervous chatter; he smiled, nodded, and subtly wrung his napkin as he struggled to anchor himself in details. He asked about the mail schedule; she replied that it came at ten. "Would you mind if I come in to use the phone sometimes?" he asked, and, "I insist that you do, by all means," Margaret said. Fujita promised, "I'll keep track of my calls," but she pshawed him.

"Why don't I look into getting a phone in the office?"

"No, no! Please don't trouble yourself," he protested.

"Oh, for goodness' sake, trouble me," Margaret said, her voice sharp from frustration.

Fortunately, the telephone rang. At its jingling, he appeared startled but also relieved. Sighing, Margaret turned away to answer; waiting for the operator to connect the caller, she turned back to the table to find that the man had vanished with no word, no sound. "Oh," she said, glancing about. The caller came on—just the librarian reminding her of the monthly book-club meeting. Margaret mumbled that she couldn't attend, then went to replace the receiver. Pivoting again, she saw Mr. Fujita stepping in from the kitchen porch, pulling the screen door closed too softly.

"I thought you might like some p-p-privacy," he said, shivering.

Heavens, thought Margaret, staring. What a bundle of *nerves!* What could one expect of a newcomer, a Japanese stranger, after last night's welcome? Swift and silent as a phantom, or Garvin's vampire, he moved with chilling economy, as if conscious of taking up too much physical space, of touching too much air. This vanishing act of his unsettled Margaret, who was a door slammer, a step-kicker, a foot stomper, a grand-entrance gal. To her, it verged on sneakiness. What did she know of a world that wished most of all to avoid notice? A world of cramped quarters and scant resources, whose art valued the miniature, whose compact citizens could never be small enough? All her life, the world noticed Margaret Kelly, or else she forced it to notice her, and she fancied being noticed.

"That door sticks. You have to slam it shut," Margaret said.

Mister Fujita frowned at the door frame. "I'll shave it, then. This afternoon."

"Oh, no, please don't bother. You just get settled in." Margaret *liked* having her door ajar. But again, what did she know of a world of warrantless, forced entries? Only what he had intimated in their long but stilted talks in Boston, then driving from the train station. She wanted to know, however. She wanted to ask him . . . everything. But not today.

Having talked at him for two hours, Margaret realized they hadn't yet discussed anything in particular: work, roles—they hadn't talked of *plans*. After all, wasn't that why he was there? Worried that she appeared like some rich, lonely crone who just liked having a man around and didn't know the meaning of real work, she started over. "So!" she said. Stepping out onto the porch, she looked fondly at her scarecrow, her hill. "A farm!" She waited for him to follow her outside. "I'm so looking forward to being a gentlewoman farmer. I've fantasized it for years."

His surprise, apparent in his stiff nod and refusal to meet her eyes, irritated her. She thought her pale cheeks, her full figure, her sweep of red hair, her dreamy eyes gave a grossly unfair impression of her essential spirit. She'd been trapped in a novel and bubble-bath body; a fitted-gown and taxi-driven body; a well- and nutritiously fed body, an easy-chair body. "Oh, farming's in my blood, you know," she said. "Yes, the family on Mother's side has kept a farm in Ireland for generations now. I haven't been since I was a little girl, but I think it's still there. In County Kerry." The man's black eyebrows raised questioningly. She nodded. "That's the way they say it: County Kerry. Backward, really. Well," she said, waving out to the hillside. "What's your professional opinion? When can we get to work?"

"Er, I'll get started today," said Mr. Fujita, his body and voice instantly relaxing. Now *this* he could talk about. "I'd like to survey the property, get to know it. Test the soil, prep some plots, mulch." Margaret nodded. "I'm not familiar with this terrain," he continued apologetically.

"It takes *time* to get acclimated," Margaret agreed. "Well, what would you be doing if you were at home now?"

Mr. Fujita blinked at her, disoriented. "In Pasadena? Um, waking up, I guess," he said. No sarcasm sounded in his voice, only confusion. "It's about 6:00 A.M. there."

"Well, no, I mean—"

"Oh," Fujita said, stiffening. "It's so different here from the West Coast and the Southwest, you see. I have some books about the area. It's just . . . I've come too late in the season, now." Clearly, the timing of her invitation had baffled him. She knew it relieved him to escape Boston sooner rather than later—to have a job, a real place to stay—and she trusted him to earn his keep. But he must have wondered: Didn't this nurse-cum-gardener know that they couldn't start a farm in the snow?

"Of course," she said, blushing. "It's what I expected, really. It's a slow time, I know. Oh, well, it gives us time to get acquainted."

"Yes," he said, not exactly brimming with enthusiasm. Stalled, they looked at the scarecrow, her dress clapping in the wind. Beyond the grassy woman, thickets of brush and toppled trees, massive boulders and construction leftovers covered the hillside like the battlements and barriers of a siege army. Further east, fat clouds crept in from the coast, promising rain. Beside the house, the one open storm shutter clacked against the garage; Fujita looked up at it and jingled the change in his pockets. "It might be useful to run down to town," he suggested after a while, "and see what local farmers are up to. I'll get on it today."

"I see," she repeated. She was beginning to see, a little. "Around lunch then?"

Mr. Fujita nodded and excused himself. She watched him stomp away toward the garage and felt fabulously frustrated; then she busied herself putting out candy for what trick-or-treaters might brave the Peak that night. How little she'd extracted from her new boarder. She knew he liked talking on the phone; that he couldn't sit still; that he was *armored*, Japanese. . . . That was a start. He also knew his place—knew what was expected of him, and he lived up to the expectations—even if *she* didn't. Beset by doubts, she tried to tell herself, "This is crazy. I don't know anything about farming. I'm not the kind of woman who just ups and does things like this on the spur of the moment." But then, she had to admit, that was *exactly* the kind of woman she was.

When Halloween night arrived, Livvie did what she had to do. After the morning's episode with Childs, she expected that any tricking and treating this year would be left to her. What man would dare lend a hand to Sig Tufteller's violent family? She almost reneged at the last minute, examining Garvin's eye, which had turned an alarming mustard yellow, but he grew hysterical. "Everybody everybody *everybody* is going out except me," he wailed, and Livvie conceded. To ground the boy on Halloween after Byron's taunts would have been cruel. Besides, doomed as she was to endure many Halloweens to come, hadn't she better get in practice right away?

Rains of October foliage whirled around them on their

descent from the hill. Livvie thought the night was too cold; Garvin thought it balmy. She said they could stay out until six-thirty, when they had to return home to pick up the cake she had made for Mr. Fujita's welcoming. Garvin thought six-thirty was too early, but the memory of the morning's spanking still lingered on and he didn't argue.

For a costume, Livvie had offered to sew together a mask or a ghostly sheet with eye holes, but Garvin wanted to capitalize on his gruesome shiners. She suggested he'd make a good Quasimodo, but Garvin preferred a boxer. She cut up one of Sig's bathrobes, swiftly hemmed its edges, draped a towel around his neck, and convinced him to wear several layers of long johns beneath. "No one will see them," she insisted, "and it will make you look more *muscular.*" That won him over; at least she got that part right. But when she tried to hug Garvin against the chill as they collected treats around the valley, he kept pulling away. She was becoming aware of a new parental unit of measurement—a precise and proper distance at which she was allowed to advance toward or stray from her son.

In the end, they returned to the hill well before six-thirty. A row of heavy Atlantic clouds scudded over Juggeston and emptied their wet loads just as the eastern sky darkened. The first thunderclap sounded as the Tuftellers made their way down Ellsworth Place toward Wellington's Arcade, the pot of gold at the end of every Halloween night. Garvin was determined to plod on, but Livvie wouldn't hear of it.

"Not without raincoats," she said. "You have enough sweets to last you a year already."

"We've only been to half the houses, Mom."

"Half is plenty," Livvie muttered. At each house they visited, the inhabitants practically jumped on them, like dogs awaiting Master's arrival, heaping treats on Garvin while dragging Livvie inside to inquire about her new neighbor. The questions ranged from the polite (Is he enjoying Juggeston? Has he started work yet?) to the unsubtle (Where's he staying? Not in Margaret's house? Do they dine together?) to the absurd (Does he really have a glass eye? Is Tokyo Rose really his sister?). While most interrogations were bearable enough, Livvie knew nothing—and

Garvin would say nothing—and she found the rain a welcome excuse to go home.

"Do we have to?" Garvin pleaded the whole way back. "Look, it's hardly even raining now. I could have tons more candy. Tons."

"You could have no teeth, too," Livvie said, leading him homeward. "And pimples. You could have a big fat belly like Byron. Now let's go, we're late."

The drenched Tuftellers held hands, rushing back toward the Peak. At the bottom they were halted by a burbling, muddy moat where the erosion of rain and years had gouged a gutter out of the base and deposited a bank of gravel on the roadside. To Livvie, it looked as if fully half the hill lay there at the bottom. My home is melting, she thought, holding Garvin back, meaning to find a dry or at least less wet approach. Thus preoccupied, blinded and deafened by the storm, she noticed the dim halo growing around her and heard the clanking chains, the grinding tow-truck gears, too late. Points of mud and rock raked her calves and neck like birdshot. A frigid wind passed around and through her as the truck sped by, great blossoms of rainwater arcing from beneath its tires. Pivoting, she glared after it. With the red, steel arm saluting her, its chain and hook swinging pendulumlike, she did not need to see the garage decal on the door to know the driver was Frank Childs. A great yowl rocketed up from her very toes, mindless, free-form, animal, until her throat stung. When her roar gave out, when she recovered enough to force her mouth shut, she oddly felt much, much better than she had in weeks. In his mud-mottled bathrobe, Garvin shivered more with fear of her than with cold, but she hugged him. So this is Halloween, she thought, when everybody's little ghouls come out. No wonder she had left this holiday to Sig.

"Let's go, honey," she said. From the stony gutter ringing the drive, they could just make out a glow from Margaret's living room windows. "Might as well," she said, indicating the moat. She grinned at Garvin, who tilted his head quizzically. She kissed his temple, placed her lips to his ear, and whispered, "Last one home . . ." By the time she got to "is a rotten egg," Livvie Tufteller was ankle-deep in water and a good length and a half ahead.

At home they changed into dry visiting clothes. Garvin's nose was pouring; a powerful wave of sneezing wracked Livvie. The cigarette she lit to calm her nerves only inspired lustier sneezes. "This isn't the best shape to meet someone for the first time," she burbled. Looking up at her hopefully, Garvin nodded and exaggerated his sniffling. "Don't be afraid, honey," she said, vigorously towel-drying his hair between sneezes. Garvin frowned sourly.

"I'm not," he insisted. Again, his mother wondered: To admit no fear, no weakness—was this new behavior in emulation of a dead soldier-father, or just a natural phase of boys?

"Listen," said Livvie. "This man, this Mr. Fujita—he's a little different, I guess, but he's just a man. Right? It's okay to be nervous," she added, "but don't be scared." Garvin frowned again, but Livvie was mostly addressing herself.

When six-thirty came around, Garvin's nose glowed red; Livvie's face felt puffy, and her sinuses were clogged. Along with a cold and nerves, and the brandy she downed to ease them, her renewing disgust at Childs made her even more tense and glazed-eyed. She wanted only to fix a hot toddy, bathe, and go to bed, but she made an effort to pretty herself up, then finished outfitting them both with umbrellas, galoshes, the works. "Just a regular old man," Livvie repeated as they stepped out into the rain and began to trudge toward Margaret's house. Halfway across the hill, the dessert tumbled onto the ground: She had forgotten to fasten the cake-pan cover.

Garvin looked at it with a sigh, then at her. "Mom . . ."

The hands hanging limp at her side curled into fists. Through gritted teeth, she ordered him back to fetch a pattern book she'd borrowed. As Garvin stomped back across the hill, talking to himself, Livvie closed her eyes and tried to catch her breath. The tough ribs and stitches of her girdle pressed into her at unnatural angles. Feeling faint, she let her knees fall out from under her, made a stool of the upturned cake pan, and sat mulling over Margaret's cockamamie plan.

"We have to *do something*, Livvie!" Margaret had said, coming around a few weeks earlier, so bright, overzealous. "Something good, something *fun*, make our own way. Now, I had a little idea—well, frankly, I've started the ball rolling on it already, but let me throw it at you."

It was not always easy being neighbor to the good Nurse Kelly. Livvie might admit that she looked up to Margaret, but she always felt like a child around her. Despite herself, she was often jealous of the easy relationship Margaret had with Garvin. For these reasons—and their age difference—Livvie had never felt comfortable socializing with the Kellys; the husbands had always arranged the social meetings. So Livvie had to wonder: What was this *we*?

"Livvie, look around," Margaret had said, glowing. "Read the papers. Women have a chance to work decent jobs with real incomes. I read that thirty-six percent of the workforce belongs to women now. Thirty-six percent!" she sang, and the phrase became her favorite litany.

Big whoop-de-doo, thought Livvie. Who the hell *else* will fill in the dead-end job that the irresponsible, self-centered, wandering son of a bitch left behind, running off to enlist? It was, after all, a woman's *duty*. When Sig enlisted, some well-meaning fool in town had sent her a newsletter, *Penelope*, an A-to-Z manual on how to fill in the vacuum left by your man and then vacate that space when he came home. "Resist the temptation to redecorate or move furniture around," *Penelope* advised. "Don't let his magazine subscriptions lapse while your man is on democracy's quest. Remember: A man's home is his castle, and it's your duty to preserve the castle as it was while your man is away." *While your man is* away*!* Livvie couldn't redecorate the castle fast enough.

Although her late husband was decidedly not an irresponsible, self-centered, wandering son of a bitch, Nurse Kelly seemed to view widowhood as some sort of liberation. It was the happy attitude of a woman who could choose not to work if she didn't care to—a luxury Livvie couldn't afford. "Uh-huh," she had said. "Thirty-six percent. So?"

Cupping Livvie's face in her hands, Margaret whispered, "We are going to farm this hill, Livvie. We're going to build a wonderful, successful business here and sing while we're doing it. We're going to get to know each other and do . . . *things*. I'm bored stiff and positively sick of being 'poor Widder Kelly.' Don't you say a thing. I know you understand. Lord, *we* didn't die! Don't tell me you adore seamstressing? Or maybe you're one of those women who suppose it's not feminine to work a physical job?" She held Livvie so close their noses almost touched, as if each woman's face was a hand-held mirror. "Look at us, Livvie. We're strong, beautiful, healthy, smart."

Not that Livvie didn't believe it, but she turned her eyes away, figuring that, even some twenty years younger, she was no Margaret Kelly. Anyway, did strength, beauty, and intelligence make for good business skills? All available evidence told Livvie that the world was filled with weak, ugly, stupid, and very successful businessmen. Yet she also knew her apprehension had deeper roots: Margaret had already talked of putting up a Christmas tree, had thought ahead to buy Season's Greetings cards, had taken the train to Boston and shopped. Margaret had finished mourning, while Livvie had had neither time nor inclination to really begin. She had Garvin, for one thing, and needed to seamstress double-time that autumn to afford the upcoming holidays. Margaret didn't contend with these things.

Still, Livvie admitted, "I'm a little intrigued. Go on."

Then, when Margaret began, "Now, in Boston last week, I met a wonderful man who you'll just *love*—" Livvie's heart sank.

"I don't need a man, Margaret!"

"What? My lands, Livvie! No, no, no! Of course not. Men? The world wouldn't be where it is now if things were left up to us smart women. We own the land we live on; we can either remarry and give it away to some wolf or else rule it ourselves, right? Smart women don't need men—just the opposite, I'd say. This man, Mr. Fujita, he needs *us*!" A habitual volunteer and do-good addict, the former nurse kept a constant eye out for whatever required her healing touch. She told Livvie how the poor man had been ousted from his home, lost his wife *and* son. Having owned a highly profitable nursery and produce business in Pasadena before the war, he'd been put in a government concentration camp in Arizona; when he was released, the Friends helped him find a temporary job in Boston at DiPassio's Garden

Store. He was overqualified, but with nothing to lose, he took the job and helped double profits within two months. Even an amateur gardener like Margaret had to be dazzled by his apparent skill, his umpteen professional awards and citations from various flower shows.

"I'd gone in just fiddling with the idea of reviving my tulip bed for next spring, and he asked me a thousand questions, Livvie, you never would have imagined: What *kind* of dirt? What color? What trees grow within X feet of the plot? What birds live here? Is the plot to the east or west? On the ocean or inland face?"

"Margaret," Livvie said, "what do we know about the farming business?"

"What's to know that we can't learn?"

To Livvie, it sounded like there was a *lot* to know, but her curiosity grew. How long had it been since she'd met someone—anyone—new? "Oh, Livvie, you *have* to like him," Margaret said. "He *reads.* You know? Except, he's dreadfully serious, at least about plants. In the detention center—oh, that's a nasty business—but he showed me pictures of the vegetable plots they worked in the desert. Mile-high grain, corn; huge lettuce, tomatoes; citrus trees with fruit the size of bowling balls—all in the desert! He had a walletful of snapshots of plants, Livvie . . . oh, but you know, he didn't have *one* picture of his family left! There I go again. But, do you see what I'm saying? You've got Garvin, and I'm going to be fifty next month. Garvin will like having a man around to do man things with. We'll fix up Jack's old office for him. He'll help us, we'll help him; it will be even. Do you see?"

In fact, Livvie did not see how having another person dependent on her could ease her situation, not really. And Garvin? What about the teasing he'd taken from Byron? Would the boy understand? Wouldn't he look at this Japanese and imagine his father's killer? Or what if Garvin did take to him? Surely he didn't mean to stay? Yes, she could use some extra income, but this Californian's thumb had better be pretty damned green. She recalled Sig's massive, blonde, bare-chested figure sweating and cursing over his meager rows of beans, pygmy-sized cabbage heads, brownish sprigs of herbs. And yet, so many miserably dull hours, weeks, months had passed since Livvie had heard, seen, or thought anything new, anything at all, that she surrendered. She agreed to a trial with this Mr. Fujita. He would move in as soon as arrangements could be made. Although Livvie saw no need to rush about it, Margaret was insistent that they must "rescue" the poor man at least by the holidays, hopefully before Thanksgiving. The women had sealed the deal with a hug.

"The holidays!" Livvie groaned, now reminded of the season approaching. Not the first without Sig, but the first since his death just before the New Year. How would she get through that? Of course, she was not without aid; no sooner had word of Sig's death spread through Juggeston than the same well-meaning fool had sent her a subscription to *Bereavement*. A modest, saddle-stitched bulletin with the distinct air of a church pamphlet, *Bereavement* offered "helpful, practical advice for war widows" on how to keep your loved one "alive." "Opening cards, receiving flowers, writing and sending acknowledgments—your supporters may not realize how demanding their sympathies can be on the newly widowed," it reminded her. "Tell your supporters just how much you can comfortably handle." She tried it for a short time—had spent a week at her kitchen table, penning belated thank-yous for bouquets and condolences (and even a few anonymous money gifts), and begging to be excused from various social functions this year. That first, December, issue had warned, "Holidays are especially difficult. Observe your loved one's presence in the family circle," *Bereavement* recommended. "Set a chair for your loved one at the dinner table."

Livvie still sat on the cake pan, shaking her head, hugging her nerves, bracing herself to meet this Japanese man—this detention-camp person, this ex-convict. . . . Had she made a big mistake? It shamed her to imagine Sig still looming over her shoulder—he'd have whipped the notion right out of her hide. She resented it, in fact—her late husband's "presence." "Set a stupid *chair*, for Christ's sake!" she grumbled. Around her, the wind grew violent, spitting rain needles, yanking back the trees so that the Peak seemed pulled off balance. Garvin would just be arriving at the house now, scattering things about, having not listened to her say exactly where he'd find the pattern book. Just like his father, he would have neglected to wipe his feet on the mat. Like Sig, he would take off his cap and forget to put it back on. He'd lie in bed grumpy and sick all the next day, refusing to eat anything, and hide the aspirin under the mattress when she turned away. She massaged her stiff right hand, her sewing hand, her spanking hand. She watched the raindrops tear into her cake like flak through bare skin.

"Fuck you, Sig," she finally told the rain, the cake, her muddy boots. Breathing in against her girdle, she stood upright. "Really, fuck you." The chair's *taken*, she thought, and bent with care to pick up the empty pan. When Garvin returned with the book a few minutes later, he had left his cap behind.

They made a great racket, clomping the mud off their shoes before entering though the back. Nonetheless, Garvin's mother felt compelled to call out a warning. "Hello! We're here!" The new man, standing in half-profile to them, was gazing out the front window, his stance formal—hands locked behind him, chin upturned—as he surveyed the swampy yard. Garvin thought he looked like a general presiding over a war room. "It's okay," his mother whispered to him. "He's just a man. Be polite."

Margaret ran to the door, fluttering about them, ushering them in, removing jackets. "Mr. Fujita," she called. The man pivoted and smiled. "Can you tear yourself away from that window for a moment to meet your new neighbors?" She bent over Garvin and stage-whispered, "He's annoyed because it rained and it's so chilly. I told him he hasn't seen anything yet and he'd better get used to it. Go on. Tell him."

"Er, yep," Garvin agreed, stealing a glance back at his mother. Nudged forward by Margaret, he reluctantly extended a hand. "Welcome to Massachusetts."

"Well, thanks, pal," Mr. Fujita said. "Put it there. Hey, the last time we tried that, we almost got beaned, didn't we? Some hubbub last night, wasn't it?"

Letting his hand be lifted and lowered, Garvin felt the man's palm, scaly and hot. Usually a polite boy, he could not even bring himself to look at the man. It made him too nervous.

"From those shiners, I think Garvin had *already* been beaned a few times last night," Nurse Kelly said, examining him. "That's a mighty impressive Halloween mask you've got there. They look better now. Did Mom give you a whipping?"

Garvin grinned. If he didn't much care for *getting* black eyes, he didn't mind having them. They made him feel tougher, and he wanted to seem tough meeting this new man. "This is my mom," he said, pointing.

Livvie appeared surprised. "Oh, hello, finally you . . ." She reached out to shake hands—hers still held the muddy cake pan. She looked at Garvin as if she needed his help to remove it. "Well, he has both arms and legs, it seems."

"I'm sorry?" Mr. Fujita said. Garvin shook his head.

"Can I take that for you, dear?" Margaret asked.

"That *was* dessert," Livvie explained. "Mud pies," she added.

"Heavens!" Margaret took the pan and the rain-limp pattern book, which she pinched by the corner in distaste, as if it were a fresh animal pelt. "Oh, well. My own culinary efforts tonight also leave much to be desired. I've fallen a bit out of practice entertaining since Jack died." She had laid out soda pop—it was flat—and a plate piled high with grease-soaked rounds of fried potato topped with Spam. "Getting ready for Mr. Fujita's arrival, I never quite managed to get to the store. Do tell him, I'm not usually this . . ." Sighing dramatically, she arranged them all near the living room fireplace—Livvie in the rocker, Garvin on the couch beside Mr. Fujita—while she stood by the cabinet bar. They all blinked at one another awkwardly until the hostess continued, "Well . . . um, brandy?"

"Er, thank you, no," said Mr. Fujita, who sat stiffly as a suitor on a chaperoned date, his hands crossed over a folded-up newspaper in his lap. "I don't care for anything."

"Absolutely," Livvie said, shuddering, then sneezing violently. "Hurry."

"I'll just have soda," Garvin said seriously, and the adults all laughed. He regarded the new man with caution. In this bright light, his face appeared even rounder, the ears larger. There was something very stiff and formal about him—particularly his neck. The way he stared down his nose, he looked like Mr. Wood, the principal, just before he would deliver a scolding. In last night's haunted sleeplessness, Garvin had formulated different theories about Fujita's background; then at recess, he returned to the high school to review the scary recruitment poster. It still didn't fit this face. He had once visited the nearby Wampanoag Indian village, though, and after careful scrutiny he decided that a Jap's features were close enough to venture a guess. He took advantage of a lull in Margaret's chatter. "Say, you got some Injun blood in you?" He used his radio gangster voice, as he often did when nervous.

A Spam-laden chip clenched half-bitten in his teeth, Mr. Fujita studied Garvin curiously, as if he were a cuddly but potentially treacherous pet, then released a laugh so guttural, from so deep within his lean chest—like a *bear's*—that Garvin cringed. He recalled the man's vicious growling when he'd chased the egg-throwing boys into the shadows.

"Garvin!" Livvie cried. With dizzying speed, she ripped the boy off the couch, a smart rap aimed at his wrist. "You apologize right now, young man!" The blurred red trails of her nail polish, the *whoosh* of her descending palm filled the air so threateningly that the boy winced in anticipation.

But Mr. Fujita intervened, hauling Garvin away from his mother and back up onto the couch, mussing his hair and booming out, "Hah! You're a real curious one, all right!" When his laughter subsided, though, he said soberly, "No, Kemosabe. Sorry. No Injun blood."

"I just *wondered*," the boy explained, rattled.

Livvie resettled herself in the rocking chair and scowled at Garvin. "We *both* apologize, Mr. Fujita," she said, though with some annoyance at this stranger's intercession. Margaret handed her a snifter of brandy, which she downed neatly.

Garvin, staring down at the newspaper, asked, "Um, can I have the funnies? I never got to read 'em this morning."

Mr. Fujita narrowed his eyes and held the paper to his chest. "Don't you wanna know what I *am*, iffen I ain't Injun?"

"I guess not," Garvin answered, eyeing his mother, deeply unsettled by her newfound taste for whacking people. After laughing and mussing Garvin's hair again, the man surrendered the *Crier.* On the pretense of getting some orange juice from the fridge, Garvin slipped away to the kitchen to escape in his funny papers. This week's episode: Blackhawk comes home from Burma.

How do people come together from opposite corners of the country, of the world? For Fujita, the California widower, it was only out of necessity and under the most extreme duress. More an ice-maker than an icebreaker, Garvin's disruption left the adults stiffer than ever as they struggled to exchange that neighborly banter designed, as Margaret put it, "to get to know each other."

"Were you born here?" Livvie asked, "here" meaning somewhere in that vast and unspecific expanse between his home in the far west and hers in the far east of this country—meaning America.

Bracing himself, the new man now accepted a brandy when Margaret poured refills, then began his much edited hearth-side tale of the *Pacific Angel.* To his consternation, the women sat rapt and unmoving, as if hearing a Halloween ghost story, until he concluded with Ichiro's fireworks: "'Bang bang bang!'"

"My lands!" Margaret sang, clapping her hands together.

"Wow!" Livvie said.

"I don't know if that's *exactly* the way it happened," the Nisei stranger confessed, his broad lips drawing to a frown. "Mom's . . . tough to pin down—about many things."

"*Thirty-six percent!*" Margaret intoned, raising her glass in what had become her catchall salute to spunky womanhood. "I like her already!"

"Is your mother . . ." Livvie began. "I was going to say 'around,' but . . ."

"Er, she's alive, yes," he said, fidgeting. "Still somewhere out west." He saw Margaret on the verge of demanding, *You don't know where?* "She moves a lot," he said abruptly. There were still so many places, in America and in himself, that he could not go. He changed course. "Well, I don't mean to bore you talking about myself."

"Not at all," Margaret protested. "We want to hear *all* about you. Don't we, Livvie?"

Leaning back in the rocking chair, Livvie grinned. "After the grilling I got trick-or-treating tonight, I'd say *everybody* wants to know about you."

The man's foot flew up involuntarily and set the coffee table rattling with the untouched pop bottles and appetizer plates and potato slivers. A slim vase of browning marigolds turned over, oozing watery green muck onto a stack of books there. With a magician's speed, he conjured a handkerchief and wiped at the books. Margaret was an avid if impatient reader; the tasseled page markers showed she was currently halfway through Yeats's *Last Poems*, Eliot's *Four Quartets*, and Hemingway's *For Whom the Bell Tolls* all at once. Impressed, and hoping to shift the talk away from himself, Mr. Fujita held the dried-off stack out to Margaret admiringly.

"I have a lot of time to read these days," she said, slightly embarrassed, placing the pile on the mantelpiece. Strumming the spines, she chuckled. "It drove Jack mad how I read. Oh, he wooed me with poetry, but after his MD training, he decided he'd done enough reading. He read nothing but *Life*, *New England Journal of Medicine*, and dime-store westerns. Remember, Livvie, how he gobbled up those Zane Grey pulps?" She turned to face them again. Set before the masonry backdrop, its firelight setting the reds and golds of her hair dancing, her posture struck Fujita as oddly theatrical—even operatic—though her wistfulness about her late husband seemed sincere. "He was always quoting Oscar Wilde: 'Maggie, my love, *we live in an age that reads too much to be wise*.'" She took on a gruff, rasping voice, and in this Mr. Fujita imagined he heard an echo of the ailing Dr. Kelly. Finding her candor at once appalling and enviable, he thought the Kellys must have parted well.

"Ha! *His* only entertainment was radio, gossip, high school sports, and plays. Well, I warn you, Mr. Fujita, this town does that to a person. Makes her lazy. *Him* lazy," she amended. "You see, Jack expected it to be Walden—away from civilization, back-to-basics, some idyllic retreat. Ha, again! Rural New England has no spunk, no imagination. Definitely no sense of humor. I'm sick of it. No, I take that back. Oh, I don't know what I'm sick of, but there's something . . ."

Disquieted by this intimate reverie, Mr. Fujita looked to Livvie for her reaction, but she had her head bowed, focused on the silky swaying the rocking caused in her brandy snifter. One pale hand tugged at the ends of her hair; it fell in a nearly black sheet so straight over her hidden face that he almost could have taken her for Japanese. More than just twenty years separated these women, he thought, when Margaret recalled him by name. "Well, Mr. Fujita," she sighed, and he sat bolt upright, fearing she meant to interrogate him about his wife, Mari. Instead, she said, "I can only imagine it's better than where you come from. But if you're one of those fellows looking for small-town enlightenment, you'd do better to turn right around. Still, you are welcomed, and I hope you feel comfortable here on Widow's Peak."

"Widow's Peak," Mr. Fujita echoed distantly, anything but comfortable.

Livvie's chair accelerated its exasperated rocking. "Widow's Peak," she muttered. "Widow's *walk*. Widow's *weeds*," she said, finding a rhythm. "War widow. *Dowager*." She emptied and refreshed her glass, then wrinkled her nose at something. "You know what I learned today from my oh-so-informative widow newsletter? I'll tell you. I discovered the *grass* widow. You know it?" Mr. Fujita shook his head; Margaret looked out the window, toward her scarecrow. "A grass widow is a woman abandoned by a man. Left. Such as a war bride *before* she's made a war widow. Get it? But does it stop there? Oh no! She can be a divorcée, or separated, or an unmarried woman who's lived with a man, or men. A mistress left in the dust, maybe. Perhaps, more specifically, with an illegitimate child. Imagine. All that in one handy phrase. What the grass is, I don't know. A grass bed? Sleeping out in the field? Sleeping around in the barn? Or just put out to pasture?" The chair creaked wildly now, and it seemed the Tuftellers had *not* parted very well. "*Then* there's the good old merry widow! Not to mention the black. So many words for us secondhand gals. But men, only the one. Widowers are never merry, are they?"

"Not this one," Mr. Fujita admitted, though there was absolutely nothing about his parting from Mari, in Gila River, that he cared to recall for strangers—or himself, for that matter.

"I suppose there might be a grass widower?" Margaret offered.

Livvie shook her head firmly. "Not the same. I actually looked it up. Sure, a man may be divorced or separated, but one thing's for sure: He's not sleeping out in the barn with the kid. Er, no offense," she told the new man seriously. "We've had a cruddy day."

"No," he concurred. "No offense."

"I'm just. . . . Okay. We have a business, we make a farm. Can we also make a pact? Can we at least not call it that? Can we not live on *Widow's Peak*, please?"

Widow's Peak. The three barely acquainted adults nodded in agreement but then looked away and silently acknowledged the thin and morbid kinship among them. Only Margaret could yet evoke her ghost with a wry smile, a sparkle in her blue eye. That sparkle in Livvie was yet a slow, angry burn. In Mr. Fujita, there was only that daze, as in one trying very hard to retrace his steps to something he had misplaced. These war years had rendered each of them—like so many in the world—grown-up orphans.

Mr. Fujita surveyed the room carefully. So cozy: the hot stone fireplace, the knickknacks, the well-worn cord rug, Jack's tarnished trumpet on a stand, the needlepoint samplers in oval wooden frames. Above the doorway hung a three-foot shelf with a web-strewn gingerbread house from some Christmas past. He eyed the antique rolltop desk in the corner, a ragged quill pen rising from its empty inkwell. This house, he thought, has led a slow, comfortable, and peaceful life. He liked its smell. He looked at Margaret and liked her. He looked at Livvie and thought he might like her, though she was a touchy one. They all looked at one another, smiling, smiling. Excruciating.

Mr. Fujita and these generous ladies would spend many nights like this, in strained and frank fireside talk of themselves, the war, gardening, more war, books, and war again. That night, however, the newcomer felt they'd fairly well stretched social frankness to an exhausting point. "Please, forgive me, but I'm a bit tired," he said, rising. "And tomorrow *is* a workday," he added, trying to sound hearty. Preparing to dash outside to his room, he saw in the rainy dark Margaret's miserable-looking scarecrow. It was not the mere fact of that straw figure that set him obsessively mulling over "grass widows"—of women abused, abandoned, alone. Rather, with her dress plastered against her curvaceous body, her bonnet limp, her wig hanging waterlogged, that grim Halloween image struck the widower as forcefully as seeing a snapshot from his own life—and of women lost to him. Shutting his eyes, he stepped out into the chilling curtain of rain and knew Livvie was wrong: There *were* grass widowers, too.

TWO

To the City of Roses

William did not become William until he was—in American reckoning—six months old. From the Fujitas' one-room apartment on First Street in Los Angeles, they could conduct their daily business in Japanese at a handful of Japanese establishments if they wished, at a close commute to both the wharf and the *gakuen*, the Japanese-language school where Tamie taught part-time.

"Well, perhaps the extra income will benefit us," Ichiro said when she landed a job offer there. "But of course, they shouldn't count too much on you. I don't plan to remain here very long." In planning things, Ichiro was a master, who would instruct his son, time and again, "Always be prepared, and you will never be unpleasantly surprised."

In keeping with this philosophy, Ichiro's most treasured possession was a seventeen-jewel Royal pocket watch. Well crafted and sturdy, the watch's gray exterior and plain roman-numeraled face could only be described as dull, but to pry it open—as Ichiro did for ritual weekly cleaning—revealed a finely sculpted magician's box of silver and brass gears. It baffled and amazed young William that the Waltham, Massachusetts, watch wizards saw fit to decorate only its innards; scallop shapes and curlicues, zigzags and crested waves and starbursts had all been burnished into the inner casing where no one but watchmakers and obsessive watch cleaners like Ichiro could appreciate them.

Toward the end of his days, Ichiro would fiddle with and refer to the timepiece compulsively, as if he expected the westward-bound steamer that would bear him home might depart any minute. By that time, however, it became clear that the Little Bull would never return to his homeland. For Tamie, too, always had her plans.

The baptism of the newest Fujita in the Japanese Union Church could not long remain secret from Ichiro, as Tamie wished, but there was just time enough to accomplish the boy's belated naming and blessing. Access through the open front doorways was obstructed by a wall of folding chairs; there the most obese and elderly congregation members enjoyed a cool breeze and survived the service without succumbing to the sweltering heat. In the poorly ventilated front of the baptistery, the Reverend Mr. Takemura, though a thin fellow, perspired so profusely that it looked as if he had already been doused himself. Mopping his face and neck with a handkerchief, he asked Tamie if they might wait for her husband (who never attended church), and then suggested they halt until some electric fan could be located, but Tamie insisted they begin immediately.

Although most of her family were Buddhist, Tamie had attended a Christian church in Japan. Its grand ceremony offered more entertaining distraction from academic study—her real religion—and speaking with the missionaries and borrowing their untranslated hymnals let her practice her English. She viewed baptism as a precautionary measure more than a religious necessity; her son would choose his own spiritual path, as she had. Further, the infant had long gone unnamed during his parents' ceaseless battles over what to dub him. Ichiro grew adamant, nearly violent, about giving the boy a Japanese name. He preferred the unimaginative Hiroshi.

"We live in America, and the boy should have an American name," Tamie insisted. "Do you want your son to be an outcast?"

"If you give him an ugly American name, he'll be ridiculed when we return home."

So they stalemated, until Tamie decided the boy had been called "the boy" long enough. *John, Harry, Jim?* she thought, en route to the church. Standing beside the sweating clergyman at the head of the baptistery, still she wondered, *Hank, George, Theodore?*

Tamie's new blue silk dress clung to her body for the heat, its high collar fastened so tightly about her throat that she teetered with a pleasing dizziness. Her eyes swept over the clean church interior, drinking in the teakwood sheen of the rafters, the simple chandelier that her volunteer efforts had helped purchase, the soft, sprung hardwood floors, all like an aged, heady wine; so elegant, so warm, she thought. If Christ still existed in some spirit—and Tamie did not close her mind to the possibility—he would be a creature of light, of nature. A carpenter-angel, he would appreciate the meticulous, light woodwork of the Japanese Union Church. He would feel at home there.

Sometimes, as on this day of her son's baptism, she thought she felt that spirit seep into her like warm rice wine, intoxicating her as she looked upon the congregation, so well dressed, so hushed, animated only by numerous colorful hand fans fluttering in rows down the pews like a regiment of butterflies. Although some craned their necks, loosened their neckties, she noticed only the smiles. Smiles, she imagined, for the obvious halo of new motherhood radiating from her, from the diaphanous veil encircling her pinned black bun down to the sheen of her rich shoes. She felt . . .

Tamie had won high marks studying English at university and immediately worked to improve her pronunciation in her early months in California. Still, she stumbled on vocabulary. With her first paycheck from teaching elementary Japanese at the gakuen, she bought a massive dictionary, a thesaurus, and a pocket style book, all of which she consulted faithfully each evening before sleeping and again while attending to the baby's cries in the middle of the night. She carried a notepad so that whenever she encountered a new word during the course of the day—grocery shopping, gossiping at the YWCA, or reading the newspaper—

she could record the term (always in context of the entire sentence) for later research. About this Tamie was most fastidious, for her considerable intelligence had not been matched by an equivalent short-term memory.

And now, in the Union Church, she felt. . . . Oh, what *was* that word? It frustrated her that she often forgot things—words, names, appointments—and became tongue-tied, particularly since her reputation as a polyglot (she spoke and read some Mandarin Chinese, and learned a spot of Canadian French one summer tutoring a diplomat's daughter) had won her teachers' admiration. "Without English, you are made just another idiot here," she had complained to Ichiro in her early American days, after being laughed off by a shopkeeper who couldn't understand her. "And I'm not an idiot."

Cradling the baby in his lap, Ichiro poked its round belly and said gleefully, "Ah! Then you bore me an idiot son? All he says is, '*ga*' and '*ki.*'" He nibbled on a tiny toe; Ichiro was especially affectionate when drunk. "Don't worry, boy, your father's an idiot, too! But we'll all be rich professors when we go home!"

The baby agreed. "Ki!"

But Tamie had only murmured, "I'm *not* an idiot."

Was the word she now sought *luxurious* or *luxuriant*? Turning from the waiting congregation, she reached into her purse for the notepad, tucked within the pages of the little style book, and jotted her memo. "I feel luxurious," she wrote. "I feel luxuriant." She looked up at the ceiling and sighed in exasperation. What she meant was: She felt like a princess.

After more minutes of waiting, the increasingly uncomfortable Reverend Mr. Takemura took Tamie aside.

"Please, Takemura-san," she said, "you must forgive my husband for keeping you all waiting on such a hot afternoon. He works so very hard at the docks. Let us begin now, and he will surely come by and by."

The reverend shook his head but appeared relieved that their time in the stifling baptistery would be prolonged no further. He asked the boy's name, and Tamie, still undecided, chose the name of her style book's author, Wm. S. Williams. The reverend directed Tamie to the baptismal, whispered a few directions, oiled the child, and in a pidgin of English and Japanese, welcomed him to the care of Christ.

"Keep your head up when talking to a man," Ichiro Fujita instructed his son regularly during the boy's growing years. "Look down to see the divine."

In addition to the often repeated "Always have a plan," William Fujita would remember this directive as Ichiro's other singular contribution to his spiritual upbringing. In the end, Ichiro accepted, forgave, and forgot about the baptism; whatever Buddhist instincts he exhibited seemed mere knee-jerk reactions to Tamie's more consistent faith. Truthfully, Ichiro thought little of religious matters, or of any world beyond the wharf, the bar, the racetrack, or his dream home in Japan. For him, the nautical miles between his native and adopted countries constituted all the universe.

That distance also lay between the shores of Nisei William's and Issei Ichiro's hearts. Although he held a steady wharf job, Ichiro remained in his mind an adventurous bird of passage, and his wanderlust and entrepreneurial zeal took him moonlighting afar for weeks or even months at a time. The patchwork, immigrant economy depended on movement, on generalization and resilience, on unofficial jobs and sometimes illegal ones. After seasonal work picking oranges or cotton down south, one might take up a few shifts at the cannery or, like Tamie, take in home laundry. Always there existed more demand than supply for things Japanese—foodstuffs, books, prostitutes—so one might sideline as a *pinpu*, if one had space enough for a hospitable brothel, or, like Ichiro, hit the road as a salesman for an Oriental trading company. Similarly, it was not uncommon for proprietors of a dry-goods store to put out their neighbors' homegrown daikon and burdock, or bathtub sake, there by the socks and girdles. In that community's younger days as a mostly bachelor society, round-the-clock card games often ran in the kitchen of a confectionery store. Ichiro was better known to the gambling sites and racetracks along the Pacific Coast than to his son, and perhaps it was this absence that allowed the boy to idolize his father, the adventurer-hero.

His parents were heroes to him, and it saddened him that he felt unequal to the hopes they had for the newborn whom Ichiro had mistaken for the heroic peach boy, Momotaro. What a burden it placed on the boy's small, rather average shoulders to be the only child of heroes. After delivering him, Tamie was never able to bear him a sibling, and it both pained and thrilled him to hear that account of the newlyweds' great ocean crossing and his own humble but violent beginnings. "But is it true?" he pleaded.

"What do you think?" Tamie would respond slyly. "Why would your parents lie to you?" And though little Billy didn't know why, he had observed that the immigrant's morality was a shifty one, not fixed like the notions taught at school or in the Good Book. He saw certain contradictions between Tamie's behavior and her outward Christian faith, as when the two splendid missionary ladies came to teach her American cooking. To William, they'd looked like bear queens, so regal in both their corpulence and their extraordinary attire, their unseasonable rugs-upon-rugs of animal furs and the foot-long ostrich plumes sprouting from their headpieces. They took up so much space! Taking as evidence the Japanese's short stature, these charitable gentlewomen impressed upon Tamie the inadequacy of her traditional diet, woefully lacking in those staple foodstuffs that were readily available in more civilized countries. In their opinion, immigration may have saved Tamie's life, and indeed, they administered their lesson in the queenly art of preparing ground beef with the grave urgency of field nurses applying tourniquets to a fatal wound. To Billy, the demonstration had the entertainment value of a magic show, as they slapped the enormous slab of flesh, as big as his whole head, onto the skillet, conjuring columns of an oily, alien smoke that made Tamie turn green. To his relief, the flat red masses condensed into smaller brown balls that he might be able to fit in his mouth, but the ladies then heaped these onto a salad, itself arrayed between two planks of bread. Though an ingenious way of consolidating a whole meal, Billy thought the sandwich excessive. "You must eat *properly* if you want to grow up big and strong," instructed one she-bear, pouring him a large tumbler of milk. "You should drink at least three glasses of milk a day."

Eager to be rid of the ladies so that she might vomit in privacy, Tamie thanked them profusely and ushered them out into the hall, whereupon the tiny flat instantly grew larger. To eject the ladies, Tamie had to assure them of her conversion. "I can't thank you enough," she told them, and she repeated her new phrase of the week: "This was a real eye-opener." It opened Billy's eyes, too. As he let forth a cyclone of burps and farts that lasted several hours, he realized that his mother—now gagging over the sink—could lie.

After that, Mom was draped in mystery—not the mystery of deception but of withholding. Once, when she was particularly angry with Pop, he asked her what led her to marry a stranger whom even nine-year-old Billy thought to be financially and intellectually beneath her, but she would not even entertain the question. For her, history started only with her son's story, with the day she delivered him to America. Everything else was pre-history, "*Mukashi no hanashi,*" as she always said. "An old story, long ago."

Whenever Tamie wished to be alone with her son, she gave her husband money to go out; when she wouldn't give him money, he could always revert to his old bachelorhood method of procuring alcohol, and he would return bruised but content. Tamie only withheld money if she suspected that he planned to gamble with it. Waving a bill just out of his reach, she'd warn him, "This is for going to the docks, not for cards. If you gamble this away—"

"I know, I know," Ichiro would reply. "I'm not stupid."

Only in his teenage years, as his father lay near death after an accident at the wharf, would William realize that the Little Bull had been a lifelong alcoholic and that "going to the docks" had been his parents' euphemism for getting drunk. As a child, he had visited the wharf often. When other boys his age learned to throw a baseball sidearm, William perfected a two-handed, pendulum-swing mackerel toss. While other fathers taught their sons how to bait a hook, Ichiro showed him how to winch up a hundred-pound net, or how a dozen fish were selected, gutted, cleaned, and packed in ice in less than a minute. If the innocent boy did not know his eccentric, wandering shadow-relative very well, he knew how strenuous working on the docks could be, and he admired his father as a champion of hardy, selfless toil. If Pop occasionally pawed his family with too rough hands and tunelessly sang songs in Japanese, well, didn't a man deserve to let loose a bit after working all day *and* night? And if occasionally his speech slurred, his eyes and face glowed hot red, or he stumbled, what of it? The man must be exhausted.

No spiritual man, Ichiro was nonetheless a *good* man, William believed. And one must automatically forgive a good man when he would jeer, "Why are you staring at the ceiling?" as the boy knelt at his mattress, hands clasped in nightly prayer, lips moving silently.

"Ask blessing for your father," Tamie would say in English.

"There's nothing up there except rust and chipped paint," Ichiro would say. "That's your chore for this week, boy. Scrape that paint."

William could not help but look up. An otherwise healthy boy, he would be dogged all his life by a stiff neck—rigid and tilted slightly back—resulting from his violent birth. "Bless my mother," William would whisper toward the chipping paint. "And Pop, too," he would say, bowing slightly toward the hole-ridden floorboards.

"I'm going the docks," Ichiro would say.

Accustomed to dualities in life, William never thought it paradoxical that his mother was more or less Christian, his father, more or less Buddhist, and himself more or less both. They attended picnics celebrating the births of the Japanese emperor and George Washington, but didn't everyone? He never found it strange that the sounds of his nursery and boyhood were a bilingual garble. Nor did it consciously occur to the child that in the whole rapidly expanding city, so many places remained closed to him. Although he remained unaware of it until adolescence, William also carried the dual citizenship common among Nisei. However dissimilar their styles, beliefs, and functions in his life, his parents seemed, to him, to meld logically and perfectly, even if they were a little peculiar.

Despite their profound differences, his parents concurred on one unshakable point: that a growing boy's hours should be filled with activity, with no time spared for idleness. William took his earliest formal study at home with his mother. At once a Japanese teacher at the gakuen and an English student at the YWCA, she practiced her vocabulary constantly—reciting first the word and then the definition in Japanese—always within earshot of his cradle. In his toddlerhood she played with him the card game she used to teach poetry; each card bore the last two lines of a five-line poem in *waka* form; by the age of six, he could recite fifty of the verses, in Japanese and English. Thus, by the time he enrolled in the integrated public school, his vocabulary was formidable, though spotted with untranslatable idioms that annoyed his teachers and inspired ridicule from his classmates, who knew that Billy Fujita was a little peculiar, too.

Though he was studious, his teachers frequently complained that he "drifted off" in class. His look became "vacant" or sometimes "haunted." "He looks dead to the world," is how one teacher put it to Tamie Fujita. William's mother knew that he didn't sleep very well. Like his father, William was a born insomniac—the Fujita men were vampires. He read and studied, waiting up to greet his father (or to help carry Ichiro to bed). His nights were also disturbed by the unsettling sounds of Ichiro trying desperately and vainly to provide him with a brother. On rare amorous afternoons, Ichiro sent the boy outside to play. But who was there to play with? His mother might add, "Don't go too far." Where would he go? Sometimes he would find a couple of kids shooting marbles or playing kick-the-can (or kick-the-cat), but usually he'd take a book out onto the stoop and wait. Once, after lovemaking, his parents forgot to call him back in until suppertime. Ichiro headed downstairs to look for him. Tamie's hands were covered in sticky rice, so it took her a moment to get the window open. Below, the boy lay on the steps with his arms covering his belly, staring straight up into the night sky. He didn't yell or cry; he didn't get up. "What are you brooding about down there?" Tamie called, only a little guilty.

"You forgot me again," he stated. Tamie grimaced at the resignation in his voice.

"Don't be ridiculous!" she yelled. "I just wanted you to get some fresh air, that's all. It's good for you!"

"In the dark?" the boy called, still lying on the step.

"It's character-building. I don't want you to be afraid of the dark like the others. Now stop fooling around down there. Pop's hungry." On his cue, Ichiro swung the door open, and a skewed rectangle of yellow hall light suddenly cast the little body into relief. "Ya," Tamie said, gulping. "He does look dead."

His teachers also complained that the boy hardly spoke in class, and when he did, he whispered. This was partially attributable to the teasing by his classmates, but Tamie knew her son had a capacity for silence unusual in a young boy. Unfortunately, the lack of space in their one-room apartment had apportioned to William the status of a family dog. His parents tended to discuss adult things in front of him as if he were incapable of comprehending human speech. They spoke in Japanese, but even when William didn't know what they were saying, he knew what they meant. They tried to whisper, but in that place one couldn't whisper softly enough. The blanket they strung between his bed and theirs, like a hospital-room partition, made a poor baffle, particularly for those nocturnal noises that were his introduction to lovemaking. Though infrequent, those nights were unimaginably long for the boy, whose only possible escape in a room offering none was to shoehorn himself into the crack behind his bed. Later William would suspect those early living conditions contributed both to his insomnia and his career, his fondness for outdoor work.

He became an isolated child, regarded as "that creepy Jap kid" by his schoolmates, who tolerated him without offering him lasting friendships. As he grew older, they also resented his studiousness and teasingly called him "the Big Brain of Little Tokyo." His rare friendships, based on convenience, tended to be struck with Negro and Chicano kids, and other Nikkei—those of Japanese ancestry—who shared the public pool on colored days, the back balcony of a movie theater, and other trappings of the second class. Devoid of much early social experience, the boy remained unworldly about common adolescent pleasures. He did not attend pep rallies or take friends joyriding (Ichiro never owned a car); his neck problems prevented him from playing sports; he fished for suckers in the sewers but did not hunt; he certainly never experienced the sort of gaming, romancing, and drinking so enjoyable to his father. He never even masturbated (where could he?) until he was nearly fifteen. In addition to regular schoolwork, his Saturdays at the gakuen, and Sundays at the church, a hefty chore schedule ensured that he was not idle. His regular responsibilities at home included watering the plants, helping his mother carry home groceries and ice, washing the windows and floors, emptying out his father's ashtrays, returning milk and pop bottles to the grocer, and pickup and delivery when Tamie took in home laundry.

In this way William Fujita was formed, and Tamie grew concerned. Who wouldn't desire such a son? Tamie asked herself cautiously, reluctant to admit his social shortcomings. Thoughtful, serious, intelligent, responsible, and hardworking, never a trouble—these assets she counted as if ticking off a grocery list, until forced to append at the last: "dull." Her insensitivity to his social development may have been unintentional, but she blamed herself. She did not oppose play or leisure in principle, but unlike Ichiro, she preferred the life of the mind and did not think to plan out these things. As for Ichiro, he saw little use for the boy to develop strong ties to other children. "It's not like we're staying here," he reminded her, burnishing his Royal pocket watch.

No, Tamie admitted it: She'd been negligent, and it was perhaps inevitable that her son should grow up to be a wallflower—*a plant man*. Much as it pained her to imagine him becoming "another Japanese gardener," Tamie saw that it suited his temperament. Though she hoped William would blossom into a *college* man (she'd stop at nothing to ensure he'd never be a *fish* man), many or most career opportunities for Japanese led to plant life, whether as farmers, migrant pickers, greengrocers, florists, or gardeners. That they were as a rule successful at this work was evidenced by the ever-increasing vitriol and violence of California's anti-Japanese network: Labor unions and agricultural organizations resented that Nikkei farmers, controlling only 1 percent of California's cultivated land, accounted for nearly 40 percent of its crop production. Tamie saw how politicians ran on "yellow peril" platforms supported by such self-proclaimed "nativists" as the Native Sons of the Golden West, whose brotherhood arose from the charming view of California as "the White Man's Paradise given by God to a white people." A political hotbed itself, the Sons' roster would shape the future of American justice, in Earl Warren, and even the Oval Office, in that glittering son, Richard M. Nixon. Not only was it boring by 1913 to be a Nikkei plant man—it was becoming dangerous.

However, Junichiro Miyake, gardener to many big Hollywood and Pasadena estates, was a particularly successful plant man—even famous. Thus, when a colleague at the gakuen found William a summer job as the old Issei's apprentice, after his rocky freshman year, Tamie accepted on the boy's behalf, and William agreed. He began what he would later call his "indentured vassalage" one boiling June afternoon on the estate of a flamboyant sporting-goods mogul who had made his fortune in baseball gear. As ever, the teenager arrived punctually, but his new boss glowered as if he'd been waiting for hours. The arms crossed on his chest were knotted and narrow as old, woody vines; his long face tapered into a scraggly goatee that made William itch to look at it. The master stood at least a half foot shorter than William but gave orders as if he were the estate's owner, not its gardener.

Heralded as "the King of Cleats," the sports mogul inhabited the estate only in winter, but he kept a skeletal groundskeeping staff year-round. Under the stewardship of Miyake, "Gardener to the Stars," the property maintained an intelligent, manicured magnificence that had intimidated many a baseball commissioner, team owner, and star-slugger. In addition to the usual flower beds, kitchen gardens, and decorative shade trees, the King of Cleats kept a full baseball diamond, a lawn-bowling area, and a grass tennis court, which William mowed and raked. His enthusiasms also extended to water sports, and more specifically *nude* water sports; the man-made pond and Olympic pool were both strategically moated by hedges, a shield from paparazzi, private eyes, wives, and the like. A lush fig tree sat on a concrete island in the midst of the pool, to the dismay of both William—responsible for its pruning (a tricky business, as he had never learned to swim)—and the pool cleaner. A ninety-square-foot maze of cut evergreens allowed privacy for "indoor-outdoor sports," Miyake explained with a snicker. But maintaining the modesty of the playboy sports mogul and his guests called for a heroic effort, and William did not cherish it.

"It's an honor to work with such an accomplished artist!" Tamie scolded her son. "Character-building! It's an opportunity to learn something *and* be paid a dollar a day!"

The old Issei did make it look effortless. How neatly he trimmed bushes into decorative patterns . . . while William cleared the droppings. After checking saturation levels, he mixed just the right proportions of soil and peat, which William lugged across the estate in a wheelbarrow (Miyake forbade driving the truck on the lawn). One of these ninety-seven-degree days, William's thoughts turned to rebellion. Forced to excavate seven barrel-sized holes by the front porch, wheel the dirt away, and wheel back seven weighty shrubs for transplanting, the teenager determined that he would tell his mother and the old slave driver: Watching the marvelous Miyake ply his craft could not be worth a hundred dollars a day. He could live just fine without that honor!

Then he saw the girl. As he huffed up to the house pushing the seventh load, he looked to the porch, where the mogul's Mexican cleaning girl worked the hand-washing machine. However unglamorous her chore, she managed to keep a pretty, unsullied appearance in her light blue dress and white apron. She expertly stuffed the wet clothes between the rollers, paused, smiled his way, rolled up her sleeves, then cranked the handle until the wrung fabric slid out the other side. The biceps of her dark arm impressed him—so distracted him, in fact, that he pushed both the wheelbarrow and himself nose-first right into one of the ditches.

"Why don't you look where you're going, stupid boy?" Miyake screeched, waving his fists. "A gardener looks at the ground. You don't look up at girls!"

Lying humiliated in the soot, facedown, William groaned, then disinterred himself with what dignity he could. Tossing back her curls the hue of red mahogany, the girl giggled and disappeared back into the house. For the rest of the afternoon, he planted the shrubs, packed them, encircled them with bricks, watered them, and wheeled the excess soil away, his plan to quit quickly dissipating in the simultaneous hope and fear of seeing the girl again. Miyake sat smoking under a shady tree during the hottest hours, calling out orders and waving his arms like a symphony conductor. At quitting time, the old man examined each new shrub, stretched, and mumbled, "Hmph. Pack the truck, then we eat. Today's work has made me hungry. Go wash up at the pool house. You want to stink for the girl?"

Truly, the boy smelled offensive even to himself; his hands and knees bristled with scars, and he looked like a mass of sculptor's clay. It was a state the unworldly teenager would come to associate with love.

"You like this girl?" the old man said, frowning. "Then tomorrow you work harder, concentrate, or I have no use for you, being so lazy."

Young William Fujita knew only enough of romance to know that he knew nothing. Tamie never spoke of it; Ichiro, who frequently enjoyed extramarital romances, did not share his wisdom at the dinner table. With no personal experience to gauge the sheer bigness of his feelings, the studious teenager found guidance in his assigned summer reading, *The Iliad*, learning that love was arduous, even fatal work. Although he had vowed there would be no "tomorrow" with the tyrannical old gardener, Master Fujita reported the next morning as Homer's *Dawn spread her saffron mantle across the world*—and he did work harder.

Unable to marshal the courage to speak with the cleaning girl, whom he secretly named Helen, he exorcised his frustration through positively Spartan labor in service to the King of Cleats. How vengefully the stouthearted Fujita mowed those lawns, decapitated the spent rose blossoms. With his Helen urging him on, even the treacherous Olympic pool moating the fig island could not cow him. All for a glimpse of her there at the porch railing, pressing wet cloth through the wringer, shaking dust from a mop—lovely, he was certain, as a daughter of god and swan.

"Still mooning over that Mexican?" Tamie jeered throughout

that long summer, though at first she feared the boy was ill. Returning from work, ecstatic with misery and weariness, he wouldn't or couldn't speak to her, only rummaged through the cupboards and ice chest as if he hadn't eaten in weeks, then dove into *The Iliad*.

Of course, such delicious, first-lovelorn agony comes to a boy only once in life and quickly becomes its own reason for being, the subject of its own passion. By summer's end, had he discovered that she requited his affection, he'd surely have quit. As it happened, she quit first, when school resumed. Still, his summer swoon did not fade, nor did the spectral Helen that the cleaning girl had conjured in his imagination. He remained productive; his study with Mr. Miyake became more and more fruitful. Outdoor labor released his pent-up energy; he so valued escaping from the apartment and the city, he learned to drive Miyake's truck in only one month. Very soon, Miyake told his parents he had discerned a real talent in the boy.

"It's as though he's possessed," Miyake said. "With his help, I could have a nursery up and running before year's end for the Tournament of Roses. I had doubts about him at first, but I say to you now, you can be proud of your son. I've come to rely on him a great deal." In fact, William was indispensable now that Miyake had decided to lease a small nursery in Pasadena. When the time came, Miyake hoped to buy the property, and with the new Alien Land Act he'd need a young Nisei apprentice more than ever. He offered to let the nursery's house to the Fujitas, if William would help before and after class. Tamie said she'd think about it.

The idea of having his own space meant more to William than he could express. He badgered his mother frequently about Miyake's offer, but she only said, "Yes, yes, I'll talk to your father, but you must have some patience."

"Sure, you'll talk to Pop," he moaned. "He'll say, 'Pft! Pack your bags! We're leaving in five minutes!'" He scratched at his underarm, aping his father's most recent and embarrassing habit—Ichiro scraped at himself all the time, all over his body, and even in public—as if his skin was on fire. His watch checking had also taken on a frenzied, desperate pace, and he'd taken to speaking Japanese more frequently, too. William believed his father was losing his marbles.

"Be patient," Tamie repeated. She had herself long argued for a bigger apartment in the suburbs, but she knew something that neither of the male Fujitas seemed to notice: Her husband was clearly dying.

A few weeks later Tamie was proved right when Ichiro entered the hospital having collapsed at the wharf one night. He had been enjoying his usual diversions—fighting, drinking, smoking, poker, and drinking, in that order. He may have noticed that the pounding he invited hurt more than usual, that the Ichi-Bomb kicked back more violently, that his cigar puffs drew less smoke, but his poker playing had improved with age: He had won the biggest pot of his life, all of $539! His cannery comrades weren't put off, though, for Ichiro Fujita was nothing if not an upright chap and a graceful winner. Instead of taking his booty straight home, he stood everyone, including himself, two more rounds. Finally he stumbled out of the bar drunker than usual, probably because he'd skipped dinner—he hadn't been hungry. "I'm just dizzy from *good fortune*," he chuckled. Then the man who daily navigated seaweed-slimed angling nets delicately as a ballerina blacked out, tripped on his own foot, and tumbled into the bay.

Two of his Caucasian buddies, only slightly less smashed, managed to fish him out but feared they were too late. They were. When they dragged him to the hospital, though, the doctor instantly determined that the near drowning was a mere *symptom* of his inevitable killer. The real culprit, Ichiro's doctor opined to Tamie, was alcohol. The man had finally just pushed his body to its utmost limits. He reeked like a moonshine still.

The doctor shook his head. "See, his skin's yellow," he pointed out. At first Tamie frowned and blinked at Ichiro, then to the doctor as if to say, "Yes, *and?*" But he meant yellow from jaundice, an indication of a progressive disease called alcoholic hepatitis. "And he's been scratching it. See?" Ichiro's itching was another symptom—along with general confusion, disorientation, mental slowing. "My bet is, his liver's inflamed, too. This man," the doctor concluded, "has got poison for blood."

Thinking Ichiro too ill to understand them, they had spoken freely in English. Searching her husband's face, however, Tamie grimaced. He understood, all right—and he smiled.

So Tamie had urged patience—they would wait until Ichiro became well again, or died. Then, summoning his family to him the next day, he made it easy for her. "Maybe you should give notice to that stupid landlord of ours," he told her, wheezing. "We'll see what happens."

He signed over what needed to be signed ("Best to be prepared," said he), wrote out a will, and worked out mortician arrangements ("You never know what may happen"), surrendered his poker winnings to his wife, and asked her to wait out in the corridor. Then he asked his son, "Do you want to continue work with Miyake? You want to move to Pasadena with him?"

"Yes, Pop."

"Your mother will want you to go to college, you know. I don't know if you can be a student of Miyake's and of college. He knows about hard work; he will demand the best from you, and you must decide. I won't have you shame me because your mother makes you go to college." He paused to rake at his skin with a fork from his otherwise untouched breakfast tray. "You'll have to take her, of course, and you'll have to watch her. She's too clever for the likes of us." He reached into the pocket of his trousers hanging on the bed knob and drew out the seventeen-jewel Royal pocket watch. "It stopped when I fell into the water. Maybe you can find someone in Pasadena to fix it."

"Sure, Pop. Absolutely."

"Come here."

Leaning toward his father, William did not know what frightened him, why Ichiro did not seem like Ichiro. Then it came to him: They had never been so close without the scented cushion of smoke, fish, and hooch. His father smelled clean now, soapy, like a baby.

"Come closer, boy."

William did it, and with one ruined, bear-paw hand, his father gave him the penultimate gift of a smack across the face.

"What was *that* for?" William yelped, stepping back.

"I always say, 'Be prepared,'" Ichiro chuckled. "Stop thinking about that stupid Mexican. You make your mother mad with that, and she's made me mad all summer. Don't be so stupid."

"Okay, Pop," the boy mumbled, rubbing his cheek. "I'm sorry."

After that the room was a flurry of activity. A parade of dockworkers came by, then the doctor ordered everyone out so Ichiro could nap. That afternoon Tamie returned with Miyake, ordering William to stay outside. Later William learned, with a mixture of irritation and joy, that without consulting him they had arranged to purchase the nursery in his name, as he was the only citizen among them. He was to hold 30 percent, Miyake 49, and Tamie 21.

"You *bought* it?" he cried. He liked gardening but maybe not that much.

Ichiro explained that it was a favor to Miyake. "He's still the master, but you will be the man of the house. Only Nisei can own land or get anywhere in America."

"I know, Pop."

"It's only temporary," Ichiro emphasized. "But it's good business, too. Better to own than lease."

Later that evening, when a Japanese couple from Ichiro's prefecture came to visit the Little Bull, he was exhausted and embarrassed. The Fujiwaras knew his family; someday they would carry word of his last days back across the Pacific. The purchase of the new house, though he knew he would not live there himself, represented to him a resignation to failure, the beginning of his end.

"This little problem," he gasped, waving a hand over his stretched-out body, "delays my plans. Ah, how stupid! So: We are buying a house. Pasadena. Really moving up in the world. Only until my strength returns, of course. Then sell it. Tell my family. When you go home."

"Yes, Fujita-san," the Fujiwaras said. "Yes, of course."

"And I'll sell it at a profit, you can bet!" he shouted, and the attempted enthusiasm sent him into two minutes of solid coughing, heaving, and panting. To William, who sat reading in the corner, his father's agony sounded uncomfortably like ecstasy.

"Yes, of course you will, Fujita-san. Please don't exert yourself!"

"Shit. That nearly killed me," Ichiro managed, finally catching his breath. "A house in Pasadena," he sighed. "Tell them. Tournament of Roses. How spectacular. And how my son is fifteen. Already partner to Miyake. Say: Only a boy, but already a successful businessman. With his own home and nursery. In Pasadena."

That night Ichiro Fujita fell into a coma, and one morning soon after, his wife and son awoke to the landlord's angry knocking, summoning them to the telephone downstairs. While his mother answered the phone, William glanced around Mr. MacGregor's filthy apartment—three times the size of his own but stuffed with ten times the furniture and bric-a-brac and occupied by a horde of mangy cats. The landlord himself was as disheveled. As a child, Fujita had always feared him—the hirsute, keg-shaped body, gnarled teeth, and pointed ears reminiscent of a wild boar's, and a disposition to match. Ever teetering on the brink of exasperation, MacGregor soured whenever a tenant summoned him to fix a pipe or check a radiator. At these times he would cross his thick, tattooed arms over his chest as if to say, This is the very last straw! And now, as Tamie listened into the receiver, MacGregor planted himself firmly by her side, rolled his eyes and tapped his foot, grumbling, "This absolutely stretches the limits of my patience."

"No need," Tamie said to the other party. "I'll come right away." She looked to her son, nodded, and hung up. To MacGregor, she said coolly, "Thank you for your patience. And oh, we'll be moving out. Come, William."

At the hospital Tamie pulled down the sheet covering Ichiro's face and said, "*Oki no ishi.*" It took William a moment to translate, *a rock in the ocean*. He looked at the corpse, amazed, as if indeed it was a rock, a meteorite that had fallen through the little narrow hospital window and landed on the bed.

"Mom," he said. "You okay?"

Sitting on the corner of the bed, hugging her arms to her sides, Tamie screwed up her face in concentration, then finally recited:

Waga sode wa
Shiohi ni mienu
Oki no ishi no
Hito koso shirane
Kawaku ma mo nashi

Years later, just before the war in the Pacific, Fujita would return to the wharf where his father had worked and recall Lady Sanuki's poem. By then the navy had leased the cannery for Liberty Ship construction, but the dock's bar remained, looking much more run-down than he remembered, less accommodating and cozy, as if it had fallen out of use. Outside its windows, jutting out of the bay, an enormous, guano-caked rock loomed thirty feet from the wharf. Ringed by warning buoys, it reminded him of his father and the waka poetry card of his childhood.

My tear-drenched sleeves are,
like a rock out in the sea
hidden at low tide,
concealed, escaping notice,
bereft of a place to dry.

Without identifying himself to the elderly bartender that afternoon, he finished his beer and was pleased to learn that the fellow still remembered Ichiro Fujita. "A heck of a guy," the old man said. "A heck of a customer, too. Business has slumped since he kicked, I can tell you, what with the goddam dry years. Thank Christ he passed before Prohibition! That really would have killed him." The bartender paused and chuckled. "In the better times, he drummed up a lot of business for my place, I betcha. I'm not kidding when I say I owe Itchy Fujita."

Fujita cringed to hear his father called "Itchy." The bartender's gruff, intense affection for the Little Bull touched him, though when the old man offered to stand him one, anything for a friend of Itchy's, he politely declined. It also pleased him that even after the long Prohibition, one could still order an Ichi-Bomb, and that off-duty engineers and seamen still placed bets on drinking contests, still challenged one another to dare the world's most undrinkable drink.

"Boys his age should prefer girls to plants," Tamie complained to Miyake one cool February Saturday, preparing his lunch in the nursery kitchen while William made the delivery rounds. The Fujitas had now lived on the second floor above the nursery shop for two months, and Tamie had fast tired of living amidst the business of growing. "As much time as he spends around them," Tamie groused, "I shouldn't be surprised if my son turns green and grows leaves!"

In evidence, she pointed to the daybed on the rear kitchen porch where, to her irritation, William frequently slept with the potted ferns and rakes and bags of peat, squandering that luxury he'd sought his whole childhood: his own bedroom upstairs. But the nursery had far exceeded that fantasy, she knew; having aspired to a mere two-room city apartment, the boy seemed lost in this four-acre strip with its greenhouses and storage sheds and boxy, eight-room, two-storied house and shop. To Tamie's thinking, the housing arrangement allotted to their lives an unhappy boundarylessness. Stuffed to capacity, the ground floor shop hemorrhaged its inventory throughout their living quarters. On busy days it was not unusual to discover that a lawnmower had been hastily rolled into the downstairs bathroom or, conversely, that Miyake had set a pair of wet socks to dry over the raised paw of the Beckoning Cat icon in the shop window. Typically a tidy boy, even William had taken to strewing things about, tossing a coat over a chair here, a schoolbook on the floor there—because he *could,* because on paper, at least, it was *all* his space.

There was a lot of space, too. Although there were three bedrooms, Miyake chose to live in a detached room out back, a shed just off the kitchen porch whose furnishings Tamie had glimpsed only briefly and didn't care to dwell on. She imagined he grew mushrooms in the darkened hovel; she imagined moss growing under the bed. Even as she voiced her fears for her son's foliating, Tamie had to observe how treelike Miyake himself appeared, with his brown, knotty arms and hanging beard and soiled boots.

Miyake gave a careless glance out to the porch and nodded. In his crusty way, the old gardener had grown quite fond of his apprentice, but he agreed that Master Fujita was "pretty crazy for botany." He stroked his goatee for a time, then shrugged. "Girls? Well, perhaps some diversion *would* be good for him. But pity the woman who marries him! He'll be married to his greenhouses. I know it." Miyake himself had never married. Judging by the contented mess in the old man's bachelor den, Tamie felt sure he never *would* marry.

"A diversion," Tamie repeated flatly. One must make some allowances for one's elders—no use insulting Miyake by saying that in her heart she didn't want her son to be a gardener, or a farmer, or a botanist. Why not some professional? A teacher? Even an artist? As if California hasn't got enough Japanese gardeners, she grouched to herself.

When Tamie first saw Mari Arai sitting on the YWCA's front stoop in March of 1914, she caught the girl in the compromising act of reading a romance novel. After reading over the girl's shoulder, Tamie cleared her throat. "Preparing for Bible discussion?" she asked.

"I'll say," Mari laughed, and Tamie thought it more creditable than if she'd blushed. Mari bowed her head slightly and began fanning herself with the book. "Oh, but I guess it helps me concentrate. Better to think about such things *before* church. Well, let me get the door for you, Mrs. Fujita."

The girl was immediately likable—polite, but not too polite; Christian, not overly so; lively enough to draw William out of his shell without being brazen. And pretty enough to please, but not to cause trouble. Mari's simple white dress looked crisp and fresh, her hair neatly curled up at the ends; her eyes were large, long, and even—she didn't blink too much, didn't stare. She had a pleasant, musical laugh and didn't giggle. Small-breasted and trim, she looked athletic but not in a manly way. Good posture, Tamie noted, and confidence without vanity. Mari Arai possessed all the attributes of an excellent "diversion."

A sophomore at William's high school, Mari had grown up in Havre, Montana. Her father, as an employee of the Great Northern Railroad, had been responsible for climbing into and deslaking the great engine boilers and other tight fits. (Not squeamish, thought William's mother. Not a girl to be put off by a man with sooty fingernails.) He sent her to California because it offered an inexpensive postsecondary education far superior to that available in the north country. As Mari told Tamie, she appreciated the opportunity but didn't much care for the state, whose prejudice was of a more virulent and obvious nature, perhaps due to the far greater number of Japanese, who all seemed to cluster together, which Mari also disliked. In this Tamie detected a certain haughtiness that made the girl appear older than her age, which Tamie found alluring, though she supposed some boys might find this intimidating. Mari had the air of a restrained wild child.

"A pretty girl like you," the fish man's widow baited her, "must have so many beaus—proposals all the time, I'm sure?"

"Well, I . . ." Mari blushed. "I'm not in a great hurry. I . . . have other things to do first."

And patient, too. William's mother couldn't keep herself from thinking, A good wife isn't too much a wife—a woman must be a wife in moderation.

"Mom," William said that evening at dinner, after enduring her long recitation of Mariko Arai's appealing qualities. "With school and the nursery, I don't have time for girls." He dumped the shoyu cruet over his inarizushi, the rice balls lined up in their sugary brown bean-curd envelopes like miniature footballs. Tamie cringed, and old Miyake shook his head.

"Girls don't take much time," Tamie said.

"That's not what the guys at school say."

"Oh, those are only the *unpleasant* girls." His mother was persistent. In the following weeks, whenever she returned from the YWCA, she would say something like, "I say, that young Mariko Arai certainly has a lot of friends. I saw her today with the Kintaro boys. How stricken they both were!" Or: "That pleasant Mariko Arai got a new hairstyle yesterday. How attractive she's becoming!"

"Good for Mari Arai," her son would reply. "Wonderful."

Finally, Tamie negotiated Mr. Miyake's aid one day while William was in school. "I would be so grateful if you'd speak with him, Miyake-san," she said. "He thinks so highly of you."

"He's a good boy," said Mr. Miyake cautiously.

Tamie thought about that; he *was* a good boy, with a good boy's contented paralysis and distanced desires. He had wanted the cleaning girl but couldn't talk to her. Why? She knew Ichiro had fancied visiting prostitutes sometimes, and while she wouldn't have William emulate his father—good boys didn't do that, not in California, or not obviously—wasn't that desire natural to men?

That evening William sulked all through dinner, and Miyake looked sheepish. Whatever the old gardener had said only seemed to harden the boy's resistance. After an hour of Tamie harrying him, he finally said, "I just wish you'd stop trying to marry me off, Mom. I don't want any marriages arranged for me. Okay?"

"How stupid you are!" Tamie shouted, throwing out her hands to him. "Why? Why should I do that?" She glared at Miyake, who only shrugged.

"I don't know. You and Pop had things arranged when he was my age."

"And look what happened to him!" Getting too excited, Tamie rose from the table and busied herself with the dishes. "Anyway," she said, "that was in Japan. In California I do things a different way; why should I impose my will on my son? Marry who you want. I don't care."

After a few more weeks of her badgering, the boy relented and accompanied his mother to the YWCA one Saturday. He behaved in this building full of women with his customary clumsiness, though emboldened by an April spirit and taken with the girl's plain, frank beauty, he finally invited Miss Arai to the moving pictures with Mr. Miyake as chaperone.

"Well?" Tamie demanded, after the date. She had waited up to hear.

"It was okay," he admitted. "But I'm not marrying her or anything."

"I don't care who you marry!" his mother chuckled triumphantly.

They both knew that her list of unacceptable brides was very long indeed. However, Tamie felt she'd done her duty by introducing him to the pretty, pleasant, and, most significant, patient Miss Arai. He continued courting Mari that spring as his work and studies allowed—only because his mother desired it, he told himself—but he methodically fell in love with her, and sometime later grew to love and appreciate her, too. By the end of that summer, Fujita imagined proposing; entering his senior year, he joked about it with her; on the first day of Christmas vacation, he hypothesized about it aloud to her; and on a rare, unchaperoned date during his last semester before graduation, he drove her to the park at Santa Monica, helped her out of the cab, went down on one knee just as he'd seen in the pictures, and told her he loved her. Mari said it was high time. Then she said yes.

Then he said, "We'll have to wait a bit. Mom wants me to go to college, I guess."

Patience took Fujita and Mari far; during their years of waiting, they loved each other well, and liked each other, too. They had never spent every waking hour together as other kids did; he never pressured her to make love, and they rarely saw each other alone. Rather, Fujita's energies were mostly devoted to becoming at once a class salutatorian and entrenching himself in the Pasadena small-business community. Mari Arai appreciated his discipline; she knew he'd be a dependable husband, and frankly, she liked having a courtier who wasn't forever hanging around. She did manage to teach him to loosen up—to dance, to socialize—so that their time together was enjoyable, even fun. She could wait. After all, she was a year behind him and had her own schooling to finish.

After taking a semester off to earn tuition, Fujita agreed to attend college if he could major in agriculture and minor in business and could complete his study in three years. The whole prospect put Miyake out, not only because he anticipated that his young partner's attention would be sapped considerably, but because he had never gone to college himself. Nature was a gardener's school—real school would only clutter the boy's head with rubbish he'd have to unlearn later.

"He must have an education," Tamie insisted.

"He's *getting* an education," Miyake groused. "To be a fisherman, you go to sea. To be a hunter, you go to the woods. Who goes to school to be a gardener?"

"I think I want to go to business school," Fujita interjected meekly. In principle, he agreed with Miyake, who was an excellent if occasionally abusive teacher. Sometimes he wished to avoid college altogether; after all, he had real, adult responsibilities, and not much ambition for more than running a nursery anyway. He liked poetry; for about a second, he fancied being an English major, but who went to school to read poetry?

"You want business," Miyake said, spreading his arms, "here's a business. You live in a business!" Tamie looked pointedly away. Miyake's green thumb wasn't green from *money*. He was a clod in business. He'd left gardening for the nursery, in part because he'd alienated more than a few of his customers; he wouldn't take orders from women. His tenure at the King of Cleats' estate had ended when the Queen of Cleats visited the winter house with her new infant prince; Miyake, beginning his work at 6:00 A.M., ignored the grand dame's request that he not run the mowers first thing, as it woke up the baby. No, Miyake didn't know how loudly money talked in America, almost as loud as sex, and sometimes louder. Neither had Ichiro. But his widow knew, and she frequently resented her measly 21 percent share of the nursery.

Despairing that William would abandon his schooling, she finally resorted to enlisting Mari's help. Pretending to be angry with her fiancé, Mari gave him the silent treatment for two weeks. One day, William sent her a note: "Now what have I done?" On transparent parchment, imprinted with pale green bamboo stalks, she jotted down the reply: "*I* plan to go to junior college, and I'll never wed a man less educated than myself." And so Fujita relented and took a dual major—business and agriculture.

On the New Year's Day before resuming his studies, a Festival of Roses float accessorized with floral arrangements by Fujita and Miyake won a trophy. Running out of time to decorate, the float's owners had contracted the nursery's help—including

Tamie and Mari—for a good chunk of money. Working alongside his future wife thrilled the young man more than he ever dreamed. He had developed a guilty taste for the slightly shabby; he fantasized dirty women—not obscene, lewd, or forward, but actually dirty. In no way shabby, Mari dressed and presented herself as tastefully as she could afford to. He loved her appearance, but when she worked outside at the nursery, with a rivulet of sweat down her back, under her armpits, outlining her breasts, and a smear of some soil on her forehead, these were the moments she stirred him most. Invigorated by anticipation of an actual marriage bed, he enrolled in a nearby college, paying his way with the Rose Bowl chunk, then earning a senior-year scholarship. Dividing his spare time among the nursery, study, and Mari, he methodically got it all: an education from Miyake, credentials from school, and the patient love he needed from Mari.

They were married by the Reverend Mitsutaro Tsuji in a bilingual ceremony in Pasadena's Japanese Union Church in 1919, when Fujita as methodically set to learning how to be a husband and lover. He found this more difficult than obtaining dual college degrees. Upon his first sexual experience, it developed that the memory of his parents' vigorous hullabaloo saturated the actual act. The sounds of orgasm would always recall the feeling of wedging himself in the crack beside his childhood bed. The polar opposite of an exhibitionist, the inordinately careful, tight-lipped lover made no sound at all, and Mari asked if something was wrong. Was it wrong not to grunt? He didn't really know. And how did *she* know, he wondered. After reassuring her that he was not angry, and that it was pleasurable—it was—he tried, for her sake, to indicate his passion a little more audibly.

Learning to be a husband was harder. At some business function over the years, smoking with the men after dinner, it always surprised him how fellows found deriding their wives a relaxing, comradely pastime, like playing poker or talking of cars. Marriage, these men seemed to say, placed an undue burden on their lives. Miyake believed this, but he'd at least acted on his conviction and remained a bachelor. It perplexed Fujita that a man—usually Caucasian—should begrudge his wife her shopping habits, yet begrudge more her desire to take a job. It *astonished* him that a husband would discuss his marital and extramarital sexual triumphs and tribulations, or if faithful, expect hearty congratulations for not having an affair. Had he missed something? He *liked* his wife; he *needed* her to work at the nursery; he *loved* having sex with her, but he wouldn't discuss it with anyone, however friendly. And certainly he watched the family spending, but he always *wished* he could buy her more. Was something wrong with him as a husband? He decided he didn't care. Burden me, he thought. Burden me.

In 1923 Mari gave birth to Toshio Ichiro, "Tony," and suddenly their lives were in full bloom. They learned how to be parents, too. They sent him to school; Mari worked and also joined service clubs and ran a women's group at the YWCA; Fujita applied his skill to growing a business and spent time with his family when he could. While there was always room to improve *himself*, he thought his life had become as good as it could get.

One day, clearing out a bedroom closet to make room for the baby's clothes, toys, and diapers, he rediscovered the musty steamer trunk his father had transported on the *Pacific Angel*. Its silken inner lining had torn in places, leached away by mold; to Fujita, it smelled of the sea. Buried away, he found the seventeen-jewel Royal pocket watch, which he'd never had repaired, and burnished its plain face. Prying the cover open with considerably thicker fingers, he still experienced a rush of confusion and amazement at its hidden, intricate patterns and complicated workings. Perhaps he should have it fixed? A new father, he thought, must be aware of time—children took so much of it. A father must know when it's *quitting* time, he thought. But then, hadn't this very timepiece, in working condition, placed the whole of the Pacific Ocean between himself and his own father? To that bird of passage with his fierce homing instinct, this watch only ever ticked off the days to his return, and no more. Ichiro had never known when it was quitting time.

Fujita pocketed the Royal and determined to think about it later, when the proper moment presented itself, as it surely must. Everything, Fujita believed, according to plan.

THREE

Under Glass

On the first day of November, that Day of All Saints, Mr. Fujita scouted all across the Peak before sunrise—he called this "reconnaissance." It would become his daily autumn ritual; he would always have to wash again before breakfast. He was eager, as he told Margaret, to learn the natural rhythms of Widow's Peak. He also wanted to secure some thinking time alone, to find out if this land could for a time be called home. Ankle-deep in cold mud, his breath lightly misting on his upper lip, he stomped across the hill, dislodged a few small boulders, hacked at brush, and, under dawn's light, drew thumbnail sketches of the topography. Squatting, he would randomly pierce the earth with his fingers, grumbling about the unsavory New England climate.

On that cool morning, his solitary wandering also took him down off the hill. Believing he must learn to do as easterners did, he began walking away from town toward the more remote farmland to see how the natives' crops fared—what they cultivated, over what area and in what manner. He didn't get very far. First he came upon an unremarkable little ten-acre plot whose main business seemed to be feed. A quarter mile down, he encountered a small apple orchard—no more than seven acres, he thought. He could see nothing of the mill from the roadway, though he could smell it, sweet, warm, and tangy. Syrup? Vinegar? Cider?

At the place identified by a mailbox reading "Pedicott Farms," now fairly well stripped of its crop, he found carcasses of what had been pumpkin and squash tossed here and there into the turned earth. As he lingered to admire the scene, a quartet of boys ranging in age from about four to ten ran out of a storage shed toward the road; then, seeing him at the fence by their bus stop, they froze. The youngest one broke into sobs and bolted back across the field toward the house; the other three stood fast and gaped. "Fine day," Fujita called. The eldest tilted his head upward to check the weather, neither agreeing nor disagreeing. Soon, a lanky, giant man emerged from the house and began loping their way, trailed by the sobbing little one and a Labrador retriever. Fujita thought it best to move on. He did not flee exactly, but by instinct he knew never to rest in one place for very long. He'd only come down for a look-see, anyway. Repeating his observation of the day's fineness, he tilted his hat brim, then turned deliberately back toward the Peak.

Thus, over the following days and in his own way, the nurseryman began the messy business of getting to know them—the land, the town, and his new neighbors. Mr. Fujita was no psychologist, no mystic, no poet. Yet, as a businessman, and part salesman, he believed he could gain insight into people's characters by observing their relationships to things—the objects they surrounded themselves with or created. Most telling was the space they chose to enter, that they considered their own. A sensitive glance over a small plot of earth could often divine the inhabitants' personalities, and perhaps fates, reflected in the landscape. Out west he had known men, high rollers, whose cliff-balancing homes would one day slide into the Pacific Ocean; Fujita's own nursery sat above a fault line.

His forays across Margaret's property revealed that its southeasterly position captured full early sunlight; its soil had warmed and dried quickly after the Halloween rains—evidence, he thought, of her own bright disposition. However, the muddy area on the southwest face of the Peak, on Livvie's property, sat in a poor position—darkened by trees reaching desperately skyward to claim and hoard the few precious drops of sun. The Peak itself prevented the western face from enjoying the benefits of the warm ocean breeze. The Tuftellers, he knew, would be the challenge—late to thaw and late to bloom. And what of myself? Fujita mused, as he would come to do again and again. Will I be able to etch my own mark on this land?

How do people come together from opposite corners of the country, of the world? With the Tuftellers, it could be achieved only incrementally, in little daily favors, squabbles, and kindnesses—a method closest to Mr. Fujita's heart. Not that Livvie was especially cool to him (he might have expected that), but her manner made clear she could take him or leave him. Later that morning of saints, she asked if he would pull down a maple bough half-collapsed on her roof; she feared another coastal storm could drive it through into her bedroom. While he set up the ladder, she asked him if he'd like a coffee or juice, and when he said no, she didn't ask again. Fujita appreciated this. In conversation, she had a distant, not-quite-paying-attention air that he recognized as the buzz of one who drank early and daily. Working on the bough, he snagged his shirt on a gutter, and the seamstress mended it for him while he waited. As they sat at her kitchen table, even her constantly burning cigarettes could not mask the scent of brandy wafting from her coffee mug. "It's a nice place you have here," Mr. Fujita offered, glancing about. The walls were a clutter of Garvin's drawings, clippings from fashion magazines, and reminder notes.

Livvie squinted up at him—the light was dim, her vision was poor—and pursed her lips. "It's small," she said. "But it's getting bigger. Big enough for just Garvin and me. Well, you know."

Mr. Fujita nodded. He also knew about the expansion of bereavement, the echoing of absence. In the kitchen, he found no likeness, nor any apparent trace, of the late Mr. Tufteller displayed. Yet, by the way he was swamped in the bathrobe Livvie loaned him, he could at least infer Sig's intimidating heft.

"You're not a talker, either," Livvie observed. "That makes a house bigger, too, when you don't talk. Margaret's a world-class talker," she said, and Mr. Fujita listened for some hint of malice or sarcasm, but couldn't be sure. "She'll put you under glass, or on the rack, just for conversation. She loves to talk." He nodded again.

"It must be difficult for her," Mr. Fujita offered, tightening the belt on that king-sized, crimson robe. The garment looked unused—its pile still plush, shimmering with motion. He thought it very possibly the most comfortable thing that had ever touched his body. Mari usually bought his clothes; he never would, never did, buy a stitch for himself. It never occurred to him. "Margaret's got a big house to fill."

Livvie snorted then, or maybe sneezed. He couldn't tell because she never once raised her head from her work. "I'd like to fix this place up," she said. "If we grow and sell anything here, I'd be pleased to have money—I'd be surprised, frankly, but pleased. No offense. I'm sure you're a whiz at home, but here. . . . Unfortunately, this isn't a California nursery. I'm not expecting much."

"It's brave of both of you," he admitted. He cuffed the bathrobe's sleeves twice; still, they extended beyond his knuckles. "Farming is hard and risky work," he said, "but gratifying. It can have real benefits for a child, too—the science, the exercise, the responsibility. Garvin might enjoy learning a bit about it." He told her about the boys he'd seen on his walking tour that morning. "They sure seemed to be sturdy, healthy fellows. I think I scared the little one, though."

"It was Margaret's idea," Livvie said, and again her tone was inscrutable to him. Then, biting off a thread: "Garvin's afraid of you, too." Busy tying a knot, she did not see him flinch. "There. Finished." She had sutured the tear very handily within two minutes; as with Ichiro Fujita, a little morning snort did not appear to impair Livvie's professional skills. This, like her directness, he also appreciated.

After he'd changed, Livvie tried to give him the robe. "No one here can wear it," she said, "and I'm trying to clean house."

"Thank you," he said at the door, "but it's such a nice one, and too big really." Stepping out, he paused on the welcome mat. "It's not California, you're right. I wish I could bring my nursery here," he said, sad and honest. "But I promise you, I'll do my best."

Tipping his hat, he excused himself, then folded the ladder to haul back to the Kelly garage. After wearing that lush robe, his shirt felt like steel wool. When he lifted the ladder onto his shoulder, its cold aluminum leg chilled his skin through the flimsy fabric. Traveling clothes, he reminded himself, *should* be worn thin. A bathrobe is worn at home. Before he could go home, he faced much traveling ahead, as well as a bitter winter, and Livvie had given him an idea. If he couldn't return to his California nursery, couldn't he bring his nursery to him, just a piece? By himself, or maybe with that boy, he'd build his own sanctuary against the eastern winter—a winter under glass.

When Margaret emerged later that afternoon, Mr. Fujita already wore a full day's grime, lying stretched out on his side by the scarecrow. Legs extended, torso propped up on an elbow, he gazed down at the ground and caressed it firmly, probingly, even longingly. On a sunnier day, he might have been a picnicker caught in a woodland tryst, lazing on a blanket, whispering poetry over a lover. When Margaret slammed the porch door—*whump!*—his body stiffened as if whipped.

"Sorry," she said, wringing her gardening gloves, yellow with red butterflies, the price tag still appended. Just as clean were her khaki trousers and yellow slicker, so that she fairly sparkled in that hazy morning air. "Well, here I am, ready for duty."

"Oh, excuse me," he said, blushing exactly as if interrupted in some intimate rendezvous. He scraped a film of mud from his side. "I wanted to get a ground's-eye view. That is—"

She laughed. "Oh, go on, have fun. Just don't hog it all for yourself! So," she said heartily. "What can I do to help?"

It embarrassed him to think that this work must not have appeared like work at all to this sparkling grand dame, so painfully bright he felt filthy beside her. "Well, you might want to change into some work clothes," he suggested. "It's pretty nasty out."

Margaret looked down at herself and frowned. "Oh." She regarded her gleaming yellow chest and cuffed hems and throttled her new gloves. "These *are* my work clothes."

"I see," Mr. Fujita said, nodding. Keenly conscious of prejudice based on appearance, he tried to judge people by their actions—which to him meant their work. In his moral hierarchy, doing one's job achieved transcendence; limbo was failure to find and fulfill one's *role*. In those early days, he first perceived his new neighbors as simple nouns: nurse, seamstress, elementary student. He tended to distrust people who upped and switched careers, and Margaret looked and talked exactly like a nurse and nothing like a farmer. Still, he tried to fight his biases. What people *said* and how they appeared was always suspect; what they did (or could do but failed to do) defined the soul. Fujita knew this: It was, after all, how he viewed himself.

"Well," he said, and he reached into his back pocket. Nervously, he drew out the folded sketches and handed them over: topographical, ground-view, and finally the thumbnail design he had made—his attempt to bring a bit of Californian warmth to ward off the harsh winter.

"A conservatory?" Margaret asked, eyes widening with delight. "Yes, of course!"

"More a greenhouse, really . . ." He bristled at the word *conservatory*. In his opinion, the one was a useful commercial property, the other a playground for the rich.

"A conservatory!" Margaret repeated, now beaming. "Oh, it reminds me of *Little Women*—Mr. Laurence's light conservatory with the tea roses and vines. How delightful!"

"Yes, a sort of conservatory," the nurseryman conceded. A working, commercial, freestanding conservatory. A glass sliver of home.

High above the Kelly house, a seagull followed a chill, salty breeze from the coast. A red-bronze oak leaf, stirred by the rush of its wings, fell onto the roof slates but was unheard by the inhabitants. Another breezy kiss slid it down, caught its stem on the jagged rim of the gutter, and flipped it into the air so that it toppled in lazy curls past the upstairs bedroom, past the protruding stovepipe end, past Margaret Kelly's face in the kitchen window, and onto the shoulder of Garvin Tufteller squatting just below the sill. A sneak attack. With no sign of the new man about, he devised to give Mugsie a start. He removed his shoes, then closed the door onto his fingers to dampen the noise.

"Aren't you supposed to be in school, young man?" She greeted him without turning from the dishes in the sink.

He whistled appreciatively. "Mugsie, are those radar antennas up there?"

She huffed and raised a sudsy hand to the network of hairpins jutting from her red bun. "That's *antennae*," she said, not turning.

After another quick glance around, he sidled up to her and reached into the sink to play with the suds. He pressed against her aproned hip, warmer and more substantial than his mother's. He loved to do this. "Um, Mugsie?" he whispered, nudging her. "Where's Mr. Fudd, Fudge . . ." he tried. He'd managed to avoid the stranger for a week now.

Margaret abruptly splashed him with a handful of suds. "You're not here playing hooky again, are you?"

"Naw. I got a bad cold, so Miss Hardy sent me home." He splashed her in return. "I kept sneezing on Byron," he confessed with a giggle. "He sits in front of me, and I got him but *good*. Mom's out for a while, so I came over."

"I see," said Nurse Kelly, drying her hands. "Some cold medicine's the thing for you, and I want to take your temperature. Go take off your trousers and lie on the sofa." Garvin gulped. "Oh, feeling better all of a sudden?" She laughed, and Garvin bobbed his head in eager assent. "That's fine. So, I guess you'll want to read your Blackbird? Check on the mantel."

"Black*hawk*, Mugsie," he corrected her, pityingly. Assuming the coast was clear, he jabbed his fist into his stomach to jerk an invisible rip cord. Calling, "So long, doll," in his bold, Blackhawk voice, he bailed out down the four steps to the living room in one mighty bound, then stopped short with a gasp.

He stood eye-to-eye with the new man. He was supposed to live in the garage. He should be in the garage.

Sunk deep and crooked into the sofa, Mr. Fujita held the *Crier* aloft and wagged it vigorously like a washerwoman shaking out a pair of bloomers. He peeped out through a neat little two-by-two-inch box someone had snipped out of a photo on the front page. A grinning Winston Churchill shook hands with a trench-coated body with Mr. Fujita's eyeball for a head. Above the photo, the banner read: "FDR's campaign: Don't change horses midstream!" Election Day was just a week away.

"Oh no," Garvin moaned, panic momentarily overshadowing his dread of the stranger. "Not the funnies, too," he pleaded. "I hope she *didn't*, I hope she *didn't* . . ."

"I just put it down for a few minutes," Mr. Fujita told him. "I got a drink of water, and when I came back . . ." He examined the square on the front page. "Coupons," he said, nodding his head sympathetically.

"Sorry, fellas," Margaret said, stepping down from the kitchen. "I got a little carried away."

"No, not coupons," Garvin grumbled, pointing to the campaign slogan. "Mugsie doesn't like President Roosevelt very much these days," he explained. "I beg her not to, but she keeps cutting him out of the paper. Boy."

"Really?" The man examined both sides of the paper. "Um, just Roosevelt?"

Too distraught to answer, Garvin just gave a frank roll of the eyes. This burden, enduring the daffy doings of dames, was something men shared—even across enemy lines.

"Well, it hardly seems appropriate to say this to you two," Margaret said, reddening, "but I've just been so irritated with everything. The war, I mean. But everything: After I heard about what happened to your people, Mr. Fujita. . . . He's a *Harvard* man," she tried. "I voted for him; I was New Deal Maggie. He said we wouldn't join the war, but he lied. I must sound silly to you—you both lost people in the war, not I, and maybe I shouldn't talk . . ." Stuck, she ruffled Garvin's spiky, sandy hair, but he wouldn't look at her, still worried about the fate of the comics. It pleased him, though, that she had mentioned that his father was a soldier. No one talked about Pop these days, and sometimes Garvin felt the figure in his drawings of Burma was becoming more real than the memories of Sig Tufteller as he had been in Juggeston.

"Well," Margaret concluded, "it just makes me so mad to look at his face sometimes."

Mr. Fujita shifted on the sofa, pulled a cushion from behind his back. They shared an embarrassed pause while Garvin began ripping through the comic section for signs of decapitation. "I met Eleanor Roosevelt once," the man began but then stopped and shook his head. "Oh, I'll tell you about it sometime."

"Aauughhhh!" cried Garvin, dramatically thrusting out the comic page. "She cut half of it out! Of all the comics . . ." He flipped over to where there *had* been a photo of the president and the first dog, Fala, as part of a children's feature.

"You shouldn't read that rubbish anyway," Margaret said defensively. Grabbing the paper, she took a glance, then shrugged. "Ah. So *that's* the bird fellow. Well, I don't see what the crisis is. Just killing each other—everyone killing each other. I'm doing you a *favor.*" She handed the paper back disgustedly. "Do you want to grow up a know-nothing thug? Why don't you read an actual book, for goodness' sake! The next best thing to a smart woman is a literate man," she instructed him. "If you're ever to get married someday, you'd better get to work."

Garvin, of course, vigorously denied having any such intentions—"not nohow, not *ever.*" The new man, an impartial observer until that point, clucked his tongue and shook his head in sympathy with the boy.

"I gave you all those novels last Christmas. Don't you read them at all?"

She had given him a vast packet of readings—a whole library, almost. Starting him out with such shaver's fare as *The Wonderful Wizard of Oz*, she did throw in tougher fellows such as Finn, Sawyer, Gulliver, and Twist—but they were not up to Blackhawk's stature. She didn't understand.

"I read 'em sometimes, Mugsie," Garvin explained, "but that stuff's not real." He meant that they had nothing to do with cowboys, Indians, knights, or the war—with his particular nightmares or dreams.

"That's why I *gave* them to you, you rascal," she grouched, untying her apron. "They're *better* than real. What's so great about 'real'? Do you think adventure, excitement, even *magic* can't happen, even here in Juggeston? Even without killing people? I was going to give you *Alice in Wonderland* this Christmas, but you're obviously not grown-up enough to appreciate it. Ah, heck!" She scooped a pair of garden gloves from the mantel and a tattered old dress, red with fifty front buttons, from where it lay draped over the sofa's arm. "I've had it with you boys."

"Where are you going, Mugsie?" Garvin asked softly. He'd hurt her feelings, he knew.

"I'm going to talk to the scarecrow and give her a new dress, since *you* said the one she has on now is so *ugly*. And no, don't think you're coming with me; this is just us women. You two boys can stay here and talk about tanks or balls or bait or whatever."

Before Garvin could follow her, she slipped back up and out through the kitchen, slammed the porch door, and left him there, trapped with the Japanese man. Slowly, he turned. The new man's black, fleshy lidded eyes had him pinned.

"It can be tough to be a guy with only women around," Mr. Fujita sighed. "Most of the time, it was just my mother and me. Yes sir, did we argue. Same thing with my boy, Tony, and his mom."

Curious, Garvin nodded. "You know what I mean, right? About those books?"

Mr. Fujita shrugged. "My comic books were Homer. You think Jack Armstrong's something, you should see Odysseus. At your age, I wanted to be Momotaro the Peach Pit Boy," he said. "I'll tell you about him sometime."

Garvin frowned. A peach didn't sound very heroic. He was wondering if he should say so when the kitchen door slammed again and they heard Margaret grumbling, "Evil bird." She stomped down into the living room, crossed her arms, and thrust her foot forward for their inspection. With a delicious mixture of pleasure and disgust, Garvin saw a glistening blop of bird dung on the shiny toe.

"It was that seagull you made friends with, Garvin," Margaret said. "Always coming around with his hand out. I told you not to feed it."

Garvin grinned, secretly gratified that his hero, Blackhawk, had been so swiftly avenged. "I guess your old scarecrow musta been napping!" he teased her.

"It's your fault," she grumbled. "I warned you yesterday not to call her ugly. She said, 'Next time, it's going to be Garvin. You tell him that.'"

Garvin went into a blinking fit. "Really?" Margaret grinned triumphantly and tromped upstairs to change her shoes. He looked out to the scarecrow, listing in the breeze, brilliant in her new outfit.

"You know," said Mr. Fujita, "some folks say it's good luck when a seagull . . ." Chuckling, he started over. "I'll tell you a secret: Seagull guano is an excellent crop fertilizer."

"You put *poop* on food?" cried the boy in outrage.

"Well, on the ground. And you wash the vegetables, of course. I know some other special secrets, too," the man said in a hushed voice, jingling the change in his pockets. "Hmm. Maybe I'll let you in on one of them, *if* you can keep a secret."

"Sure I can," Garvin said, though it made him nervous to imagine what sorts of secrets this stranger might possess.

"I want to show you something," the new man said. Opening the door, he motioned for Garvin to follow him outside.

The seagull atop the scarecrow's old bonnet launched skyward and soared in slow circles just within feeding distance. Fujita shaded his eyes with a flat palm to watch the bird's flight, hoping it augured an extension of the relatively warm weather that had returned after the rains. "There's the devil who bombed Margaret," he said, pointing.

Garvin remained sober as they approached the offended straw woman. Buying time to organize his lie, Fujita straightened her dress and hat, then pushed a large rock to buttress her center post. "Now," he began, pulling Garvin around to face her. The boy's shoulders stiffened at his touch. "That stuff Margaret said—well, women know a lot of things. There's something to it; scarecrows are touchy. I learned this trick in Arizona from a wise old Indian chief who knew General Custer." Actually, he had read about the ritual in a library book; he thought it might have been Slavic in origin, but the boy wouldn't know that. He produced a shiny nickel from his pocket and handed it to Garvin, who warily took it in his palm.

"The coin's not for you," Fujita said. "See, the scarecrow spirit is just like anyone else, the chief told me. It expects to be treated with respect and trust; it wants to be spoken well of; it hates gossip. It doesn't like people who are mean-tempered or ornery, especially to their parents." Fujita paused to consider what other lessons the imaginary chief could impart to right the world. "Extravagance," he added. "It hates sloth."

"What's sloth?" Garvin mumbled.

Fujita pressed ahead, piling it on. "Greed, narrow-mindedness, paranoia."

"What's paranoia?"

"It hates cheaters. More than anything, it hates complainers," Fujita said. "No, more than anything, it hates *waste*."

Dubious, Garvin frowned. "What kind of spirit is this? It doesn't seem to like anything."

Fujita hemmed. "I suppose that's right," he admitted. He pointed to Garvin's hand. "Except, most of all, just like you, it loves getting presents. Makes sense?"

"Go on," the boy said, undecided.

"Anyway, the chief told me the surest way to make sure a scarecrow protects your land is to plant something valuable inside of it. You know, like wampum. If you do this, the scarecrow spirit will be warm all winter. By spring, it will be ready and willing to watch over your crops, and things will be able to grow. And sometimes—just sometimes—it gives you back something even more valuable than you gave it originally. Sometimes it's money—like the tooth fairy, except better. Sometimes it's just happiness."

"Maybe you're trying to fool me," Garvin said. Fujita only shrugged. It seemed to irritate the boy, who looked away in silence toward the chimney of his own house. "I don't know when to believe anybody," he said at last.

"Okay. You don't want to even try it. You don't believe in anything. So, give me back my nickel, smarty."

"Hold on a second, I'm thinking," the boy said, clutching the coin. They both looked around at the yard, now rapidly taking a new shape: the hundreds of soda bottle–sized holes in the topsoil, a wheelbarrow filled with uprooted boulders, the bundled tree branches leaning against the garage, the staked-off greenhouse site. Fujita watched Garvin intently for a spark of interest.

"What's the chief's name?" young Tufteller asked. "Huh? The Indian who knew Custer. If you're on the level, then what's his name?"

"Hold on," Fujita said. "I'm old, it's been a while. Let's see . . . Tuzigoot. Yes, that was it."

"Tuzigoot? That's a name? What does it mean?"

"You know, for such a little guy, you've got an awful lot of questions stuffed in you. I don't know exactly what it means."

"Well," Garvin said softly, "can't you pretend it means something?"

"I don't have to pretend," Fujita insisted, saddened by this big-eyed, hopeful boy so ready to depend on his machinations. "He's a real person, I mean. You get to be my age, you just don't remem—wait. Dust devil. Yes, I think that's what he said. You've never seen that, but it's what they have out west in the desert. All the time. You know the tornado in *The Wizard of Oz*? That's what they're like, but smaller—sometimes the size of a house, sometimes only as big as a man. Red, and if they touch you, you can't breathe, you're covered in dust, and it feels like your skin is being torn off by sandpaper. Yes, that's what Tuzigoot means. That's what the chief was like, too. A tough guy. If you don't believe me, feel free to look it up."

"Okay," Garvin sighed. "So, what do I do?"

Fujita began to reach for the dress buttons, but propriety made him hesitate. This curvaceous scarecrow was no bloated, straw hausfrau attired off-the-rack; she shared Margaret's intimidating fashion sense and wardrobe. "Hmm. Scarecrows are usually men," he said. Averting his eyes, he unfastened the middle section of its collar-to-hem buttons until its wire-and-hay belly was exposed. "Now, bury the coin right there, right inside," he said, "so no one can see it or steal it."

Garvin looked apologetically up to the scarecrow's bespectacled face. Closing his eyes, he thrust hand and coin into her grassy innards.

"Gently, nice and deep, where it's warm," Fujita instructed. "Good. Now slowly remove your hand. We'll wait and see. This late in the year, we'll mostly work inside. We'll let the stock germinate in the greenhouse and transplant it later. But just wait until spring comes."

The operation accomplished, the men grew bashful under the grass woman's gaze. After gingerly refastening the dress buttons, the Nisei patted Garvin on the back, and the boy didn't recoil or shriek. "See, Garvin? I think she's smiling. Now, wherever you go, whatever you do, she'll watch over you all year. But remember, this is just between us, right?"

"Right," Garvin agreed. Tentatively, he shook Fujita's hand. As they walked back toward the porch, he asked, "That Indian . . . did you learn that in camp?"

"What?" Fujita hid his alarm. "Who said anything to you about camp?"

"I went to camp, too," Garvin continued wistfully, "the summer before Pop left. We took a field trip to Mashpee to see real Indians. I found an arrowhead in the woods."

"Oh. I see. You must have done a lot of interesting things there, huh?"

"Yeah, but that was the best part." He paused. "It was fun."

"I'll bet."

"I guess you know all about Indians."

"I knew a few in Arizona. And Tony, when he was about eight, like you, he—"

"Eight and a quarter," Garvin corrected. Although hearing him, Fujita became distracted on the porch by a rusted nail stabbing up at them from the top step. He removed it with ease but began to scrutinize the stoop with the intensity of a bloodhound. "Eight and a *quarter*," Garvin repeated.

"Don't be in such a hurry," Fujita said, now searching the kitchen doorway. He extracted a nail from the jamb. "Anyway, at your age, give or take a quarter, Tony went to school with some Indian boys. I'd take them all fishing together sometimes, and they'd always catch more fish. They were pretty rambunctious fellows, I can tell you, always raising a ruckus in the back of the car, but they sure knew how to be quiet when it came to fishing. Could sit for hours without making a peep—barely even blinking—until Tony got so bored he couldn't stand it, and I fell asleep. They never wanted to go home. I'd wake up from my nap, and there'd be this huge pile of perch lying next to me. One thing I know about Indians is, they're expert fishermen." Shaking his head, he paused to attack another nail. "Well, some of them are. Better than Tony and me, anyway."

Garvin considered this, trying to remember his geography lessons. "They fish in Arizona? Can you fish in the desert?"

"Not much, though you can hunt other things. But this was before, in California."

"Oh." Garvin spotted a nail Fujita had missed and gave it a yank. "Mom said your son was in the army. He died, right?"

"Right," Fujita said. It was almost a whisper.

"I know about that," Garvin said. Fujita only nodded. "The Pacific theater," Garvin recited. "My pop was there, too. In Burma," he added. "Was your son in Burma?"

"No. Tony . . . moved around a lot. In the South Pacific. I don't think Burma's actually in the Pacific. Indian Ocean, maybe. It's Asia, anyway."

"Oh. You ever gone there?"

"No, I haven't," Fujita said, meaning Asia, not only Burma. Scanning the door frame a last time, he nodded to say that it was safe to enter.

"Say, do you want to see my bike?"

"Later, pal," Fujita said. "You do your house chores and schoolwork first. And you'll help me when you've got some free time. But you always do your work first."

Garvin retrieved his book bag from the kitchen table. "I guess I knew you'd say something like that." The way he slung the weighty sack over his shoulder moved Fujita. Stepping out onto the porch again, they took a last glance at the scarecrow, who did not seem put out by the invasive surgery. "Well, see ya, Mr. F." Garvin said.

Fujita reflexively bit his tongue. In no way did he let himself indicate to the boy that the use of that nickname belonged to

Yoneko, who was beloved of Tony, and who bedeviled Fujita himself. It gave him a stab of pain, but he liked it; like a stone in the shoe, it would remind him to stay unrooted, keep focused. As young Tufteller started across the Peak to his own house, Fujita pointed to the scarecrow and warned, "Remember, she's always watching now."

"Was that a cheap shot?" he inquired of himself late that night, in his biweekly letter to the national menace, Tamie Fujita. "Values!" he wrote, then crossed it out. "Guidance," he wrote. "What boy doesn't need that? When Pop died, I was older, and I already had a job I liked, and Miyake. I had busywork to distract me." He paused, knowing full well that he secretly counted on this farm and Yoneko as similar distractions now. This made his writing more cranky. "I came here to work, sure, but not as a *baby-sitter*. Children take time, slow one down! Still, mustn't I find some *small* way to involve the boy? To help distract him?"

And, he wondered, can I do it without derailing myself?

This question became more pressing when he went down the next day to send the letter. Opening the mailbox door, he discovered that two postcards from Yoneko had arrived together after some lag time in the forwarding order to Juggeston. He slipped them out as gingerly as if removing bait from a jaw trap.

> GREETINGS FROM DETROIT!
>
> Auntie says you're setting up shop with two ladies of the Caucasian persuasion? Or setting up house maybe? She hasn't sent me an address, though. When are you moving out of Boston? I guess someone will send your mail on? I hope you're wherever you're going to get this, or oops! What an embarrassment with those ladies! Well, it's good for you, having some hobby besides chasing me around. So, Mr. F. to the damsels' rescue! Or are you still "just the old farmer"? Hee hee. — Y

"Stupid girl," Fujita grumbled. "'When are you moving?' As if you'd told me where the hell you were and I could have told you!" Relatively speaking, however, it was a sermon of goodwill—perhaps the kindest words to pass between them in years. The postmark indicated that it was sent from the Berkshires. The other, apparently sent from Providence, bore a picture of New York's Times Square.

THE GREAT WHITE WAY
You're a real nuisance, Fujita-san, sniffing around like that! I really wish you'd stop. It's embarrassing. Just write to Auntie—none of my friends, darn it! Sorry. I'm up and down a lot lately. Just don't hound me, OK? —Y

P.S. — Oh, I got the money but told Auntie to keep those seeds and stuff. I'm trying to travel light, you know. (And I don't exactly have time for gardening!) She won't ask you, of course, but Auntie really wants one of those tiny garden shovels. Can you send her one? —Y

Rechecking the postmarks, he was infuriated that *neither* bore a legible date. One had been run through by a broad pen slash. The other—stamped at an improper angle—was a red semicircle and the truncated "Providen." "Ah, cripes. Is she going north or south?" Fujita huffed. "Tiny shovels! God! And her fool postscripts are longer than the messages." She talked that way, too: just a river of unstoppable afterthought. He knew he lacked some vital antenna for understanding the girl. Although they shared a history of violence, pain, misunderstanding, and mutual loves, he frankly didn't know her all that well and so was confounded. Such mood swings! Such wandering and aimlessness! To what end? And such meanness: stringing him along, keeping always in touch yet always out of his reach. He might have taken this as a kindness—her deference to bonds of the past—but to him it was torture, for he suspected she held his future, too.

Immediately, he returned to the office and his secret book to find addresses for War Relocation Authority stations in New York City and Providence (Detroit was unlikely, and he'd badgered Boston plenty), then prepared to fire off his queries. By now it was a form letter, a snare with only a few dates and place names changed: *The girl is a runaway; she might be in danger;*

please, Fujita begged, *bring her home to me.* "Home?" he muttered, not for the first or last time. Along with these pleas, he gathered miscellaneous mail, presents, and supply requests and stuffed it all into a shopping bag. Stepping outside, he paused by the scarecrow—her bifocaled crystal eyes had an eerie way of following a person. Sniffing, Fujita turned to look out over Juggeston. "Time to meet the new neighbors, I guess," he said. Without setting off any alarms, he thought. *Carefully.*

"Everybody knows Alf Wellington, and Alf Wellington knows everybody!" A portly, balding man some four inches shorter and wider than Fujita, the proprietor of Wellington's Arcade mopped his sweating red face as though the evening outside his shop could not be more balmy, even as the Californian hugged himself against the chill. "And now you do too, hey?"

"I'd really like to see your p-place," Fujita said through chattering teeth. Your warm place, he thought.

"Well, sure you do!" laughed the shopkeeper, with all the grinning confidence of a master of ceremonies at a roast. "After all, it's going to be your second home!" With that, he raised his arms to hug all that could be seen, as if he were proprietor of the town itself—an impression that was not unfounded. Except for the events surrounding the Meeting, Alf explained, his hybrid pop shop/grocery/band hall/historical society offered the village's only real leisure alternative to staying home or driving to the sea coast. Across the public parking lot from the shop, Fujita had seen a garish, roadside shingle blaring in gold-glittered letters: JUGGESTON'S VERY OWN ARCADE WELLINGTON! The landmark had caused fierce enmity between Alf and the previous mayor, who insisted that it might be mistaken (as indeed it often was) to indicate that the entire square—the parking lot, Civil War statue, meetinghouse, and even Town Hall itself—constituted the arcade.

"In depression years," Alf said, "I was Juggeston's *only* center of commerce, so my sign outlasted the mayor." Then, embarrassed, he asked, "How long have you been here? How are you settling in on the hill? Things okay up there? Have you been to meeting? How do you like us so far?"

Overwhelmed and shivering, Fujita renewed his efforts to move inside. "Say, let's take a gander at your shop. Looks really lively in there."

"Well, sure! My pleasure!" Alf glanced proudly back at his domain, but his round body remained firmly planted before the door. Just smiling, so broadly—too broadly. A chill ran up Fujita's neck, his built-in radar. He'd played this cat-and-mouse game with many merchants—the gushily sincere smile replaced by a slammed door, the welcoming tin placard YES! WE'RE OPEN! flapping on glass, and a hand-scrawled cardboard sign: JAPS KEEP OUT. That was out west, though, Fujita reminded himself. He glanced at his bag, weighed his options, then began to push past.

"Wait!" A hand gripped Fujita's elbow, and he clenched a fist and spun around. Alarmed, the shopkeeper stepped back. "Wait, please," Alf repeated, nearly whispering. "I was just wondering . . ." Looking down, he straightened the welcome mat with his toe. "How is Maggie—um, Mrs. Kelly, doing?"

Struggling to breathe again, Fujita unclenched himself and scrutinized Alf's expression—tender, attentive, searching; clearly, the man loved Margaret. How crippled Fujita felt to have mistaken love for hate. What's happened to me? he thought. "Mrs. Kelly's fine," he said. "Just fine."

"Well," Alf said, stepping aside, again bursting with propriety and charm and words, words, words, as naturally as switching on a light. "Well, hey! Why are we standing out here? Come on in and familiarize yourself with the place. Now, in here to the right . . ."

The main pop and grocery shop itself occupied the first floor of the Wellingtons' enormous house, but Alf had built several additions over the years, in seemingly random order and with whatever resources were overstocked at the time. Patrons could also relax on the benches out front, surrounding the Civil War statue; in warmer weather, most preferred to bask there, adding to the thick carpet of squashed cigarette butts and sharing sections of the *Crier*.

Juggeston was a temperate town, and the Wellingtons sold no liquor, but people could choose from a few watery local beers or a great selection of tonics. Attached to the shop was a smoky, brick-built room with some mismatched diner tables, a player piano, a makeshift stage with a real PA system, a pay telephone, and no shortage of war miscellany. On one wall hung a poster-sized chart of aircraft silhouettes for differentiating American and Allied planes from Axis. Someone had taped magazine caricatures of the German führer and the Japanese General Tojo to a dart-board. Beside this hung a war-bond poster, and another of a cartoon soldier, his lips stitched shut: "Button your lip! Loose lips sink ships!" Didn't Friends practice pacifism? Fujita wondered. In his ignorance, he'd imagined Juggeston as a Thanksgiving greeting card: men wearing top hats, women in plain bonnets, both sexes sporting simple buckles on their shoes. Obviously, not everyone in town was even Quaker, but the majority attended meeting (he thought he'd better try it himself one day). He'd hoped that the war—and its images of the enemy—would not extend to this remote, rural town.

The lounge itself seemed expressly designed for loose talk, judging from the half-dozen men within, gabbing and playing a lackluster round of five-card stud. Yet when Alf ushered him into the room, the players fell as silent as if the Battle of the Atlantic depended on them. Fujita nodded around the table as Alf rattled off the introductions too quickly: "Harrold, Charles—"

"Go by Chuck, to pals," the man said, his tone not quite establishing that relationship. Fujita tried to pin the names to the men—all rather similar-looking, middle-aged, wrinkle-faced, hair in varying stages of balding or graying. Alf charged onward.

"This is Pete. The smokestack there is Fred." Rubbing an unshaven cheek, the first man unbent his long body like a tree from over his cards and his decimated pot to nod. The second coughed and waved a spewing cigarette in their direction. "And over here . . ." Coming to the last and youngest, Alf mussed the fellow's hair, which was so thickly greased that a pencil-sized spike remained erect like a lightning rod.

"Darn it, boy!" Alf said, recoiling in mock horror. "Don't you know about oil rationing? There's a war on, you know!"

"I do my bit," the young man grumbled, patting his hair back in place. "I'm closed up, aren't I?" Grinning, he threw a thumb over his shoulder toward the window and raised a splint-encased hand. Blocking the entrance to the garage across the street, a placard read: TO AID NATIONAL DEFENSE: NO GAS SOLD BETWEEN 6 P.M. AND 6 A.M. REQUESTED BY THE FEDERAL OIL CO-ORDINATOR. The Childs of the signpost matched the name sewn onto the breast of his olive jumpsuit. Gas fumes surrounded him like a cologne. Fujita saw that his face and hands were chapped and dry as a mummy's, and a flaky, white patch of psoriasis snaked up from his forearm to the tip of his elbow.

"Of course you're closed," said Harrold, or possibly Charles. "It's poker night."

"And this here's Casanova," Alf said at last. "But we call him Frankie."

"It's *Frank*, Alf. Jesus *Christ*." The eyes turned onto Fujita clearly indicated that whether it was Frank or Frankie, Childs wasn't about to invite this stranger into a first-name relationship, much less shake the hand Fujita now extended toward him.

"Dammit, Frankie," coughed Fred. "Shake the fellow's hand and play cards."

Instead, Childs puffed himself up like a peacock and rose jerkily from the table, knocking his chair backward and clenching his fists, as if emulating a movie cowboy summoned to a shootout. The youngest there by at least twenty years, he carried more bulk than appeared while he was sitting. He looked strong, or at least sturdy with something like baby fat.

"So, Tojo. You're the new man at Livvie's place, huh?"

"Don't go getting all hotheaded again," said Charles. "We playing cards, or what?"

Fujita iced over, ready for trouble. The others chuckled and remained easy.

"Frank," Alf called sharply.

Intent on the stare-down, Childs said nothing.

"*Frank!*"

He did not turn but deflated considerably as he released a breath to reply, "Jesus, Alf. *What*?"

"Have you gone loony on me?" Pinching Childs's earlobe between a thumb and forefinger, Alf said, "Pick up the chair, boy. You don't come in here and knock my furniture around. What in heck's wrong with you?"

"He's just a hothead," Charles offered to the room, if not exactly to Fujita. "All that grease up there's melting his brain."

Stricken, Childs glared around as if contemplating fighting all six, until the air gushed out of him and his arms fell limp. He lifted the toppled chair with his foot but did not sit again.

"Come on, Frankie," Harrold urged. "Play some cards." He swallowed a laugh but in the end could not resist adding, "Don't get your dandruff up." Even Fujita could not help smiling.

"You think this is funny?" Childs shouted, growing bigger, brandishing his splint. "I think it's goddam sad, you jokers sitting around here yukking it up with a goddam Jap. It's funny that you got two ladies and a little kid alone up there with *this*?" He aimed a finger at Fujita. "Something's goddam wrong here! I'll tell you: Sig Tufteller would not find *this* funny."

As Childs pointed a second time, Fujita neatly grabbed the splinted hand as if offered a friendly handshake. "Whoa! That's quite a grip you have, Frank!" he told the grimacing mechanic, straining to sound casual. "Say, you ought to be in the service. A big, healthy-looking fellow like you—and with such strong convictions. If I were your age, I'd enlist."

Childs looked stunned, stung. He yanked his hand free and backed away to the exit.

Feeling cheap, Fujita struggled to ease up. "I know about you, Frank. My son thought the way you do. He took himself too seriously, too."

Childs violently shrugged one shoulder, as if to free himself from an unseen hand holding him back, and stormed out, leaving in his wake silence and a scent of gasoline. A metallic taste filled Fujita's mouth, and his pulse boomed as he turned back to the card players.

"Er, this lounge is available for private parties!" blurted the master of Arcade Wellington, with a forced cheeriness that made even Fujita wince. The card players returned to the game, their jollity dissipated. "Concerts, school plays, bingo . . . anything. Except, the ladies have a monopoly on Thursdays, when they . . ." He paused, blinking vacantly toward the gamblers. "Well, frankly, we don't exactly know *what* they do. Thursday's

Lil's night. I'm not allowed in here, so only God and the women know what they do in here."

"And the Shadow!" coughed Fred. The men chuckled. "They drink hooch and play poker, I'll bet."

"Sometimes they sew, I think," said the ladder-limbed man named Pete.

"You're both wrong," amended Harrold. "They just sit around and plot how to make our lives miserable! They knit our names into a quilt."

"Harrold's hit it on the head!" Alf said, laughing more easily now. "Anyway, it's the closest thing we have to a watering hole. Used to be, we made live music here. Jack Kelly and I and a few other players rehearsed here. Say, you don't play an instrument, do you?"

Fujita began to confess his tin ear when he saw atop the battered piano lid, marred by cigarette burns and coffee rings, the sheet music for "Slap That Jap Right off of the Map!" Plunging his hands into his pockets, he shook his head. Alf caught it, too, and blushed. "Well, those were happier times."

A phone rang on the wall behind the card table. "Alf?" a stern woman's voice called from another room. The shopkeeper gave a start, then bustled over to answer it. As one, the card players murmured, "Uh-oh." Margaret had told Fujita about this rite at the arcade: how the wives of Juggeston—seething over a cold dinner table—ritually rang the shop to deliver summonses, then entreaties, then threats. Around suppertime, the local operator never asked, "What number, please?" They needed only to tell her, "Food's on and he's not home yet," to be connected to the lounge.

"Now, settle down, Doll," Alf cooed. "No . . . *Doll* . . . I'm telling you, I haven't seen *Harrold*," he said loudly, winking to the quarry.

As Harrold scrambled for his coat, however, a severe, elaborately dressed woman appeared at the doorway in a cloud of cigarette smoke. Noticing Fujita, she murmured, "Oh, yes, mmm hmm," as if he had asked her a question. Without taking her eyes from him, she reached out to tear the phone from Alf's hand, cradled the receiver on her shoulder, and stepped to the card table. She stabbed her heel firmly on the tail of Harrold's coat, which hung to the floor, pinning the poor fellow down in a half-sitting position.

Right away, Fujita recognized Mrs. Wellington, whose appearance matched her temperament. Of the Juggeston women he had seen in passing, only Lil Wellington dressed as expensively as Margaret, yet her well-labeled attire seemed to dangle from—more than suit—her coatrack-thin frame. Her prodigious application of cosmetics only served to blur the finer lines of her face and accentuate its naturally harsh angles. "Lil appears a bit *hard* at first," Margaret had warned him, "but I guess a heart beats under there somewhere." If so, it was impenetrably armored under a rhinestone brooch shaped like a floral bouquet. Its bristling crystal bulbs reminded Fujita of a sea urchin. Hugging this woman could be painful, he thought, glancing at Alf.

"Why, the rascal's sitting right here, Doll," Lil snickered, stepping back to free Harrold from his chair. "And a sorry sight he is, too, tripping all over himself." She lowered her voice to a grave whisper. "Really? Oh *my*. I'll just *bet* that's right, Doll. Yes, he's withering already."

As Harrold's footsteps retreated down the stoop, across the gravel parking lot, Lil thrust her pointed chin into the air, swept the room with a triumphant let-them-eat-cake look, and demonstratively ignored Fujita, as if he were no more noticeable to her than a bug. Margaret had also warned him that Lil's youngest brother had died in combat in the Pacific that summer.

"Uh, Lil, honey? This is Mister . . ." Alf said. One of the card players—the tall fellow, Pete—shook his head gravely.

In a voice harder than her marble pop-shop counter, icier than her ice cream vats, she said, "Well, here you are."

"Here I am," Fujita said evenly.

Without another word, the woman turned her back on them, and Alf and Fujita followed her out into the main part of the store. "And here we are," Fujita said, unloading his pile of letters and papers onto the counter—daunting but organized. Some were urgent communiqués to the New York and Providence P.D.'s, and to the more cryptically addressed contacts in those cities—the WRA office and JACL chapter and AFSC. Another, to a Boston industrial-supply firm, bore legions of ten-digit numbers and sketchy descriptions of metal, mechanical, and electrical items. Some ten pieces of regular mail were unpronounceably addressed—Ichioka, Munemori, Kitabayashi, and Tanaka. He produced two neatly wrapped packets of cash: one for a money order to wire to an R. Yamaguchi in Rivers, Arizona, the other to buy postage for the letters and a small crate addressed to a federal penitentiary in Montana. He bought fifty stamps for himself, too. Amazed, Lil and Alf traded glances.

"Gosh, you have a lot of friends," Alf observed, more coolly now.

"That's some network you have there," said Lil.

Her tone was recognizable to the Nisei—the usual suspicions of some sinister espionage, secret meetings, fifth-column intrigue. He knew well how significant deaths could make a person act unlike, or opposite from, his or her true self. Lil hated him at a glance, but perhaps at night they shared the same nightmares.

Though prepared to overlook any trespasses, he had tasks to accomplish and grew impatient. "If you feel it's too much for you," he said, "please tell me now and I won't take up your time. I'll drive on to another town."

"We wouldn't hear of it," Lil said with an ugly grin. "You've come so far already. Get to work, Alf." Without taking her eyes off the stranger, she shoved the pile to her husband, who slid down to work at the far end of the counter, weighing, sorting, stamping.

"That's very kind of you," Fujita said, thinking it wasn't kind at all—it was their *job*. "I'll just browse a bit, then."

Retreating into the grocery aisles, he found much shelf space empty. As if this were a point that pained him deeply, Alf called, "I'm sorry to say our stock's pretty lean just now. Rationing and all. We try to get people what they need." Nodding, Fujita fingered a can of olives as though reading Braille, then flipped open his coupon book. The wartime coupon system secretly gratified his frugal part—perhaps his Japanese part. Selective shopping came naturally to him, and rationing measures only codified his own practical, private point system. As newlyweds, with their money sunk in the nursery, he and Mari had frequented wholesale and discount stores. Even as business took off, he still would rigidly compare prices at length, buy in bulk. Since camp, though, he'd become subject to sudden cravings, as if he were pregnant. While he suppressed such impulse extravagances as olives, he liked to look at them in stores. The loss of twelve points for a poor-quality sixteen-cent item finally did not seem worth it.

"Is that what you're looking for, mister?" Lil asked in a noticeably aggressive tone.

"Lil, honey," Alf admonished, "the man knows what he wants and doesn't."

It saddened Fujita, this little whatnot arcade, this patchwork grocery, this most general of general stores. What saddened him wasn't the woman smoking furiously at him; the smells of chocolate syrup and butterscotch, and the cool, sticky marble counter, transported him beyond Lil's loathing, beyond this nowhere town and its mean-spirited mechanics and awkward farmers to another, better, and now unrecoverable place. He marched up to the shopwoman.

"Mrs. Wellington," he said, "I'll bet you could make a heck of a banana split. You have no idea what a treat it would be for me."

Lil seemed mildly surprised that Japs ate banana splits, but she shrugged and rolled up her sleeves. Business was business. While she prepared a bowl of Breyers choco-nilla swirl, he perused Juggeston's unofficial historical museum. Lining the walls of the shop was a hodgepodge of old news clippings, maps, letters, and photos from the town's not very remarkable past. Alf finished weighing Tamie's package. "So how do you like it here so far?"

"Very much," he replied as warmly as he genuinely could. "I've been busy working on Mrs. Kelly's property, you know. The soil is rocky, and there's a lot of landscaping to be done. We're building a greenhouse—that's the challenge. I've located good wood for it. With the scrap, I thought I might build a shelter up top for the civil patrols—"

"My, that's considerate of you," Lil interjected.

"Well, what with the rain and snow you must get up here in winter."

"I'll bet it's a lot different from what you're used to, eh?" The veins of her face strained forth, pinching the skin, as she scraped the ribs of the cardboard vat with a dull gray scoop. "All that swell Pacific sunshine. Palm trees. Things like that?"

"Yes, I suppose it is."

"I'll just bet there are a lot of things you find strange in our parts."

He drew a deep breath and gave her a controlled smile. "Yes, well, you know: 'East is east and west is west,'" he recited, "'and never the twain shall meet.'" Then an unsettling thought came to him. To Alf he said, "I understand the farmer's market is held right here."

Alf nodded. "Wednesdays and Saturdays in good weather. People come from all the neighboring towns. The only other grocery is seven miles away, and it carries lousy produce, but here we get the best goods because we invest in quality. Most places give fifty cents on the bushel for cabbage, for instance, but we pay out sixty-five."

"*Sixty*," Lil corrected him.

"Hefty wages, of course, but it's just good business. Why, we were so busy for a time, Lil and the town board almost got a Boston company to build a train station right here in town. Track-laying started in spring '41, but they quit when the war broke out. That would have been a boost for Juggeston, I can tell you."

"They'll begin construction again, I'm sure," Fujita suggested, "once things get back to normal, once we win the war." Both hosts froze—Alf despite himself, and more discreetly—to eye Fujita, trying to decode this loaded statement. "Juggeston will be a boomtown, then."

Alf cleared his throat. "Well, yes, that would be nice. At least the farmers are doing better these days—thank God for that. Funny how a war can improve some things. Well, I'm all for the farmers. That's why I came here. I came to Juggeston because Juggeston just looked like it *needed* me."

Lil bisected a brownish, frozen banana and flanked the bowl with the halves. "I wanted to be a farmer," Alf admitted. "I pictured us out there hoeing, surviving on what we grew ourselves.

Well, *you* know." Spritzing the mound with too much whipped cream, Lil laughed wickedly. "But Lil wasn't too keen on being a farmer's wife," Alf admitted. "So we bought this place, instead." Lil grinned, ploinking five Queen Anne cherries on the mound. "It's true, I can't even grow grass by myself," Alf confessed, smiling winningly.

Recalling that Alf's victory garden by the horseshoes court looked indeed more like a coming-out-with-your-hands-up garden, Fujita smiled back.

"Well, you'll see the market for yourself before you know it," Alf said. "We're sure you'll fit right in, of course. Isn't that so, Lil?"

"Sure it is," she answered, chillier than the ice cream she finally plopped on the counter, placing it not before her customer but at a conspicuous reach.

Grimly determined to wait, Fujita hooked his feet in the bars of the stool and sat rigidly with spoon upraised like a palace guard with his halberd. Biting the insides of his cheeks with his back molars, he set his jaw, aimed an unwavering smile at the woman. Having waited a very long time—too long to remember—he could wait again as long as it took this woman to do her job.

Smile. Lil rose to the occasion, smiling back, looking rather sweet, the pucker lines mostly fading from her lips. *Smile, smile.* Shifting her weight slightly, she propped herself up with a fist on her hip. *Smile.* Her severely penciled eyebrows crinkled down above her nose, slid into an annoyed frown. *Smile.* Shifting again, Lil asked, innocent as a schoolgirl, "Well, aren't you hungry?" The last syllable flew high and trilling as some small spring bird.

Smile away, far away, smile like a statue of Buddha. "That, Mrs. Wellington," said Fujita, lowering his gaze to the crystal urchin protruding above her right breast, "is really the most extraordinary . . . no, compelling . . . no, *exquisite* brooch I think I've ever seen."

"Oh." He watched Lil Wellington's hand snake up from her hip, across her apron skirt, over the buttons of her dress. Covering the jewelry with her palm, she looked as if she was swearing in to office. Then, the wrinkles of her mouth revealed themselves again and she grinned. "Oh, *this* bauble?" she said, and she slid the overflowing dish toward him. "Well, really, it's nothing."

Yes, he had waited—so much waiting, Fujita did not know quite how to proceed with this dessert, as if he'd forgotten how to eat. Tentatively, he ran his fingertips over the thick glass, textured with four-faceted points. Delicately as a surgeon giving an inoculation to some tender, intimate body part, he probed its wobbling crest of whipped cream with the spoon tip. So rich, luxurious, so daunting. Feeling unworthy, he fought back more than a twinge of guilt as he pierced the white shell, tapping a spring of chocolate syrup. He lifted a slow shovelful and let it hover, teasing the air beneath his nose, just kissing the skin of his lips, before taking it inside him.

Cold, yes. Exploding sweet and bitter, clinging to lip, incisor, tongue. Cold in his esophagus, cool in his stomach. "Mrs. Wellington," he murmured, "you don't know how long it's been." Swept away in sensory memories, he set to devouring it with such rapture—cooing, groaning, sniffling and sighing—that the proprietors could only gawk behind the bar. Shoveling, shoveling, frenzied, faster, the spoon hand moved with such velocity they might have thought the man, skinny as he was, had starved his whole life. The banana emitted a tropical air, a Pacific air to Fujita's thinking—an air of Sunday family drives to the waterfront in Los Angeles, the click of a change purse, the jangle of frugally doled-out pennies, racing, gulping, and the clank of two spoons as he and Tony fenced for the last remaining cherry at the muddy bottom of the bowl they shared.

"Bill, I don't think we'll starve if you and Tony have your own bowls," Mari used to scold him. "You can both have a cherry. You can pay another penny for an extra cherry."

"It's too big for him to eat alone. You want him to grow fat and toothless?" he would say. "You want *me* to get fat and toothless?"

"You'll never be fat. You're already half toothless. Another cherry won't hurt," Mari insisted, not knowing that he always let Tony win the battle but only after bringing the cherry to his edge of the bowl, to the edge of the boy's defeat. In its way, the ritual was his method of teaching the boy life lessons in adversity, in conflict and commitment. In its way, the Sunday-morning treat made up for the wrestling, the football Tony could not play at school (he was too small), for the swimming lessons Fujita could not give, and for the infrequency of their fishing trips (since his own father had squandered and eventually lost his life working in a fish-processing station, Fujita could never really bear the things). It was, Fujita believed, his way of teaching his son to stand firm when people inevitably tried to steal all the cherries.

There at Wellington's, he could almost hear Mari's reply: "It's your guilty way of treating yourself without paying full price for it." True, he could never eat a whole sundae himself without growing ill, and it did irk him to pay all to eat half. Still, the Fujita men *liked* this ritual; they liked these manly duels. "*You* like it," Mari would say. "And it's not manly, it's childish." Fujita's love needed those Sundays, the touch of those stainless steel epees clicking.

He heard it now, the click, click, click, and looking down saw that he'd made very neat work of Mrs. Wellington's monstrous concoction—only the five uprooted cherries remained, flooded in a muddy film. With a certain ceremonial care, he lifted the cherries, one by one, dangling by their stems—frightened, he imagined, like sacrificial virgins carried to the monster's cave—to his open jaws. His nausea grew with each swallow, the sweetness now unpleasant. Holding the last, unsacrificed cherry above the bowl, he remembered another part of the ritual, Tony's great pleasure in trying for years to teach his father a crude parlor trick. How did he do it? It only worked with jarred cherries, not fresh-picked. Trying to remember, Fujita popped the fruit, stem and all, into his mouth, then closed his eyes and rocked back so far he almost fell off the stool. The muscles of his mouth churned and flexed and danced. Then he felt the soft rubbery stem loop over into itself. Opening his eyes, he looked at the glasses and jars and cutlery and posters and photographs behind the counter, behind Alf and Lil, wary and transfixed. Holding his palm open beneath his lips, he poked his tongue forward.

Out popped the stem, tightly tied into a small red knot.

"Mrs. Wellington," he said sadly, dropping the little bow into the empty glass boat. "I guess that was just about the very finest ice cream sundae I've ever had."

Lil Wellington stepped back and placed her hand to her throat, struggling for the words, "Oh, my! It's just ice cream. I mean, really, it's just . . ." She looked away in embarrassment, but Alf leaned over the bar, wide-eyed, as though watching a lion at the zoo during feeding time. His wife swatted the back of his head. They blinked at Fujita for a long moment, until Lil recovered enough to ask, "Seconds?"

"On the house," Alf urged, ignoring Lil's glare.

"Thank you, no," Fujita said, out of breath. "I actually don't feel too well now." Lil mustered the generosity to offer him a glass of water, and it touched him—after these years, the smallest kindness felt as vast as a stay of execution. Rising stiffly from the stool, he rubbed his stomach for their benefit, though that was not where his ache lived. "Margaret and the Tuftellers are probably holding dinner," he remembered aloud. "Well, as you say, I'll probably be back here a lot."

Wandering back toward Widow's Peak, he kicked pebbles from the roadside, recalling one of his father's more memorable precepts about the difference between East and West: Westerners sought God only in the sky; they walked with their faces to clouds, and so stumbled. "Meet another man face-on," the Little Bull had urged, "but look down when you have something to say to gods." So Fujita looked down in shame, poured curses against himself into the earth. He felt sorry for Lil Wellington, he confided to the worms. And Childs . . . well, he was young. "I mustn't lose my temper," he said. Seeing the raised mailbox flag set his heart thumping, but he found there only paid bills Margaret had set out. "Control, control," he urged, tromping tiredly up the hill. Halfway between earth and sky, he glanced up enough to envision how the greenhouse panes would catch the moon on such a night. How warm it would be.

Up top, the scarecrow almost appeared as if she'd been waiting for him—and not patiently. Though she greeted him with open arms, she wore what seemed a rather critical, crystal-eyed stare that reminded him of one of Mari's harsher expressions, and he shivered. "That *could* have gone better," he muttered to the grass woman, through gritted teeth.

With time running out on the season, Fujita exorcised his anxiousness in physical work. Making a priority of the greenhouse, he conducted his lieutenants in an orderly campaign of landscaping—felling trees and shrubs, moving boulders, mixing concrete, building glass frames. Weekday mornings, Garvin hopped the fence on the way to the bus to check the progress. He'd catch his breath, impressed by the ravaged landscape, the leafy corpses whittled down into points at the base like huge spears, the holes great and small piercing the earth everywhere. "It looks like we've been bombed!" he'd comment, laying down his books, and Fujita would lay aside his ax (or spade or rake) to nudge the boy onward. "I know, I know," Garvin would say, "school first. No need to get grumpy."

"Who's grumpy?" the farmer would mutter grumpily. Mid-November in Juggeston could not decide if it was mid-September or early December. As the weather fluctuated, so did Fujita's moods, and so did the radio news of battles won and lost. (That news came only by radio, for one thing that didn't change was the president; the campaign and then FDR's unprecedented fourth election had rendered the *Crier* a site for presidential beheadings those weeks.) "I'm not grumpy, I'm *busy*."

Trying to be patient, Fujita made an effort to educate his workers. He explained that what seemed like random destruction followed the meticulously detailed maps he'd plotted. These considered such matters as walkways, irrigation, light access, which beds' longevity relied on an ocean face, et cetera. Opting for the southeastern exposure, he decided on a standard, even-span greenhouse attached to the garage—an iffy business all around. The site had good drainage, the best light, and close proximity to water and heat sources, not to mention to Fujita himself. The greenhouse would effectively prohibit parking in the garage, as the fumes were too dangerous. Since it would have to contend with the strongest winds from the Atlantic, they left some trees standing as a natural windbreak. It wasn't quite a conservatory, but it wasn't his nursery, either. He couldn't exactly ask Margaret to build the most expensive possible, freestanding greenhouse, reroute her property's heating systems, and suffer major relandscaping and light loss to the main house. After all, he assumed—though he didn't mention this to Margaret—that he would be off again within a few months to locate Yoneko.

On the whole, the good soldiers did what they were told, but they all needed to be told, and that fact frustrated him. One wet morning, Margaret got the Dodge stuck in mud while extracting a high, woody shrub chained to the truck's bumper. Pushing it from behind, Fujita was about to say, "Ease it out," when she gunned the motor and the spewing tires caked him top to toe with sludge.

"Whew!" Garvin whistled. "You look like Al Jolson in the pictures!" The unflappable Fujita flapped a great deal then—the man they knew to be about as talkative as the scarecrow at home could barely control his rage when disturbed at his work. "It's all right," he grumbled, spitting out mud. "We have all the time in the world."

As he poured the concrete for the greenhouse, the others turned to preparing the actual garden plots. They roped off patches of land to mimic the lines of his detailed maps, a series of concentric steps, divided by walkways, radiating downward from the hilltop. "It's like magic!" Margaret called when they'd finished. From up top, the beds looked like cells of a gigantic hopscotch court. "We did that, Livvie!"

The new recruits did their best to stay out of Fujita's hair, but they'd caught the bug. Hungering to know more, to be of more use, they pestered Fujita to teach them. "Tell us everything you're doing," Margaret said. "Leave nothing out."

"Be tough with us," Livvie added, and Fujita noticed that she relaxed a bit as the four of them were busy together outdoors. It seemed to distract her and Garvin from goading each other.

So he walked them through it. In addition to the greenhouse, he did some sacrificial transplanting those weeks, wanting to see how cold it became, how quickly, to what effect; which mulch should go where; which herbs and vegetables might survive winter in shallow glass hotbeds warmed by manure. Some plants liked winter: Parsnips, for example, fared well in frozen ground, the cold turning the starch content to sugar. It was all new to Margaret and the Tuftellers, and throughout their labors they bombarded him with questions:

"Why plant these beneath the apple tree? Won't it take up all the sunlight?"

"Why do you mix the berries and vegetables?"

"Isn't it too rocky here?"

"Sig and Jack used to dig up nightcrawlers here for fishing. Won't the worms eat the roots?"

"Did you go to school to learn all this?"

To which he replied: "It's a small tree; there's enough light, and its leaves make a natural mulch and compost. Do you want to do this every year?" And "Why not? Nature doesn't discriminate; neither should we." And "No. There will be a wooden planting box, here—a pyramid—and a trellis to elevate plants with shallow roots." And "Of course not. They eat dirt; they do half of your tilling for you." And "Watch nature. See how things happen naturally, then do things naturally. Diplomas don't make things grow; nature makes things grow. I went to school to learn to make money."

His professorial tone tickled the women. In his element, the serious, mysterious Fujita found himself slipping from his businesslike manner on occasion to brighten uncharacteristically. He described how various plants interacted with light, water, and one another to explain his map—asparagus here, Brussels sprouts here, broccoli there—and the women cooed, but Garvin said, "Yuck. What a waste!"

Fujita took seriously his commitment to keep the boy busy. "I've got a real important job for you, pal. Come here." He led Garvin in a circuit around one patch skirted by thin, twine-drawn rows of herbs like a moat. "These herbs are Umbelliferae, good for attracting wasps that hunt down caterpillars and aphids and other pests, see. Know how they do that?"

"Uh-uh. They sting 'em, I guess."

"Worse. You know from school that they collect pollen and eat the nectar from flowers, right? This herb patch is their mess hall. So, they fly here and have dinner on these herbs, right? Then what do they do? Well, they're like young boys: They don't like to eat vegetables any better than you. They know they've got to get some nutrition, so they put up with it, but then they fly along . . . you know, 'buzz, buzz, what's for dessert,' they say. They sneak back into the garden—in secret surveillance—and, bingo! A sweet, fat caterpillar on the cabbage! Some of the fellows, they swoop down, grab their prey, and take it back to share with their buddies. But the women are the ones to watch out for. They don't bother with sharing or snacking. They just stick the caterpillars but good, and lay their eggs inside the dead bodies to incubate."

"Neat!" sang Garvin.

"Neat is right," said Fujita. "And these herb beds . . ."

"Underbelly," said Garvin.

"Er, Umbelliferae. These will be your responsibility, pal. You'll put up a wire fence around here, and you have to check it each morning before school. Weed it, remove vines, make sure no rabbits get in, look for mouse droppings, things like that. Okay?"

"Roger Wilco," Garvin said, saluting, yet happily more at ease than Fujita had ever seen him.

At the end of one shortening mid-November day, as the scarecrow's back glowed red in the setting sun and her shadow fell far down the hill, the three spouseless adults collapsed together on the porch, sharing their surprise at the pleasure they took just from being together, along with that exquisite ache and exhaustion that had always been Fujita's addiction. That rush of exhilaration when the lower back began to clench and quiver, so that merely standing became a daunting, new experience. The stripping of sweaty work gloves, baring hands moist and tender as new-hatched chicks. And all the calluses and scrapes and pricks and blisters that made a scoreboard of the body, that one could mark the fact with heartbreaking certainty that something has been accomplished. He leaned on the porch railing; they sat on the steps. Livvie nursed a tumbler of scotch and watched Garvin somersaulting on the lawn; Margaret rested her red hair on Livvie's shoulder. "You know," she said, "before now, I never walked all the way around the property before. I don't think I've ever quite looked at our hill this way."

"I wish my half had this view," Livvie said, gazing toward the coast.

"Wouldn't it be grand if we had a table of some sort out here? To look out over our farm, our very own," Margaret sighed. "I'm so pleased. No, that's not right. I feel," she began. "I feel . . ." she tried again, closing her eyes. "Like a well-loved meatball nestled in a big heap of warm, overcooked noodles." She turned a bright, content smile on Fujita, who had nothing to say to that. He looked away, down, anywhere but her eyes. "Well?" she teased. "You can't just let that pass. You can't just let a woman tell you she feels like a well-loved meatball and get away with saying not a blessed thing. Some response is called for here. Right, Livvie?"

Livvie looked at Garvin playing, then up to Fujita—pinned, blushing, looking lost—and then more curiously at Margaret. Whatever she saw there only made her shake her head and raise her drink to the new man. "A toast!" she said. "After all this work, here's to something actually *growing.*"

"But the work is its own reward, too," sighed the Protestant in Margaret Balford Kelly.

Pushing himself even further upright on the railing, as if awaiting sentence, the nurseryman gazed at the scarecrow shuddering in the wind and thought, *Work will set you free*. At the time, the phrase—wrought in iron above locked gates halfway across the world—was known to the Jews of Auschwitz and others that the Nazis found so loathsome in their country, but not yet to tiny Juggeston. Had Fujita known, he might have cringed but would think it anyway. As sure as those Puritan settlers who had migrated to that region before him, the Nisei pilgrim believed that work would free him from fear, from grief, if not from death. He counted on it.

"Amen," said the Nisei softly, "and amen."

FOUR

Demimonde

"If you were stranded on a desert island," Bill Fujita hollered into the wind, heading down the winding LaLoma Road from the Sunday drive back toward the arroyo, "and you could only take three kinds of food with you, what would they be?"

"Here we go again," said Mari. She knotted her scarf tighter beneath her chin to save what little of a hairstyle the wind had not ravaged. "Can we put the top up, please?"

"That's an easy one," Tony hollered back, leaning over the front seat between his parents. "Dr Pepper, definitely. Corn on the cob, and . . ."

"Bologna," Fujita finished for him.

"Yeah, that's it. As Grandma would say, 'Indubitably!'"

"Not *natto*?" his mother asked teasingly.

"Natto's like eating slugs!" Tony mimed retching, though truly, the slimy, fermented beans made him queasy.

"Don't talk to your mother like that," said Fujita.

"Can we put the top up, please?" Mari repeated. Above them, the wind rushed through the fronds of the great palm trees, which swayed contentedly as if under a scalp massage. A precise wind, it always spilled just over the lip of the arroyo, at the entrance to the Colorado Bridge, where Fujita now signaled his turn.

Physically and socially, the arroyo cutting through Pasadena separated the city's higher and lower neighborhoods—those San Rafael hilltop mansions that Fujita called "Estate-side," and the center of town, which he called "down here." On his daily delivery rounds Estate-side, Fujita usually took the Colorado Bridge, the fastest route, offering a terrific view of both the Rose Bowl and Brookside Park below. Trickle-down was Pasadena's natural order. Just as the flotsam of clockwork rainstorms tumbled down their steep streets to fill the arroyo's gut, so Pasadena's elevated society and their money occasionally trickled down to mingle with the valley people. Not all valley people, though. Brookside Park housed the infamous "Plunge," the public pool where young Fujita had been deterred from learning to swim on those Tuesdays allotted to coloreds, and where it was said the piss-greened water was changed on Wednesdays. In more prosperous times, runoff from San Rafael nourished an economic demimonde of colored workers: servants, houseboys, mother's helpers, gardeners, pool cleaners, launderers. The depression, however, saw the Colorado Bridge renamed "Suicide Bridge," and more hill people began plummeting into the arroyo, though still the bridge offered the same terrific, final view.

"Okay," Fujita called. "Here's another one: If you were stranded on a desert island and could only take five pieces of clothing . . ." Mari laughed at his absurdity. "It could happen," he protested, aware how easily it could happen, without even leaving home. Bankruptcy could be their desert island. From 1930 on, the nursery's finances had suffered sympathy pains as some Estate-side catastrophes trickled down in tangible ways, such as rubber checks. Yet there were benefits, too. For that Sunday's constitutional, the family had cruised the wealthy hillside as if on a botanical garden tour. In what Fujita thought a bizarre response to their neighbors' misfortunes, many of the luckier or savvier hill people contracted ever-more lavish gardenscaping. It was as if they hoped to stave off foreclosure by maintaining a wealthy appearance through their lawns: Let them sell part of the property to pay for it, as long as the remainder looked like Versailles. Miyake, the old master gardener who still looked over Fujita's shoulder every day, saw nothing odd about it; to him, a well-kept garden was a necessity, not a luxury, especially in such tough times. Maybe a *vegetable* garden, thought Fujita. With his college degrees, he remained always more a businessman than a gardener. A good thing, too, in 1937, as Fujita steered them over the arroyo across what he could fortunately still think of as the *Colorado* Bridge.

"It could happen," he insisted. "Best to be prepared. Say we go on a family cruise and—"

"Just walking by a travel agency gives you a rash," Mari said. "A drive to Orange County is a safari to you."

"Yes, well, I have been feeling a little crazy these days. Maybe it's time to throw caution to the wind."

"Brother! I'll believe that when I see it," Mari said, untying her scarf, unwilling to surrender *that* to the wind, at least.

The troubled Pasadena hills were distant and exotic enough for Fujita. "Ah, I lead such a boring life," he admitted happily to the warm air, content just to reach the opposite bank of Suicide Bridge. How he loved going home.

Fatherhood: Fujita thought it his fulfillment—the greatest upheaval life had in store for him. Mari Fujita, who read romance novels but never, ever quite believed in their happily-ever-afters, secretly feared her husband was inordinately unprepared for parenthood—that plenty of surprises awaited him, that his need to control and protect their lives must surely be revealed for an illusion. There would be Tony's illnesses, broken digits, truancies, little heartbreaks, wrecking the car. While Fujita lectured the boy on industry, at study or in the shop, Mari foresaw the tempest when Tony would discover the limits on his life and in his skin—a lesson her husband couldn't pass on because *he* hadn't seemed to realize it yet. When the time came, Tony would surely refuse to follow in Pop's horticultural footsteps—now that would be upheaval! Yet, perhaps due to the perpetual anticipation of uprooting Ichiro had imposed on his own boyhood, Fujita grew into a resolute homebody. Determined that his own son should surpass him, he would not imagine anything could go wrong.

He lived full days after December '37, as the Sino-Japanese war raged, when he at last assumed the mantle of garden supplier to the stars. His mentor, however, kept closer ties with friends and calabash relatives in Little Tokyo and so noticed that distant war seeping into Los Angeles, its quiet skirmishes between Japanese and Chinese, both in the streets and in the local political arena. Although Miyake never expected to gain citizenship—this was forbidden by law, and he supposed no amendment would occur in his lifetime—he had seen the burgeoning net of immigration and naturalization laws raised before the U.S. shores, barring further entry by his countrymen. He had heard the decline of his mother tongue, noted the floundering of the Japanese associations, now effectively set adrift from the Japanese consulate. Thus, at sixty-something years old (he never said exactly), the time had come to realize the dream of dreams, *kin'i kikyo*, to surrender his share of the nursery and return home wealthy—well, not as rich as he'd thought, hoped, or been promised, of course. This, in lieu of stranding himself among the other Issei *kimin*, abandoned by Japan to the whims of a hostile country.

"You would never overreact a wee tad, eh?" Fujita asked him that December night at dinner when Miyake announced his decision.

"He wants to get married," Mari teased. "To find himself a village girl!"

Usually so talkative at the table, Tamie glanced away, saddened. No girls, village *or* city girls, were forthcoming from Japan. No wives, no picture brides. California and Tokyo had put an end to girls like her long ago, and in America the maestro gardener was doomed to remain alone.

"Married," Miyake huffed. "I go home to *die*, not marry!" He shook a finger at Fujita. "Bad times ahead for Japanese. Sinking the *Panay* is just the start. Think you're so smart, college boy. Have a plan for everything, sure, but never think ahead."

On New Year's Day, Miyake sold his nursery share over to Fujita for a few thousand dollars—calling it a birthday present—and passed his room keys into Tamie's keeping. "Now we'll get Mama out of the house, get them some space," he chuckled.

"Now Mama has some space away from them," Tamie sniffed.

Fujita hired an especially skillful part-time assistant named Lum Chen from Chinatown, and Mari and Tamie took shifts in the shop. Thus, despite his increased responsibilities, he could continue to spend time with his family, if less of it. Together the male Fujitas learned to throw a football and build a tree fort.

"Bill's worked so hard," Mari said one day, watching her boys trying to have a catch out back, awkwardly flailing baseballs at each other's feet. "He's making up for lost time."

"He's just a late bloomer," Tamie told her.

Though Miyake would always be the master, Fujita with his degree knew more about growing a business. Once in command, he increased profits and established new distribution channels; for example, he gave bulk-purchase discounts to a retail group in Chinatown—a move his mentor had refused to make. He drummed up twice as much business among Caucasian clients and funneled the income into a stall at a profitable outdoor market in Los Angeles. As his professional profile improved, he won spots in local business clubs and joined the Japanese-American Nurseryman's Association. He even accepted an invitation from his alma mater to lecture on urban and suburban agribusiness strategies at a time when colleges had only just begun to conceive of such subjects.

Concerned that her son overextended himself by expanding too quickly, Tamie watched his success with a mixture of pride and dread. Lately, he'd begun to negotiate to buy new trucks, but what was wrong with the *old* truck? "Depreciation," he had laughed, and Tamie had to look up the term. "Capital investment." So cocky! A big shot, know-it-all! Never quite resigned to the idea that her son had irretrievably become a plant man, she had to admit that he'd achieved much—maybe not *the* American Dream, but an American dream. Still, she worried. Like old Miyake, she sensed rumblings, and she feared them. The trade papers reported union efforts to restrict Japanese agricultural workers—always some petition circulating, a politician mouthing off. The Chinese . . . at least Tamie forced herself to question her deep distrust of Lum Chen, the twenty-five-year-old helper who had proven himself loyal and hardworking.

Strong, sharp-witted, and charming to clients, he'd been a great asset to their family, but who knew what complicated machinations lurked beneath that facade of dependability? Chinese were *zurui,* Tamie thought. You had to watch them.

"Mom," Fujita protested, as they helped Tony with the shop inventory, "we're doing great. We have a devoted clientele, diverse investments, and dependable staff. What's to worry about? You don't even have to work at the shop. You could *retire* if you wanted." The men traded conspiratorial grins. Tamie frowned sourly.

Retire?! How smug! "I'm still part owner, you know," she fired back. "I'm looking out for my concerns." Tony giggled but avoided his *obaasan*'s eyes.

"There's nothing to worry about," Fujita sighed, "but fret if you like."

"It's a free country," Tony added, adopting his grandmother's accent and laughing.

She slapped Tony on the arm. "May you avenge your baachan and torment your father as he torments me."

"I promise, Grandma!" Tony laughed. "I promise!"

It was 1939, and Tamie watched with a blend of satisfaction and dismay as her potent curse came to fruition. The year that German troops rolled into Poland and Czechoslovakia, Tony turned sixteen, entered high school, and joined the fray of adolescence with a vengeance. His concentration was crippled, he dropped and broke things at the nursery, miscounted in inventory, overslept and missed the schoolbus. His hard-won high grade average crumbled. "It's hormones," Mari offered. She had expected it.

"It's the war," Tamie said. From the classroom buzz at the gakuen, she knew how expectation of America's imminent involvement in Europe's war had laid low many relationships between Pasadena's sons and families.

"It's the war *and* hormones *and* a girl," Fujita said, certainly.

Truly, Tony devoured newspaper articles and comic books and pulp war novels to the detriment of his studies, which seemed trivial by comparison. He cultivated a healthy loathing for fascism and determined to enlist when he could, readying himself for his call of duty by joining a gang of like-minded budding patriots who undertook their own brawling basic training around Pasadena's parks and L.A.'s alleys. "He acts more like his grandfather each day," Fujita told Tamie, who nodded in worried agreement.

Fujita knew for sure that a girl lay behind it all when Tony came into the shop one midnight of his sophomore year looking as if he'd jumped face-first into an empty swimming pool. Despite his wounds—and the tears Mari wrung from him, angrily swabbing them with alcohol—Tony was in jolly spirits. As his mother leaned close, scanning his face for cuts, it became apparent that he had been drinking—the smell mixed with a cheap perfume and cigarette smoke. Streaks of brighter red, mingling with the blood on his cheeks: lipstick. Battered but happy, loose-lipped from drink, Tony confessed that he'd fought over a girl. Her name was Yoneko.

"Talk to him, Bill. If I hear any more, I may scream," Mari said, storming out.

Uncertain what to say, Fujita assumed his most annoyed, authoritative expression. Slumped back in the chair, glassy-eyed and smiling, the boy looked strikingly like his grandfather. Recalling that Ichiro had killed a man at Tony's age, Fujita steeled himself. His son would not be a drunk—happy or not. Pulling up a chair, Fujita sat with his arms crossed like the stern old landlord MacGregor, scourge of his childhood. "Come here, son."

"Yeah, Pop," Tony said, flopping forward, his head bobbing as if set on a spring. So trusting. Fujita wondered if he had made such an easy target for his own father.

"No, come closer."

Fujita swung. The blow caught Tony full in the ear, and Fujita cringed as the boy somersaulted back over his chair. The unprecedented action stunned them both. Although Tony had certainly absorbed harder blows that night, he remained sprawled on his back until Fujita yanked him upright.

"You'll never come in here drunk again," Fujita said. "Got it? Or do you want another one of those?" His fist raised, hovered, then lowered. "Good. So. What's-her-name. You got in a fight over this girl?"

"Yoneko Yamaguchi, Pop," Tony said, rubbing his cheek. "But you don't understand—see, she was—"

"Stop. I don't want the details now. Here's the plan: You'll straighten up, *excel* at school, cut out the drinking—out, cut, completely—and bring this girl around to see me. If you don't, I'll have to kill you." He paused. "You'll make your mother mad with that, and she'll make me mad, and I don't want to be made mad. Understand?" Echoing Ichiro's last words made Fujita grimace; he felt brutish and ugly, but effective. "Straighten up and fly right, and you can keep seeing this Yoneko."

"Mom won't like her, Pop. Grandma will hate her."

"We'll see about that later."

Yoneko Yamaguchi: When Fujita first saw the girl the following spring, she was smoke to him—from the smokiness of her eyes and voice and even her movements to the smoke that literally clung to her sleek figure like a cape of mystery. He knew Tony stood hidden in the wings of the Union Church's tiny theater, fanning dry-ice mist across the stage with a cardboard flap. Still, he marveled at the spectacle: The vaporous tendrils meshed naturally with Yoneko's full, jet hair; a sharp, magenta spotlight made her already brilliant red sheath dress glow like a hot coal; the very air seemed a shifting, pulsating rainbow beneath the colored arc lamps. Fujita had seen few theatricals of any sort; in a stage audience he was a believer; he would have no disbelief to suspend, if not for his mother's persistent fidgeting in the seat beside him.

"She looks like a Filipina," hissed Tamie. "I don't like her." For Tamie, Yoneko's ambition to an acting career was already a strike against her. Her Saturday rehearsals precluded her attending Tamie's gakuen class (the Yamaguchis didn't require her to learn Japanese—strike two). Protesting that he didn't need the classes, since Tamie spoke Japanese at home, Tony had dropped out to sign up for grip detail at the church—strike three. "It's a free country," his wounded obaasan had said. "You're my worst student anyway." And, Fujita knew, his mother would count the girl's stage persona—the play's sultry femme fatale—as strike four.

A stale, moralizing melodrama, the play detailed the lives of two couples—one good and chaste, the other wicked and sexy—who somehow exchanged partners. The Villain (identified by his penciled-on, handlebar mustache) first seduced the Heroine (with the bonnet and parasol), leaving the Hero (a proper hat and white shoes) high, dry, and frustrated until he too succumbed to the curvaceous siren in scarlet (Yoneko). From the moment Yoneko entered, Mari sat unmoving, Tamie frowned, and Fujita suppressed a stirring in himself uncomfortably like arousal. He tried not to notice the extraordinary lines painted about her lips, lids, and lashes, the sheen and slopes of her tight-fitting costume, or the visible effects of the icy mist on her chest.

"That gown is shamelessly sexy," his mother whispered. "Her makeup is ghoulish."

"She's supposed to look like that," he whispered back. "She's an actress."

"Not a very good one, I'd say. What do you know about acting, anyway?"

"Nothing, but as much as you do," he mumbled. "It's just a play."

"Ssshhhh!" Mari commanded, and the surrounding audience echoed her.

After the final curtain, Tamie announced, "She looks like a tramp to me—"

"It's only a play, Mom," he repeated. Despite its ridiculously predictable plot, its characters flat as pancakes, and its moralizing as subtle as a boxing match, he greatly enjoyed the show, the lights and sets and costumes. He was proud of Tony's smoke effect. Less concerned about the production values, Tamie complained of the girl's obvious exhibitionism, her vulgar *publicness*.

"Mom, you talk like it's a burlesque show. She's just acting sexy—it's just a role," he said. In his cautious, inexpert opinion, Yoneko performed that role pretty well, too. It was the play's greatest fault; who wouldn't prefer the vivacious siren to the chaste and boring damsel?

"Oh, he's a sexy expert now!" Tamie grouched. "She looks like a gold digger."

"What gold?" Fujita demanded.

He looked pleadingly to Mari, who only said, "Her voice sounds forced, insincere," as if she'd been mulling over it for some time.

"She shouts like a hakujin!" agreed Tamie, shouting. "Take my word for it: This one should be thrown back in the water."

The overstuffed church lobby began buzzing and shifting as the performers pushed out of the greenroom to meet family and friends. Over the sea of mostly black heads, Fujita saw Tony slip through a wall of bodies, tugging a hand, arm, and then eventually Yoneko. Tony glowed, his face hot, sweaty, excited, and dappled with spots of greasepaint and lipstick. His hair stood on end; it looked unwashed.

"Hey, Pop, Mom! Hey, Grandma," he blurted. "How'd you like it? You wouldn't belieeeeeve the goofs. Say, this is Yoneko."

Now in a luxurious, silvery dressing robe, the young woman stepped forth to greet Tony's parents with a deafening chirp so at odds with her sultry appearance. "Hiya, Mr. F., Mrs. F.! It was grand of you to come." Not her stage voice at all, Fujita thought. More like Darla of "Our Gang" holding her breath. Oddly, when the girl saw Tamie, she bowed—not a Japanese greeting, but an actress's flourish. As she rose, though, her full-lipped, painted smile fell when she looked at Tony's father. Through a moment's chitchat, she kept finding him with her gaze, strikingly direct but unreadable, darkened by her false, glittering lashes. Leaving to change her clothes, she halted at the greenroom door to stare once again.

"She's . . . very energetic," Fujita offered. He shot his mother a silencing look.

"She's a masterpiece," Tony corrected him dreamily.

Driving them all into the big city, Fujita treated the curious girl to dinner at the Little Tokyo Chinese restaurant, the Far East Café, so the family could get to know her. Tamie lost her appetite; she cringed whenever the girl spoke. Everything about Yoneko seemed theatrical, designed to overwhelm. She waved to waiters and ordered dishes, then as quickly decided she'd prefer another dish and waved them back. Swishing up to go to the ladies' room, she returned, forgetting her purse. It took ten minutes to choose dessert. Utterly gaga, Tony kept dropping his silverware.

Unaccustomed to being with young people, women, and especially such a showy young woman who stared at him so, Fujita felt edgy sitting beside Miss Yamaguchi—a bit dazzled, and so his observations of her were imprecise. Every feature either shimmered or glimmered or shook—the full, smooth folds of her eyelids, her carefully constructed hair, her polished shoes, her lips and burnished nails. Flamboyant, chatty, flighty, and scintillating, she seemed to Tony's father the kind of girl who never thought about anything before she did it; she was, in short, wholly unlike a Fujita. Although her family lived in Nihonmachi, she spent the school year with her Aunt Rose in Pasadena, where she could better become "acculturated." The public school had far fewer Japanese and Nisei, "which is plenty fine with me," she said. Having taken beauty classes outside of school, she dressed, coifed, and accessorized in fashion, studying magazine pinups and trying new styles on for size—new hair colors, too. She knew how to make herself look as close to a girl next door as a Japanese girl could look.

When they dropped her off at her aunt's house, leaving Tony to say good-bye and walk home, Tamie insisted on moving to the backseat—she'd squished between the adults in the front rather than sit beside *that girl*. She exaggerated her stiffness as Tony helped her shift seats. Stepping away from the car, Fujita was left with Yoneko, who returned his uncomfortable smile with confidence.

"You don't remember me, do you?" she whispered, searching his face for signs of recognition. Fujita went blank—only stared back. Even in the dark, her very eyelashes seemed to sparkle. No, he thought he'd remember her if they had met. He looked to the car; Tamie gripped Tony's shirt as they tried to shoehorn her into the rear seat. Taking a step back, Yoneko stood with arms open, presenting herself as evidence. "No?" she asked.

"I'm afraid you have me at a loss," he admitted, trying to sound warm rather than perplexed.

"It was a long time ago," she said, nodding. "It took me a while. I remember you looking bigger—darker, too. I remember your hands. Strong . . ."

"My hands?" Fujita began, as Aunt Rose's porch light flashed on. Then Tony slammed the car door, Mari knocked on the window, and a woman's voice called out Yoneko's name from the house. She turned and waved to her aunt, then waved good-bye to the women in the car, her gestures as grand as always.

"G'night, Mr. F.," she said, and before Fujita could question her further, she was up the porch steps with Tony.

My hands?

"She even does her makeup to look like a hakujin," Tamie complained before they'd pulled out of Rose's driveway. "The loudmouthed harlot. The strumpet. The . . ." She paused, her breathing labored. "The demimondaine."

"The *what?*" Fujita asked. In the rearview, he saw his mother waving her pocket vocabulary notebook at him. "Jesus, Mom," he groaned, and wondered anew at his mother's bizarre enthusiasms and dark talents. He wondered, in fact, if she, like Ichiro, was losing her marbles—and if it was hereditary. "What's all this about looks, anyway?" he asked, envisioning that face that he was supposed to know, and frankly finding nothing wrong with the girl's *appearance*. Of more concern to him was her admission that she'd been held back a grade in school (what had she done?), and her ambitions of traveling to this resort or that big city, owning this automobile or that gown in *Vogue* (she had better get that movie contract). "Well, they're young. He won't be with her for the rest of his life," he assured the women. "It's just infatuation. You have to be patient. Boys will be boys."

"You're telling me?" Tamie said, unappeased. "I am patient. But I don't have to like it, and I don't have to act like I like it, either."

Of course, this was the surest way to solidify the teenagers' resolve to romance, Fujita knew. He allowed the kids to continue dating, strongly suspecting that Tony's interest in the girl would fade when she returned to live with her parents in Little Tokyo over summer vacation. It did not. Of the many characteristics that had trickled down from Ichiro to Tony, the vehement sense of purpose was undiluted.

"You ever been with a Caucasian?" Fujita overheard Lum Chen asking in hushed tones. The young nursery assistant had erected a virtual altar of blonde starlet pinups in the storage shed, where he and Tony sometimes spent their lunch hours that summer in monklike contemplation of that overwhelming mystery—sex with a round-eye. Sometimes they laughed and hooted over unsavory jokes they would not knowingly share in front of the boss. One day, loading a wheelbarrow with sacks of peat, Tony's father inadvertently eavesdropped on what sounded like an argument over the desirability of Caucasian movie stars.

"Um, Vivien Leigh," Fujita heard his son saying excitedly.

"Oh, yes," agreed Lum Chen. "A fair size. Okay, okay . . . Judy Garland."

"Hey, come on, don't talk about Judy Garland," Tony said defensively. He paused, then chuckled. "Elsa *Lan*chester! Hah hah."

"Yikes, Grand Canyon, but chilling. How about Ingrid Bergman?"

"Ingrid Bergman! You're loopy. Look at her: They're close together and *beady.*"

Beady? wondered Fujita.

Was it a generational difference, or just his own native thickness—since he'd never kept company such as his hired hand or, well, his son—that prevented the plant man from deciphering their juvenile humor? Or both? Other than half glimpses snatched through a wall of shrubbery while working on the estate of the decadent King of Cleats, he had never *seen* a naked woman except for Mari. He'd married young and well, after all. He wasn't a consumer of pornography; it just never managed to fall into his hands, and it seemed rather a wasted effort, anyway; and he wasn't one of these young sleep-about teenagers. For whatever reason, Fujita was both disturbed and fabulously perplexed by the conversation until both younger men, of a single mind and voice, suddenly gave a victorious shout: "Bette Davis!! Hahaha!"

Picturing the beautifully bug-eyed star, Fujita suddenly and sadly understood the boys' standards for comparing the celebrity round-eyes—this catalogue of famous "Caucasian cunts."

The term, even in Chen's soft speech, sounded like broken glass to Fujita, who momentarily froze there in the shed, baffled and angry. Of course, he was familiar with the sport of hypothesizing *men's* organs based on more visible extremities—feet or hands or noses, he recalled, thankful that his own penis bore little resemblance to his wide, flat snoot. But he never understood the pleasure of this recreational supposing-about-penises, and this business of women's eyes was just imbecilic. Did Swedish women have *blue* vaginas? Not to mention the hazel-, brown-, or *green*-eyed women across the planet. He never visited the prostitutes, Japanese or occasionally Chinese, that his father had so appreciated, but he knew at least how some johns held a related, but inverse suspicion about Asian women's epicanthic folds, as in "is your slit slit *down there*, too?" Perhaps Tony had heard it in a school cafeteria, or at Boy Scouts, and would empathize with his grandfather's frustration. In 1941, as in 1895, the difference between slits and round-eyes was that the first theory was open for exploration—virgin territory, as it were—and the latter could get you lynched.

Fujita knew all this but really didn't care. Tony's crudity bothered him, but what *infuriated* Fujita was the tone this game took. Beyond the absurdity, the boys spoke of the women with a blend of both reverence and cruelty that he couldn't abide. It sounded like *revenge*. He could do nothing about Lum Chen, but stepping into the storage shed, he hauled Tony up by the arm and ordered him to go help his mother in the shop. Glancing around at the gleaming starlets pinned over every wall of the shed, he noticed that Lum Chen posted no Chinese pinups (but then, how easy were they to find?).

"This is not your home, Chen," he said. "It's *my* place of business, and it had better look like that in five minutes. Got me?"

Leaving the red-faced Chen peeling his pinups off the shed walls, he stormed away after Tony. Beauty is in the eye of the beholder, but fantasies, in Fujita's day, were something else. *You ever been with a Caucasian?* A world-class economizer of effort, Fujita would never, ever have even considered the pointless question in his own boyhood. It was like pornography: Such thinking, at the least, was doomed to leave you hot and unhappy. Perhaps that was the sort of thing young people were thinking about, with their diet of movie magazines and romance novels, but not Fujita. Or, well . . . he'd wondered a little. But bred deep within him, in every nerve, bone, and synapse, was that warning siren that could never, ever be turned off.

In his concern, he began to think more kindly of Yoneko. If the boy was so gaga for her, why spend his idle hours at this stupid game? *She* could be a pinup, Fujita thought. He'd hate it, of course, if his son dated an exhibitionist (he assumed that all models were indeed exhibitionists). But no two ways about it, the girl was exceptionally alluring. And Nikkei. Throughout the following fall semester, he forced himself to be content with the teenagers' continuing romance, conducted at a distance from the Fujita women, believing it might keep Tony out of some kinds of trouble. Then one December day in 1941, as the season began its annual race toward the Tournament of Roses, he returned from deliveries and checked in at the shop to find a message about a call from the high school principal, reporting that Tony and Yoneko were caught late for class, smoking cigarettes and kissing behind the gym.

"Goddam it, Tony," he muttered. Wondering if Tony had read Homer yet, he made a mental note to speak with his son about the matter—love, sex, dedication, the works. But he never had the opportunity to do it.

FIVE

Go Safely

On one of their reconnaissance missions together, the ever-vigilant Garvin Tufteller discovered that deer had been chewing on the crabapple trees and other bushes. Something had been pawing at one of the misty hotbed boxes, too. He reported this to his mother and Mr. Fujita. "What sharp eyes you have, honey," his mother exclaimed, squinting at the nibbled foliage.

"Good work, pal," said Mr. Fujita. "Deer could be a serious problem for us next year."

Hesitantly, his mother offered Mr. Fujita use of Pop's rifle. "I don't know how to use it—and don't want to—but feel free. There's a bag of bullets and cleaning stuff in my attic."

Mr. Fujita shook his head. "I've seen too many of those recently," he said with an intensity that surprised Garvin. "I can't even shoot spitballs, anyway."

"I'll do it," offered Garvin helpfully. As their defender from rabbits, mice, and caterpillars, he supposed that deer should be his responsibility, too. He'd never shot anything, but the idea intrigued him. He remembered Pop carrying home this or that bundle of bloodied feathers or sometimes a pelt; once he'd driven home with a hefty buck draped over the car's hood. The grown-ups only chuckled. "I'm *serious,*" he insisted, with a stamp of his foot that made them laugh.

Garvin felt left out of a lot of jokes lately; he was always missing something. And just *what* he was missing gnawed at him, for he had suspicions, he heard rumors. One recess period that week, he'd found some sanctuary from boredom and being teased in working on his watercolor in the art studio. When Franklin Bunkinson interrupted him by singing, "Garvie Warvie, how's your Jap today?" Garvin didn't even look up—this was the usual fare. He just snorted and told Franklin to get lost. However, the teasing that day held a new twist. "I hear things are really comfy cozy up there," Franklin said in a girlie voice. He batted his lashes and went into a kind of convulsion, massaging himself all over, wriggling his hips and making kissing noises. "I hear it's really lovey-dovey."

Before Garvin could blink, he had sent the murky fluid from the brush jar soaring in a splendid arc directly onto Franklin's white shirt. The gray-brown-black explosion impressed him. He began to rise, but Franklin dashed away screaming down the hall. Deciding he could always kill the coward later, Garvin held back, brooding. *Lovey-dovey?* Haunted by the image of Franklin's silly and ecstatic writhing, he recalled the recruitment poster of the winged enemy dragging away the naked lady.

Now, in the field, watching his mother and Mr. Fujita having such a gay time together, *ignoring him,* he swelled with confused outrage. When his mother bent to kiss him, he noticed she wore a lot of makeup. Crossing his eyes, he saw that her lipstick gave him a Rudolph the Reindeer nose. "What's so darned funny?" he wanted to know, wiping his face with his sleeve.

Mr. Fujita managed to rein his laughter in first. "Er, sorry, pal," he said. He combed his fingers through his messy hair and stared at the chewed branches. "I appreciate your offer, but we'll cook something up."

"*Not* venison, though," Garvin's mother said, and again they laughed.

Sulking, Garvin didn't even bother to ask, "What's venison?"

What the four coworkers "cooked up" indeed took a culinary approach. Together that night in Margaret's kitchen, they all had a chore. First, the men collaborated on Operation Fireball. Fujita set Garvin at the table before two lobster pots, each containing three gallons of water. The mission: Break a dozen eggs into each, add half-cups of Tabasco sauce, thoroughly blend the brews, then load the formula into two hand-pumped pressure sprayers. "See how small the mouth of the nozzle is?" Mr. Fujita said. "Any shell bits will clog the hole, so you have to mix and filter the stuff *really* well."

"I know, I know," Garvin said. He pumped the plunger wildly, shooting the man with air.

For Operation Hairball, Mr. Fujita asked Margaret and Livvie to collect their old orphaned or torn stockings and instructed Livvie to sew up any holes.

"Must we be so military?" Margaret asked. Garvin groaned. "Oh, fine. What do I do?"

"You'll give me a haircut," Fujita replied, handing her a metal shears. "Yes, a haircut. I'm plenty shaggy enough. With the stockings, we'll make bells full of hair. See? The deer keep away because they smell people around. And if they don't . . ." He patted Garvin on the shoulder.

"Operation Fireball!" Garvin howled, waving the Tabasco bottle.

Mr. Fujita arranged himself in a chair with a towel about his neck. Margaret clacked the shears tentatively. "*Shaggy* isn't quite the right word," she said. "*Ravaged* is more like it."

"I haven't had a proper cut since, well, I guess since Mari passed away," he admitted. "It's hard to find a barber these days," he explained. "One that will serve me, anyway. But I have chopped at it myself in the mirror once or twice."

"It certainly looks it, from back here." Margaret combed away from the forehead, down the neck. Mr. Fujita closed his eyes contentedly. She didn't need to comb too rigorously—the hairs were straight and thick as bits of fishing line. Her first snip severed a swatch barely larger than a fingernail. In this way, she continued so gingerly, she might have been removing sutures.

Pausing after every snip, she'd scrutinize the mess, wait for inspiration, then swoop back in to peck at a hair or two.

"We have to fill those stockings," Fujita reminded her. "So snip away. Don't be shy."

"Don't hurry me," Margaret said, yanking his hair. "You want to look nice, don't you?"

"Nice? I don't see what that has to do—"

"If you rush me, I may *slip*. Like that time I was cutting Jack's hair, he got me so mad I accidentally sliced off a chunk of hair *and* scalp. Poor dear! I had to give him three stitches—more painful because I couldn't stop laughing."

Gulping, Mr. Fujita tried to melt into the chair back as she absentmindedly waved the scissors in the air, fading into some happy reverie.

"Margaret, at that rate we'll be here all night," Livvie said, abandoning the hosiery at the table. "Here, let me do it. I'm sick of sewing, anyway."

"Uh-oh, pal," Fujita said to Garvin. "They're using my head to settle their professional rivalry!" The boy grinned back at him. The women laughed.

"We'll each do a side," Livvie teased. "Last one to the ear's a rotten egg."

Margaret smiled but could not mask her disgruntlement as they traded places and implements. "All right," she said, "but mind the shape."

Nodding, Livvie drained her glass, then began fingering the unkempt head before her, regarding it as gravely as a seer with a crystal ball. Mr. Fujita gave an involuntary hum at her massaging. Pausing from his toil at the hot-sauce pot, Garvin looked up and watched them, watched them hard, as the man leaned his head back against his mother's waist, as his mother pulled the head to her. His face briefly flashed into and faded from a sour scowl, but whether the tableau had any special significance for the boy or he was merely exhibiting his natural distaste for haircuts in general was lost on the adults. Margaret occupied herself threading a needle, zeroing in on the eyelet through her bifocals, which she held at arm's length. Livvie concentrated on separating the dark tufts, binding them with bobby pins from her own hair. Mr. Fujita sat staring blankly, as if he'd dozed off with his eyes open.

"Okay," Livvie whispered to herself. "Got it." In contrast to the nurse's focus on detail, Livvie took a seamstress's approach—shapes and outlines. She launched into a whirlwind of bold, swift slicings. The man's head became a panic of scissors-flash and flying black flecks, so suddenly he and Margaret both gasped. Inches at a time, the salt-and-pepper cascaded down his back, her clothes, the chair, onto the floor.

Fixated, Margaret emitted an occasional "Oh!" and "Careful!" and gradually, "Goodness, to think that under all that hair—"

"What?" Fujita asked, straining his eyes upward. "What's happening up there?"

"Hmm," Livvie said, as her shearing began to wind down. "This is getting interesting."

"How *dashing*," said Margaret. "Livvie, get that bit by the ear."

Livvie took a few final chops, stepped back to view her work, and whistled. "Wow!"

Even Garvin, who thought little of cosmetic matters, marveled at the change. The man appeared years younger. The cut exposed a strong jawline melding into high, etched cheekbones. Margaret and Livvie also regressed several years, dancing and twittering around Fujita, giggling like schoolgirls.

"So much fuss," Garvin grumbled. "So childish." In their distraction, he took the opportunity to spike the deer repellent with a double dose of Tabasco. A good thing, too, for the man's hair, though spiky and unkempt, was not as voluminous as it had seemed before Livvie tamed it.

Mr. Fujita bent to examine the sweepings on the floor, where most of the salt from his salt-and-pepper now lay. "That's all?" he said, scowling. Then he noticed the women staring at him. "What?"

"You have to see yourself," Margaret said. "Wait, where's my purse? I'll find a mirror." As they scuttled about searching, the women continued to twitter, plotting a trip to the hair salon for themselves. "Yes, we should have makeovers too!" Margaret said, finding her purse and digging into it.

Fujita grimaced. "I'll cut your hair," he offered, holding up an empty stocking as if he intended (and indeed he did) to do it on the spot. They froze and regarded him scornfully. Weakly, he said, "Or maybe not."

Returning to her search, Margaret caught her breath. "Oops, I forgot," she said. "This came for you this afternoon." Along with the compact mirror, she drew out a wrinkled postcard. With uncharacteristic aggressiveness, he swiped it from her hands.

With a photo of the Berkshires, Yoneko's postcard didn't even bear her hallmark postscript this time. Just this message—clipped, pointed, and angry:

> Are you ever a piece of work!!! "A runaway"! "Bring my little girl home"! You'd better stop snooping and making waves. It's dangerous to corner people. We may get lost and never be found. — Y

"I'm sorry about that," Margaret said. "It slipped my mind."

Folding the card in his hand, Fujita shook his head. "Please, don't concern yourself . . ." Margaret certainly looked concerned, though—and curious. Apparently, she'd looked at the card. "Er, a girl from home," he said stiffly. "We've had some little . . . arguments."

In the tension of that kitchen, they could all almost feel the vibrations of Margaret's lips, quivering painfully to prevent herself from asking, "Arguments?"

"Well," Livvie said. Her voice seemed to boom like a cannon. "Anyway, don't you want to see my handiwork?" She grabbed the mirror from Margaret's hand and passed it over. After fleetingly displaying relief, Fujita's face grew wide with shock at his new, tidy reflection. Moon-faced, is how Mari had put it—the Man in the Moon.

"Gosh, it *has* been a while." Hiding his embarrassment, he faced Garvin and turned his head from side to side. "Ah, what do dames know about it? What do you say, pal?"

Garvin hesitated, detecting new threatening lines in the man's face, however kind and radiant the expression. Also, it was unusual that anyone bothered to ask his opinion. After a bout with Tommy Taylor, Juggeston's barber, the trimmed, brushed, tonicked, and decaped Sig would only rise from the chair, wipe hairs from his chest, and grin into the ceiling-high mirror: "Garvin, you're lucky to have such a handsome pop." Now scrutinizing Mr. Fujita's cut—almost military, short with a swirl—he blushed and pronounced, "It's okay. It's sort of like Blackhawk's hair."

"Good enough for me," Fujita said distractedly, rising. "Let's get ready to bag some deer, then."

Allowing him some privacy to collect himself, Garvin filled the pump sprayers and the women gathered up the bits of Operation Hairball. Laying down the mirror, Fujita glanced again at the postcard and noted the "N. Amherst, Mass." postmark. Pocketing it, he shook his newly shorn head to clear it, then lifted the sprayers.

As they passed outdoors, Fujita groped for the light switch. With a flash, the powerful lamp illuminated much of the Peak, creating a shadow play of their silhouettes—the farmers and the scarecrow—on the low-hanging bellies of the clouds. They looked up in fascination, Margaret and Livvie and Mr. Fujita, with his new, clean-cut face catching moonbeams, and watched the dark projection of Garvin hanging the first hairbell on a shadow tree, like some perverse, solitary Christmas ornament. Only a handful of the most determined stars could be seen. Perhaps someone could see the Peak even off the coast? If German technology had so progressed as to shell this far inland, those lurking boats must also know that nothing on this hill was worth destroying. Still, they decided to kill the light, anyway.

Averting his eyes from Margaret's dressing gown, robe, and slippers, Mr. Fujita entered the kitchen in a chilled panic. By instinct, Margaret hastily went to tighten the belt closing her robe, then caught herself and shrugged. "Oh, well, you've caught me in my morning glory," she said, sleepy and amused. "You look alert this morning. I suppose you've already plowed the east forty and read the paper?"

Not up for repartee before coffee, the man merely nodded and rubbed his hands together as if to ignite them. She lowered the flame beneath the percolator and poured two mugs. As they sipped together, Margaret noted the bags beneath his eyes, more severely swollen than usual. "One of your arctic nightmares? Do you want to talk about it?"

"It's just a dream I have," he said. "It wakes me up sometimes. Ridiculous. It's nothing." Pausing, he rubbed his new, spiky hairstyle. "Say, you know, this short cut saves time in the morning."

Margaret huffed at this obvious, evasive maneuver but was too tired to pry. She had suffered a sleepless night herself. Following her usual routine, she had poured her water, propped herself up on her four pillows, donned her reading glasses, and enwombed herself in a blanket and a favorite novel. She dove in: "It is a truth universally acknowledged that a single man in possession of a good fortune must be in want of a wife." After several minutes, she realized she was repeatedly rereading the opening line to *Pride and Prejudice.* It had so often swept her away, a direct tributary to her dreams; yet, last night, its current carried her nowhere. "What an extraordinary statement," she whispered, as if reading it for the first time. Shaking off a sense of foreboding, she forded on to, "However little known the feelings or views of such a man may be on his first entering a neighbourhood, this truth is so well fixed in the minds of the surrounding families that he is considered as the rightful property of some one or other of their daughters." Clapping the novel shut and turning off the light, she had felt herself beset by self-doubt, frustration, and unsatiated curiosity. Couldn't sleep a wink, for brooding about the new man, whom, she realized, she'd almost forgotten *was* a man.

Neither spoke until after they'd had a second mug of coffee, when they planned a trip into Boston. He'd raised the brick skirt for the greenhouse and now wanted to make a run for the remaining supplies and some "other errands." Margaret literally bit her lips shut to refrain from prying about the postcard from North Amherst. They decided he'd also drive her to Cambridge, where she and some girlfriends volunteered once a month to wrap gauze bandages for the Army Medical Corps. Ordinarily, she and Paulette Pedicott took a bus to Gloucester, headed in to

North Station, and liked to walk across the bridge past M.I.T. into Harvard Square for tea and scones before work. Logically enough, Mr. Fujita suggested they might give her friend a lift, too. But Margaret refused with such an abrupt and alarming "No!" that they both stiffened in shock.

What in heck was that? Margaret wondered. "Er, the greenhouse is the most important thing now," she said, back-pedaling. "My little gossip club mustn't interfere with your *work*." Seemingly convinced, Fujita nodded, but his full lips drew down in contemplation of gas coupons expended—of extravagance.

Paulette Pedicott bore a too-striking resemblance to Lil Wellington. She was okay, really, but motherhood over five children (her fifth, a girl, only a few weeks old) had made her bitter. Her participation in the ladies' club—her only excuse to leave Juggeston—had a desperate flavor to it. She sulked whenever they had to skip a meeting, tried to make a job out of fun, and disliked outsiders. Over ten years, her friendship had grown clinging, as she increasingly coveted what she declared to be Margaret's "freedom." Enslaved to the boredom of her own, housebound life, Paulette had a skill for sniffing out the slightest morsel of gossip, and with four hyperactive boys, the frenzy spread quickly, if not always intentionally. "When do we see your new acquisition?" Paulette had once teased her, meaning Fujita. "Where's your mystery man?"

She wanted to shield him from Paulette, if only for a while, and hoped it didn't seem that she meant to hide *him* from her friends. When the mystery man finally said, "Well, it's very generous of you, donating your time to the war effort," she tried to detect some injury in his voice but couldn't be sure.

"I'm not interested in Mr. Roosevelt's war effort," she insisted. "His 'arsenal of democracy.' This is my *peace* effort. Well, it satisfies our yen to Christian charity, anyway," she said, sounding more irritable than charitable. "Of course, it also gives us a chance to dress up."

Margaret did so simply that morning, lazily for her. At her vanity, she shuffled through a packet of folded, colorful scarves, holding them up to her hair, face, eyes. Nothing looked right. Was it the change in season? Or in her life? She wondered if Mari

Fujita had owned such things, to sit hours shuffling through them at her vanity. She decided on the dour military look of her Mangone suit, exaggerated black hound's-tooth cutting across a cinched-waist jacket and the underside of a knee-length black cape. Smoothing the lap of her wool skirt, she felt more armored than dressed.

Joining Fujita in the car, she made a peace effort toward him, too. "Sorry. The thought of seeing the girls today has made me grumpy," she said, wringing her white, gauntletlike gloves. Too floppy—should have brought the slimmer ones in black suede. She fixated on his strong, scarred hand, waving her apology away, then gripping and flexing on the steering wheel. She looked back to her own. She had nice hands, she thought, still the hands of a young nurse—shapely, nimble despite some nasty cuts and calluses from her new horticultural life. She wondered, how did Mari Fujita care for her hands, her skin? She knew no way to ask. And why did he never speak of his wife, anyway? It was . . . well, *odd*. Infuriating, too. And that postcard. Who's this "Y"? How hard it was to be a proper kind of friend to someone when he eluded being known. "Well, it's a good thing to do," she sighed, gloomily sliding her gloves on. "Doing anything is a good thing to do."

Mr. Fujita nodded approvingly and smiled out to the road before them.

Arriving in Cambridge, they took the long way down Mass Avenue past Central Square, festooned with autumn color. Outside the tobacconist, an ensemble of college boys in matching crimson sweaters sang under the baton of a fat little conductor, unhearable through the car's glass. Suited men with hats and pipes dug into overcoat pockets for change at the news kiosk. Ever since Jack had passed up that practice in Cambridge, she felt she really belonged there, and the first and last glimpses of the Charles River always made her glum. Yet, thinking of the town and of her own husband—now that she was thinking of wives and husbands—distressed her more than usual. Why, she wondered, do I come to Cambridge at all? Appearances, perhaps—to be looked at by the ladies' club, envied and pitied: See what poor Margaret endured with the Mick country doctor, banished to the provinces, starved for civilization! Margaret thought: Can I help it I was spoiled? How Ma hated herself, the Irish farm girl with her squelched accent, the shopping sprees and teas and humiliating deference to her in-laws—she would die to make you appear Boston Brahmin debutante. Oh, pitiful, how you despised her—made love to the romantically poor Jack Kelly like a stake through her heart and followed his big-fish American dream to the little Juggeston pond. Your revenge exacted, what was left? Where were the teas and horse shows and society pages? You left what you loved for Jack or for spite? He had to go—*you* could choose to be not-Irish; you had nothing to prove.

Margaret snickered at herself so bitterly that Mr. Fujita looked alarmed. She could have asked him to turn right around then, but for his own secretive errands. "It's nothing, nothing," she said, waving him off. "I was just thinking about something." He nodded and drove on, enjoying the street scenes, the return to some semblance of a city, and Margaret enjoyed watching his enjoyment. Still, after his cool reception at Wellington's, she worried for the stern, dark man sitting beside her. In Cambridge, as in Juggeston, Fujita was who he was: the Enemy's doppelgänger. Would he set off alarms, even in a town as intelligent as this? And how would the ladies, gathered in their Christian charity, react upon seeing him? And Paulette? Groaning, Margaret recalled they had canceled the last meeting, on Mischief Night.

At her direction, Mr. Fujita steered the Dodge up curbside before a little yellow diner across from Harvard Yard. "One moment," he said, hauling up the parking brake, killing the ignition, fumbling with the keys. "I'll come around." In the second he sat checking the sideview mirror for traffic, Margaret saw within the facade of knee-high-to-ceiling windows, fogged by coffee steam and conversation, the blurry but unmistakable outline of Paulette's blue, veiled hat with the black sash and feather pin. Her narrow blue-gloved hand was waving. Mr. Fujita opened the driver's side, admitting a rush of coldness, and slipped outside. Still rooted in her imagination, seeing herself through the curious eyes of the ladies' club, Margaret gasped,

"No!" Too late. The ever-prompt gentleman had already rounded the car and stood rigidly beside her open door, stiff and courteous, she realized, as a chauffeur.

Thinking fast, she met his eyes with a brilliant, cinematic smile, offered up a limp white glove, and whispered urgently, "Take my hand." Knowing he would hesitate, she hissed again, "*Do* it!" The poor man's eyebrows arched questioningly, but he stepped around the door and thrust his hand to hers as if he would hurl her out of the car. Letting herself be lifted up, she placed one hand intimately on his shoulder and allowed the other to linger enclosed in his slightly more than long enough for the ogling ladies' club to be certain he was no chauffeur. Then, with a flash of teeth, she projected herself onto the pavement. Keeping an eye on the restaurant window as an actress before a dressing-room mirror, she adjusted her hat and waited for him. "Well," she sang, her face animated, "here we are, at last, at last!"

They turned to face the diner entrance, the steamy glass vestibule clogged with her ladies' club. The proprietor had cunningly arranged a display of potted ferns and moderate-climate flora on the windowsills, creating the impression of a hothouse. GET IN OUT OF THE COLD said a hand-painted sign by the door, which Fujita read aloud and longingly. Punching his hands into his pockets, he jangled the keys there and made a brrrrr! noise. "Are th-those your friends?" he asked through chattering teeth. "So I guess I'll b-be off, then."

"Can't I convince you to come in and meet the girls?" Margaret asked. Then quickly, "Yes, why don't you?" eliciting another of his noises, a sigh closing into a loud "hommmm," clipped short by a nasal huff. This was the sound of his irritation when she interrupted him at work. She could paralyze the man with a question; when hunched over a shovel or propped on an ax, a simple "Will you want lunch soon?" could set his universe toppling pell-mell into chaos. Yet he seemed allergic to just outright saying "no." He pretended to deliberate, waiting to be released, dismissed, brrrrr!-ing at the sharp wind exploding off the Charles. Nurse Kelly, determined to bring him back into the world, knew what she had to do.

Here's what she told herself: Let him say nothing. Insist: He must be a gentleman and escort you to the door. To set an example, yes, that you, Margaret Balford Kelly, respect this man. If he offers some observation on the course of the war, compliment his understanding. Should he remark on world finance, bow to his business savvy. Laugh at his jokes even if they're not funny. Fine, let him blink at you, crazy woman. Be firm, make him freeze until he says it: Yes, of course, I must. Brrrrr!

Slip your arm through his, keenly aware how thin his coat is, old, unlined, a West Coast covering, a coat for show. Be conscious of the silk lining your own jacket, the rich cloth rubbing, the soft skin of influence. Recall the price tag, the sales girl kowtowing. In the law of equilibrium, exchange your body's warmth for his arm. Wonder, does he miss this? Does he miss women, too? Realize you're not Mari Fujita. Realize, too, the possibility that you may be repulsive to him. Feel at a loss, never having known what it's like to be repulsive to anyone.

Wave back at Paulette. Walk him toward the door, not too hurried. Ask him: "Do you know any good jokes?" and feel him shrug against you, his bafflement. "I don't know *any* jokes." Resigned to understanding nothing of your whims, he knows you're bonkers but is a sport and won't let on. But what's this wanting, wanting to show him off—for you, not him? Why bring him to this alien hen coop? He couldn't care less about the judging, frowning housewives: See poor Margaret, the desperate widow with her Jap! Here I am, girls. Here he is. No use denying you've been wondering, you've been imagining, you've been talking. Yes, Margaret, what are you trying to prove?

What Margaret told herself was: Make them like him, respect him. Make things right, or what good are you?

Patting Fujita's arm, she promised, "We'll make this quick, painless."

She allowed him to open the door to a warm scent of coffee, of omelets and hash, and the flurry began. Waves, hugs, kissing, scrutiny all around. "No, it hasn't been *that* long, Paulette," she said. "We last met seven weeks ago. Girls, this is Mr. Fujita. This is Paulette, Mary Simon, Jane, and Meredith—oh, honey, your knee looks to have healed marvelously, doesn't it? And where is Mary Elkin?"

That was Paulette's cue to snipe at the absent woman. "Oh, Mary," she said, her voice more sniffly than usual, "Mary *Elkin* is occupied with some very important something or other with her mother-in-law from Florida. Pneumonia, you know. Too old for New England winters." Sneaky as Lil Wellington, though less false, she sidled up to Fujita. "I understand you are also new to our corner of the globe—"

"Mr. Fujita is a warm-blooded creature, too, aren't you?" Margaret interrupted. "He's a businessman from California." Mr. Fujita removed her cape and hung it on the vestibule coatrack. "So, how are your boys, Paulette?"

"Oh, they're big," laughed Paulette, grinning, grinning, in the superior manner that those who measure their worth by stretch marks take toward the childless. "Big pains-in-the-Rumpelstiltskin, that is."

"Well, Mr. Fuchida," said Meredith, of the bum knee, before Margaret could inquire about Baby Pedicott, "you've had us just *bursting* with anticipation. Do stay for tea."

"Yes, won't you stay and tell us about your business? We'd love to hear all about you."

Margaret looked helplessly about the steamy vestibule. Paulette, bored mother of five, practically sniffing him, licking her chops. Little Mary Simon gaping as if the man had eight arms and was covered with fur. And Fujita himself, his hair cut, his wide, bright face, his strenuously forced smile threatening to eclipse the entire restaurant. Allow him to leave, Margaret Kelly!

"Oh, I told him I'd love for him to stay, but of course not everyone can afford to take a day off on any old workday just to humor ladies of luxury like us. He's got *business concerns* to attend to downtown. Yes, please don't let us hold you up, Mr. Fujita. You've got more important items on your agenda today."

"Yes, it's true, I've some appointments," he stuttered. "Though your offer is very kind, thank you. And it's a pleasure to meet you, ladies," he added. "So. I'll be off then?" he said to Margaret, dog-paddling, swimming in place.

"Yes. I'm sorry you have to go," she said, surprised to realize that she meant it—and that she found herself longing for that hand-ruining farmwork, too. Sadly, she determined to show these middle-aged biddies that this Jap in his battered coat was a good man, a man capable of being trusted, befriended, even by her, and he had been a father and husband—*a man in possession of good fortune*—and yes, he was even capable of being loved. Yes, even by her, Margaret Balford Kelly. "I'll see you this evening," she said. Letting the remark swing in the diner air like a pendulum, she escorted him to the door and sent him off bewildered, doubtlessly wondering what kind of childish madwoman he'd attached himself to.

What Margaret told herself was: Give the man just a shred of peace, Maggie. To the women, she said, "Ladies, I'm famished. Let's eat, then go do some good."

"What was *that* about?" Fujita asked himself aloud as he sat before the Dodge's steering wheel. Boy, people sure do change in social situations, he thought. *Women* do. He sat idling a moment, appreciating the old university buildings. As he had never traveled outside America, and lived mostly in the perpetually fresh West, Harvard Square looked, felt, even *smelled* older than any place he had ever seen. In Gila River, of course, he had lived in proximity to ancient Indian structures far older—Tuzigoot, Casa Grande, Montezuma's Castle—but those were camouflaged, built of and into the land, and he had not exactly been allowed the liberty to sightsee then. Mari Fujita, who had seen Japan, would have been less impressed; the history of Cambridge would fill only a thimble compared to some of the venerable temples she had visited. Even Tony, hopping among minute South Pacific islands, alternately chasing and fleeing the Japanese frontlines, had become quickly—if fleetingly—more worldly than his father. But Tony went to war to liberate himself from history; he would ultimately have preferred the bars and cafés, shops and game halls, of the newer Cambridge. Lining Harvard Square were a few modern storefronts—some half-finished, then aborted a decade earlier—a buzzing news kiosk, and plenty of automobiles, to be sure. Across a large, second-story lightbulb bulletin board, like that in Times Square, fluttered the letters: V2S POUND UK. Turning off Mount Auburn onto Brattle, passing Longfellow's house, he thought he'd have liked Tony to attend Harvard.

He became soundly lost for a half hour. The longer he drove, the more aggravated he grew, mired in the same bottlenecked intersections, seeing the same landmarks crawl by. On past the common, past Copley Square, Newbury Street, he cruised miles of what he believed the most idiotic street system ever laid by man, until he turned around and finally hit familiar turf in the North End.

He hoped to keep his visit with his old bosses short—in, hello, out, good-bye—but as expected, Sally DiPassio insisted he wait until she made him lunch for the road. "You look skinnier than when you first came here!" she cried. "Jesus, Mary, and Joseph, there's nothing left to *pinch!* You look like you haven't eaten since you left here!"

"Of course he hasn't," said the bearish Bud DiPassio, also twisting a sizable chunk of Fujita's cheek. Hiring the internee to work at his garden-supply store, Bud had been instrumental in Fujita's release from Gila, and Fujita was at once unnerved by him and extremely grateful. "Yankees don't know about food, Sal. Don't they feed you up in Swellville, Bill? Bet you don't eat like you did with us, huh?"

Fujita had to admit it. He once wrote Tamie that the feedings Sally administered saved his life. "In my entire *life*, no one's fatted me up the way you did, Sally."

"Diplomatically put, my boy!" Bud roared. "But business before pleasure. Gimme your list. I'll load the truck; you look too weak to do it yourself. Sally, this boy's gotta get some meat in him."

While Bud loaded the Dodge with garden and greenhouse supplies, his wife heaped wrapped sandwiches on Fujita and stuffed his pockets with small links of sausage and jars of tomato paste. While she was at it, Fujita requested a few staples from her larder unavailable in Juggeston—oils and proper olives—but begged to be excused from lunch since he was on the fly, heading down to the War Relocation Authority office. That reminded her of something. "Ey, wait a minute! Somebody left you a letter at the shop. I'll bring it out to you." Zooming away and back out to the Dodge, she handed him another sack of groceries. "There, it's in the bag." Before he could read it, he endured another bout of hugs, kisses, and pinches. He felt he would suffocate as small, round Sally—short even by Japanese standards—swallowed him between the folds of her vast chest. At last he tore the envelope, examined the postcard within, and gasped.

"Who brought this? *When*?" The DiPassios shrugged in unison. Maybe a week or so? "How do I get to . . ." He glanced at the card again. "Quincy Market?" He managed to divine directions, say good-bye too abruptly, then pulled onto the street too fast.

Behind him, he heard Bud shouting, "Bill, my boy! You come home to the roost any time you get sick of Swellville!"

Home? thought Fujita. Maybe the mist in his eyes prevented him from seeing the speedometer. Or maybe he sped just out of panic. Whatever the reason, the cop sitting against his car by the bustling Quincy Market waterfront plaza did not look pleased when Fujita skidded to a halt inches from his feet.

"Step out of the vehicle, Flash," said the cop, whose name tag read "Gunnison." Whatever wasn't blue on him was orange—his cheeks, mustache, hair. After frisking Fujita and noting the name "Dr. John Kelly" on the Dodge's registration, he said, "Okayyyy, Dr. Kelly. How about unlocking the back door." A full foot taller, the cop leaned over his shoulder, sniffing, as Fujita fumbled with the keys. "What's that *smell?*" When he made Fujita remove the submarine sandwich from his pocket, it surprised them equally to discover a twenty-dollar bill wrapped around it. This was certainly Bud's work; if Livvie sometimes felt like "lost property," and widows were treated like ghosts, widowers, Fujita had learned, were treated like orphaned children.

"Well, look at that," Gunnison sneered, peeling off the bill and pocketing it. "I'd surely like to know what deli you eat at. Me, I only ever get my subs in wax paper." He unwrapped the sandwich gingerly, as though it might possibly be a disguised bomb. Taking a pencil from his clipboard, he pried the lunch open and probed its contents. It was stuffed with capers, just the way Fujita liked it. He gritted his teeth. "Looks good," the cop said flatly, handing the mess back. "Remove your hat."

"My hat," Fujita echoed, handing it over. Gunnison slid his pencil eraser around the lining, squeezed the brim suspiciously, then returned it. He fished around in the crate of garden supplies. "What are you . . . a *tree* doctor?" Discovering the assorted metal fittings, wires, and gear for the greenhouse, he whistled and slammed the door. "Gimme your license."

Reading the ID, Gunnison scowled, abruptly shoved the protesting Fujita into the Dodge, and in a blink handcuffed him to the steering wheel. "Stay here," he muttered, and before Fujita could protest further, he stomped out of sight behind the car.

If there were more or less decorous or graceful postures to assume when chained to a steering wheel, Fujita could not imagine them. Accustomed to being conspicuous, he breathed deeply, willed himself to ignore the staring crowd and focus his energies on the marketplace itself. The view was familiar as he glared down the corridor of storefronts. So Bostonian: identical rows of red brick with kelly green wood trim; cobblestone walks covered with pushcarts; obsolete dung scrapers before each doorway; a roasted-nuts aroma over all, and military uniforms everywhere. A huge flock of young people milled about the plaza, mostly crisp soldiers with young girls, gabbing and laughing open-mouthed in pairs or groups. One awkward boy in navy whites balanced two paper cones brimming with popcorn in one hand, unwilling to extract the other hand from his sweetheart's grip. Nothing about the boy struck Fujita as anything but plain—not the pale face mottled with freckles, nor the sandy-blondness of his crew cut, nor the doughy build of his frame—but all uniforms reminded him of Tony now (and in 1944, everyone seemed to wear some sort of uniform). The girl, too, looked pretty without being the least bit remarkable. A thin blue band pressed her hair flat and back down to the collar of a matching blue jacket; both hair and jacket were well cut but too mannish for Fujita's taste. He couldn't help noticing that her skirt ended a hair's-breadth shorter even than the current fashion, maximizing her shapely but thick legs, like Ann Miller's.

The longer he watched, trying hard to steady his breathing,

the more this boy and girl next door faded into the crowd, and the more all the marketgoers seemed to melt into a distressing, hakujin homogeneity. Filling with irrational loathing, he imagined this girl's strong legs would soon bloat into those blue-veined peasant ankles, ravaged by the cold Bostonian winters. Her dirty-blond hair would fade to dirty gray. Why, on his first shore leave, this blandly handsome couple would beget yet more blandly handsome freckle-haired, sandy-faced little boys and girls next door.

The Melting Pot.

During his time in the North End, a few of Fujita's Italian neighbors—who had only recently left Ellis Island behind and were enrolled in naturalization classes—spoke of it with elation. But Angel Island was not Ellis Island; Fisherman's Wharf was not Quincy Market, and in California the term was uncommon. Fujita's young home state demanded from its newer arrivals and their children acculturation—not assimilation. In an intimate sense, antimiscegenation laws forbade "melting," and people seemed more or less resigned to holing up in their own little tribes, like colored dots splattered on a Seurat canvas. Fujita had always associated "assimilation" with the East, and for him, moving from camp to Massachusetts had been like holding his nose and diving headfirst into the Melting Pot. He thought it would be okay. Alone in the greenhouse, or in his room over the garage reading a novel, or hand-washing his work clothes in the sink, he was not conscious of his race, his skin; both depended for definition on other people. In solitude, listening to a ball game or a war report on the radio, he would find himself rooting for the home team and think he felt American. His transformation, or his anesthetization, was so complete that after these years the first coarse remark of each day could take him utterly by surprise, like a man who realizes painfully that a KICK ME sign has been taped to his rump. Yet at times like this—looking out at Quincy Market, left for over fifteen minutes now chained to Margaret Kelly's car, the cuffs cutting into his angrily flexing wrists—he did not feel "melted" at all. Here he was the yellow nigger. In Yankee Boston, and in Juggeston, he felt like an impurity, and very, very alone.

Then, startlingly, in the rearview mirror, dwarfed by the blue-and-orange bulk of Officer Gunnison, stood one person who looked like him. Not *the* one—not Yoneko—but a distraught, middle-aged man in a janitor's apron, his eyes refusing to follow Gunnison's pointed finger to the Dodge. Scowling, the Nikkei held up a window squeegee, pointed to it, waved a hand in Fujita's direction, and emphatically shook his shaggy, black head. The cop crossed his arms, then nodded and excused the window washer, who rounded the Dodge at a safe distance and began chatting with the bland youngsters as he resumed his swabbing. Only then did the Nikkei regard the prisoner; and the shame, the loathing in that glare, made Fujita feel more truly fettered than the handcuffs. Pointing at him, the worker shared some joke with the girl with Ann Miller's legs, who laughed with relief.

"*Inu*," Fujita hissed to the window, because he could at that moment think of no English word that would serve to return the Nikkei's loathing in kind.

He let the cuffs chafe his wrists raw and found the sensation pleasing and bracing. He told himself he understood this displaced Nikkei's delusional desire to melt—it was survival, not a betrayal. Yet, observing the trio laughing at him, each so determined to melt into someone else, he insisted to himself that *he* preferred loneliness. Being part of a community, Fujita knew, gave a false impression of strength, of heft. In his experience, heft equaled burden, a hampering weight. Social ties and friendships made a man slow and visible, an easy target; needing others fettered a man to history; it made you a sitting duck.

Hugging beneath the store window now scraped free of grime, how bold they were, those lovers. Boldly furnishing the homestead not yet built, pointing to ads promising bigger, newer, better household goods—currently war materiel—the couple seemed certain first of victory and then of prosperity. Bold, Fujita thought, as Tony and Yoneko. Slumping over the steering wheel, he shut his eyes, but the image of the marketplace lingered like a travel slide thrown onto a screen. No matter that the handcuffs kept him from reviewing the postcard in his pocket; he knew this scene; he'd memorized it in an instant. Painted on the same corner where he now sat parked, at nearly the same angle, it read, "Greetings from Quincy Market—Boston, Mass.!"

> I was here but now I'm gone, I left my name to carry on, those who know me, know me well, those who don't can go to heck. (Read that on a bus.)
>
> It was a nice time while I was staying here, though cold, but I prefer cold after camp. I know how you feel about having me around, so I didn't try to see you. (Miss me yet?) Ah well. Until my next happy haunt. —Y

Neither the nastiest nor most teasing of postcards, this message was nonetheless the most painful. No stamp or postmark—she had been here, right under his nose. "I made a simple *mistake,*" he whispered, but there was nothing simple about his many fatal mistakes in Gila River. He dropped his head to the steering wheel, and his nose sounded the horn. Like a sleepwalker startled to consciousness on some precarious path, he jolted upright and saw Gunnison in the rearview mirror, walking angrily in his direction. The bleat also startled the girl with Ann Miller's legs and her beau, and one of the popcorn cones slipped from the boy's grasp. Rather than being annoyed, they just eyed the mess and laughed, being of that enviable age when even accidents can inspire romance and glee. Any accidents, Fujita thought, from spilling popcorn to pregnancy. Miserably, he watched the girl follow a giddy impulse to wrest the other cone from the boy and dump its contents over his head; this inexplicably sent them spiraling into a passionate, almost violent kissing embrace. They didn't even care that people were watching.

The big, orange knuckles of Officer Gunnison yanked open the driver-side door. "Okay, doc, here's what we got," Gunnison said. "You were doing fifty-five at least. That's ticket material. On top of which, I wonder as to the whereabouts of the physician who owns this car."

"He's dead," Fujita confessed. "Of pneumonia."

Gunnison huffed. "I also wonder if you know there's a serious rationing effort going on. All this meat and metal and crap you got back there—I wonder, in fact, if you aren't undermining this country's war efforts by dealing in black-market goods with your friend over there." He bobbed his head toward the window washer.

"My friend? What is this garbage? I don't know that man."

Gunnison shrugged. "That's what he said, too." He removed the cuffs. "Now, scram."

Why the smug, orange son of a bitch! "What about my ticket?"

"This will take care of the ticket," the cop said, patting the pocket containing Bud's twenty. Content to leave it at that, he turned.

It was absurd, it made no sense—no more than speeding down to this vast public mall, this sea of bodies, expecting to find Yoneko weeks after she'd passed through. It made no sense that amid such harassment he drew his line at that stupid little lunch, that dumb sandwich that he didn't really want to eat anyway. It made no sense, it was *absurd* that it was finally the soft sourdough lips stretched wide, the slice of cappicola lolling out onto the front seat like a severed tongue that made him call, "Gunn-i-*son!*" In three short syllables, Fujita's voice modulated from a whisper to a shout. "Don't you tell me to scram," he growled to the enormous blue back, "after you lock me to my car, rob me, and then *stick a damn pencil in my lunch!*"

As the cop turned, a hand on the truncheon hanging from his hip, his expression showed the blend of confusion and bemusement that prevented him from beating the crap out of the crazy Nip. "Your lunch?" He actually looked a bit frightened. "Jesus, are you people screwy," he whispered. "Look, Togo, get lost or I'll take you in just for the fun of it."

"Fine!" Fujita said, getting out of the car. "I'm not going anywhere until you give me my goddamned ticket." He stepped right up to Gunnison, head raised fiercely, his nose barely reaching the man's raw chin.

The cop took a step back. "You *want* a ticket?"

"That *is* the law, right?" Fujita said. "I was speeding, and as a *citizen* and taxpayer, I have a right to expect my goddamned public servant to do his stupid job." He reached into the surprised policeman's pocket for the twenty and waved it at him. "How much is a speeding ticket?"

By now Fujita had attracted an enormous crowd, murmuring and whispering on the cobblestone behind them. The cop hesitated. "Ten?" he asked.

"Ten? What, you don't know?" Fujita demanded, rolling his eyes. He pointed to the Dodge, then the curb. "But I'm in a no-standing zone. What about that, eh? Eh?"

The baffled lawman had to admit it. "Five more." He drew up the ticket and handed it to Fujita, who beamed with maniacal pride and handed over the twenty. Even as he said to keep the extra five "as a donation," Fujita was as mortified with himself as he had ever been. *I've lost my mind,* he thought. Gunnison seemed to think so, too; he only laughed, climbed back into his cruiser, and put it into gear. "You better slow down from here on in, doc," he said, recapturing some of his cockiness. "Now have a nice day." Fujita waited until the cruiser zoomed by him and lobbed the ruined sandwich at the lawman's taillights.

"You pumpkin-headed moron!" he shouted, but it was not the first time one had detained him, both in and outside California, and probably wouldn't be the last. "I've seen worse," he grumbled, rubbing his throbbing wrists. As he stepped up onto the cobblestone curb, the crowd dispersed away from him. "Christ," he snapped at one bag-laden matron, who backed away from him in terror. "What's wrong with you, woman?" For a second he considered following the old biddy—maybe she'd drop her bags and run? He might like that. Maybe if I just walk through the market, I can start a stampede, he thought grimly. Through the crowd, however, he spotted the Nikkei, glaring at him with tangible loathing, and the sheepishly staring sailor couple. Now his reaction to them grew irrational: He hated the Nikkei bitterly and felt a powerful compulsion to apologize to those kids, to give them some paternal advice, some benediction. Remember your *parents!* maybe, or, Forgive your parents! But of course, this was as absurd as the Nikkei's fantasy of melting into ordinariness among the Boston Caucasians. It made no more sense than how he had alienated the girl he now chased across the country, when she had every right to expect solace and love.

"Go safely," he whispered to the biddy, to the window washer, to the young romancers. Pulling away, he watched the lovers receding in the rearview mirror, entangled as if adjoined at the hip. It occurred to Fujita then that he witnessed a leave-taking, a farewell kiss. He floored it back toward Widow's Peak, speeding the whole way home.

Returning to Widow's Peak after his encounter with Gunnison, Fujita found waiting for him his mother's first letter to Juggeston. Still smarting from the afternoon's humiliation, he considered putting it back in the mailbox for a few hours. But then, expecting some version of maternal comfort, he opened the letter. The censor's office had been getting sloppy lately. At first Tamie Fujita had enjoyed challenging the faceless, mad clippers by spotting her letters with insults and other miscellaneous "security risks." In the early days they dug their fountain-pen nibs into the paper, proudly signing their inspectors' numbers to the ever-present stamped box: "Detained Alien Enemy Mail—EXAMINED—BY. . . U.S.I. & N.S." (Similar stamps had also appeared on Fujita's own letters from Gila River.) Models of discretion, the anonymous censors once snipped through her correspondence as avidly as Margaret edited FDR out of the *Crier*, so that the delivered letters looked like paper-doll cutouts. But the war had stretched on too long; the censors now made do with black ink strikes here and there. Once, one broke every rule and scribbled tiredly, "Come on, Tamie. We surrender. How about giving us a break?"

Fujita's mother wrote that her hearing would take place soon and she feared they would send her to the "disloyals" camp at Tule Lake. "Only then," she wrote, "do you have my permission to get me out of here."

"Oh," grumbled her son to the flimsy sheet. "I'll have your permission, will I?"

"I prefer the federal jails," she wrote. "I may confess I'm related to the emperor so they'll hang on to me." This part so outraged Fujita that he read it that night to Margaret.

"Now, there's a spunky gal!" she laughed, and she sang out her celebratory statistic: "Thirty-six percent!"

Irritably, Fujita read the letter's conclusion,

> The point is, do what you want or need to do. Why waste your time writing to me? Don't be stupid! Who cares about my bank—what can I buy here? If you want to send something, send books. You think too much, but always about the wrong things. You have your own problems, and I expect you to bear yourself honorably in this new job. (And where else do you have to go?) You see to that demimondaine who ruined my grandson and find out her situation. I told you she was no good, but you didn't listen. Well, it's a free country. I'll see you after we win the war.
>
> The Emperor's Niece

Growling, he slipped the letter into his pocket—another reminder, an IOU, a stone in his shoe. As the coming winter slowed his work, he would spend many hours trying to devise sane responses to his mother's insane letters, grumbling all the while about madness and heredity. Yet in each letter he imagined he detected traces of the Pacific Coast—of citrus and clay, Mexican food and sun showers—soaked into the very paper, and it always set him back to work with renewed vigor. No one could infuriate him so expertly as Tamie.

The final week of November certainly demanded vigor, as the weather turned emphatically gloomy and the days shortened. While Margaret and Livvie saw that the assorted plant-test sites were roped, tilled, and mulched, Mr. Fujita turned his will to Garvin's education and to the greenhouse. To build it right, he used double panes, cheaper to heat and useful in controlling moisture levels. For heating, he made do with the coal-fired hot-water heater in the attached garage. "A dodgy business," he told Garvin. "Like us, like people, baby plants are very fragile. The fumes can be poisonous to them, so you have keep the atmosphere really clean."

Garvin took to cleaning the furnace and flues with heroic concentration. He didn't mind the filthy job, though. He loved the ash, how it filled his ears and nose and left a tarry ring in the tub at day's end. He also used it to draw elaborate stick-figure armies on the garage floor. With his sharp eyes and tiny hands, the boy proved a valuable tool in precise work such as stringing electrical wiring, but always Fujita made sure to explain the big picture. He told Margaret he regretted not imparting to Tony more of the sense of labor; born into the nursery, Tony learned the work automatically and out of necessity, as any household chore. Garvin had chosen to learn, so Fujita patiently explained that the wiring fed many electric fans that, with several vents with louvered shutters, kept air circulating, reduced condensation, helped to control temperature and carbon dioxide levels. "Like us," said the *sensei,* "plants must be able to breathe. See?"

To Margaret and Garvin and Livvie, those green recruits, each morning brought new improvements that seemed spontaneous, almost magical. Suddenly the greenhouse would sport a wall of glass panes or row of slate tables, or an exterior airtight with fresh epoxy. And did leprechauns rig the hydrating system with spaghetti strands of pin-pierced wire casing, all snaking to the precise water regulator?

No one believed it, of course—not even Margaret, even though Jane Austen was once again lulling her to sound sleep, so she never actually saw Fujita up in the glass house at one, two, three in the morning. From the haunted gutters beneath his bloodshot eyes, the stubble on his cheeks as he sucked down four morning coffees in haste to return to his toil, even Margaret could see that he was obsessed with transforming Widow's Peak into "his little piece of California."

"You're running yourself ragged," she scolded, in her I'm-a-nurse-and-I-know-best voice. "At least wait until I've made you some proper breakfast."

"Winter won't wait," he said, rising and excusing himself.

"You poor man," Margaret whispered, watching him go out. "We've got to find something recreational for you to do. You'll blow a fuse."

The good Nurse Kelly did understand his anxiousness. Once the thing was done, the seeds set germinating, the routine established, there would be more than enough time to wait—for plants, grief, and hopefully, war's end. Among the four workers, only she had yet weathered the first anniversary of widowhood, or that most dreaded hallmark of all—the first Christmas in bereavement. What hope could the new year promise Mr. Fujita? Only a birthday alone, a mother in prison, and facing those milestones of losing Mari and Tony—alone in a frigid, foreign landscape.

Then one morning just before Thanksgiving, Margaret awoke to the din of metal smashing metal, so incongruous with the picture out her bedroom windows, the wispy beginnings of the season's first snow flurry. Delighted, she hopped out of bed and crossed to the window, the floorboards sending a thrill of coldness up into her soles. Looking out, she saw Mr. Fujita, his head enveloped in mist, hammering a rubber strip to a trash-can lid—raccoons had been in the garbage again. Setting the can upright, he used it as a stool to rest. He looked up into the sky, appearing both furious and awed, and released a puff of misty breath—perhaps a curse? Then she saw a stab of pink as he reached out to the air with his tongue, as a child will do, and it occurred to her he might never have *seen* snow before. Standing, he then spent a solid fifteen minutes pacing circles around the scarecrow, staring up to the clouds, talking to his grass companion in cotton-ball breaths. It both endeared him to her and made him seem more alien than anything else.

"He talks to *her* more than he talks to us," she griped to herself, and then to Livvie later that afternoon as they walked down to meet Garvin's school bus. It concerned her that the man didn't take any leisure, or that his few leisure activities all seemed like *work*. Oh, he'd been at some carpentry and tinkering and letter writing but pursued these with such intensity they hardly fit into the rest-and-relaxation category. Everything he did was toward some purpose, like fixing the radio cabinet in Jack's old office or jazzing up some part of the house. "His idea of taking a *break* from the greenhouse is mending a floorboard. It's all so . . . utilitarian."

"You act like that's something to complain about," Livvie laughed. Unused to fixing things around her own house, she appreciated Mr. Fujita's handiness. That week he'd fixed a leak in the tub and put in her storm windows.

"I don't think I'm complaining. Well, yes, I am. He's too serious. I just think he ought to do something, you know, for fun. Not just do things that need doing."

"So he likes work. After all, he *is* a workman. That's why he's here, right?" Livvie asked pointedly, and Margaret blushed. "He does like to cook," she suggested. "What I wouldn't give for someone like that. Sig couldn't even boil water without burning it. I wouldn't mind someone cooking for *me* sometimes."

"You'll get your chance," Margaret said. "He wants to make Thanksgiving dinner. 'Something unconventional,' he said."

"Something Japanese?" Livvie asked. "Well, I don't like turkey anyway."

"Something Italian. Some very complicated recipe he's wanted to try for a long time." Margaret shook her head tiredly. "But as you say, cooking is work, too. I mean, he might take up the harmonica. Play baseball. Join a choir. Read Zane Grey novels, even. Or make model ships in bottles, or whatever. Do you think? Livvie, what do you think?"

"I think that's ridiculous."

"Oh. Well, something frivolous I mean. For himself. You can't trust men who are helpful and pragmatic all the time; inside, each one is a martyr, hoarding resentment. It's our duty to keep him from being too serious, to force him to have some fun. With his hands, he could be a sculptor, or a surgeon, but everything he makes is so—" she wrinkled her face in distaste, "practical."

But the dour handyman surprised them all with a Thanksgiving feast that was lush, luxurious, and sloppy. There was wine, and a steaming oxtail soup, and a dish of marinated clams, and fresh-baked sourdough bread, and wedges of baked mozzarella. The centerpiece was a Sally DiPassio recipe. She had described it as "the food of love" and said that in old Italy, prostitutes would prepare the dish for their lovers. *Spaghetti alla puttanesca*: the spicy, aromatic mist of crushed tomato and anchovy, sprinkled with chopped garlic and shallots, nonpareil capers, and hot red pepper flakes; bolstered with chunks of salty kalamata olives; topped with fine ribbons of fresh, sweet basil from the hotbeds of the Kelly/Fujita/Tufteller farm. Inhaling the rich steam,

Margaret took just one bite and knew the dish had been prepared with love—a full, strangled passion lived inside the man seated stiffly across from her.

They voted to ignore the advice of the *Bereavement* newsletter, figuring that those absent would have some other place to dine. Outside, in the dark by the scarecrow, in the birdbath where the Annisquam Witch had anointed herself, a thrush ruffled his cold feathers and decided it was well past time to migrate. Launching westward, it flew a few rings above the chimney of the Kelly house, rubbing its back feathers against the fragrant warmth as down below, inside, the new family of Widow's Peak lit candles for Sig, Jack, Mari, and Tony, giving what thanks they could.

SIX

"The Whole Thing"

Billowing, oily fumes threaded themselves among the long clouds above Oahu, over the same tiny, fortified inlet that Ichiro and Tamie had viewed from their porthole on the *Pacific Angel.* From sea level, the smoke and clouds over Pearl Harbor appeared to interlock like the fingers of black and white sumo wrestlers setting to a match. To the terrified sea birds, however, piercing that handshake and racing away from the explosions, the pathways were only gray. Some flew against the prevailing wind, eastward toward Molokai, Lanai, Maui; those light-feathered creatures had to fly very high and very far to escape its unnatural reek.

Failing his father's advice, Fujita proved unprepared for the Sunday that finally spurred his country into war. Gearing up for the Tournament of Roses and the holidays were keeping him too busy to read the papers or listen much to the radio. Tony helped very little—mooning about the shop over Yoneko, breaking things. Unusually grumpy, Tamie expressed her distrust of Lum Chen by shadowing him, criticizing his work, ordering him to petty tasks. "Get out, all of you!" Fujita finally yelled that morning. "If you're not going to help, at least don't hinder my work!" The family abandoned him for a church service and luncheon (even Tony went, to see Yoneko) and planned a leisurely shopping afternoon in Little Tokyo. Thus distracted, Fujita didn't think much about it at first when his longtime terra-cotta supplier, Harv Clemens, first broke the news that Japanese warplanes had bombed Pearl Harbor.

"Gosh," Fujita said, writing a vendor's check, not really listening. "What do you know about that?"

"Well, I heard this on the radio," Clemens said. "I thought I should tell you, Bill. I mean, I think things may get pretty hot around here for Japanese."

"And I appreciate it, Harv, really." Fujita, alert in an instant, opted for caution. What had it to do with him? In fact, he didn't know where Pearl Harbor was. China, maybe? "Um, what's Pearl Harbor?"

"Hawaii, Bill! Pearl Harbor, *Hawaii*."

Friendly as their acquaintance had been, Fujita knew Clemens to live in a perpetual state of alarm. The potter suffered from imaginary, imminent ailments—bunions lurking just beneath the skin of his toes to insidious cancer cells plotting to infiltrate his organs at any moment. "That's some news, Harv," he said, not quite believing it. Perhaps the broadcast Clemens heard was an Orson Welles radio play.

"I know you're an upright fellow, Bill," Clemens said, "and you know my sympathy is with you. If anything queer happens, I'll stick by you, and plenty of others will say the same. But you should look after your ma. Let me know if you need anything."

Fujita promised to call if the need arose. Long after the potter had departed and the door chimes fell silent, a ringing still sounded in Fujita's head. "Ridiculous," he said. Not about to close shop, he returned to the stack of purchase orders. After a while, however, the notion began to nag him, so he flipped on the radio, and that's when he heard the news from the ravaged Henderson Field.

His first thought was, My son will definitely be drafted now.

He listened for a half hour, feeling punchy, intoxicated. The house was warm enough, but Fujita chilled over, sensed the hairs bristling up his stiff neck. Only brief snatches of the broadcast settled on him: "Japanese planes of war," he heard, "countless Americans dead," and "surprise attack." He'd counted on Roosevelt, voted for him—no American boys would fight in foreign wars, the president had said.

Fujita thought, They've attacked us, and now my son will go to the war.

Nearly hysterical, the announcers already scrabbled to pin responsibility on the base commanders. "If there were errors of judgment . . ." the radio posited, as if this alone could make sense of such a catastrophe. "If there were derelictions of duty . . ." Much later, after the shock, when he had already been ousted from his life, Fujita would recall the news media's second assault on the navy. Whether nature or nurture, this damage control through blame was among those few instincts Fujita believed were truly *American.* In the moment, however, he only wondered, Why them? "Blame Military Intelligence," he grumbled. "Blame the *Japanese.*" Blame the *world.* Thus, he intuitively groped to express a dread in him that he had yet to see clearly, much less find words for. Don't blame *me.*

So he sat unmoving until jarred back to clarity by the bleating telephone. A representative of the Japanese American Citizens League introduced himself, but the words faded in the static of Fujita's incipient headache. The man was calling through JACL directories. "Avoid crowds for a few days. Don't talk about the war with anyone," the caller advised. If someone forced a discussion, he said, "you should demonstratively show your feelings about this country."

"What in hell does that mean?" Fujita said. "Thanks anyway." Hanging up, he decided to fetch his family. Just in case. He locked up the shop, closed the shutters as an afterthought, climbed into the truck, and drove slowly to the Union Church. He looked around. Quiet. Streets deserted but the same old streets. The few pedestrians didn't stare or behave oddly; maybe it would be all right. He wondered how he should "demonstratively show his feelings." Drink more Ovaltine? he thought. Whip out my mitt and have a catch?

Parking in front of the squat church building, he met a grave

Herb Nicholson. A thin-lipped man with light gray hair brushed back to reveal a scar, Nicholson stood a full six inches taller than Fujita. Known as an honorary Japanese, he was an ex-missionary to Japan and a devoted friend and sometimes-minister to the Union Church. His zeal, though admirable, unsettled Fujita as much as his height. Herb was "a whole lot of Christian," as Fujita once put it.

"Haven't seen you at church in a while, Bill," Nicholson said, looking down at Fujita through small, wire-rimmed glasses that pinched his potato nose.

"I've been here in spirit," Fujita said, shaking the man's hand, then accompanying him toward the entrance.

"It's a bad business," Nicholson said. He ran his fingertips anxiously around the brim of his fedora. "I'm sorry about the whole thing."

"I don't know what the whole thing *is* yet, Herb."

"You'll find out in the meeting," said Nicholson. His long face drooped even longer, cloudy with earnestness, as he held the door open.

"Actually, Herb," Fujita said, halting by the door. "I came for my family."

"Oh, I see. Uh, Bill . . ." Nicholson pointed to his forehead. "Your hat."

"Right. Sorry." Guiltily, he followed the tall man inside.

First greeted by posters bearing kanji characters, he started down the aisle and then stopped short, chilled by the seating arrangement. To his left, the gray, white, or dyed heads of the Issei section marched in prim, tidy order, the eyes directed down, ashamed, or to the plain cross above the altar, pleading. On the right hand, the pews sprouted heads of shining black, slouched and slumped. Set not in rows, but distributed in uneven clusters, the young people's half looked to Fujita like poorly planned furrows of cabbages, sown by drunkards. Such segregation of the Nikkei generations was common at special bilingual gatherings, but on that infamous day Fujita found the deployment sinister. The center aisle unfurled like a bed of coals, or a tightrope, and for the moment only he and Herb Nicholson dared walk it.

He had then what Tamie called the "mirror moment" that she assumed all Nisei must eventually experience. He saw how the younger people's eyes were aimed at the Issei, red with anger and betrayal; and yet he also had to notice how *alike* those columns of pews appeared when contrasted with the light-haired ex-missionary walking down the aisle between them. Following Nicholson, he hesitated, as the question arose, Where should *he* sit? That it was a question infuriated him, as he scanned the pews to see Mari and Tony seated to the right with Yoneko, and his mother to his left with her Issei friends. As a nonchurchgoer, he wasn't one to talk, of course, but if a family *attended* church, shouldn't it attend *as* a family? But how familiar it felt, hovering there in the middle. It was the story of his entire neither-here-nor-there life. He could not claim to be among "The First" sitting paralyzed by shock to his left; yet he had been The First Among the Second, and a half-generation gap lay between himself and the majority of those sulking on the right.

"Shit!" Fujita grumbled. No sooner had the word left him—its echo bouncing like an escaped frog down the aisle, and all eyes turning on him so that he realized he'd forgotten the splendid acoustics of this hallowed place—than Fujita felt he could almost *see* his outburst rocketing toward the long back of Herb Nicholson, who cringed as if the word had become material—as if he had been blindly beaned with actual shit.

Slowly pivoting around, the tall man pinned Fujita with a thick-spectacled stare. "It *has* been a long time, hasn't it, Bill?" Nicholson tried and failed to grin.

Humiliated, Fujita slipped into the pew beside his wife, who hid her face with a hand. Beside her, Tony rolled his eyes, whispering, "Way to go, Pop." Beside him, Yoneko giggled. Across the aisle, her Aunt Rose gaped at her potential in-law as if he were a lunatic, and a few pews down, Tamie would not even look at him. As he gazed on the rows of heads now aligned to face Reverend Mr. Tajima, it occurred to him that they all looked like ducks in shooting gallery. With this earliest intimation of what "the whole thing" for West Coast Issei and Nisei would look like, Fujita finally began to accept, on that most infamous of days, that in the eyes of his country he was Japanese.

Could there be any doubt? No, not when the Fujitas returned to the nursery to find themselves barred from the driveway by legions of upended saplings, mounds of soil and gravel spilled from sacks dragged from their orderly rows and gored by sharp objects. The lath house, an open structure roofed with thin slats and used for shading tender new plants, lay felled by one of his own axes. The whitewashed shop facade was pocked with green tomatoes, steer manure, eggs. Painted letters cut across the front windows, bold as blood and pitch: GO BAK JAPS! and WAR!

"Yes, well," Fujita mumbled, amazed, looking down. "Oh no." From the ground, he lifted a beheaded persimmon, about two years old. The dried-out root system dangled from the pot's cracked bottom; the stalk had been repeatedly and cruelly hacked at with a machete. "No!" He brushed the roots as tenderly as if caressing a lover's hair. Defacement was one thing—a racial and occupational hazard even in Miyake's day—but what made a human being do . . . this? Then, an explosion of glass sounded, and he found that he no longer held the sapling. It had materialized inside the shop, beyond the graffiti, now edited to read as the more cordial cheer, GO JAPS! "That's better," Fujita said, believing he now understood the thrill of painting those letters. How sublime was that lashing out, how exhilarating it felt to loathe. Beside him, he heard the whizzz of the rake arcing from Tony's shoulder, then the crash, and Tony's grunt. And suddenly, WAR! was no more.

Mari slapped her husband. Tamie began shrieking at the men to stop breaking *her* windows. "You childish idiots! You *simian* idiots!"

Many more arguments would follow. A few hours later, driving home from filing a report at the police station—where Pasadena's finest had been oh-so-very-helpful, basically ignoring the Fujitas—they passed the Chinada grocery store, newly festooned with an enormous banner: WE ARE AMERICANS. "Oh, Jesus Goddamn Christ!" Fujita snarled.

"I don't like the downward turn your speech has taken lately, Bill," Mari said. "And I think that sign's a good idea. For the nursery, we should—"

"No, we should *not* do that," he fired back, digging in. "Not now, not ever, because *that* is horse shit. Because we run the Fujita family nursery, not the goddamned Fujita Family Circus, and *that* . . ." Even as he jabbed his thumb toward Tamie in the backseat, the one noncitizen among them, he regretted saying it but could no longer stop himself: "is a Fujita, and unlike Chinada, I'm not willing to shit on my parents or any Issei just because this moron state has gone bonkers."

"Don't talk about me like I'm not here," Tamie said. "And watch your language."

She was trying to sound angry, but her voice quavered more with fright than fury—such an alien tone that Fujita glanced worriedly into the rearview mirror. Hugging herself, Tamie turned to watch the banner fade out of sight. What was her word? *Simian?*

"I'm sorry, Mom," he said, but she didn't appear to notice. "Mom, I'm sorry."

"And it's a good idea, as Mariko says. You should listen to your wife. I picked her because she was smart."

Fujita bit his lip and frowned at Mari, who shrugged. "Listen to your mother."

Parking the car, Fujita only sighed to see that during his visit with the police, someone had again used his nursery for target practice. Steer manure and bonemeal cascaded down the front steps, but Fujita strode over this as on a red carpet, made a beeline to the bedroom closet, and dug out his father's steamer trunk.

"What do you *think* you're doing?" Mari screamed at him when she found him sitting on the bed with the twenty-two-caliber rifle across his knees, reading a pamphlet on how to clean it.

"I'm exercising my goddamned, God-given American right to shoot things on my property," he snapped back, squinting at the instructions.

"You can't even shoot gophers. You don't know anything about guns, anyway." This was true. Ichiro won the weapon in a card game, then put it away and forgot it. Only Miyake ever fired it, usually at garden pests, though once or twice he'd knocked off a few blackbirds, which he barbecued in teriyaki sauce sprinkled with goma seeds.

"I know where the thingy is," Fujita said. "That's all I need."

"The trigger, you mean."

"I know, I know."

"The *thingy*," Mari said scornfully. "Put that away." Attracted by the commotion, Tony and Tamie took Mari's side. Tamie slapped her son on the arm. Tony laughed. Traitors.

Outgunned, he placed the twenty-two back in the trunk and stewed until another argument flared up that night. The Fujitas ate dinner around the radio, leaving the room only to go to the bathroom or answer the telephone, which rang constantly. Tony begged to be allowed to drive to Little Tokyo, where Yoneko was staying with her parents, but Mari forbade him "absolutely, positively."

"Pop?"

Irritated that the boy meant to pit them against each other, Fujita found himself repeating, "Listen to your mother, Tony." He huffed. "Besides, there's a blackout in L.A. We'd have to drive so slowly, we wouldn't get there until tomorrow, anyway."

"What if I take the Red Car in?" the boy insisted.

Fujita shook his head. "Tonight it's not safe. Tonight the family stays together."

Unsatisfied, Tony phoned Yoneko at each break in the newscast until her father finally ordered her off the line and forbade them to talk again that night.

"Her parents are as concerned as we are about your safety, I'm sure," Fujita said, trying to be reasonable and fatherly. "It would be dangerous for her to go out now."

Tony sulked. The teenagers, too, had argued. "*She* doesn't want me to come, anyway. She said that if you say to stay in, I should do what you say."

"She said that?" Fujita asked, surprised. Tony shrugged. "Smart girl."

Tony shrugged again. "She always says that. She thinks you're some kind of hero or something."

"A hero?" Fujita thought aloud. The word itself seemed foreign. Especially tonight. Looking down at his hands, with tiny arcs of potting soil resting under their nails, he recalled his unresolved conversation with Yoneko on the night he first met her—

or thought he first met her. "Well, what do you know?" he mused.

The rest of the night passed like a séance. Like all the neighboring houses, the nursery remained darkened and silent, but for the glow and murmur of the radio, which the family surrounded like a crystal ball in whose midst the slain of Pearl Harbor might appear to reveal the future. Like their neighbors, the Fujitas listened fearfully for reports of the Japanese—as if the invasion might be channeled through the radio speaker itself. However, the Japanese this family sought in the radio were not only the enemy.

Mari's parents, the Arais, had the misfortune of taking their vacation abroad during the holiday month. She had begged them to wait. "You'll miss Christmas and New Year's and Bill's birthday," she complained. They usually helped out during the Tournament of Roses, too. *Shikata ga nai,* it can't be helped, her parents insisted, and the phrase would become an Issei mantra throughout the war still so new to them. Their schedule was inflexible. A couple only had one golden wedding anniversary; however far the heart and mind might range, honeymoon sites and first passions were immovable, and theirs were in Nippon.

Mari's own spouse of twenty-two years was thinking of Miyake, who if still alive, would also be listening to the radio but from his garden. The master would spit and confide to his flowers his worry for his apprentice, who "planned everything but didn't think ahead." Now unable to communicate with his mentor, Fujita regretted not trying to do so before, though Miyake was a bridge-burner, a terrible correspondent who could write no English and, Fujita suspected, wrote poorly in Japanese, too. It occurred to him then that if he'd surpassed two fathers, he had also lost two. He'd never kissed his surrogate father; they'd never shared a hug. Now that he thought of it, he could remember no touch at all beyond a swat at the arm or a less frequent pat on the back. Yet, that dark night, holed up in his nursery, considering the life Miyake had taught him, which was so perfect for him, he struggled with the antenna and hoped. If the war could ride those shortwaves bridging the Pacific, maybe love could cross back that way, too. Pinched by nostalgia and regret, he wanted to kiss his own son, who had, somehow, long ago become too old to kiss. The next morning Fujita expressed his love in the only way he could: He allowed Tony to stay home from school, "just this once," to work with him.

"I need you here," Fujita said. This was true: After a fitful night, even two extra cups of coffee barely woke him, and Lum Chen had neither reported for work nor called. Few customers came by, but Fujita hauled the radio into the store and tried to approach December 8 as any other Monday. Mari and Tamie began readying the holiday stock, packaging poinsettias, tagging the remaining Christmas firs. The men cleaned up the vandals' handiwork. At lunchtime Fujita needed Tony's help loading the truck for daily deliveries, which he resolved to make on schedule. In living life, as in watching theater, Fujita was a believer. Persist, he thought, and the customers will be there. Yet his regular two-hour route to a dozen estate gardeners took only forty-five minutes, as four of them, all Issei, did not show up to receive the deliveries. Persist, he amended, and the customers will return. On the way home, his stomach began to bark at him from nerves and hunger, so he stopped at the five-and-dime for a paper and four sandwiches. The elderly Jablonskys smiled and looked right through him, taking care with his order—nothing unusual in that. Persist, he hoped, and the *whole thing* will be all right.

Whatever "the whole thing" will be, he thought, and already it seemed a woefully inadequate phrase for those perils he imagined—feared—lay ahead.

By the time he returned to the nursery, his wife and mother were gone.

"What do you mean, 'gone'?"

"Gone, Pop," Tony repeated. Rising to surrender the chair behind the desk, he looked dizzy, even faint. The blotter was riddled with phone numbers and curlicue doodles. "I don't know where. Three men from the FBI just flew in and blitzed the place. Here's the phone number. They said . . . they said they were rounding up suspects and asked to see Grandma."

"*Suspects*? Did they have a warrant? Where's your mom?"

He flailed his arms helplessly. "Mom went with her. I don't know about the other stuff. I mean, they just came in . . ."

Fujita stalked to the phone and requested the number written on the blotter. No, he thought, waiting for the operator to connect him. Better call a lawyer first. He rummaged through the drawer beneath the cash register, then through the desk drawers. By his watch, fewer than thirty hours had elapsed since the attack on Pearl Harbor. How could someone become a suspect so quickly? Too quickly, he decided. Despite himself, he had to be impressed with the Bureau's swiftness, if not its efficiency or accuracy: If they were less hasty, would they have targeted *his mother* as someone worth arresting? He should definitely call his lawyer first.

"Where the hell's my address book?" he demanded.

"They took it with them, Pop."

Fujita swung on his son as if he were responsible for the whole affair. "For Christ's sake, Tony! Did they take anything *else*?"

"Just some road maps," Tony said, "my geography homework, and Grandma."

He threw the sandwiches and paper on the blotter and saw again, and more fully, the bright red headline screaming: WAR! The operator chimed in again, "No one's there, or they're just not answering. Do you want me to try again?"

Unable to form words, Fujita released one long, silent breath until he felt absolutely empty of air. "No, I . . . um, what's your name again?" It seemed for some unclear reason important to know. She told him, "Eveline," long *e* and long *i*. "Right, Eveline. Could you connect me to a business number for the attorney Myron Ichioka in Pasadena?" When the operator hesitated, he snapped, "*Eve*line, it's urgent!" That was why it had been important to put a name on that faceless voice, which now sounded so hurt as it continued, "Well, you'll have to spell that for me." Gritting his teeth, he said, "M-Y-R-O-N: Moron," he growled, feeling mean. "Er, Myron. And, I-C-H-I-O-K-A: Ichioka." He sighed. "I'm sorry, Eveline. It's been a rough day."

Throughout that nightmarish afternoon, he relied on Eveline to steer him to countless other dead ends, empty offices that were, he learned upon his fourth attempt to find Ichioka, all on the Bureau checklist. When Eveline at last connected him to

Myron's assistant at the Japanese Association where Ichioka served as treasurer, Fujita learned that his lawyer, too, had been arrested. Not just the association officers, he was told, but Buddhist priests, schoolteachers, newspaper staff, even kendo instructors—folks Fujita knew from picnics, the nursery, and business settings, from the gakuen or Tony's baseball league—all community leaders, just swallowed up as if by an earthquake.

"Well, what the hell am I supposed to do?" he demanded of the attorney's assistant. "Can you come to the Bureau with me?"

"I'm not going *near* there," yelped the frazzled young man. "And I'm busy. Look, you're not the only one, but you're on your own. Sorry about your ma."

Defeated, Fujita slumped in the chair behind the cash register. After such a prolonged and intense connection, he now found himself oddly longing for the voice of Eveline. He even felt a pang of guilt when Mari returned to the shop.

"Mom's all right for now," his wife said, throwing her gloves onto the desk in a manner that forbade further questioning for the moment. Ashy circles of mascara cupped her eyes, and she drooped so that he feared she was sick. Draping her coat on the back of his chair, she then pulled him up and into the main house, leaving Tony to mind things. In the vestibule between the shop and the den, she began shedding her clothing, leaving a trail on the floor—first her hat, her sweater; in the living room, she tossed away a light silk scarf; in the kitchen, she dropped her purse but did not stop there. Passing onto the kitchen porch, the back courtyard, she unbuttoned her blouse. Fujita looked about anxiously—Lum Chen or some customer might be lurking about—but no, not today. "Um, Mari?"

At Tamie's quarters, she reached down into her camisole, withdrew a key, unlocked the door, and pulled him in. He saw in the flash of sunlight that the room had reverted to the messy state it had as Miyake's old bachelor's den. The FBI's roundup was about as tidy as an earthquake, too. Momentarily blind, Fujita heard Mari scuffle about on the floor, then a bump, her hiss, a creak. She flipped on a tiny reading lamp and sat down on Tamie's low bed; in her lap, she cradled a gleaming cherrywood box with ebony and pearl accents. Its key, too, lay nestled beneath her undershirt. Opening the case, she removed a fistful of bills, mostly twenties, then handed the box to her husband. "Torch it," she said grimly, then she finished removing her blouse and lay down to nap on Tamie's bed, the money still clenched in her fist.

Hesitating, Fujita searched the mostly unfamiliar contents: postcards featuring a great military ship, a hillside landscape scene, a duck; Tamie's college degree, recommendation letters, grade reports, various citations and awards; a thin student's notebook, utterly filled with hiragana and including what looked like a child's treasure map. Buried beneath, he found two bundles: the cards with the short poems bound in blue ribbon and, in an orange ribbon, two years' worth of letters, unaddressed or hand-delivered, the last one dated 1896. Faltering, the letters resumed only a year later, sent to the gakuen. On those parchments, a lush prose defied easy translation. Fujita could read some kanji, as in the plainer news items in the *Rafu Shimpo*. Yet, any but the most advanced Nisei and even Kibei would have struggled with these secret columns exchanged between scholars, except for the tiny island of Roman characters embedded there, reading

Let this sad interim like the ocean be
Which parts the shore, where two contracted new,
Come daily to the banks, that when they see:
Return of love, more blest may be the view.

Surrounding Shakespeare's sonnet, the rest was less clear. Script handwriting was tougher than printed characters. Already daunting for their advanced vocabulary, the letters were more forbidding for their intimacy, for the joyous or agonized or silly metaphorical calisthenics of a learned correspondent who was, translatably, in love with Tamie Asakawa, and later with Tamie Fujita.

Naturally, the Shakespearean imagery seemed to hark back to the lines Lady Sanuki had wrought in waka form four centuries earlier. The seaside lovers mingled with seaside mourners; in addition to the ocean, the unseen rock also lay between the imagined lovers and the shores of two countries. "Oh God," Fujita said, feeling the need for a drink and thinking of his father. He strained to read further. "I need a dictionary."

"Burn them, Bill," Mari said suddenly. He had thought she was asleep. "I promised her."

"What? No! Why should I burn them?" As he continued leafing through, his amazement mounted, but his concern did not—what he could interpret was in no way treasonous. "There's nothing incriminating in here—not in the *government's* eyes. And anyway, I need to go over—"

"There is and you don't," she said emphatically. "*He* teaches English for the Japanese Navy. Get it?"

"You knew about this?" he said, gaping. Mari rolled on the bed, turned her back on him.

"Honestly, I don't know much." She sounded exhausted. "I do know you shouldn't snoop through her letters, but ask her. That is, after you've gotten rid of those things."

He observed his wife, whom he respected and adored, in this ransacked room on this nursery Tamie had acquired for him, sleeping beneath the Tokyo mayor's wall hanging depicting Tamie's ambitions for her son on the Gold Mountain. His mother had made a lot of choices for him, he thought. Then, feeling like a shadow puppet on a stick, Fujita carried the chest out to the property's deepest corner, where he kept an old oil drum for burning leaves and brush. Ask her, he thought. For fully ten minutes, he hovered by the drum seeking courage to dump the contents of this hope chest—wasn't that what women called it? He retained the waka poem cards, but before he could decide to retrieve the letters, he sparked them with a match and watched them shrivel with the finality of a funeral pyre.

When he returned to Tamie's room and Mari insisted, "Later, I'll tell you later," he felt startlingly easy settling onto his mother's bed and pressing against his wife's back, as if he sensed that Tamie would never sleep there again. Even when Mari undid his trousers and pushed them to his ankles with her feet, it felt not so much disrespectful or invasive as untimely. Yet Mari had been told "no" so many times and in so many ways that day, he supposed she needed a "yes," and he did not refuse her. When did his mother ever refuse him what he needed? And it surprised him to discover that he needed a yes, as well.

While not quite managing to see his mother during the blurred weeks following Pearl Harbor, Fujita became convinced of the authorities' resolve to keep her safe and treat her humanely, and simply to keep her, regardless of what he did or said. In a handwritten note, she assured him she could get on fine and ordered him to see to his own business tending "my nursery." She again enjoined him to recall her care in choosing Mari for him. "Mariko has many good ideas," she added, in the first chapter of their wartime correspondence. "She's a mother, too, and you must always listen to her. I'm sorry that I may have to miss your birthday, but Mariko will make your birthday manju this year. Of course, in some things a wife cannot replace a mother, and you will not have my manju until I come home, which cannot be helped, but Mariko knows my recipe, and she has my utmost faith and trust."

Mom might not make such a bad spy, he thought, rereading the cryptic note. Decoded, it seemed to say that he should heed Mari's advice about imitating the gaudy banner on Chinada's Grocery—he should take steps, as the JACL put it, to "demonstratively show his feelings about his country." He also realized that by "utmost faith" and the manju business, Tamie meant she trusted Mari to leave any explanation of the mysterious "hope chest" to *her* when released.

"Whenever that may be," he grumbled to his wife, who shrugged and patently refused to discuss the matter when he pressed her to "make my manju a little early."

As instructed, Fujita went on about his business and barely noticed the gossip blazing throughout Pasadena's white and yellow communities. Newspaper editors battled over what had come to be known as the "Japanese problem," as California now referred to the ever-expanding "whole thing." From Fujita's vantage, a greater Japanese problem was the rumor that wolf packs of Filipinos in L.A. were killing Japanese. "Stay home," he would order Tony, yet the boy would elude him, and he was always too busy to enforce it. In addition to seeking decent legal help, he dizzied himself trying to prevent the nursery's physical and financial ruin. From his Presidio in San Francisco, Lieutenant General John DeWitt dropped a significant bomb on a cherished Pasadena cash cow, deciding to relocate the Rose Bowl game to Durham, North Carolina. Although an entire, wholesale subindustry existed to supply the Tournament of Roses, the tiny Fujita nursery had always profited during the festival selling dethorned garlands, single stems appended to ribboned lapel clips, and the like. Every day he revised his markdown signs: X-MAS TREES 25% OFF! Left with an enormous surplus of miniature rosebushes, Fujita tried to dump them at his outdoor stand in L.A., but the war, the editorials, and the boycotts took a dire toll. FREE POINSETTIA WITH EVERY X-MAS TREE!

On December 29 he decided: Persistence can only take you so far. Finding some old paint in the garage, he was preoccupied knocking off Chinada's patriotic banner when four men from the Justice Department came to search the house. Oddly, the officers just shrugged upon discovering the twenty-two in his closet. Apparently more fearful of him shooting pictures than people, they only confiscated his camera, along with his shortwave set and binoculars.

"Fine, take them!" he shouted, painting away, ostentatiously trying to treat their visit as routine. "Do I sit around listening to the radio eating bonbons? Do I have time for bird-watching?" he demanded.

Do I have time for Justice Department morons? he thought, stabbing the dot beneath the exclamation point. In the hysterical weeks that followed, he endured a very long list of morons. In early January, the bank froze a business account he held jointly with Tamie. This came at an unfortunate time (when is a *good* time to have one's assets frozen?), since he was besieged by legions of vendors seeking payment amid rumors that the military would oust Japanese from the Coast. In mid-January, the tax people breezed through but were easily persuaded that Fujita would be filing a loss for that year. Only the insurance moron, who was supposed to come about the vandalism damage a month earlier, never visited the nursery. By early February, Fujita was convinced that WE ARE AMERICANS! splashed across his floundering business had devolved into a synonym for WE ARE MORONS!, but at least he still felt safe. He was still, partially, a believer.

He hadn't time to read what the journalist morons were up to (he left that chore to Mari), or he might have realized just how completely vulnerable they were. Free to snipe away at Little Tokyo, the fourth estate was hell-bent on discovering a fifth column in California, though too slowly for the idiot governor, Culbert Olson, who impatiently spouted unproven sabotage rumors as fact, while the state attorney general moron, Earl Warren, found the *absence* of sabotage "the most ominous sign in our whole situation." Sometimes Fujita couldn't avoid newspapers, such as the day he drove in to his troubled outdoor stall in L.A. He fleetingly considered starting a fight with the cranky old greengrocer next door who was always jockeying for position; their stalls sat between two lampposts, and Fujita's neighbor resented that one of the posts partially obscured *his* stall, even though he'd paid a lower fee because of that deficiency. He had shoved Fujita's table aside to be obscured by the second lamppost, but the Nisei let it pass so he could eavesdrop as the neighbor and a customer discussed "the Japanese problem." The customer, a sandy-haired office type about thirty, was nattily dressed as if headed to an important meeting. He was nodding his head vigorously and crowing, "Right! Ditto!"

"Yes, sir," said the red-faced old crank, who continued reading from the *Times* spread open atop the produce. "'A viper is nonetheless a viper,'" he read, with reverential ardor, "'wherever the egg is hatched.'"

"Absolutely right!" The customer's head bobbed wildly, as if set on a spring. "Sure, some of 'em are born here, but damned if *I* can tell which ones."

"That's right. You *can't* tell. Hawaii's probably ninety percent yellow, and if we don't keep an eye on the shifty buggers, you think it won't happen right here in the U.S.A.? Do you?" demanded the greengrocer, and for emphasis he stabbed his finger into the article, forgetting about the tomatoes, so that the hemorrhaging fruit drenched the newsprint. "Pack 'em up and herd 'em off, I say!" he sang.

Fujita braced himself for violence, but oddly, despite the old crank's eloquent call for vigilance, the men acted as if they couldn't see him at all. For a hopeful moment, he thought that maybe he wasn't as *visible* as he'd previously imagined, until the familiar figure he spotted at a competitor's booth across the street dispelled the notion. Backed by a brown apron, the white button pin shone like a headlight on the chest of Lum Chen: I'M CHINESE! Having never known what it was like to be frightening to anyone, it took Fujita a while to consider that perhaps the crank and his customer *avoided* seeing him because they feared him. Perhaps they didn't really wish him harm but only wished him gone. He'd lost his patience for gray areas and fine distinctions, so he obliged the gentlemen. Swiftly rolling up the Fujita Family Cut Flowers banner and collecting the assorted chains, padlocks, and cooler boxes, the nurseryman turned his back on the harmonious love fest, climbed back into the truck, and having shut down his business, rolled out into the City of Angels for the last time.

Fujita felt safe because he could, unlike his wife, discount what was happening around him as mere stupidity, as temporary insanity born of fear. After all, such calls for expulsion of Japanese were hardly a new phenomenon. With effort, he maintained a faith in people's essential sensibleness; it would all come out in the wash, thought Fujita the believer. It shocked him, though, when Mari showed him another article, by the popular syndicated columnist Walter Lippmann, who was decidedly not a moron. Avoiding the whole issue of proven sabotage, Lippmann likened California to the deck of a battleship. "'Everyone should be compelled to prove they have a good reason for being there,'" Fujita read, suppressing his own impulse to say, "Ditto." They should administer IQ tests, he thought, still steamed by that fool greengrocer. They should pass the Boob Exclusion Act. Lippmann, whose power to convince and web of syndication were so vast, very reasonably argued that an evacuation from the Coast did not comprise an infringement of civil liberties since "under this system all persons are, in principle, treated alike." Unlike Mari, Fujita had faith in principles, too. "It's not just us, and it *is* war, after all," he said, to Mari's ritualistic and increasingly irritated, "Oh, Bill, oh, Bill."

Tony reacted in his own fearsomely youthful way to the war.

With his country mobilizing, squandering himself at geometry seemed more wasteful than ever, even treasonous. The day after the FBI snatched away his grandmother, Tony went to volunteer for the civil defense at Yoneko's request, then the couple moved on to offer assistance to the Pasadena police, which sent them home when they admitted their Japanese language skills were weak (in Tony's case) or nonexistent (in Yoneko's). No matter that the young lovers were never summoned to duty; the thrill of their personal war effort added extra fuel to their romance.

"Why, I thought . . ." stammered Tony's principal, when Fujita answered the phone call one February day. "That is, I thought you'd be gone by now. I meant to ask for your family's new address."

"Gone?" Fujita echoed, uncomprehending. Had Walter Lippmann triumphed, but not told William Fujita? After spending all day sitting by his silent cash register poring over the spreadsheets, he was feeling far too cranky for guessing games.

"We'll miss Tony around here. He's a live one—a real firestarter—but a solid student when he wants to be. If he put the screws on, I'll warrant he could win a scholarship to one of the state colleges." *Miss him?* thought Fujita. "He just needs to harness that energy," the principal said. "That nonsense with the smoking and the tardiness and brawling . . . he'll get it out of his system. Young men need to sow their wild oats sometime, and I suppose it's better to be done with it *before* college."

"Smoking? Tardiness?" asked Fujita, who had never significantly sown much of that sort of oat. "What brawling?"

"Why, that business I wrote to you about," the principal said. When Fujita remained silent, he added, "In my last progress report?" Apparently, Tony had skipped school for over a month; once caught, he told the school officials the family was preparing to relocate outside of California. Intuitively, Fujita sensed he should play along with the lie for now. He cautiously thanked the principal, asking him to send the final report card to the nursery.

"I thought you'd have your mail forwarded, but with times as they are . . ." The principal sounded positively chipper—that instinctual heartiness he assumed with parents at sporting events and PTA meetings. "It's a very dodgy business, this whole thing. Well, good luck and bon voyage." *Bon voyage!*

That night Fujita obsessively rehearsed what he'd say and do, stalking about the nursery, mining for traces of the Little Bull in himself. He heard the front gate swing open; by the time it clanked shut, he had drawn his belt from his trousers and planted himself at the store entrance. His expression must have been more severe than he thought, for when Mari entered, the doorbells jingling crazily behind her, she beheld him and screamed. He saw from her puffy face that she had been crying. Dropping the belt and going to her, he began softly, "We need to talk about Tony."

Violently waving him off, she told him the official news sent to the YWCA that night via the JACL. With Ivy League penmanship, the flowing signature of President Roosevelt on Executive Order 9066 made the rumors concrete, authorizing the forcible exclusion of anyone, anytime, anywhere, without hearing or trial.

"That doesn't mean anything," Fujita reassured her, not wholly convinced himself. Despite his business understanding, he never had a mind or interest for politics, and he found it hard to imagine that such broad, macrocosmic proclamations could trickle down into what he considered his unnoteworthy but secure little life. "It's just a *precaution*," he said.

"If that's not writing on the wall, I don't know what is," Mari Fujita replied, with much more conviction. "I love you, but brother, are you naive."

WESTERN DEFENSE COMMAND AND FOURTH ARMY
WARTIME CIVIL CONTROL ADMINISTRATION

Presidio of San Francisco, California

May 3, 1942

INSTRUCTIONS TO ALL PERSONS OF JAPANESE ANCESTRY

Living in the Following Area:

Pursuant to the provisions of Civilian Exclusion Order No. 33, this Headquarters, dated May 3, 1942, all persons of Japanese ancestry, both alien and non-alien, will be evacuated from the above area by 12 o'clock noon, P.W.T., Saturday, May 9, 1942.

No Japanese person living in the above area will be permitted to change residence after 12 o'clock noon, P.W.T., Sunday, May 3, 1942, without obtaining special permission from the representative of the Commanding General, Southern California Sector, at the Civil Control Station located at:

Japanese Union Church
Pasadena, California.

Such permits will only be granted for the purpose of uniting members of a family, or in cases of grave emergency.

The Civil Control Station is equipped to assist the Japanese population affected by this evacuation in the following ways:

1. Give advice and instructions on the evacuation.
2. Provide services with respect to the management, leasing, sale, storage or other disposition of most kinds of property, such as real estate, business and professional equipment, household goods, boats, automobiles and livestock.
3. Provide temporary residence elsewhere for all Japanese in family groups.
4. Transport persons and a limited amount of clothing and equipment to their new residence.

The Following Instructions Must Be Observed:

1. A responsible member of each family, preferably the head of the family, or the person in whose name most of the property is held, and each individual living alone, will report to the Civil Control Station to receive further instructions. This must be done between 8:00 A.M. and 5:00 P.M. on Tuesday, May 5, 1942.
2. Evacuees must carry with them on departure for the Assembly Center, the following property:
   A. Bedding and linens (no mattress) for each member of the family;
   B. Toilet articles for each member of the family;
   C. Extra clothing for each member of the family;
   D. Sufficient knives, forks, spoons, plates, bowls and cups for each member of the family;
   E. Essential personal effects for each member of the family.

All items carried will be securely packaged, tied and plainly marked with the name of the owner and numbered in accordance with instructions obtained at the Civil Control Station. The size and number of packages is limited to that which can be carried by the individual or family group.

3. No pets of any kind will be permitted.
4. No personal items and no household goods will be shipped to the Assembly Center.
5. The United States Government through its agencies will provide for the storage, at the sole risk of the owner, of the more substantial household items, such as iceboxes, washing machines, pianos and other heavy furniture. Cooking utensils and other small items will be accepted for storage if crated, packed and plainly marked with the name and address of the owner. Only one name and address will be used by a given family.
6. Each family, and individual living alone, will be furnished transportation to the Assembly Center or will be authorized to travel by private automobile in a supervised group. All instructions pertaining to the movement will be obtained at the Civil Control Station.

Go to the Civil Control Station between the hours of 8:00 A.M. and 5:00 P.M., Monday, May 4, 1942, or between the hours of 8:00 A.M. and 5:00 P.M., Tuesday, May 5, 1942, to receive further instructions.

J. L. DeWitt
Lieutenant General, U.S. Army
Commanding

SEE CIVILIAN EXCLUSION ORDER NO. 33.

Amidst a whirlwind of planning, packing, securing the house and nursery, Fujita chanced to look out the shop window one splendid spring afternoon. Normally, the sight of a man bearing a tool belt, a hammer and nails, warmed Fujita like a shot of sake, a living ode to progress through manual labor, of the kind Whitman celebrated. But in the armed, dour-faced soldier, he saw not the splendid father of fathers of sons celebrated in his favorite poem; when the man lustily drove the nail into the telephone post outside the nursery, Fujita did not marvel at the rapturous flexing of fabulous muscle. For an anxious moment, he thought he saw a coffin-maker at work.

They descended like carrion birds, like vultures and crows. They came to their Nikkei neighbors with pickup trucks and wheelbarrows—these were common. One drove an old ambulance; another brought an empty perambulator. That was Mrs. Toler, Fujita could see, as he drove by her block an eighth mile down Lincoln Avenue from the nursery. When he glimpsed her pushing the black-and-silver baby stroller like a shopping cart into the garage where the Yamamoto family had laid out their furnishings, he just had to brake, in the manner of one drawn to a roadside accident. Idling at the curb, he sighed with a guilty relief: *He* had someone to help ward off the scavengers. Or so he hoped—he had doubts about the potter, Harvey Clemens, who would lease and run the nursery in his absence.

On this warm, late-April day, the evacuation sale looked like any suburban garage sale—a spring-cleaning-before-the-kids'-summer-recess sort of sale. A narrow woman with round spectacles and a fragile demeanor, Mrs. Toler didn't work outside of the home, yet Fujita always associated her with dark libraries. What most distressed him about his regular customer was not so much how she seemed to coo at the booty piled in her pram—a stack of china, a set of water glasses, a hearth shelf radio, and a camera. Rather, as he watched the disconsolate Mrs. Yamamoto run weeping into the house, what struck him most forcefully was that Mrs. Toler had not bothered to remove her apron. Why this oddity so incensed him Fujita had no idea. But the thought of it. . . . Had she been at the sink washing the dishes and thought, *Oh, fudge! There's a chip in my great-grandmother's teacup?* Had she then decided to just nip across the street to the neighbors' house and plunder their possessions?

It was beyond all reason, and Fujita was a rational man. Pricked by the absurdity of it all, he allowed himself to be absurd, too. As Mrs. Toler reached the curb and gingerly lowered the front wheels of her baby carriage onto the road, he slammed the truck into gear. He did not stop to extract the metal and canvas roadkill from his grill until he reached home.

On the train to Tulare—the "assembly center" from which evacuees would be assigned to various internment camps—the Fujitas did not play their usual travel games; that first week of May made it crystal-clear what they would actually choose to take to their desert islands. The Army had handed down instructions to bring only those goods listed on the posted evacuation order and what few personal items they could carry. Mari could not part with her mother's ceremonial tea set; she brought her wedding gown, a King James Bible with magnifying glass, and a collection of romance stories. Fujita had packed copies of all his business documents and the lease leaving his nursery to the care of Harvey Clemens; the Tokyo mayor's scroll; and the set of waka poem cards he had studied and loved as a child. He also took his father's seventeen-jewel Royal pocket watch—still broken, but what use in knowing the time when you have nowhere to go? True to his word, Tony stashed a two-pound bologna in his trunk along with two hidden cartons of cigarettes, a set of comic books, his first-baseman's mitt, and a regulation baseball.

The teary-eyed Clemens drove them to the Union Station in the newly renamed Clemens Nursery truck and blushed when Mari hugged him. Fujita noted that his wife was in a hugging mood; she administered hugs to people who needed it—to crying girls, children lost in the throng, lonely old people, white women from the Federated Missions. She hugged the Reverend Mr. Tajima, who had arranged to send his family to Ohio but lingered to see the very last of his flock off on their journey. Despairing that she meant to hug every single soul at the station, Fujita, who was unfortunately in a yelling mood, barked for his family to "keep up! Let's go!" It would be easy to lose one another. "So many people," Fujita murmured. Immediately, he thought of a dozen more efficient methods the Army might use to channel the traffic. But the depot swelled and shifted like an uneasy sea, all aswirl with bodies and voices, prayers and spat epithets. And last-minute sidewalk sales: A graying Issei man had managed to drag a fat, white refrigerator with him. In broken English, he was haggling with a bald hakujin in an apron, a local restaurateur, perhaps, who stuck firmly to his offer of ten dollars. Somewhere, a dog yelped.

As they were funneled between columns of rifles fixed with bayonets, he felt himself and the station growing smaller, like the shrinking Alice in Wonderland. Ahead of him, one short, uniformed figure stood strangely out among the press of bodies. The man pivoted sharply to face one of the stony sentries, and Fujita felt a momentary wave of betrayal to see a Nikkei in U.S. officer's colors. This in itself didn't account for the strangeness Fujita sensed. No, the colors of his coat were off, different from the other surrounding uniforms. That still wasn't it, though. Inching forward, he saw that the man was at least fifty. An Issei, *and* paraplegic, the sleeve of his officer's coat folded up at the elbow, its cuff pinned neatly in his armpit. Standing rigidly as, well, an army officer, the Issei engaged the younger soldier in a stare-down.

In the crowd, no one moved; indeed, no one could move. Something about such sentries, anywhere in the world, makes one need to taunt them, to force any human response. This impulse belongs primarily to civilians, though. Not veterans, thought Fujita, finally realizing how uniforms had changed between the world wars. Not men like the Issei, who held ground before the tunnel of M.P.'s, compact and stout and scarred as a pit bull terrier. Not taunting, but he did mean to force a response. When finally one junior officer raised an uncertain salute, the Issei dropped the duffel from his one intact hand, returned the greeting primly, then moved on. It gratified Fujita to perceive how the M.P.'s slackened, how they strained to find one another with sideways glances full of question. At that moment, the also stiff Fujita felt himself entering a battle, too, a battle against bitterness that would last the rest of his life and that began with an assault of hands: from behind, lifting his hat, brushing his hips, reaching between his legs, patting his hot armpits.

A regular uniformed cop with a leather bandolier finished frisking him, then turned to Mari. "Hey! Now wait a . . ." In a rush of possessiveness, Fujita interposed himself between the cop and his wife but was yanked away by anonymous claws. *Move along, guy!* His baggage was wrested from him, flopped on a table, wrenched open, dug through. He had packed so neatly, so tightly, and now he couldn't get it closed again. *You're gumming up the works, fella.* Yoneko and Aunt Rose, who were left alone when the girl's parents were taken into Justice Department custody, had to sit on the case while he and Tony struggled with the latches. *Move it along. Christ, are you people stupid.* Numbered tags were affixed to their lapels, similar to those he used to price plants at the nursery, and they were swept on again until the ever-tapering press of soldiers became corked by Yoneko's frightened aunt. For such a tiny woman, Rose presented a resolutely impassable barrier, inspiring a stream of mild oaths from all directions.

"Auntie, they won't hurt you," Yoneko said, sounding to Fujita surprisingly grown-up. "They're here to *protect* us. See? Like Buckingham Palace. Just walk right through, like this." She shoehorned her way past, and with her chin thrust high, she strode down the tunnel of armed boys as grandly as a princess through a procession of court guards. As if she did not notice that the protective bayonets were pointed inward at her. Fujita shook his head, but it convinced Aunt Rose to shuffle onward. Whatever else Fujita thought of the girl, he'd always said she was a darned good actress.

"What the hell is that?" said a voice behind Fujita. "Looks like a piece of a bomb." The official who had mangled his luggage was examining a mechanical device the size of a cigarette case, a white dial on its metal front. On the inspection table sat a gaping suitcase, a white shirt lolling to one side like the tongue of a giant clam. It belonged to the haggling Issei, who had apparently managed to pawn off his icebox—for ten dollars, Fujita felt certain, seeing the man's satisfied grin as the inspector pondered over the thermostat. At last they'd caught a subversive.

Onboard the train, the initial cacophony quickly exhausted itself as the evacuees' panic gave way to both boredom and a low, humming dread. Two seats behind the Fujitas, however, Yoneko and Aunt Rose chattered the entire way. "Well, it'll be something new," Yoneko said. "It's much better to think of it as a road trip, like a vacation." Unsure of their destination, both Yamaguchis had dressed up as if going out for a day at the fair.

"It's been so long since I've had a vacation," Aunt Rose said cautiously.

"Lord, the whole family's stupid," Mari hissed to her husband, who squeezed her hand reassuringly. The soldiers had drawn every window shade at the journey's outset, and Mari, ailing from claustrophobia, buzzed beside him like a beehive. She clamped her eyes shut and pressed her head back against the seat, as if she sat in a roller-coaster awaiting its initial plummet.

Yoneko had defied the Army's advice and brought considerably more than she could carry. Among the effects that Tony hauled for her was a packet of dramas and music scores, and makeup and sewing kits. She told Aunt Rose she might establish a youth drama club.

"Oh, I'm sure we won't be away that long," Aunt Rose said. "But you could play the flute, and we could have sing-alongs."

"If they start singing now," whispered Mari, "that old bat will get a flute right up her nose!" When the soldiers crowded in the aisle to distribute boxed lunches, Mari squirmed so violently that Fujita had to restrain her from bolting.

"Oh! Lunch!" Yoneko sang. "I'm famished!"

"I can't breathe!" Mari gasped, massaging her chest, and to her worried husband it seemed that she *didn't* breathe until the journey's end, when the window shades were raised. Then it was Fujita who stopped breathing. In time, he might understand and possibly forgive the Army, the governor, the War Relocation Authority, and President Roosevelt. What he could not forgive and would never forget, not ever, were the new neighbors he saw in that first sun-bleached glimpse. What sort of reception did he expect? What sort of town would agree to host The Enemy?

Beverly Hills certainly would never have them, he thought, as the train finally chugged over the last hill before the converted Tulare Fairgrounds and Racetrack. Of course it wouldn't be the Rose Bowl. Only a lowbrow, low-rent, low-tax town, Fujita knew. A low-everything town with no options but lots of guns. It felt as if the train had dragged them back into the nineteenth century, smack in the middle of the hillbilly feud between the Hatfields and McCoys. On run-down stoops to either side, whole families, and rather large ones, gathered with pitchers of lemonade and fully loaded twenty-twos across their knees, as if waiting for the Independence Day Parade to pass by.

"*Ultrapatriots*," Fujita would sneer derisively, whenever, over the course of his entire life, he would feel bold or secure enough to summon up his rage and recall the armed yokels he saw that day. As in: "Who the hell do they think they are, *guarding* us? We're locked up surrounded by soldiers with machine guns, and these Yahoo vigilantes, these ultrapatriots with their twenty-twos are going to catch us running away? Who's going to outrun machine guns? The stupid, whiiiii . . ." Groping to put his visceral fury into words, he would find himself always stopping just short of completing the epithet he'd heard but never used before that first Tulare day, when his spite needed to find the correlating term for Jap slant-cunt, for greaseball nigger kike. He meant "white trash," though with more clarity he'd suppose that this particular trash's "whiteness" was incidental, and that the term didn't nearly convey the exact swamp-bottom quality he divined in the stoop-watchers. That moment in Tulare would come to symbolize the whole war for him, as syphilis first reveals itself in a small chancre. As if, inexperienced in hate, unsure what to do with it, the Nisei had poured everything into the first tangible receptacle he could find. The ultrapatriots.

At Tulare, with the wind knocked out of him by the powerful new emotion, Fujita needed Yoneko to restore him. As they disembarked and approached their new home, the girl positively bubbled. "Look at that, Auntie!" she cried. "A fairgrounds!" Only when they had shuffled in through the gates, beneath the grandstands, across the track, into the center of the field stuffed with earlier arrivals did she seem to realize that they were all to be locked away. The grandstands were full of sallow faces, and a chorus of young boys hooted at the new arrivals, "You'd better go back where you came from! You won't like it here!"

They were given their luggage and herded immediately into a low-set building, wooden with a corrugated tin roof. Corralled into a long hallway, they waited until assigned their new "apartments" and given their "beds," the large sacks they were to stuff with straw. The Fujitas' quarters were filled still with the odor of the previous inhabitants—perhaps some of the same thoroughbreds whose winning tickets had allowed Ichiro Fujita to purchase the nursery for his son. "How nice," Fujita grumbled. "A manger scene." Stumbling with Aunt Rose into the stall beside the Fujitas', Yoneko began to weep.

"Hah!" Mari whispered bitterly. "That should finally shut her up."

Their weeks in the Tulare "temporary assembly center" turned into months, and they had *almost* managed to rid their little stable space of the horse-piss smell when word came down they would be moved again to a concentration camp farther inland, to Arizona. That was John Wayne territory. That was more "West" than the West Coast. To the Fujitas and Yamaguchis, the name, Rivers, Arizona, was unknown, but it sounded wet, thus promising, until acquaintances on the advanced building crews mailed back warnings. The new site was named Rivers not for the Gila River, a meager artery insufficient to irrigate the vast no-man's land in the Casa Grande Valley; nor for the parched Salt River, which more often than not was indistinguishable from any other clayey depression in the desert floor—better for catching rodents and serpents than fish. "'Here in the Big House, there are rattlesnakes,'" Fujita read aloud to his family, "'and scorpions—some spiders—so write to your friends back home and ask them to send bug spray. Tons of the stuff. Have them send a fan, too. Almanac's predicting the hottest summer in fifty years.'"

"It can't be any hotter than here," Tony said.

"Spiders?" said Yoneko. "Rattlesnakes?"

The site in fact received its name from Jim Rivers, the first

Pima Indian killed in action in the war to end all wars—since 1939 known as World War I. The two camps comprising Gila River, Canal and Butte, sat tucked in a tiny corner of a reservation apportioned to the Pima, who would doubtlessly have preferred that an instantaneous metropolis *not* be plopped on their shrinking home. Yet the natives had more experience in evacuation and relocation than the Japanese and their descendants, and the tribal leaders understood that the memorandum authorizing the War Relocation Authority to use their lands was not a request. Relative newcomers to the area themselves, the Pima were accustomed to sharing the neighborhood with phantoms. Before them; before the Japanese Americans; before the U.S. government, the white settlers on horseback, and even before *horses*, an anonymous civilization carved from the valley a city whose exact nature still eluded desert visitors. Multistory apartment buildings of cool brown clay, or some vein of an ancient canal system, still arose from the fiery earth, then melted again under storms of dust, more worthy of the name Phoenix than the modern sprawl forty miles north. Hohokam, the Pima called those early architects, that lost people more easily erased from history than its monuments. Apparently, no one knew for certain what became of the Hohokam. How could entire peoples just disappear, utterly forgotten, without explanation or trace? For the Pima, such questions could and must be lived with, so perhaps that community was better prepared than most when government contractors rolled over their alfalfa crops and planted yet another phantom population, another city. Rivers would soon swell to become Arizona's fourth-largest city, its population falling slightly short of the Poston camp farther north. And in the blink of the desert's eye, the rocks would swallow them again.

At least the desert colony did provide more space than a horse track. Months living next to the Yamaguchis had driven Mari and Fujita to their wits' ends, and they happily anticipated being rid of them. In addition, because the Pasadenans had been the last to arrive at Tulare, the temporary employment office had already meted out the good jobs. Fujita did not know how arable Gila River would be, but wouldn't anything be better than the clerkship he'd been assigned at Tulare? Only Aunt Rose wept when she heard that she would be moved again; she'd grown accustomed to her stable.

"Come now, Auntie," Yoneko said gamely. "Just think how fun it will be to go out there, all that unspoiled landscape. You'll get to see the Grand Canyon and everything!"

Aunt Rose, whose knowledge of American geography was minimal, nodded helplessly. Actually, they drove nowhere near the Grand Canyon. Their roundabout path (the driver headed south to avoid having to navigate Death Valley) did convey them past such graceless towns as Delano, Lost Hills, Idyllwild, Cathedral City, and Mecca, but unfortunately for poor Aunt Rose, these again remained shrouded by window shades. The only view permitted the prisoners was a bump of a town called Felicity on the California side of the Colorado River, where the bus made a rest stop.

"The only thing felicitous about this town is its toilets," mumbled Fujita, whose bladder and bowels had vied for his attention ever since leaving Tulare. Once emptied, he reboarded and relaxed enough to nap as the bus rattled on past Yuma and Mohawk. Mari poked him awake a few hours later, and still groggy, he joined the passengers filing off the bus one by one. Disembarking pained him; after the darkened journey, the daylight glare hurt, and he shielded his eyes. This August sun, like everything in the Southwest, was bigger than elsewhere; it was a ten-gallon sun, a Texas-sized sun, with no merciful thing to impede it as the newest of Rivers' twelve thousand boarders settled into their new homes.

SEVEN

Juggeston Comes for Christmas

As the holidays of December 1944 approached, the outlook on Widow's Peak worsened, as feared, expected, demanded. The weather slid into a pattern of snow, rain, sleet, then snow, rain, sleet again. Mr. Fujita locked himself away in the greenhouse more frequently, where Margaret could sometimes see him frozen at the window, alternately depressed and amazed by the relentless white tumbling from the sky. At night he stalked restlessly about fixing things or else hid in his room vigorously hammering something—he wouldn't say what. Like a relay runner awaiting a baton, he stationed himself at the mailbox every day, dancing from one foot to the other and shivering, watching for the postman. While she could only intuit what anxieties dogged him, Margaret expected that these forlorn holidays would hit him the hardest.

Rolling in like a glacier from Pasadena, Herbert and Madeline Nicholson's Season's Greetings card bore postscript tidings neither comforting nor joyous. When Fujita wordlessly handed it to Margaret, she knew enough to understand its portent. "Harvey Clemens seems to have vanished(?). We'll try to find out more. Please, please don't lose faith, Bill," they urged. The nurseryman's faith in his proxy at the *Clemens* Nursery had evaporated long ago. Then, in the brown envelope from an anonymous Connecticut P.O., came a goodwill packet from the girl named Yoneko. "God rest ye merry Mr. F., and ho ho ho. Well, me and Auntie appreciate all the presents, and there's nothing wrong with a little bribery now and then, but you're really overdoing it. I'm sort of strapped myself these days, but here's a little something for you." Drawing out the photo, Mr. Fujita gave a strangled, animal cry. He didn't even seem to notice or care that Margaret hovered breathlessly over his shoulder. She resisted reaching out to the shaking widower—she was learning.

"I'll leave you alone," she whispered. Turning away, she was astonished to feel his grip close on her elbow.

"I'm all right," he said, not sounding all right at all. "I'd like you to see . . ." He pointed. "That's us. My family." Allowing herself only the briefest glance, Margaret saw a desert, a shack, a cactus, a star, the nurseryman, the pretty, small-boned Mari Fujita, and the shirtless, mugging teenager, Tony. Silly as it was, it shocked her how *Japanese* they appeared, those figures she'd only imagined before, now brutally made flesh. Firmly believing that friendship *should* be color-blind, Margaret realized then how familiarity had rather blurred Fujita to her. She had come to appreciate his individual qualities and contours as something like endearing, off-white quirks—and she had viewed her attitude as sound and just. Yet, this clan frozen in the camera's eye reminded her of what she'd either conveniently or generously forgotten. For all her probing after the details of his life, she now shied away. Reluctantly, she followed his pointing finger near the photo's margin, where the curvaceous outline of a woman had been scissored out. Running his finger along the rough edges, he said, "And that's Yoneko."

After the photo, the disconcerted Margaret thanked every last god for Tamie Fujita. Wielding a mother's magic, Tamie saved the day with a perfectly timed and appropriately inappropriate note of holiday cheer that so aggravated the widower, he risked Margaret's "Thirty-six percent!" to show it to her. Mrs. Fujita wrote that she had learned to sing "Silent Night" in German from a fellow inmate. "It's called *Stille Nacht*," she wrote, "but you sing it the same. (Wake up, censors! Get out your phrasebooks!) Today is December 8. That means I was arrested three years ago. Fancy that." She signed it, "The Emperor's Niece."

"Goodness," Margaret laughed, trying to lighten his mood. "She sounds happy about it." How Margaret liked Mrs. Fujita without even knowing her!

"My mother's lost her marbles," muttered Fujita. "It runs in the family."

Through her Medical Corps volunteering, Margaret had learned of a tiny, understaffed private hospital on the North Shore, and she called to offer her services. She could get out of Mr. Fujita's hair and also put her nursing skills to use. Depressed as the residents of Widow's Peak felt this holiday season, she could only imagine how low the patients might be.

Beginning with her usual gusto, she just took a bus out to the shore and sniffed about the hospital until she'd located the chief surgeon. An imperious, loud-voiced man whose desktop was decorated with preserved organs, Dr. Masters stated flat out that he was running behind and had less than no time to spare for an interview. To Margaret, he didn't seem busy at all, sunk back in his plush leather chair, his feet flopped up on the desk blotter. Jingling his pocket change, the surgeon eyed her coldly, top to toe, in a blink. In the slant of his pure white eyebrows, so bushy they could make Groucho Marx blush, she immediately read his clinical analysis of her. The symptoms: mink stole, heeled shoes, neatly colored fingernails. The diagnosis: a rich housewife with a guilty conscience and some free time before the kids' holiday from boarding school. In Dr. Masters's business, the ability to make quick assessments and snap decisions was imperative, Nurse Kelly knew. She also knew that haste often led to improper prognoses. She gripped her handbag and waited.

"Well, yes, what would you like, missus?" he asked curtly. "No, don't tell me—"

"I'm a nurse," Margaret interrupted, unperturbed. "I *was* a nurse. I'd like to help in whatever duties the hospital administration can assign me."

Sighing, Masters put his feet down and leaned over his desk.

Deep dark grooves ringed his eyes, and his jaw bristled with gray stubble. Although he admitted he needed nurses, needed hands in general, and needed women on those wards full of soldiers, Dr. Masters's eternal problem—like Mr. Fujita's—was time. "No offense, missus, but nurse or not, the holidays plus a mink stole usually equals valuable hours of training for one day's labors, after which a lady's so upset I have to console her for another fifteen minutes before she quits the same afternoon. Get it?" He picked up a specimen jar, a marble-sized tumor suspended in the fluid, and swished it around as if it were a martini. "I don't suppose you have military experience?"

"Certainly not," Margaret said, but she understood him. Throughout that December, the Battle of the Bulge had stuffed the Eastern Seaboard hospitals to capacity with those young Americans who'd made it home for the holidays. They often came to the North Shore having been bumped from hospitals in Boston and Providence, and some came from places as far away as Connecticut and New York. They began their journeys much farther away, from places such as Belgium, Germany, and France, places that seemed as distant from Juggeston as Oz.

"Well, it gets rough around here, missus," Dr. Masters said. "There's work here; we have bodies and bodies coming through. Especially at Christmas. Soldiers get careless around the holidays; they start thinking of home instead of where they are. There's work if you can stick with it. There's no goddamned jollity around here, I assure you."

His brusque manner reaffirmed Margaret's belief that Mr. Fujita certainly had what it took be a surgeon, in temperament as well as manual dexterity. The doctor and nurseryman would like each other, she imagined. Neither looked women in the face, and neither could see her earnestness. Fujita had exhibited surprise when she'd told him she wanted to volunteer to help the war casualties. He said she was brave.

"Oh, I'm not squeamish," she had said. "I've changed bedpans in my time, drawn blood, given enemas, and irrigated abscesses. I can work in the kitchen, too, if they like. You'd have to get up pretty early in the morning to dream up something I wouldn't do. I just want to help."

Nonchalantly lifting a jarred, preserved heart as if returning his toast, that's exactly what she repeated to Dr. Masters.

She went to work. As the chief surgeon had predicted, being a nurse for a country GP was no preparation for his hospital. She would recognize some wounds and often feel she recognized some of the boys. Broken bones were common enough when Jack had been physician to the high school sports teams; so too were occasional gangrenous infections when, say, a local boy might catch his toes in the blades while mowing a lawn. But Dr. Masters explained to her that medicine, like every other industry, had considerably modernized during the war.

"I don't imagine that many Massachusetts farmers use napalm-jellied gasoline on their cabbage patches," said Dr. Masters. "I don't suppose they dust their crops with white phosphorous."

During her tenure at the hospital, Margaret encountered many ailments unknown to Juggeston, though sometimes it was difficult to tell what ailed a patient—she couldn't *see* them. Apparently, the field doctors in Belgium, Germany, and France were unable or unequipped to practice the new modern medicine. Many casualties arrived at the North Shore looking like half-finished statues; lacking time or resources, field medics often resorted to enclosing the boys in full-body casts.

"They look mummified," she told Mr. Fujita. "I'll stick it out at the hospital, but it sure can crush you sometimes."

As she talked of the wounded soldiers, his wide face whitened and his eyes glazed over—thinking of Tony, she was sure. "Yes, you are a generous woman," he said, and it was curt enough that she knew she could not follow him into that photograph he inhabited with his lost family.

In that off-season, the greenhouse had become Fujita's place. Garvin helped him out sometimes, but he was mostly busy preparing for some holiday art fair coming up at school. Livvie was kept in relative isolation, seamstressing double-time, mending Juggeston's holiday finery. Sometimes they all dined together and discussed how their days had passed, but conversation grew ever more sparse. Livvie drank more, Mr. Fujita fidgeted more, Garvin moped or sometimes sat apart to draw. Little good news passed among them. Fujita confided that his queries, entreaties, and threats to the man running his nursery continued to go unanswered, though he pointed out that the place always got very busy around Christmas—he *hoped* to hear from Clemens after the New Year, once his caretaker's workload lessened.

Nurse Kelly kept uncharacteristically quiet those nights. The things that occupied her days in the hospital began to wear on her, but she guessed these were best omitted from dinner conversation. Then one night she came home especially distraught, knowing that the day's events at the hospital demanded she speak with Fujita but edgy about approaching him. She changed twice before dinner, first splattering her front with cooking oil, then dropping a full gravy ladle on her shoes. She became snappish with Mr. Fujita: "Stop *fixing* things! It's time to eat!" At table, she compulsively wiped her silverware with a napkin during the meal, which she barely tasted. Afterward, they settled into the living room around the radio as had become their custom, but ignoring her dessert, Margaret merely sank into the couch, massaging her temples and jaw. Between war reports from Europe, the station mercilessly replayed "I'll Be Home for Christmas." Finally, she rose from the sofa and switched the radio off.

"Mugsie," Garvin called, his voice floating up from behind the couch, where he lay hidden on the floor, drawing. "The news is coming on again soon."

"And Walter Winchell," Fujita said.

"Oh, I know plenty about Belgium," she said gravely. "I see its sickening details every day." Intuition told her she should not bring this up; she just had to. "The news tells you how many miles this way or that way we've moved or the enemy's moved," she said bitterly, "but they don't tell you what it looks like, really. Shells, they say, tracers. It looks like fireworks, they say." She told them how the field doctors encased the casualties in plaster casts when there was no time for surgery. Then, pouring brandy, she told them of the boy she had befriended that morning. One of the body-cast boys.

"He looks an awful lot like your Tony," she said carefully, eyeing Fujita, who hardly blinked. "In that picture from a few

Christmases ago. He's Nisei. He was impressed I knew that word, so he chatted me up." Fujita took a drink and mustered a little smile for her, perhaps amused that the one Japanese word spoken in the house in months should come from Margaret's mouth. She pressed on.

"He had an angel's face—an angel's: scarred, but round, hairless, shining. You don't bother asking the boys how they feel, but I asked if I could do anything for him. He was cocooned in this cast, and chafing around the collar, so I had to scratch his neck for him. He's from San Francisco, and he'd enlisted a year before Pearl Harbor. His name is Bob Ito."

She paused and looked at Fujita as if expecting some sign of recognition. He shifted in his seat, but his wide face remained unreadable. "It's a very common name," he said.

Margaret nodded. "Well, I saw they were going to cut off both arms above the elbow because there were ink marks scratched into the plaster. You learn to smile, too, no matter what. He was so relieved to be scratched, he kept me with him for a half hour, almost chirpy, talking about growing up, his girlfriend, how he hadn't seen his parents since 1940 because he hadn't been allowed back in camp. They don't even know what happened to him yet. I kept thinking of you," she said quietly. She could have stopped then, left them all wondering. Certainly, she didn't want to pain anybody. Yet Fujita, for whom the tale came closest to home, never frowned, wept, or said, "Shut up, Margaret"—nothing. And it bothered her fiercely. She feared for him. "Well, he told me that at first he hated the Army because after Pearl Harbor they assigned him to KP detail, but he had trained as a paratrooper, so they finally called him to Europe. You know what he said? He called it his 'big break.' He was thrilled because a paratrooper makes higher pay than KP, and the guys were better to him—you know, because they depend on each other—and he used to joke around with them, talking some Japanese and pretending to be an enemy soldier stabbing himself. Is this funny? Mostly, he loved to jump, and he told me how the parachutes gave a great jolt when they opened, and that there were four cords, one at every corner, to steer with. I could tell he was aching to act it out for me, but he couldn't move. A reserve chute is attached to the chest in case the main chute fails. Safest thing in the world, he said, when you do it right. At a height of six hundred feet, you're only in the air for about ten seconds, he told me. That fast, you have to look up when you jump, because if you look down, chances are you'll fall headfirst and get tangled in your chute.

"Later, Dr. Masters came in and told me Ito hadn't spoken a word since he arrived. But he sure talked to me. Then he clammed up and his face went red. He apologized and said his bowels had moved a while ago, but he didn't want to say anything. I called some orderlies to lift him up. When they raised him off the bed, I saw his back and shoulders were covered with pen markings. They all showed where bullets or flak had entered him, but they hadn't taken them out yet—no time. They just sent him home for the doctors to care for him here. I counted them. There were seven."

She paused to gulp at her drink as though parched. Across from her, Livvie scowled, and Mr. Fujita made a good effort to turn to marble. It was then Margaret noticed Garvin, leaning over the couch back behind her, pencil in hand, wide-eyed and breathless. They'd all forgotten he was there. She dropped her head and muzzled herself, until the boy whispered with intense urgency, "Go on."

In a way, she thought the story's moral particularly apt for Garvin, but she looked to his mother. Livvie's face was strained in concentration, but slowly, she nodded her assent. Rubbing her temples again, Margaret went on. "He was yelling and yelling then, and they sedated him just to change the bag, and he was crying, and just before he turned hazy-eyed, he waved at me. He said, 'Mom.' And it's not so unusual or anything. There are lots and lots like him. So many."

Stopping herself, she reached back to pat Garvin's hand—to reassure him, but also because she couldn't pat Fujita's. "I'm a little emotional tonight." To Fujita, she said, "But there *is* a point to this. See, I told him about you, and I thought it would do him a world of good . . . that is, I hoped . . ." Slapping herself on the knee, she made a final push. "Oh, I'll just say it: Won't you come visit him?"

"Me?" Fujita asked, his wide face stretching in honest shock. He shook his head.

"I think he just wants to see—" she began.

"Margaret, really!" Livvie interjected, throwing a sympathetic glance at Fujita. "See *what?* One of his own kind? What are you saying?"

"Heavens no!" the nurse protested, cringing. "It's just that maybe you know some of the same people? Have a connection, things in common. I mean, I know it would be hard for you, but won't it be good for you to talk—"

"No!" Fujita blurted. His jaws clenched so tightly they quivered. Standing, he turned away to the fireplace.

"Well, why *not?*" Also rising, she matched his pitch and tone.

"This is really getting out of line," Livvie said. "Leave him alone. Just stop now."

"Well, why not? I don't get it. I mean, he's been where you come from. I was talking to him, and I kept thinking about you: He never says anything! How can he just say nothing? You don't talk to us or anybody that I see." She splashed her drink on her skirt. "When he was calling for his mother. God. I don't think she's going to see him again. If I was a parent. . . . All right: I'm *not* a parent; I've never been one; I've *had* two parents, though, I loved two. Oh, you have to see him."

Shaking his head, Fujita channeled his distress into stoking the fire. Again, running interference for him, Livvie demanded, "Why? This soldier is supposed to be what, a *replacement*? It doesn't work that way," she said with undeniable authority.

"'Why?' Because it would help him," Margaret said to the stiff man's back. "Don't you feel a duty?"

"A *duty*," Fujita echoed, vengefully stabbing at the logs. "I have nothing in common with this boy. I don't *know* him. Sure, I feel bad for him; he's had a tough time, but I don't see—"

"Well, so have *you,*" Margaret said, almost accusingly. "Maybe it would help you."

At a loss, Fujita turned, shrugged. "Oh, I don't know," he said, with elaborate evenness. "Some people have it a lot worse. I don't complain."

"That's exactly my point: You never complain. You must be

wretched, yet you don't ask for anything. I mean, what about your mother? I can help her, call people, call my lawyer, help with legal fees . . ."

"She doesn't actually *want* to come out," Fujita replied, embarrassed.

"Oh, come now. What if I—"

"I think that's enough," Livvie said, tipsy but the only one clearheaded enough to see how haunted Mr. Fujita looked, and how Garvin seemed to find this as frightening as Bob Ito. "Dying soldiers!" Margaret might as well have disinterred their respective dead and strung them from the ceiling as decorations.

"I know I shouldn't talk, but I seem to be the only one who *does*. I want to help," Margaret said miserably, hanging her head. "I mean, I don't . . . I don't understand."

Apparently, neither of them understood. Across the room, the father of the slain soldier Tony Fujita replaced the poker and shook his head. For once, he wasn't polite. "Margaret," he said, "I am deeply indebted to you, and I'm devoted to working here and repaying your kindness, but I'm not comfortable talking about these things. I don't like talking about myself, and anyway, there is really nothing nothing nothing to say."

"Except, 'We'll be going now,'" added Livvie. "Come on, honey." Garvin sprang up to fetch their coats while the adults simmered.

"I know what the problem is," Margaret whispered after a cold silence. "It's language. I don't know about others, but the Englishman and the American have no verb for an active *peace*. Do the Japanese?"

"What a Margaret sort of thing to say!" Livvie muttered. She had to laugh. It eased them all.

Fujita steadied his breathing and sighed. "I don't know. But how about *pacify*? *Appease?*"

Margaret shook her head toward the radio. "You may hear Lowell Thomas say, 'The warring nations of China and Japan,' but never, 'The peacing nations of, oh, Australia and New Zealand.'" Livvie raised her eyebrows questioningly. "Wherever. My point is: Warrior, pacifier—no 'peacifer.'"

"Pacification," Fujita tried. "Pacifisting."

"No, that's being pacifist, not *waging peace*," Margaret said. Fujita shrugged, stumped. Just before they all separated for the night, she waved a finger at them and pronounced seriously, "That's the problem."

Now Fujita had *three* ghosts. More, even. Locked away in the late Jack Kelly's office with his faithful, all-bones companion hanging by the stairwell, he added Bob Ito to his brooding—envisioning the white plaster cocoon riddled with particolored ink marks. What a Margaret sort of *conversation* that was, he thought. The good nurse. But how irritating the best nurse can be, plying her trade—that angel of the bedpan, that saint of the painful injection, that nightingale with the rectal thermometer. *Does it hurt when I touch there?* That bared nerve, that tender vein. Margaret's diagnosing had nearly unraveled him. To her, there was nothing that a sensible woman couldn't diagnose and treat by talking—pain, worry, hate, anything. The world waited to be helped and healed; Nurse Kelly believed it could be.

He also pondered the Nikkei he had seen at Quincy Market, and how he had wanted to say, Hey, how are you? Where were you these past years? What have you seen, and how did you come here? But they had repelled each other like charged clouds—what turbulent fury might their meeting have sparked?—just as he had felt repulsed by the idea of merely talking to the broken-bodied Bob Ito. Why did the notion seem so preposterous to him, so impossible? Why did it make him feel as brittle as that stupid skeleton? But that's how it is in men, in Japanese-American men. No, he corrected himself, that's how it is in me. Mulling over Margaret's request, Fujita felt as shamed as a patient who has lied about a severe sickness for fear of the treatment.

"What's the hell's wrong with me?" he wondered aloud to the skeleton. It required greater intelligence and eloquence than Fujita felt he possessed to articulate why, but he thought he knew what it felt like to be one of the body-cast boys.

Bob Ito lingered with Livvie, too, as she kicked off her snow boots, scraped the muddy soles on the mat, dumped them into the chest by the door—all the while wondering how to exorcise him. Tucking Garvin in, she told him a bit more about Sig's final illness. "It's sort of like when you get the flu," she said. She'd previously withheld the details of malaria—it was an uncomfortable death, for sure, but was it anything compared to hole-ridden statue the boy would dream about that night? "That's not that way Pop died, honey," she said, and searched his face intently for a sign of understanding.

After a thoughtful pause, Garvin only said, "Okay." And he closed his eyes.

After kissing him, Livvie made a beeline for the kitchen. Her hip rammed into a wooden something as she groped for the light above the table; the pull string tangled, then snapped in her fingers. Hissing, she fumbled in the dark to the counter, palmed the glass cabinet doors above, located the smooth, swollen bottle. The refrigerator light helped her find milk and a tin saucepan, but she shut the door again to nestle in a more pleasing darkness. Gingerly fingering the knobs of the stove and the cool ceramic beneath, she imagined this was how blind people lived—sharp sounds, the hollow bang of tin on iron, the suck and pop of the cork, the lush splash of the brandy and one more for good luck, the gurgle of the milk, the hiss and poof as the gas burner ignited. By the time she finished a cigarette, a skin had congealed over the potion; she skimmed the top, stirred in a teaspoon of honey, and left the dishes for morning. Cupping the warm mug in both hands, she felt out each step with her toes as she climbed the stairs. They creaked louder in the dark, as did the floorboards leading into her bedroom.

Usually, she washed her face, sat at the rolltop, and read bills or letters as she drank her soporific, then tried to go to sleep. This night, however, she slumped onto her bed and downed the warm liquid, listening to the winter creak of the house. Hypnotized by that sound, she felt herself dozing off and barely avoided spilling her drink. The room was too hot, so she tried to lower the heat, but the radiator knob was stuck in place. She crossed to the window, parted the curtains, and tried to raise the pane—also stuck. Outside, the fat moon glowed nearly like daylight.

Releasing her hair from the constricting comb she'd worn all day, she walked to the bathroom. To soothe her exasperation with Margaret, she let herself indulge in the sort of pampering that had long ago come to seem pointless. She washed her face and hands, then massaged night lotions into her skin. After brushing her teeth, she removed her wedding band and set it safely away from the drain, then undressed and filled the basin with warm water. The muddy streaks on her work trousers required thorough soaping and a night's soak. When she withdrew her hands from the suds, she noticed a pale, puffy ring of skin encircling her fourth finger. She peeled off the thick, itchy socks and her shirt, tossed them into the hamper, and was about to grab a robe from the hook on the door when she noticed herself, clad only in her undergarments, in the mirror. It struck her that her work attire that day had almost entirely been Sig's. She chuckled. "Well, now, Livvie Tufteller," she said to her reflection, and she took a brush to her hair, "nice to see you. How have you been?"

Alone, was the answer that sounded in the creaking rafters. Frustrated, worried, bothered, fearful, alone.

As sewing orders poured in, she had less and less free time to participate in the farming activities. Margaret and Fujita, in their shared proximity, seemed to grow increasingly close, or close enough that the presumptuous Nurse Kelly felt free to step up her intimate needling, her meddlesome do-gooding, her callous healing. Livvie worried about—and frankly resented—Garvin's apparent attachment to the man. With all the hush-hush business of the mystery girl, his mother in jail, his own nursery slipping away, Mr. Fujita was bound to wander off again soon. It might hurt the boy. "I'm jealous," she admitted to the mirror. But more, she feared how his *presence* hurt Garvin. Spending so much time hanging around in the greenhouse, Garvin hardly ever played with classmates anymore. When he'd finally confided to her his suspicion that "lovey-dovey" was afoot on the hill, that he'd heard many rumors at school, she'd been overcome by the same sensation she had just before hunting down Frank Childs to sprain his finger. She'd repeated the same instructions to Garvin—ignore gossips, count to ten, and so on. Mr. Fujita's a nice man, she'd said, and a good farmer. This was true, and

Garvin agreed. Nothing inappropriate is going on, she'd said, but of that she felt much less certain. Though she had no real evidence of a romance blooming on the other side of the Peak, this evening's encounter left her feeling more than ever like a child sent away by herself so the adults could be adults together.

Mostly, though, she felt alone. After she had counted forty-eight brush strokes, she heard a soft, heavy object thud in the room behind her. She gave such a start that she dropped her brush into the toilet bowl. Breaking into a sweat, she tiptoed back into the bedroom and fetched a deep iron saucepan from beneath the windowsill, left there for years now to catch drips from the leaking window frame on wet nights. Thus armed, she approached what she sensed was the source of the sound, one of the two closets flanking the bureau, the messier one reeking of mothballs. Tensing, she swung the door open.

A large storage box had fallen from the shelf above. "Damn it!" Livvie whispered, more relieved than angry. As she kneeled to inspect the box, she recalled the contents: old shoes and clothes, sacks of gloves, purses with tarnished clasps and chain straps—all unused, nearly forgotten. She plunged her hands into the half-spilled pile and rummaged down to the bottom, where her fingertips grazed treasure. There: real silk, honest silk, and lace of a delicacy she could no longer afford to buy. She drew the garment out and held it to her face. Although the moonlight made the nightgown shimmer nearly white, she remembered its color, a silvery pink, like the inside of an oyster.

She held her breath and glanced around the room—to the closed door, to the space under the bed, to the open window. Stripping, she stood for three minutes before the bureau mirror with the nightgown draped across her front. Had anyone seen her there, she might have seemed caught luxuriating in a moment of vanity. Really, it was a memory she was after—that of the woman who'd worn this splendid piece for Sig's delight. Guilty as a chambermaid tempted into her rich mistress's wardrobe, she felt too rough and clumsy to wear such a delicate item now. Hearing Garvin peeing in the hall bathroom, she froze. Only after the sounds of the flush and his door closing did she raise the silk sheath above her. Fearing to tear the lingerie, she stood rigid and shivering, waiting for the fabric to slide over her of its own volition. It tumbled down easily, naturally; she had lost weight since she last wore it. She straightened the nightgown as gingerly as if it were made of cobweb, sat back onto the bed, hardly daring to breathe. It was not a winter garment, but no matter. She stretched her arms across the wide, queen-sized mattress from edge to edge and began to doze off. And as if the nightgown were made of stuff no less rigid than plaster, she slept exactly like that, unmoving, throughout the whole night.

Margaret did not mention Bob Ito again. Fujita didn't know if the boy had lived or died, but he did know that his failure to comfort Ito gravely disappointed Nurse Kelly, and he tried to make amends in his silent way. Margaret lacked his patience, so on Christmas Eve day he gave her the handcrafted present he'd labored at for months, hammering away in the night; that afternoon, when she returned from the hospital, he asked her to cover her eyes and step outside.

"Oh, I think I'm going to like this," Margaret said, grinning. "You'd better blindfold me. I'm serious. I *will* peek. I won't be able to help myself."

Fujita shrugged, then set to binding her eyes with a clean kitchen towel and led her onto the porch where the gift lay covered by a tarp. "Be careful, there's still a little snow. Just stand right there," he said. For a long moment he watched her—how trusting and silly and happy she looked, beaming with anticipation. A thrilling queasiness filled him: Gift-giving, teasing, making someone wait—he'd been out of practice. Impatiently, she cleared her throat. "Oh, just a second." He slipped the tarp away, stepped behind her. "Um," he said, unknotting the blindfold. "Ta da."

Margaret gasped. "Oh, my! Look at . . . how wonderful! A *love*seat," she crowed. Dazzled by the craftsmanship, of a kind that one only saw in the most offensively expensive stores in Boston, she hesitated from sitting in the new swing chair. Heavily varnished cedar, sparsely decorated but intricately molded to all a body's contours. Simple but elegant, elegantly simple.

"Well, not exactly," he mumbled. "More a swing, I think."

"Come, sit here. Let's see how it works."

After folding the dingy tarpaulin, Mr. Fujita sat down beside her, and the result of his labor pleased him. He had shaved the seat to comfortably cup one's bottom and allow the legs to kick freely while swinging without cutting off the blood under the thighs. From it, he and Margaret could see out over the scarecrow's shoulder across all of eastern Juggeston. In the far distance ahead, the obelisk-shaped lookout tower on Halibut Point was a shining sliver about to be melted by the overcast night rolling toward them. Further off, the Wingnersheek Beach barracks were already obscured from sight. There, right about now, a new batch of men tromped out of the mess hall and across the hilly sand dunes, nestling inside the buried gun emplacements and picking their teeth clean of dinner scraps. If the scarecrow's keen crystalline eyes could see all this, however, the pair on the swing could not.

For a moment, they both forgot the war and Bob Ito.

Margaret kicked the snow off her boots against the porch railing and sighed. "This is a nice moment," she said, watching an old dress of hers flap like wings behind the scarecrow. Fujita shrugged against the chill. He wore only a light sweater and bib overalls, and his arms and neck were coated over with goose prickles. In the deepening dusk, a circus of southbound black swallows rose and fell in wide arcs, bent-backed and curved-winged, like the barbs of lazy archers' arrows.

"Yes," Margaret whispered, "this is so good. This house is good. This hill is good. Even being fifty is better than I expected." She slid her fingertips along the lacquered wood between them, and rested her hand on the back of his. "And this swing was a grand idea."

After Fujita's long silence, she continued softly, "Well, it's Christmas. Time for peace, time for house peace. I'm sorry about those things I said. I admit, I don't know a whole lot about what your life was like before, or while you were away. I'd like to. If you have friends or family . . . well, this girl that's troubling you—I take it she's your daughter-in-law . . ." It wasn't coming out quite right. She breathed deeply for a moment and decided to change her tack. "What I mean is, this is your new home, really. For a while anyway. I know you've been writing and getting letters . . ." She felt that her mouth was full of wet cement. "I know you: You're proud, independent, but no man is an island, or, well, some women are, perforce, I suppose." *Shoot me*, Margaret thought to herself. "Well, you know that you can have anyone come here, stay here . . . at least in the office. I guess you'll tell me about all that, if you want to, someday. And if I can . . . be of use . . ." She had meant to say "help," but thought better of it. "But this . . ." She waved out toward the scarecrow, the greenhouse, the tiered gardens, their *nojo.* "This is something different. I feel rich when I sit out here; I feel lucky. I have a good feeling about this arrangement. I think we'll grow enough to sustain ourselves and to trade. And I hope you enjoy it here, because I do. A lot." After another pause, she asked, in a mock-annoyed tone, "Do you? How *do* you feel?"

Fujita stiffened slightly. "Like a door that's halfway open," he said, sadly and with effort. He looked away for several minutes. "I was thinking that maybe I should put an armrest here," he said, extracting his hand from beneath hers and patting the wood between them. "With holes to hold glasses and bottles, maybe an ashtray for Livvie. There's enough room." He gave her a weak smile.

"Oh, no you won't, and that's that!" she said. "There's room for *elbows*, and that's perfect just the way it is!"

"Well, yes. Okay. Sure." He nodded. It drove Margaret mad the way his speech always seemed so undirected, even when he spoke to her, as if she only eavesdropped on some inner dialogue. Yet, when he whispered from miles away, "She's not my daughter-in-law. Not exactly. But there's some business between us," she knew how strenuous even that thimbleful of discourse was, and she refrained from pressing him further. Then, patting her hand with his, he said, "Um, thanks. For your offer."

They swung their legs together, synchronized. From above the porch roof, two owls swooped away on their nightly foray in the woods.

"Yes. I knew this porch needed something," Fujita sighed. "It's a good place to sit out and talk." Margaret chuckled; she took this as a promise. For one wordless hour, Margaret and Mr. Fujita watched the snowy fields below dim from gold to orange to purple to gray and finally to black.

At Christmas dinner, they considered following the advice of *Bereavement*: "Set a dinner place to recognize your loved one's presence" and so forth. Far from sure if it would be useful, helpful, or wise, the adults watched for Garvin's cue. What would be best for him? they wondered. And for us? Of course, it fell to Margaret to suggest it. "Well, there's no harm in it, is there? It might be nice."

"*Nice?*" Livvie asked, her tone tinged with a hardness uncommon even for her. "Are you kidding?"

"At least the table will seem less empty," Margaret said, hurt but trying to smile. "It seats eight, with the leaf insert."

"Oh, boy," Livvie laughed, shaking her head.

When Garvin and Mr. Fujita began hauling extra chairs out from the basement, they discovered the eighth chair lacked two legs. "I can nail a couple two-by-fours to the front," he suggested. "C'mon, pal. Help me look." The two trudged back down the stairs.

"Oh, *forget* it already," Livvie called after them. She tamped her cigarette pack on the tabletop. To Margaret, she said, "Jack was a good man, truly. If Mr. Fujita wants a séance too, fine. But Sig's not invited. He's lousy dinner company, anyway—just can't take him anywhere. This year, I'm enjoying myself."

"Livvie, really," Margaret whispered, eyeing her neighbor's empty glass, thinking that Mrs. Tufteller was enjoying herself just a bit too much this holiday.

"No, Margaret, really. You know that even if he wasn't *dead*, he wouldn't *be* here because he'd be back at our house screaming about bills, passed out drunk under the tree, or maybe vomiting on it. Maybe *shooting* it, for Christ's sake!" She grabbed a candelabra from the table.

"But Livvie," Margaret tried. "For Garvin's sake. What about him?"

"Margaret . . ." Livvie began tensely, but raising the candles to her face, she accidentally singed the end of her hair. "Ah, hell!"

she yelled, squinting against the odor. "All right. I'm such a lousy mother, I don't know what's good for my son. Fine. Let's ask him. Hey, Garvin!"

"This isn't necessary," Margaret said, anchoring her fists on her hips.

"Yes, it is," said Livvie. "Sure it is, because it's for my sake and for Garvin's sake that I don't want the son of a bitch here haunting me anymore!"

"Stop *now*," Margaret hissed, as the dust-covered Garvin and Fujita reappeared in the doorway. Disoriented, sensing hostility, the boy glanced back and forth at the women.

"Okay," his mother said, placing her hands on his shoulders and steering him to the table opposite the empty chair. Pointing, she asked, "Honey, does that look like Pop to you?"

"Now wait, be fair, " Margaret insisted, stepping beside the chair. "Garvin, we're wondering if it wouldn't be nice to have a place at the table so your dad and Jack and Mr. Fujita's family can be with us for Christmas dinner." Not only confused, Garvin looked frightened; he backed away from the chair. "Or, well, so we can remember them," she admitted.

What the boy couldn't express in words he conveyed through gestures—a shrug, a frown at the empty end of the table, a step backward. The symbolic faltered, the absolute prevailed. Pop was either there or not. Sig Tufteller was not a broken chair.

"Pop's dead," he said, simply and with certainty.

With that, Garvin stomped away to tend the fireplace; he liked to poke the logs. To the adults, it felt as if he'd taken all the oxygen from the room with him. Like rocks in the sea, they stood anchored in place, unbreathing, silent, clustered but alone. Considering the unhappy moment with some reverence, they shared the thought, *It's our first actual fight.*

"Maybe just one chair would do," Mr. Fujita suggested. He carried the chairs back to the basement, where he wrapped them in sheets and slid them neatly into the crawl space.

"Well, it's nice just to remember," Margaret said, nodding, and she too left the dining room, to check the turkey and count the glasses until she stopped crying.

"It's a creepy charade," Livvie said. Shrugging, she rounded the table, flopped into the empty chair, and filled and drained her wine glass.

Since Margaret wouldn't, and Mr. Fujita couldn't, Livvie let Garvin say grace. Livvie raised her glass in a farewell toast to *Bereavement*—her year subscription was just about to run out. Dinner was passed, dessert served and picked at, and dishes washed—the meal could have been just a dream. And afterward, when Garvin went to torment the fireplace, the adults smoked a cigarette—even Mr. Fujita—and made plans for the farmer's market in spring. "If farming doesn't work out," Fujita said—and it was the first joke he shared with his new friends—"maybe *we* should start a newsletter."

They did their absolute best—the Bunkinsons, Wildmons, Wellingtons, Pedicotts, the Adamses and Fredericks, the Woods, Does, and even Frank Childs—the shrinking Christmas choir of Juggeston. At the foot of the Civil War soldier in the town square, many gathered in defiance of the December night's iciness to share what might be called joy. The joy of a brisk walking-off of potatoes and chewy winter stews, of showing off new home-knit mufflers, and of stretching their throats in song. The busy pleasure of meeting again with people who knew them, knew their families, and would talk knitting and tractors and property taxes and toothaches—who knew of these things and cared. That Christmas Eve, however, the fact of a dozen absent boys subdued the congregation; in place of magic fell mystery. Sleet drops stabbed down onto the tiny square where in previous years fat snowflakes had sprinkled them like manna. Even Baby Pedicott, bundled papooselike against her father's chest, seemed to sense that this Christmas, her first, was not right. As she squirmed restlessly, one of her four brothers complained, "Dad, it's *dark*."

"That's so Santa will come . . . maybe early," said Pete Pedicott, the treelike farmer whom Margaret called Peter the Potent. "He only comes when the lights are off."

In deference to the wartime blackout, the tree remained unlit; usually a dazzle of primary-colored lights rivaling that of many larger towns, its mound of shadowy pleats wore a dull spiral of cranberries and popcorn. The only illumination came from scattered tapers during a vigil for peace prayers; but that dim glow was sufficient to see that again, their tree's crest was bare, abandoned by the O-mouthed electric angel with the seventy-watt innards. Her lighting had always cued Jack Kelly, whose lusty puff into his trumpet signaled the commencement of carols. Without either of them, how would the singers know when to begin?

Alf Wellington believed he knew. In the gloom of the vigil at the tree, Alf most keenly felt the vacuum, and the burden, left by the doctor. Though the shopkeeper was renowned to be friendly to every man, he had been intimate with only one. So he tried in his clumsy way to compensate for the lost Jack Kelly. A Christmas pageant needed a fool; it would be Alf, the queer little shopkeeper, the paragon of professional heartiness, with his awkward, Kringle-like body and perfect, blessed tone deafness. He clapped his palms together, yanked off his mittens, and laughed, just laughed at nothing.

"J-j-jesus, Alf," Frank Childs stuttered. "What's wr-wrong with you. Let's start already. What a crappy night."

"You're really getting into the spirit, eh, Frank?" Alf said, determined not to let the mechanic get him down. Slipping his fingers through the handle straps of his accordion, finding the keys, he sandwiched the wheezing box forcefully and simulated a brass fanfare, as if he would restore breath to his dead friend through his fingertips. Defiantly, he howled against the sleet, "Hark the herald angels sing, glow-ry . . ." So the carolers of Juggeston set out to brave the long, cold trek from the Civil War statue up to the Peak.

To the audiences en route who rose from dinner to listen from steamy bay windows—clans ringing the elderly and poor of health, or mothers who, like ventriloquists, manipulated infants hung on their hips to wave, throwing tiny voices, "Merry Christmas!"—to these, the weak carols sounded sad and alien. Even the most tone-deaf, even Alf could immediately discern the absence of the trumpet, and how the harmony, eviscerated of young tenors and baritones in wartime, had split into isolated bass and soprano lines, growling and shrill. Even Alf, the one-man band who bravely compensated, choking himself into a cracking falsetto, a teenager's octave—even he heard it. Keenly conscious of what they didn't hear, the makeshift choir set their faces against the sleet and did their best.

"They're coming," Garvin said, poking half-crumbled logs around the fireplace with a hearth iron. The adults, halfheartedly festooning the living room with garlands and pinecones, stopped to listen. Margaret pulled aside the front drapes, revealing no movement but sleet and drips from the icicles suspended below the miserable scarecrow's arms. Garvin huffed and dully watched for them to hear, many moments later, the honking of Alf Wellington's accordion rising weakly to the crest of the Peak.

"Garvin? How on earth could you hear that?" Margaret asked. He rolled his eyes.

Mr. Fujita joined her at the window. "They may have trouble getting up here," he said, frowning out at the icy slope. "I should salt those steps. Don't want an accident."

"You *already* salted them," Margaret scolded. "Goodness, will you calm down? How do I look?" In her reasonably subdued Christmas reds and greens—a combination only she could get away with, since those colors naturally belonged to her—he thought she looked lovely.

"You look very well, Margaret," he said. "Brilliant, but very well."

"I look ridiculous, like a holly wreath. They'll expect me to wear black, of course. An *armband*," she complained, though she did wear a choker necklace of black velvet. "Black, black, black—Quakers, mourners, and Coco Chanel. I won't make myself look like a nun. Oh." She caught herself. Garvin even mustered the energy to grin. Hair, suit, socks, tie, and shoes, Mr. Fujita might have been made of coal. "No offense," Margaret said.

"You think I should go change?"

"Don't go anywhere. And don't plan to spend the evening hiding and fluttering around like you do. And don't be nervous; when the carolers come, be friendly, mingle. Remember, it's *Christmas*," she pleaded. "Don't let's mope around anymore."

"It's Christmas," repeated the new man, sounding almost as

glum as Garvin felt. "This means I have to meet more people in one sitting than during my whole time in Juggeston. I don't think I 'flutter around' really," he said, immediately fluttering into the kitchen to check on the toddies.

Already two toddies merry, Garvin's mom laughed and hammered a pinecone wreath above the hearth. "Boy, do you flutter!" she called. She lightly kicked Garvin back from the fire. "Doesn't he? I'm talking to you, Grumpy. Hey, don't you want to help us deck the halls? Get ready for Santa?"

"Nah," Garvin mumbled. He replaced the poker and plopped himself on the couch. This first Christmas of grief brought the realization that Santa Claus, angels, and wise men existed no more than his father.

Finished fluttering, Mr. Fujita resalted the steps "just to be safe." "It's nice of them to tough out the weather all this way," he ventured cautiously. "Eh, pal?" Garvin shrugged.

"God!" Margaret exclaimed. "They sound *awful*!"

Truly, they all agreed they'd never heard such a pitiful wassailing as the weak voicings of the Woods, Feltons, Does, Pedicotts, and Wildmons now nearing the crest of Widow's Peak. "Angels We Have Heard on High" sounded hollow as a dirge. They all had to laugh, even Garvin. Drawing a deep breath, Margaret straightened her dress and looked back at him. "Okay, Garvin, enough moping," she called, placing her hand on the doorknob. "It's show time."

"A gardener, you say?" whispered the big-boned Paulette Pedicott, mother of five little Pedicotts, to Alf. "I saw him once in Cambridge, but he hardly said a word. Margaret said he was a *businessman* of some sort."

Alf Wellington trudged ahead, tight-lipped, as their gossipy group approached the slick gravel drive up to the Peak. The choir had shrunk even more. Passing through the town, various singers peeled off from the group as they arrived shivering back at their own homes, yelled a final "Merry Christmas!" and darted back inside. A dozen or so singers remained, though—the hardy, the drunk, and mostly the curious. What oddities awaited them at the final stop of the night?

"Why the hell are we g-g-going up there, anyway?" Frank Childs wanted to know, eyeing the treacherous climb. The flat feet that had exempted him from conscription always gave him difficulty in snow, he claimed, and especially on such tricky surfaces. "I mean, Jesus Christ—"

"Because it's *Christmas Eve*, Frank," Alf barked. "What's wrong with you?" He tried to stare down the big mechanic but felt silly hugging his accordion.

Glassy with sleet, Frank smirked and held his mittened hands up. "Well, that settles it then," he said. "The S.O.B.'s not going to be Christian, is he? So we can go home." He began to back away. "Anyone else coming?"

"Well, the rest of them are!" Alf said, wanting to brain Frank with his accordion. "They're our neighbors."

Frank shrugged. Bending down to pack a slushball—the good, tight kind one can make with really wet snow—he turned away, acting careless. "Okay, you're all a bunch of goddamn traitors, but suit yourselves," he called, and he hurled the icy projectile into the Kelly mailbox from point-blank range, leaving it with a ringing dent. "Banzai!" he yowled, then disappeared again into the sleet.

There was a miserable, sleety silence until Alf gave a trill on his accordion, which seemed to revive everyone.

As they began their ascent, Pete Pedicott said, "He never comes to meeting."

"I think Margaret has him on a pretty tight leash," Paulette snickered to her potent mate.

"And what's *that* supposed to mean?" Alf grumbled.

"Oh, nothing. Just that they seemed very . . . comfortable together."

"So? She's nice to people," Alf said, scowling. "And he's polite enough. A little touchy," he remembered. Tense as a harp string, actually, but then, Lil had that effect on people. "Well, we'll all see for ourselves pretty soon, won't we?" he urged. Still, the gossip kept flitting about him like mosquitoes.

"They met in Boston, that right?"

"He's a widower, isn't he?" an anonymous voice chimed in from behind.

"I heard he moved into her house," said another.

"You believe everything you hear?" Alf retorted.

"So he's like a handyman? Not a butler or anything?"

"He works for her," Alf sighed. "Who knows. It's not our business." He hugged his squeezebox and wheezed out the opening to "Angels We Have Heard on High," walking ahead. Beside him, he heard Potent Pete and the orchard man, Charles, murmuring about the greenhouse, impressed, surprised, a little envious. Behind him, he might have heard a whisper, "I don't know. It's not right," or maybe he just thought it.

". . . Glow-wo-wo-wo-wo-wo-ria . . ."

Then they were abruptly flooded in porch light. Mrs. Kelly's stylish scarecrow opened her arms to them. From inside, sounds of laughter, women's, a child's, a man's. Then, unlatching; warm light and wood smoke; and behind the screen door, two adults filled the threshold. Her: fine-boned, radiant—too made up though, in her deep burgundy dress, emerald lace shawl. Over her shoulder, rigid, all in black—could be a butler: the Japanese stranger.

"Merry C-c-christmas!" yelped Alf, his voice cracking, still frozen into tenor range.

Margaret Kelly pushed open the screen door. "It's about time! Please, come in." How inviting her tone sounded to those carolers. How warm the living room behind her, the smoke of burning oak and pine; how warm the scent of hot rum, the crooning radio within, and everything. Everything but *him*.

Him, standing just inches behind her: "Please, do come in."

"Yes, quickly! You all look frozen stiff! We thought we'd go out tomorrow and find a crowd of snowpeople on the roadside!"

How warm her "we"! Even Alf—*even tone-deaf Alf*—heard this and had to wonder: Is something funny going on here? And is it right?

Him: "We have hot cocoa and toddies—any takers?"

Alf looked around at the choir, wet and crumpled, shellacked in ice, ogling the pair in the doorway waiting to receive them. That's exactly what it was: how they stood, side by side, toasty warm, and who was this man to stand there and *receive* them at the door to Jack Kelly's home? How they stood close, not inappropriate, but intimate—that's how it seemed to Alf, who felt the cold carolers waiting for him to conduct them. He had passed into this house as a friend more than anyone. Looking around the porch, he thought, Something's changed—but what?

"Hello, Maggie," Alf said, looking away from the carved wood structure beside the door, wiping his feet. What a long time since he'd crossed that welcome mat. "I like your new . . . porch swing. Sturdy."

Margaret laughed boldly, almost haughtily, as one can with old friends. As if something in her popped open, like a piñata, she rushed to embrace the shivering shopkeeper. His accordion honked as she planted kiss after kiss on his fat, frigid cheek until it glowed again. "Okay, okay. Half the toddy, double the rum!" he said, and the band fairly charged up onto the porch behind him, two and three at a time.

"Coming right up," Mr. Fujita said, and his smile appeared more taped on than anything. Livvie and Garvin came to the door, greetings swirled all around, and the new man slipped in and out, silent but watched. He took coats and disappeared into the back hallway, the private part of the house few had seen. Caps, gloves, and mufflers he hung by the fireplace. He fetched chairs, brought matches, lit cigarettes. Moving the coffee table closer to the couch, he dealt out paper coasters. He told Garvin not to play in the fireplace, and the boy listened. He disappeared into the kitchen, reappeared, then tapped Margaret's shoulder from behind; she turned her head and leaned back and placed her hand on his shoulder to brace herself as he whispered in her ear; she whispered back, and he left and returned with a tray of cups and a metal pitcher and a key. He crossed the living room and used the key to open a low, chestnut cabinet, and he drew out a bottle and fixed drinks at Jack's bar. No, that wasn't right. Not poaching a dead man's bar like it's your own.

"Sit down, Mr. Fujita!" Margaret said, at last. "You're doing everything!"

At least, the carolers were relieved to learn, this Japanese had not settled in the house but had fashioned a room out of the late doctor's office. After the guests had thawed a bit—the rum hitting the spot, then hitting it again—he offered to take a few of the men up to his room to show off a radio he had just finished rebuilding from spare parts. After asking if Mrs. Kelly was up to entertaining alone for a bit, he fetched coats and gear for the fellows. The garage was less than thirty feet from the house, but he bundled up like Admiral Byrd setting out for the Antarctic. Shivering, he sprinted ahead of them through the snow with little Garvin Tufteller at his heels.

Turning round the corner of the house, the followers saw that Jack's office—where their children had been delivered, where all had received treatments and advice for ailments, marriages, finances—had doubled in girth. Wrapped by massive faggots of straw and brush, the garage looked like a stable; a visitor from one of the Catholic coast towns might have mistaken it for a gigantic, prize-winning crèche left dark in the blackout.

"In-su-la-tion," Mr. Fujita explained through chattering teeth, struggling with the icy latch. Of course, the Juggestonians understood that the Japanese Californian would probably never acclimate himself to New England. He always looked cold when seen at his chores about town; even before locals had put their fall jackets in storage, his nose trickled and he wore sweaters so thick and hot one could barely stand to look at him. "The furnace for the greenhouse is in there," he said.

Inside, the office appeared to be about the same, still smelling of ether and tobacco. The new man slept on Jack's old daybed; his few possessions sat in the sterile tin and glass-doored medicine cabinets. The skeleton still swung beside the coatrack; the Gray's anatomy chart hung above the wide cedar desk; issues of *Life* from 1941 on remained undiscarded and unread in a wicker basket in the vestibule. The shiny, wheeled instrument cart stood beside the daybed, stacked high with books; and the extendable magnifying lamp, into which they'd all gagged "Aagghh" under Jack's searching gaze, was now used for another kind of reading.

"It's so . . . *clean*," Alf observed, surprised. "You travel pretty light, I guess."

Mr. Fujita shrugged. "Come on in," he urged the lagging carolers stomping up the stairs. "And feel free to look around. I guess you all know this room pretty well."

Attached with surgical tape to the lamp was a cropped, overexposed snapshot of the fellow's family: his wife shielding her eyes with a hand, and his muscular, spiky-haired boy, about eighteen, making a defiantly funny face, eyes bugged out and tongue lolling to one side. They stood in front of what looked like a toolshed adorned with a wooden shingle, with APT. 9 and a set of numbers burned into it, *The Fujitas* scrawled in ink script below, and a buglike Japanese character beneath that. A moat of fine desert flowers ringed the hut, punctuated by foot-high pinwheels. Beside the shack stood a leprous-looking prickly pear cactus draped with a string of flowers and berries, crowned by a limp foil star.

The most obvious additions to the office was the looming, skeletal remains of an outdated Westinghouse cabinet radio anchored in the office's center like a mechanical bear, stripped of its oak body, wire entrails spilling. When Garvin switched it on, the glass bulbs vibrated and hummed until a dim glow ran up the filaments within and then grew to a brighter orange, and static stuffed the room. After delicate fiddling, Mr. Fujita hit on a program. That week most broadcasts reported Axis troops gaining ground in tiny, far-off Belgium, but the hiss cleared onto a Christmas show featuring the crooner, Bing Crosby.

"Say, friends," Bing said with strained heartiness, and that deep, bubble-bath voice conveyed a crackle of pine fireplace logs, the smell of cherry pipe tobacco. "Wherever you are tonight, whether you're in the snows of New England or up in the Northwest or on the warm, tropical beaches of the Florida coast, I really hope that you're getting into the spirit of this Christmas thing. I don't mean just sitting back in your easy chair listening to us have all the fun. I mean, throwing back your head and opening up your hearts and singing as loud and as pretty as you know how." The men gathered in Jack Kelly's office blinked at one another, apparently too shy for Bing, who urged, "Gang, singing is a lot more fun than you'll ever know unless . . . unless you give it a whirl sometime. You don't know the words, why, hum a little, tap your feet, or, gee whiz, do *something*. Ready?" Then Mr. Fujita began singing along softly as the radio orchestra sawed out, "I'll Be Home for Christmas." The widower did not have a fine voice—not like Bing's, of course—but emboldened by toddies, ether, and gas fumes, the gruff men of Juggeston did what neighbors would do: They joined him in a round and sang, "If only in my dreeeaaammms . . ."

Afterward, Garvin parroted the announcer in the deepest little mumble he could muster. Mr. Fujita told the guests that his son, Tony, had had a fine voice; he'd taken radio-appreciation classes in school. Having mastered so-called Standard American, the "unaccented English" of Ohioan Midwest, he once hoped to be an announcer. Garvin chirped, in his broadcast voice, "Maybe that's what I'll be, too."

As the visitors shuffled toward the door, young Theo Bunkinson, Fatty Franklin's older brother who had anonymously pelted Fujita with eggs, stopped to look at the photo on the lamp, then felt a hand on his back and jolted right up. Removing the picture, Fujita said, "This is what Christmas looks like out west." He handed the photo to Theo, who held it and passed it back like a grenade.

"Hard for you white Christmasers to believe," Fujita said, "but out there, you have to cover yourself during the day or you get burnt. You can make tea just by leaving a mason jar with some water and leaves out in the sun at noon—yeah, no kidding. In summer, you can fry eggs on the rocks. At night . . ." He went to stick the photo back onto the lamp but then slipped it into his pocket. "Well, nights are a different story. Nights in the desert can really get down there."

The carolers filed back out into the snow and waited as Mr. Fujita struggled with the latch. "Of course, you fellows don't believe it, those kinds of extremes," he said. Breaking into a run toward the house, with Garvin close behind, he shouted, "I'm sure you think all this rain and ice is swell! So you won't mind if I meet you inside!"

The choir soon called it a night—Jack Kelly's remote, hilltop house was their last stop—and they headed home, trudging across the Peak in their heavy boots, sighing, grinning, or snorting. The cracking beneath those heels—thin ice sheets frosting the seven-and-a-half-inch layer of mulch below—sounded like far-off gunshots.

"It just ain't proper," said Pete.

But seeing Margaret and the office had revived Alf's memory; he thought about Jack, who had acted on what was just and good but never, ever concerned himself with what was considered proper. "Well," Alf said evenly, "*he* seems okay, really."

"Yeah," Pete said, backing down. "But *it's* not right. You know what I mean." He pointed down the icy slope. "Greenhouse or no, this ain't farmland, that's for sure. Ladies and gents: We're looking at forty acres of fool's gold here."

To this they all nodded and shook their heads. They searched the night sky for shooting stars or airplanes. Their gazes floated beyond the fence, out over the valley where there had been no tree-lighting this year, no trumpets or angels, out toward the ominous darkness over Halibut Point. Alf scanned the yard puffy with wet snow and half-hidden boulders, almost expecting to see the doctor himself sitting up on his fence, popping a Lucky into his lips. Nothing. Nothing but the what the scarecrow wore—Jack's old stethoscope, glinting in the porch light. If her enhanced hearing let the scarecrow eavesdrop on the hushed, hearthside tale Fujita now began for his friends, the Juggestonians had to make do with regular old, human, nearly frostbitten ears, which they bound in muffs and hoods and scarves. As they eased down the slippery drive, the grim carolers didn't notice the minute icicle that fell from the scarecrow's face and shattered on the protruding granite at her feet, tinkling like laughter.

EIGHT

Rikutsuppoi

Winded from his climb, little Tom Fields reached the top of the camel-backed Sacaton Butte, lurched to a halt beneath the towering saguaro cactus, and cried out in amazement. Only five years old, the Pima boy had braved so many perils in his day—the pit vipers, the scorpions, the fierce-jawed Gila monster that inhabited the valley—but never had he dreamed of such terrors as the growling earth-moving machines he saw below him. They spewed smoke, mowed rust-colored stripes through the alfalfa crops, even rerouted whole streams. Naked skeletons of houses rose from the desert floor—so many, so clumped together. He marveled at the new towers; erected overnight, they loomed high as the butte itself, and on top, gun barrels poked out like hungry beaks from a nest above a cactus. Then the earth jumped, opening like an angry mouth with a tongue of fire, breathing clouds, but he could not hear what it said. Only after Tom had scratched his head did the roar of the huge earth mouth reach him across the distance. It shook and shook the entire valley, even the butte, to the tips of Tom's ears, which he covered with his hands. "Aaahhhhh!" the boy yelled back. Terrified, he bolted straight back across the crest, then skidded down the other side. Running away from the construction of the new Butte Camp of Gila River, Tom knew that his tribal home was no longer safe. But it was getting interesting.

Barbed-wire fencing encircled some 790 acres of desert that was the foundation for the Fujitas' new home. Administered by the War Relocation Authority, or WRA, Gila River's Camp II comprised forty-eight blocks separated by firebreaks and clay roads, arrayed in a crescent around the Sacaton Butte, the firehouse, and a water tower. Based on photos in WRA literature, Gila was, in Yoneko's estimation, "the prettiest of all the camps." Its orange double roofs and whitewashed boards were more attractive than the usual tar paper employed at other internment centers, and more heat-reflective, too: In summer months averaging 109 degrees, the Fujitas' barrack in Block 60 felt only like a Dutch oven, not a steel forge. The ousted Pasadenans counted this as a minor blessing as they began forging new lives in their second relocation.

After the shock, the anxiety, the disorientation of another uprooting; after the sunburn, the heat-sickness, the food poisoning, the bowel troubles from the fluorinated water; after scrambling for camp jobs and "apartments"; after petitioning the camp administration and electing internee representatives; after patching together jerry-built schools and playgrounds; after outfitting an at least passable hospital and firehouse; after all the basic organizational brouhaha that made Fujita feel really alive for the first time since Pearl Harbor; after all this Fujita and his neighbors found that they had built of their prison a city.

Also without realizing it, the Fujitas had molded something like a home of their twenty-by-twenty-foot cubicle on the corner of the unimaginatively named Ninth and F streets. Random homey touches sprouted up in barely perceptible increments. For example, Fujita did not recall finding or bartering for the lumber to construct the simple hutch by the door, sheltering family keepsakes from the omnipresent Gilan dust. There were also the woven grass doormat, which Mari swept twice daily, in vain; the photos of Tamie and Ichiro and of Mari's parents, of whom they'd heard no news since the fall of 1941; and Tony's glass jars and terrariums that housed his menagerie of deadly pets.

A sense of a truer home trickled in by mail. Fujita would later tell Livvie that the Gilans could have survived without a mess hall, living on desert fruits and underground springs, and could manage without doctors, police, firemen, priests, or the pretense of a representative government. Yet, in Fujita's opinion, the near biblical importance of the Sears & Roebuck catalog could not be overestimated. Some carried it rolled up in their pockets like a baby bottle or security blanket—like an umbilicus to the outside world. Children read it as a book, imagining heroic adventures and romances for its models in beekeeper hats and wading boots; in school, how many confiscated paper airplanes bore its unlikely art on the nose-cones—not Betty Grable or the Flying Tigers insignia, but a double boiler, garden rake, or lamp? For teenagers, it was a barometer of more or less current fashion "out there" while its girdle ads doubled as pornography. And how many Gilans, trapped in the open public latrines without toilet paper, had been rescued by those pages?

Yet, for each of some twelve thousand Gilans, even the sacred catalog offered no escape from the one obstacle looming before them as solidly as the surrounding fixed-gun towers. The Japanese have a term, *rikutsuppoi*, a powerful little totem that has no English correlative, though Fujita believed his mother tongue needed no word so sorely as this one. It loosely translated as "smacking too much of a logic that ignores reality." Examples of rikutsuppoi abounded at Rivers: as self-defeating behavior, useless bureaucracy, impractical and unenforceable regulations, and of course the myriad, contradictory rationalizations for that part of the war Herbert Nicholson, and now Fujita, called "the whole thing." Particularly irksome to Fujita was the rikutsuppoi manifested in stupid questions, such as those put to him one day by a young sociologist who begged "just a few minutes" of Fujita's time—a few minutes of rikutsuppoi that stretched into a few hours, and eventually years.

The twenty-six-year-old internee and Ph.D. student, Lincoln Osawa, asked the Fujitas to fill out a survey and possibly give follow-up interviews. "Do I have time to fart around with questionnaires?" Fujita growled to his wife—they growled to each other frequently now—but Mari favored it. Without the benefit of her husband's exhausting, cleansing work in the camp vegetable beds, she'd had too much time to think at Gila and had an awful lot to say with no one to really say it to. Never good at consolation, at talking things out, her husband thought that both Mari and their marriage were steadily becoming unhinged. By cinching their lives closer together, internment had suffocated their passion, as two flames will falter in a close space choked of oxygen. His usual nervous habits now irritated her, and she had her own annoying rituals—her obsessive and futile efforts to keep the doorway free of dust served only to fill the room with a swirl of particles that made Fujita's eyes and throat itch constantly. She was sharp with Tony, cool to Aunt Rose, and often downright icy to Yoneko—whose parents had been shuffled about early on, and finally sent to Crystal City, Texas, stigmatized as the camp for "real traitors."

And Mari had taken to reading the most god-awful mail-order pulp romances—nearly one a day, trading them with other addicted ladies at the makeshift YWCA—which Fujita rather snobbishly supposed only enhanced her unhappiness. Talking to Osawa, he hoped, might be a release for her. Tony said he didn't care, he could participate in the survey or not. Yoneko was disappointed no one wanted to interview her, and Fujita said she could take his place, but Lincoln wanted "just the family."

The survey was for an independent study Osawa had arranged when the war caught him near the end of doctoral work. The way he said it, he sounded as if he wasn't a prisoner himself, as if he were merely some field anthropologist infiltrating an underdeveloped tribe of pygmies. At that time, Fujita didn't know quite what a sociologist did—indeed, he never fully understood it, though after the interview he knew at least that he didn't respect it. To Fujita, a sociologist was a more annoying version of a psychologist. Or perhaps a politician, Fujita thought, discerning in young Osawa something of a politician's slimy chumminess. Still, in those conditions, could Fujita deny anyone's efforts to continue their work and education? Even fraudulent work, even silly education? In that fall of 1942,

Osawa's plans for his work were veiled to Fujita, who imagined that only some stuffy professor in some stuffy cubbyhole office would care to read his opinions on such idiotic questions as: "(1) What are your feelings about the Evacuation?" Or, "(2) What do you miss most about your life before the war?" Or this little gem: "(3) What percentages of yourself do you consider American and Japanese?"

Mari replied that (1) The Evacuation was among the most shameful episodes of the American twentieth century (though what else would one expect of the West Coast?), and she went on to elaborate for some ten pages. (2) Privacy, cleanliness, her church group, her parents . . . oh, how much time did he have? And (3) Fifty-fifty, and I'm not budging.

Tony's more straightforward answers would relegate him to a mere footnote status in the dissertation. (1) It's dumb, but it's wartime, and he's happy to do his bit. (2) Dr Pepper, his Caucasian friends, driving. (3) 100 percent and zero. Next question.

On question 1, Fujita rolled his eyes and replied: Feelings? Who had time to have feelings? Feelings, under such circumstances, were a luxurious waste of time. On item 2, he concurred with his wife: privacy, though he missed his nursery immensely—all of it, and in this he included his mother, as if she were a lath house or a plant. He avoided saying how he missed the illusion that he wasn't the only one on the planet not a moron, a madman, or a crook. Nor did he say that he missed lovemaking with his wife, which they'd done regularly and energetically before evacuation but only twice since then, and not only for practical reasons. This was the sort of dirt Osawa yearned to dredge up, he imagined. Addressing question 3, Fujita let himself be fiercely direct: "It took you twenty years of schooling to devise that stroke of genius? Jesus." This doubtlessly eased Osawa's conscience when the time came to take a red pencil to his manuscript.

Mari liked the tidy, formal Osawa, though, and pointed out her husband's hypocrisy. "Lincoln's just doing what we all have to do: Adjust, make do. You're always saying, the glass can be half full or half empty. One can do something or nothing. Those are *your* words."

Fujita had always considered himself a half-full-glass sort of person, spawned from a generally half-full-glass sort of people, but life at Gila stretched all patience. He often felt that he'd been imprisoned in an enormous, outdoor post office; in addition to the myriad forms to be filled out and the ridiculous questions put to him, there was the standing in line at the latrines, showers, mess, mail room, dinner, administration building, canteen, everywhere. For Fujita, "making do" meant finding something useful to do, and building a new city from dust provided one with plenty of busywork. Before the first camp nursery opened, he found a satisfying job in the surprisingly successful vegetable crops. That he made about ninety-seven cents an hour mattered little. He loved that wide-open nothingness; since living in his parents' one-room, Nihonmachi apartment, he couldn't get enough space. He loved filling the parched red-brown with the new green, and he stayed outdoors as much as possible. When you were busy, wasn't any situation bearable?

Only Miss Yamaguchi and the war could sustain Tony's interest for very long, and these gave him an advantage over his parents. He had a long-term goal: He wanted to serve in the armed forces, return a hero, and marry his sweetheart. With such clear purpose, he didn't need busywork to distract him from thoughts of home. Tony said he couldn't care less about being returned to Pasadena. He wanted to "see Europe." Despite his semester hiatus from school, Tony studied diligently enough for the makeshift Butte High School, figuring that it would improve his chances of winning a decent assignment if the Army called for internee volunteers.

"What the hell else is there to do?" he complained one lazy afternoon, stretching beside Yoneko on the Fujitas' low stoop. "Maybe I'll be prom king." They were sunning with a brown-mottled gecko, the newest addition to his growing zoo of desert pets. The bored city boy delighted in dangerous, unpredictable things, and he'd collected an impressive menagerie of lizards, spiders, scorpions, ants, and snakes—all beasts with whom he felt some kinship. With a vast mail-order library, he became an expert in their care, diets, mating, and life cycles.

"Who do you figure will be the prom *queen*," said Yoneko.

"That Michiko? Or maybe Grace Seko?" She knew he fancied both.

"Oh, I don't know," Tony teased her. "They're both good girls."

They were good girls. They led A-plus, active lives. Butte High Yearbook committee, Junior Red Cross, that sort of thing. A pretty girl from a grocery family, Grace lived just around the corner in Block 61. In class Tony had complimented her on a poem about the evacuation that she wrote for the *Girls' League Gazette*. He probably thought that poetry writing was very *sensitive.* "You're in my class now, buster," warned Yoneko, who didn't write poems but was sensitive anyway. "You'd better watch what you say!"

"Don't worry." Tony laughed, stretching back on the stoop where they sat smoking. "I only like *bad* girls. I like you," he said, and kissed her indiscreetly. Constant observation by the guards in their fixed-gun towers, by the giant saguaro cacti on the buttes, and by other inmates allowed few stolen moments; once-private behaviors perforce became public, a part of what older folks generally referred to as "the moral decline of wartime."

At the moment, his father was watching him, spying around the corner of Block 60 and fretting. The elder Fujita couldn't understand how being *bad* was a sort of game for young people—old Pop Fujita didn't understand that any more than he understood Tony's fascination with bugs and reptiles, which he found both juvenile and unnecessarily hazardous. He could not imagine a teenager's boredom so profound that *only* peril provided any stimulation. Fortunately, he didn't know just how dangerous the hobby was. Only much later would he hear of the secret tunnels and holes through which Tony occasionally snuck out of camp at night, hunting new specimens or fishing with a Pima friend. Fujita would never understand *that.*

Still, Tony underestimated his father. When Fujita broke from his shift in the crops to fetch his work gloves and spotted the couple lipping each other, he found it distasteful but didn't fear for the boy's moral character. Even Yoneko, he supposed, was good-hearted, though he suspected her to be a bad influence.

They didn't cheat, swear, or steal, and while camp grew rowdier with infighting, Tony had given up brawling for boxing. They were only as surly, restless, deceitful, and distrustful as other teenagers. And couldn't any internee empathize with distrust? Rather, what gnawed at Fujita most about his son—and about evacuation and internment, about "the whole thing"—was the waste. Stretched lazily on the stoop in a T-shirt, a Camel behind his ear, the cuffs of his mail-order jeans rolled up nearly to his knees, Tony looked like a poster child for able-bodied waste. It was the pinnacle of rikutsuppoi, he thought, that as wartime manpower needs worsened, all 120,000-something of them had been made wards of the state. Tony looked like Fujita's version of a bum.

Of course, Tony's father also knew the myriad benefits of having an idle teenager: The boy wasn't being bayoneted, shot at, bombed, hand-grenaded, land-mined, or torpedoed by some German, Italian, or Japanese teenager. And vice versa. By refusing the "nonalien enemy" induction, perhaps the dumbshit politicians and generals had inadvertently saved his life? Out of indebtedness, Fujita decided on Day One, Gila time, to be "Swiss about the whole thing," the very model of a neutral prisoner. A live-and-let-live man. He cooperated to the extent that he donated blood and bought war bonds. He never complained about his quarters or the crappy and sometimes poisonous mess-hall food. He was not an *inu*, a dog, a squealer, an informant-collaborator for the administration; neither would he squeal on suspected inu to those secret resisters or vigilantes who hunted and beat them. So long as the war and draft continued, he decided he'd lie and say that he supported the internment policy if someone asked his opinion (no one ever did). In short, he decided to keep quiet, keep busy, and play along.

Let him do something that's not dangerous, Fujita told himself, rounding the corner and startling the lovers. Spotting him first, Yoneko nudged Tony, who called upon one of his more grotesque talents to hide the cigarette. Fujita caught it, though—an undeniably skillful bit of . . . oh, Tamie would know the word. *Légerdelangue*? A sleight-of-tongue: With the same dexterous tongue that could knot cherry stems, he flipped around the half-smoked butt to hold it inside his closed mouth without burning the roof or using his hands. "God!" muttered Tony's appalled father.

Necessarily, Yoneko did the talking. "Hiya, Mr. F.," she said, all smiles. "Off kinda early, aren't you?"

Ignoring her, he peered into Tony's calm face, wondering just how long he could hold it in there, the smoke *and* the butt. "Good news, son," he said. "We're eating dinner here tonight. Mom's making inarizushi, and she mail-ordered two cans of natto. Okay with you?" At the mention of the sluglike fermented beans, the besieged boy's eyes grew wide and teary, and a hollow moan came from his throat, but he had a stubborn streak to match his father's patience. "Well? What do you say?" The teenager held fast until Fujita feared he meant to literally smoke his brains out. "Oh, spit that out already," he said, "before your head catches fire." In a fit of phlegmy coughing, Tony launched the projectile onto the dirt, and because he was expected to—because teenagers *needed* to feel disapproved of—Fujita frowned and barked, "Don't you have something better to do?"

"Well, no," the boy croaked honestly—the only words he could manage.

"Well, *I* do, and I need my gloves," he huffed, and having done his curmudgeonly duty, he pushed past the young lovers.

To be fair, Tony tried to occupy himself, especially in exercise. He did push-ups, sit-ups, and wind sprints. He lacked stamina, though. He also tried a stint at the camp's paradoxical model-ship factory, where the Navy, deciding that Nips were handy at making tiny things, farmed out the delicate piecework to the very contractors imprisoned for "military necessity" and fear of sabotage. Used for identification, the hundreds of models mimicked or prototyped ships of every weight and class, from minesweepers to aircraft carriers. Models used for buoyancy tests had to be absolutely precise. With his experience in radio electronics, Tony had the necessary nimble fingers, and his first model was excellent, but doing one was enough for him. He said he felt like a toymaker; though it was war-related, the work felt "childish."

As part of his war effort, Tony also took up boxing, and one day Fujita agreed to watch his bout with a Negro WRA worker, Jim Little, a friendly, mild-mannered giant and amateur light heavyweight with a neat record of fifteen wins and one loss by a TKO. The pugilists had fashioned a ring by staking off a sandy plot with twigs and twine, in the area between Block 59 and the amphitheater. Fujita shuddered when he saw the guard. With his native distrust of people who took up too much space, Fujita didn't know what to make of the dinosaur Tony had chosen for a sparring partner. To the WRA, Jim was only a gopher—he drove to various nearby farms for mash and grain, then returned with the rancid loads to the livestock pens—though one armed with a truncheon. Initially mistaking him for a guard, Fujita thought it perverse that his son should take a shine to one of his captors. Would others resent Tony's friendship with Little, tag him an inu? The way Big Jim's knuckles swelled inside the boxing gloves—not padded enough by half, Fujita thought—Tony's father mostly feared for the boy's face.

The children who gathered from several blocks around for these after-school bouts hooted and gasped and cheered as if watching Joe Louis and Max Schmeling. Largish for a Nikkei, Tony stood five-seven with a two-foot reach, while Big Jim packed a solid foot on top of that. Thanks to his daily calisthenics, Tony had grown quite muscular and moved with a natural quickness, and he did an admirable job connecting with his more experienced opponent, but Little floored him with one punch. It happened so fast that Tony's father didn't really see it until the boy lay flat on his back, gasping. Amazed by the big man's speed, he guiltily thought, Hmm, I'd like to see that again.

Rising painfully, Tony obliged him. Like a myna bird harrying a grizzly bear, Tony again scored a number of light hits, which Big Jim received with a certain sad, resigned boredom. He barely blinked until Tony went into his windup—what was intended to be the knockout punch. Leaning his weight to the back, right leg, he let fly, his punch arcing way out to the side. Bad habits die hard, and this was Tony's worst habit, having begun his fighting career as a slugger, not a boxer. The stance gave the blow momentum, but threw him off-balance, with his head and sides left vulnerable. With the merest shift in weight, like a tree swaying in the breeze, Jim leaned away, and the force of Tony's swing carried him down and to the left; as he looked back over his right shoulder, he recognized his weak position too late. Jim cocked his right arm back and hammered straight out like firing field cannon.

Returned to his back, coughing in the cloud of dust, Tony wheezed, "I know, I know. 'Straight, from the shoulder.'" It was Big Jim's constant criticism, it was Tony's mantra. Turning his head, he spit a gob of blood from his mouth. When Jim hauled him up to a standing position, Tony's eyes crossed and he wobbled a bit like a rag doll. "Shit, Jim!" he said, putting his glove to his lips. "If they sent you to the front, we might be outta here by New Year's."

"I wouldn't go. You the only cat crazy enough to want to go." Jim looked down, kicking the dirt back behind him with his boots. "Most sane folks are hoping to get deferred, and you looking to get in. Well, it's your hide," Jim said. "Let's go. Again."

Fujita shook his head in disgust. Deciding he had better things to do than watch his son be pounded into jelly, he turned to leave.

Fujita always assumed that big people with slow movements must also have slow thoughts. That the big, slow man was a Negro garbage hauler who beat people up for recreation also led Fujita to form some unwholesome preconceptions from a subconscious place long ago and far away. But that day he thought Big Jim had shown, in both boxing and speech, flashes of brilliance, and soon he came to know and become very fond of the giant he'd mistaken for a guard. Any ounce of aggression in Little remained tucked neatly inside his boxing gloves when he took them off. His voice matched the bigness of his body, and he cruised the camp singing basso like a living Tops of the Pops, always up on the latest hits and dance trends. He could talk hepster as if he taught Cab Calloway himself, and he could cuss like nobody's business. Jim instructed Tony in military English, too. There were all sorts of cryptic obscenities developed by the fighting men in the war, and despite his dislike for the military, Jim seemed to know all of them: *Snafu* ("Situation normal—all f-ed up") and *Fubar* ("F-ed up beyond all recognition") and *Ffufu* ("Face facts: U f-ed up"). Mastering profanity more easily than boxing, Tony devoured this and any other knowledge of military life Jim could impart. For the war that had already cast such a pall over their lives was drawing even closer, scudding in with the clouds of the approaching Gila winter. When December 8 looped around again, a year after the war had snatched Tamie away, it came back to the desert. It was looking for Tony.

"I'm dreaming of a whi-i-i-ite Crissmassss . . ." Big Jim Little's voice boomed through the apartment in Block 60. Cramped as it was with Fujita and Mari and the Yamaguchis, Tony's friend Calvin and his nephew Bobby Tanaka, the room could barely contain the mass of Jim. He bowed low to the women, as was his custom, saying, "*Ohayo,* Mrs. Fujita. *Ohayo,* Aunt Rose." Tony barely managed to grab the vase from the table Jim upset with his rump.

"Merry Christmas, Jim," Mari laughed, carefully trying to shoehorn him into the little room. Yoneko's Aunt Rose giggled.

Big Jim bore gifts from the world outside, but none so appreciated as the Brownie camera to record the holiday. The celebration seeped outdoors. For Mari he brought a turquoise necklace, and for Aunt Rose, a thin silver chain beaded with tigereye to fasten her glasses around her neck. Fujita got a book on Pima gardening. The pink sundress he bought for Yoneko was cut for a child—he'd had to guess her size—but she said it was lovely and cried. Tony's gift was much needed headgear for sparring; like his grandfather, his strongest feature was his chest, and he was developing a cauliflower ear. "This'll keep you from going deaf," said Jim guiltily, pressing it down over Tony's head.

"Mm, *dashing,*" Yoneko cooed. "It looks like a pilot's helmet. C'mere, flyboy," she grr-ed like Mae West. "I do love a man in uniform." Fujita pulsed with anger at her. She fixed the chin strap by Tony's right ear and gave his head a playful little cuff. Curious to see if the new equipment worked, her Aunt Rose boxed his left ear a bit less playfully. "Stop it, Auntie," Yoneko said. "Say, I hear the recruiters are already reviewing folks in some of the other camps. What do you think of that?"

"I think that's too bad for the other camps," said Big Jim, also slapping Tony.

"Gila River will have the best enlistment rate," Aunt Rose declared proudly, and she punched Tony in the ribs. "We'll see Toshio in a real uniform soon." To Fujita, her tone indicated that she, like her idiot niece, found the prospect appealing.

"Boy, if they'd let me go," Tony said, "I'd bloody some noses. That's why I'm working out with Jim. Right, Jim?"

"I ain't involved in this." Jim glanced sheepishly at Mari and mumbled, "Crazy kids."

"Just forget it, Tony," Mari said, and there was nothing playful in the way she cuffed him. "Don't even think of it."

"Mom!" Toshio Ichiro Fujita took after his paternal grandfather in other ways, too. He was constantly and keenly aware of where he was and where he wanted to be; he could not bear the thought of spending the duration at Gila. And like the Little Bull, he was a staunch believer in "being prepared." While waiting for the Army to activate a segregated combat team of Japanese Americans, he would relax his exercise regimen for nothing—not even Christmas. Irritably, he challenged Big Jim. "Either let's go spar, or get this thing off of me. I'm safer without it." He removed his shirt and untangled the laces of his gloves.

"Tell him, Bill," Mari insisted.

But Fujita, who was still being Swiss about the whole thing, distracted them all. "Okay, gang," he said, brimming with Christmas cheer. "Let's line up for that photograph." Later, when he said, "Let's take one of just the family," Yoneko sulked, correctly taking it as a retaliatory dig at her, but took a step to the side. Arranging them by the prickly pear cactus halfheartedly dressed as a Christmas tree, Big Jim snapped the photo of all the Fujitas together.

When the women went back inside, before they set to it, Tony explained to Jim, "You got pride, at least. You're free to fight for your country. And I'm saying I've got a duty to my country, too."

"You've been reading too many Captain America comic books. You know about Jim Crow? Army's got yellow Jim

Crows, too. You'll be licking out latrines 'til they ship you off to get you shot. I can think of only about a million better things to do. You'll die soon enough; ain't no use hurrying it up. *Pride*," Big Jim sneered, and he promptly KO'ed his opponent, to Fujita's silent applause. "Only fighting *I* do 'round here is to knock you on your ass."

"That's easy for you to say," Tony coughed.

The tension in the *koya* remained thick that season, aggravated by the arrival of the promised "loyalty review" questionnaires, the applications for leave clearance that might liberate them. Mari demanded that they gather in the mess hall for some semblance of a family dinner to face the baffling documents together, though they did not unanimously agree that they should *respond* as a family. Indeed, they couldn't, for the forms were similar but not identical. The original form, designed for men Tony's age, bore the Army Selective Service seal and was intended to divine their loyalty and willingness to serve. Taking the army's cue, the WRA designed its own knock-off forms; having suffered recent bad press (proper Americans were furious that their tax dollars were spent to "coddle Japs"), the WRA was eager to weed out, then kick out those internees deemed "loyal." Both forms, however, bore questions that were again the typical rikutsuppoi.

To certain, key loyalty questions, affirmative responses indicated a healthy patriotism that could earn young men the privilege of being drafted out of camp, or could clear the way for others to be released, under restrictions, to work or school. No one could go *home*. People who answered those same key questions with negative responses were presumed disloyal, either quarantined like lepers in separate camps to fester in their own dissension or prosecuted as draft dodgers, called "No-No Boys."

"We must answer them individually," Fujita insisted. "Conscientiously."

"Oh, yes," Mari said, as they arrived at the two most sinister and absurd questions of all—those one-word answers that separated Us from Them, Fighting Men from No-No Boys. "Sign as your conscience dictates, Tony. *But*, if you enlist and return alive, I promise you a fate worse than death. And put out that cigarette."

Tony said nothing but exhaled defiantly.

"Put it out, Tony," Fujita snapped. "And Mari, Tony is free to make his own decision, like a man." Mari huffed and rolled her eyes.

"Are you willing," Yoneko read aloud, translating for her aunt, "to serve in the Armed Forces of the United States on combat duty whenever ordered?" Aunt Rose gasped.

"Say yes, Auntie," Yoneko instructed the anxious Issei, though taking it upon herself to answer on the bewildered woman's behalf. "Let's just get out of here already."

"Sure, you'd look fine in a crew cut, Rose," Mari sneered. "You'd look terrific jumping out of an airplane. 'Forget it,'" she said, writing it on her own form.

"I don't suppose women are meant to answer that," Fujita said. The question, he knew, was aimed at teenage boys, and he knew what his own would answer. He looked to his own application. Waving his pen back and forth like a knife-thrower aiming a toss, he read: "'If the opportunity presents itself and you are found qualified, would you be willing to volunteer for the Army Nurse Corps or the Women's Army Auxiliary Corp?' Good Lord."

"Oh, and *you'd* look fabulous in a nurse's dress!" Mari said, but to her irritation, her humorless husband wrote, "I am not a young man. Nonetheless, I might serve in the WAAC *if* the camps were closed, my family freed from imprisonment, and our rights and property restored. In case of an attack on the mainland, I would of course defend my home. In Pasadena," he added. He squelched a wave of panic rising in him; he'd not heard from Harvey Clemens since Tulare.

"You don't need to write an essay, Bill," Mari grouched, reading over his shoulder.

"I know what I need to write," he said. Of all wartime indignities, the following question so incensed Fujita, he stormed out of the mess hall to fetch his dictionary. Returning, he constructed a purposefully muddy response meant to buy time, for Tony and himself. He was stalling until he knew the right thing to do. Like a bubble swimming up from a deep, underground pool, a plan was coming to him, though he couldn't see it yet. He still hoped to remain Swiss about the loyalty question, but the world demanded: Are you Us, or are you the Other? It offered no choice but forced you to make one, and he was on the verge of choosing to become a saboteur. Before appending his signature, he waved the paper about as if to dry the ink.

"What are your feelings on this, Pop?" Tony asked, holding up his own form, thinking induction an inglorious route to freedom. "You feel I should go, right?"

"What's all this about *feelings?*" Fujita said irritably. "Is our situation helped by feelings?" He knew his answer was important to his son—but how important? Tony obviously had some youthful havoc yet to wreak on the world. Only in the war might he carve out a space for himself, a war he saw in black and white: The Allies were good, the Axis evil. Because his skin already associated him with the Axis, the boy was rotting with self-loathing. Not fighting meant floundering in cultural limbo; shame would eat the boy alive. Big Jim might say the alternative was to be cannon fodder in a white man's war, or possibly against other yellow men. Maybe Tony could skewer Miyake with his bayonet. Or drop an incendiary bomb on his maternal grandparents. Or vice versa. What kind of choice was that?

"I don't think what I feel matters much in this case," Fujita said, and Mari hissed.

"Oh, God, Pop! It *does* matter," Tony cried, with a shocking ferocity. He whipped his cigarette onto the floor. The skin on his fists whitened as he strangled the form. He looked as if he would cry from his frustration. "I hate—"

Fujita waited patiently, then slowly realized Tony had nothing else to add. Not *I hate it here.* Not *I hate the army* or *I hate Nazis* or *I hate what's happened to me.* Not even *I hate* you, which wouldn't have surprised Fujita. That was it. Just "I hate."

If one went to war out of hate alone, mustn't that destroy a man? Would such a man come home?

"I'll tell you what *I* feel, Tony," Mari barged in, unable to bear it any longer. "I feel better having you alive and in one piece."

It was out of love that Fujita decided to sabotage Tony's war effort. It was for love that *he* had to be the one to say "no-no." He looked to his own response in his hand, edited to read: "Will you swear allegiance to the USA[1] and faithfully defend the

United States from any or all attack by foreign[2] or domestic forces[3], and forswear[4] any form of allegiance or obedience to the Japanese emperor, or any other foreign government[5], power, or organization[6]?" To which he wrote: "(1) I always have, and still do, senseless as some of its citizens (and lawmakers) have become. (2) See my answer to question # 27, above. (3) Such as whom? Would this include, for example, a military coup by the Army? And is "the United States" meant to imply "the federal government"? Suppose, for example, another Civil War develops, and part of the Union seeks secession. (4) "Forswear *v.* 1. to give up, to renounce, *he forswore tobacco.* 2. to deny or renounce under oath." If the former definition applies, I cannot properly answer this question with a one-word response, for I never bore any allegiance to the Japanese emperor in the first place. If the latter, and in light of my answer to item # 28—1 above, then the question is just redundant and stupid. (5) It's my duty to point out to you that this same question, as applied to Issei internees, obviously depends on whether or not they are allowed to remain in the United States. Prohibited from naturalization, threatened with deportation, they'll assume any answer to be incriminating. (6) What is the nature of such organizations? Does this include professional societies and business interests abroad? International partnerships between U.S. and foreign firms? Some precision, please. I look forward to your reply. Yours very sincerely."

His responses were intended to bog down the reviewers, who would accept only yes or no. If he were confronted, he'd give negative answers in hope that a bit of his own muck would splatter, saving Tony from conscription, blame, *and* shame. The father would be dragged into court, saddled with a criminal record, removed to a federal prison or Tule Lake, or even deported, while the son, the former nonalien Japanese enemy, might remain guiltless but suspect by association—and safe.

"How do I feel?" Fujita asked distantly. "If your country calls you to service, you'll do what you have to do," Fujita said, knowing now what he'd have to do himself. "Until then, you'll stay put." He wanted to touch Tony's hand, but the boy might explode if he did. "Of course, we'd prefer if you could stay

Stateside. It would be nice, for example, if you could find some essential work and put your radio skills to use." Some deferred, essential work, he thought, wondering what skills would make Tony essential. An essential boxer? A necessary zookeeper? Mari wouldn't look at him. Tony frowned. "Don't sulk. There's no shame in that. The army needs good electricians. But you'll have to decide what to do if you're chosen for combat, and if you have no compelling responsibilities at home."

"At home?" Tony echoed bitterly. "Right." He signed his form, reading aloud, "'Yes, Yes.'" Mari kicked her husband's leg under the table, but Fujita didn't flinch—he never took his eyes off his son.

"We all have to decide for ourselves," the Maybe-Maybe Man repeated, signing his own loyalty review.

Apparently, the War Relocation Authority shared Yoneko's aesthetic sense that Gila was "the prettiest camp," and when Eleanor Roosevelt, *Eleanor Roosevelt herself,* decided to visit her less fortunate countrymen, the honor of hosting the first lady fell to the "model camp" at Rivers. Why that great woman should wish to visit such a grim place was a mystery to Fujita. Yet, niece to one president, wife and distant cousin to another, and politically active in her own right, Mrs. Roosevelt doubtlessly possessed a distinct worldliness and sophistication. As a product of *shashin-kekkon,* a transcontinental picture marriage, the Nisei accepted the mismatching of married couples more easily than most—not to mention occasional blood-matching of distant cousins. However *Mr.* Roosevelt had disappointed the Democrat nurseryman, his admiration for the wife remained pure. In that fine lady he saw a savior, one with the influence and the moral gumption to actually do something about "the whole thing."

"She could tell her husband a thing or two," he said aloud to Mari. He determined then to speak with the great lady, if he could manage it, on her tour of the vegetable crops, though he feared he might turn into a pillar of salt. Planning ahead, he revised the many letters he'd fancifully penned to her husband, never meaning to send them. Watching him from the threshold, which she swept for the third time that day, Mari said he looked like he was getting ready for a date, like he was writing a *love* letter.

The great day found Fujita laboring over an acre of daikon radish, his already foul mood enhanced by the vile pesticide vapors he pumped over the leaves—his most-hated chore. It had taken him several months in Gila to notice that his thick, full hair hadn't required a trim since Tulare; Mari complained that its brittle ends broke off on their pillows at night. In wartime, the protective mask a sprayer normally wore could be put to other, better use. Fujita made do with his fedora, now mottled with the poisonous drops, his Sears & Roebuck gloves, two bandannas wrapped about his face and ears, and a hanky covering the back of his neck like the lobster tail of a feudal Japanese war helmet, so that he looked like a cross between Billy the Kid and a mummified beekeeper. This outrageous headpiece and the steady pumping of the sprayer deafened Fujita to the first lady's entourage as the cars rolled up the dirt firebreak behind him. It also prevented him from hearing the rattlesnake he was dangerously close to disturbing. Noticing the scaly blur a split second before stepping on it, he abruptly lurched backward. As his comrades in other parts of the field ran to greet the president's wife, he mistook their flight for cowardice—he thought they fled from the snake, which was fast, but not that fast. It posed a danger only to Fujita, who desperately tried to recall whether loud stomping or motionlessness best repelled vipers.

As Mrs. Roosevelt's great black car neared the crop beds, what had looked from afar like a scarecrow in the field now revealed itself to be a man frozen on one leg like a martial artist practicing a defensive pose in emulation of a stork, or an actor in a Noh drama. Yet, a veteran of Japanese cultural exhibitions, the first lady saw his gracelessness and knew better. Some ritualistic harvest dance? she wondered, and with a gloved hand directed her driver to take a detour off the firebreak. *A mad beekeeper doing a Hopi dance!* thought the grand dame, as Fujita came into view.

Intent on the snake, frozen as the predicted pillar of salt, Fujita failed to notice the black car until its regal bumper almost touched his rump. He did not need to hear the wavering, marble-mouthed, "I say there, hello, can you hear me," to know it was the president's wife parked behind him. Gulping, he pressed himself back against the car's searing metal hood and inched away from where he'd lost sight of the snake. Then he saw her, and what a whirl of confusion he felt, able only to look down as Mrs. Roosevelt placed a rich heel onto the red desert floor. His relief to have a car handy—something to jump up on if the serpent returned—was tempered by a surge of prejudicial irritation: Having women in the field, even this excellent woman, made him uncomfortable. Too dangerous. He admired her courage, braving this den of vipers. Out here alone with me, he realized, when he saw the train of coworkers running back toward them, behind the carfuls of guards and camp staff, all clearly disgruntled that the first lady had ditched them at the firebreak. Alone but for her driver, who admittedly looked strong enough to snap Fujita's spine with a pinkie, and the nervous administrator Mr. Johnson.

"Why, hello there," she said. "I'm Eleanor Roosevelt. And what's your name?"

I'm Eleanor Roosevelt! Wasn't that just like her! Bashfully, Fujita gave his name and offered what felt to him like the smile of a sane person, forgetting that two bandannas still obscured it. This muffled his voice, too, and the first lady misunderstood.

"A pleasure to meet you, Mr. Fuchida," said Eleanor Roosevelt, though the wrinkling of her queenly nose made it seem she did not find the experience pleasurable. The slapdash mask he still wore prevented him from smelling the pesticide, though he had clarity enough to remove his glove, caked with mud, before shaking her hand. "Well, what are you working at here?"

She wants to know about my radishes! thought the ecstatic plant man. Keeping one ear and two eyes out for the snake, he blathered about Gila's twelve hundred acres of vegetable crops and the one thousand acres devoted to seed farming, alfalfa, and feed crops. He estimated the total tonnage of Gila's food production to be five thousand (its value about $320,000); of this, nearly one hundred cars of surplus had been shipped to other camps. "Mung beans, Chinese cabbage, Irish potatoes," he recited through his bandit's mask. To Mrs. Roosevelt, it sounded like wunh weenh and whydwee wabbazh and whywish bonayno. "Italian parsley, Swiss chard, Armenian cucumber." A world's fair of international foodstuffs! "Not to mention the cantaloupes, the shiro uri, and the daikon." In his confusion and awe, he nearly forgot about the snake as he bent to disinter one of his huge, beloved daikon radishes. The first lady, who was beginning to regret this detour, hoped the fellow in the sinister mask didn't mean to make a present of the root, which looked alarmingly like a human arm. His ungloved hand glowed red with the fresh pesticide, causing the woman to think, Perhaps he's a burn victim? He wears a mask to hide hideous deformations? It also reminded Fujita of his mask. Whipping it off, he simultaneously smelled the poison-filled air and heard the nearby rattle of the snake he'd recently offended. A tabloid headline flashed through his mind: ELEANOR ASSASSINATED! POISONED BY MASKED JAP KILLER!

He bent down because this thought and the noxious fumes, the morning's exertion and his present excitement, made him suddenly woozy. And he was also looking for the snake, which was *very* nearby, he heard. Mrs. Roosevelt gasped when he raised the huge, dirty root in offering, but sensitive to other people's customs, the diplomatic lady returned what she mistook for an honorific bow.

The "pits" that gave a pit viper its name, young Tony Fujita had instructed his father, were heat-sensitive pockmarks on the sides of its face, rather like radar dishes. Without sharing Tony's queer hobby, even Fujita could see that the wedgelike head peeking from beneath the automobile belonged to the horned rattlesnake, the southwestern sidewinder. And a woman's stockinged ankle radiated more heat than steel-lined work boots, or even the sort of calf-high leather boots a chauffeur wore. The irritable "rattle" was formed by its shedding skin; after each molting, a new ring of skin remained on the rattle's "button." Although Fujita could not see the snake's body, he knew some species reached seven feet in length and fifteen inches in diameter. This was much longer and about as round as the massive daikon that had so startled Mrs. Roosevelt and which was Fujita's only weapon now in her defense. Swiftly, he took aim.

The driver, whose day at Gila had given him the willies, also mistook Fujita's gesture—for that of an assailant. To his professional eye, it appeared that a hostile and perhaps crazy Nip meant to clobber the first lady with what looked like a giant radish. No matter that he caught a vegetable rather than a bullet—that brave soul had spent years practicing for this moment, and he never wavered. He planted himself in the line of fire like the trunk of small tree.

This, Fujita saw, was a big mistake. The scuffle further provoked the rattlesnake beneath the car. Whacking the huge driver aside with the two-foot radish, he whipped the heavy root across the snake's snout. Like the driver, the creature seemed more stunned than wounded. Its rattle grew fiercer. Terrified, the patriotic internee then grabbed the steel pump sprayer and brought it down on the wedge-shaped head. It seemed to do the trick, but he repeated the action fourteen times, until Mr. Johnson could get out of the car to stop him. By this time, the bruised driver had shoved the first lady into the car and was now making an abrupt semicircular turn, nearly mowing down the ragtag band of field workers just making their way back from the firebreak. For weeks, Fujita's colleagues would refuse to speak to him; they blamed him for their missed opportunity to meet the president's wife, who now turned around in the black car to watch the poor lunatic beating on the ground with what looked like a bucket. This did not surprise the driver, who had always maintained that the Japanese were crazy, an inherently sneaky, barbarous people who ought to be "exported" or just shot. Though too breathless to speak, what that good lady thought was, *I don't know—maybe it's a mistake*. So perhaps, as she and Fujita lost each other in a wall of red dust, it didn't matter that he found his letter to her still folded in his overalls pocket, the letter that began, "Dear President & Mrs. Roosevelt: Nations, like individuals, make mistakes . . . "

One happy result of Fujita's humiliation before the first lady was that Mr. Johnson of the WRA had seen the whole affair from inside the royal car. Although the administrator snickered to read Fujita's letter, out of both pity and admiration he made sure that it was delivered. That Mrs. Roosevelt might have been gassed to death while in his charge convinced him that Gilan field workers needed reasonable protection, and he vowed to order some decent gloves and masks for handling the pesticides. "Well, some good came out of all this," Fujita told Mari and Tony, trying to sound upbeat. "You see, Tony. An individual can make a difference, if just a bit."

"Oh, brother," said Mari in the doorway, sweeping the homily outdoors right along with the red desert dust.

Mr. Johnson also caught Fujita's act of patriotic bravery in slaying the viper. While as a rule, Maybe-Maybes were treated as No-Nos, Johnson respectfully did Fujita the favor of ignoring his wishy-washy responses to the questionnaire. Far from casting doubt on Tony, the boy's association with Fujita the hero led some officials to hope they were drafting a chip off the old block. Fujita felt like his head had been placed on the block as he still waited to be interrogated or whatever, for he didn't yet know about Johnson's gracious pardon.

When late spring brought his draft-induction notice, Tony could barely hide his relief.

The close call in the daikon patch had warmed Fujita to Tony's zoo. He preferred sharing the apartment with Lucy the rattlesnake, safely enclosed in her glass house—one less snake to meet out there. Although he didn't care to watch Tony feed her—usually some rodent approximately the size of Eleanor Roosevelt's ankle—he sometimes helped Tony clean out the cages and jars. The shared activity was reminiscent of their days of backyard catches at the nursery. Now that Fujita had failed as a saboteur and Tony would ship out soon, they struck an uneasy peace. It was agreed that he and Yoneko would split the responsibility of feeding the beasts when Tony went into training. Fujita even learned their names. Nudie wasn't really a newt, but Tony called him Nudie because just after he was captured, he began shedding his skin. Looking at Brenda the black widow and Harry Tarantula made Fujita itch. Yoneko couldn't even look at them. Tony reassured them that the jars made secure prisons. He also kept a scorpion named Karl after Karl Bendetsen, a chief government advocate and planner of the relocation, and a beetle family (the Baileys), warring tribes of ants, a jumping mouse named Jesse (for Owens). He'd also captured a baby hare, which, in his last act as an internee, he ceremonially liberated by the front gate with his family in attendance. Painfully, the Fujitas watched him grow teary-eyed as it dashed away, seeming to slip right through the chain-link fence to be swallowed into the earth. Tony never did find the reptile he most coveted—an actual Gila monster. Perhaps there were no Gila monsters in Gila River? Tony swore the creature existed—it looked like an onyx-studded blackjack ringed with gold bands. If he could have caught one of those, he said, he'd gladly chop up the others and sacrifice them to the monster's appetite. Yoneko thought he'd still have freed the hare, which he followed out of Butte Camp an hour later.

Tony surprised them all by writing frequently while training in Minneapolis, and once he'd entered combat, he even radioed in telegrams when he could. Despite Jim's reservations, he never drew KP duty, nor was he sent ahead to punch land mines. For, if his grandmother had been arrested for teaching Japanese, Tony now won a special assignment because he'd learned the language, however shakily. As in all things, Tamie had been the first to predict it. When her letter finally made its way to them, it read:

> Dear Son (and you censors out there),
>
> I am fine though horrendously bored. I am now in North Dakota, I think. They moved us away from that old nunnery—to Terminal Island, then out here—but I am still surrounded by a bunch of old nuns! I am treated well enough by the staff, though I become aggravated by their (get your scissors out boys) ______ very often. Your father would have commented, I'm sure.
>
> I am told the Army needs Japanese teachers. Of course,

the hakujin teachers are adept at reading medieval folk tales but do not know words for "torpedo" et cetera. Well, well. I offered to teach and named my salary, but my kindness was met only with rudeness. I am sorry that I became angry, but I told them, if you fear that a 61-year-old woman will sabotage the war for you, wait until you have to draft my grandson out of camp only to learn that his Japanese is worse than the hakujin's.

They said, If you irritate the Army, it will be worse for you.

I said, You'd better not irritate me.

Now they are afraid of me. It is their loss.

I will write again when I'm not so busy. I hope this finds you and finds you well. Kiss my grandson for me.

"I told you we shouldn't have sent him to the gakuen," Fujita complained to Mari.

"She's your mother," Mari replied. "Besides, it was the radio classes, too."

Whether it was the Japanese or the radio classes, Tony did not head off to Camp Shelby with the all-Nisei 100th/442nd Regiment. Instead, he found a role in the South Pacific theater with Military Intelligence Services as a translator and began training in Minneapolis.

"Minneapolis?" Yoneko asked. "Is that where they make cheese?"

"Beer, I think," said Big Jim.

"No, no. That's Milwaukee," said Calvin Igawa, Tony's quiet Pasadenan friend who, Fujita vaguely noticed, had begun hanging around Yoneko more frequently since Tony left. A heavyweight studier after Fujita's own heart, Calvin knew his geography, too. "Beer and cheese is Wisconsin. Tony's in Minnesota. Land of Ten Thousand Lakes, they call it."

After months of training, Tony secured permission to visit Gila before shipping out to Hawaii. Big Jim drove Aunt Rose to have tea with friends way over in Canal Camp, so the young lovers had managed two hours alone. The exertion did not tire him, it exhilarated him, and when Jim and Rose returned, he put on his gloves and went three rounds with his old sparring partner without getting knocked down once. After the workday, the Fujitas and Yamaguchis took their mess trays outdoors for a picnic in the dry, eighty-degree night, and then the Fujita men sat on Sacaton Butte. Away from the rows of shacks, the crickets' night-song was a roar. Tony offered a Camel to his father, who shook his head.

"Listen," Tony began, "I asked Yoneko today." Nervously, he blew a smoke ring, and another little one through that, a trick he'd picked up in training camp along with basic first aid, some Hawaiian pidgin, and advanced Japanese and radio electronics. He'd also learned the difference between bullets and boxing, flak and fists, and the value of time. In the bright moonlight, he checked his watch. Fujita thought his voice had grown deeper.

"You asked her what?"

"To *marry* me, Pop." He sounded exasperated.

"What?" Fujita said. Then he thought about it for a moment. "No," he said.

"I'm not asking permission," Tony said, twirling the butt end of his cigarette in his fingertips, weaving a curtain of blue smoke like a holy man with incense. His jaw set with a new determination, a new authority. Was it just maturation, Fujita wondered. Just the army? A canine barking echoed across the camp. Listening to the lonely cries, Fujita scanned the earth radiating out from his shoes across the butte. Corpses lay strewn as far as he could see—dried husks of corn and beans, the woody skeletons of cacti, a bleached bovine shin bone. No, he decided, it was freedom. Tony could—would—walk through that fence the next morning free to make what decisions the army allowed him.

"You see, I'm not asking your permission," Tony repeated. "I just sort of wanted to let you know. I don't mean we're going to run off and get married today or anything."

"That's a good thing!" Fujita said, unable to collect his thoughts. "What's the hurry?"

"I mean, we're more like engaged. Engaged to be married. I

didn't want to tell Mom yet—for your sake, you know—but I wanted to tell you. I know you don't like her. She can bug a fellow sometimes. But I was talking to some of the boys at MIS, see, who got me thinking. I don't plan on dying; I might, but I don't, you know, plan on it. When I come back, you can disown me or whatever—"

"Now wait a minute—" Fujita cut in.

"Until then," Tony continued, "I have to suppose I might. You know. Die. So, I'm asking you to do something for me. Like a last request. I just want you to look out for her, take care of her even. MIS will send a portion of my pay home to my parents. So I want you to take care of her; there's been lots of fighting, even shooting, up in Manzanar and Tule. Once I leave here, I don't think I can come back—I'll know too much to be among all these Nisei," he snickered. "So if something bad happens. . . . And if you get out, go somewhere, I'd like you to take her and Rose with you. Pop?"

"Let her live with us?" Fujita asked. "Outside?"

"Yeah, like they do in Japan."

"Daughters-in-law move in with their men's families."

"Pop, please. I'm sort of fighting this war for her. For you and Mom, too, but I'm fighting so I can come back to her whether you like it or not. Please. Pop?"

"I'll take that cigarette now." From Sacaton Butte, looking above the barbed wire at the shadows of saguaros surrounding them like spies, Fujita felt suddenly elated, though it would take time to understand why. If only hate sent a man to the wars, what was left behind to lure him back? Wasn't love the only real fighting chance a man had if he was to get back home?

"If you're engaged," he finally said, "you'd better try extra hard not to get hurt. Now you've got *three* women who'll make your life hell if you do."

Then Tony was gone again. The Fujitas and Yamaguchis watched the gates slam shut, the familiar red cloud trailing away. Then Mari pivoted back toward Block 60. "Get out of my way," she said to Yoneko, with an iciness Fujita had not thought her capable of. She brushed the crying girl aside like a bug, like one of Tony's beetles. That day, from dawn to dusk, in every crack in the bare-wood apartment she hunted down every pebble, every thread of brush, every hardened rabbit dropping, and every cursed mote of the Rivers dust that could never quite be swept away.

NINE

What the Scarecrow Said

Garvin listened to the descriptions of Gila River as attentively as if he were planning to write a school essay about it, only interrupting to prod for details—the boxing matches, the model warships, the color of the snake. To Livvie, what Fujita euphemistically referred to as "the whole thing" sounded worse than she'd imagined, while Margaret had always imagined the worst, and so was surprised when amusement and fondness crept into his recollections of Eleanor Roosevelt and Tony's odd talents. Fujita's relationship with Yoneko confused both women and even irked Livvie some. "Tell us again," Livvie said, "why you don't like the girl." Fujita began jiggling the change in his pocket.

"Well, she's annoying," he said weakly.

"Annoying," Livvie echoed, and this annoyed him, too.

"Right. Well, she's terribly emotional."

"Oh, I see. You know, that's what my father says about my mother. Just like that: '*Terribly* emotional,' he says. He thinks being emotional is terrible, too."

"Well, it's only a phrase, really—just a saying." Fujita jingled away like a bell harp.

"Like 'awfully excited'? Like, 'I like her an *awful* lot'?"

It had taken him two days to get his story out: Christmas Eve and much of Christmas morning. There remained events he could not speak of, not yet, but they viewed his tale as a great gift, as sure as the model plane for Garvin and vase for Livvie, or the winter clothing they gave him. They all appreciated how their travel to far-off Rivers, Arizona, helped ease them past the holiday.

Nurse Kelly had told him, "We have to relive unhappy moments sometimes in order to heal," but excusing himself, heading off for another sleepless night in the garage, Fujita felt far from healed. Rather, he felt drained, as if from blood loss, and he doubted he had strength left to vault the anniversaries looming before him. At least he suffered no nightmares that night, on the cusp between Christmas and what Margaret called Boxing Day. He'd never heard of it. "It's the best part of the holidays," she had explained. "After the shopping, the cooking, the drunken uncles and children fighting over toys, Boxing Day is the day allotted to real friends. We usually used to hold an open house," she said. Stricken, Fujita had frowned so sourly, she had blurted, "But not this year!"

"Friends?" he'd said, a little coldly.

Late that insomniac night, he repeated it to his roommate, the office skeleton. "Friends?" However, as he faced what he feared would be the hardest weeks of his life—the anniversaries of losing Tony and Mari, not to mention the new year alone and his forty-eighth birthday—he longed for any relief, whether from friends or perhaps even Juggeston's Society of Friends. On Boxing Day morning, he sought Margaret in the kitchen. "Friends," he said tentatively. "It sounds so . . . friendly." Herb Nicholson, the ex-missionary Pasadenan, had been Quaker-raised and schooled; he had foreseen much more clearly than Fujita how "the whole thing" would test whether "a whole lot of Christian" was Christian enough. Proving his faith and friendship, Herb had been a founding member of Friends for the American Way, a frequent visitor to the camps, and had once been jailed himself for his role in easing the lot of the Nikkei; he and his wife, Madeline, had been prepared. The war, however, had made Fujita a whole lot of skeptic, and it was reluctantly that he told Margaret, "I might go to meeting, I might not. It's just a look-see. Tell me again what they believe in. They're pacifists, right?"

"Some are, some join the Army. They're hard to pin down, really. No clergy, no formal creed, except it's assumed we all have a personal connection with God—the Inner Light, they call it. You sit silently; no set service or single speaker. If you're just a tourist, it's not much of a show."

"The Inner Light," Mr. Fujita repeated. "It's like meditation. It's Buddhist."

Margaret mulled over that for a moment. "Whew, this is tough. It's like . . . a wholesale religion rather than retail. In meeting, you sort of quietly hunker down with God to hash things out without a middleman. Then people may just stand up and announce that deal—maybe an observation about the foliage outside. Maybe they get an idea, say, to oppose the draft, and they bat it around for a while. A long while. Too long for my liking."

"They vote on things," he prompted. "It's like a business-association meeting."

"They reach a consensus, yes. A 'sense of meeting.' This meeting does."

"And how do you get to be a member, again?"

"You go to meeting, help with services and events, and then you just decide to. The decision is what counts. It takes a certain amount of . . ." She chose her words carefully. "It takes maturity to be a Friend. Self-discipline. That's why I was never a Convinced Friend. I was what's called an Attender. I went, but wasn't Convinced. I wasn't ready."

"You could have joined, though."

"I wasn't Convinced."

"I see," said Fujita, though he actually did not see. His experience of religion had been mostly limited to the *retail* variety—pamphleteers and missionaries—the hard sell, the pushy traveling salesmen whose trade seemed to depend precisely upon catching the customer unawares. Among all things one must ready himself for in the world, he thought it odd one must "be ready" to join a religion, too, even one with such sketchy tenets. "And how does one get 'ready'?" he wondered aloud.

Margaret sighed. "I'm really not the best person to ask. If you're so interested, go with Livvie."

Asked if she thought he was "ready," Livvie only laughed. Her explanation of the Friends' meeting was vastly more simple, and inviting. "Margaret thinks too much," she told Fujita, shrugging. "I go to *not* think, or not in the usual way. It's a time-out. You're left to yourself but not alone. You see people, but they don't demand much of you. It's helped, actually. You're welcome to come along with me."

"It wouldn't hurt to just take a look at the place," he agreed, and although he meant to head back to his room, he found himself continuing eastward down the drive into town. The meetinghouse where Juggeston worshipped was plain and unobtrusive as the neighboring arcade was ramshackle and gaudy. It sat to the west of Town Square, at a respectable distance from where Wellington's and Town Hall elbowed each other. A trinity of green storm shutters adorned the whitewashed face. No railing guarded the front porch, and the granite wall skirting the grounds stood at most a foot high. No crucifix, no busts or statues, no tortured saints or gargoyles—only a plain-lettered sign revealed the building's function: JUGGESTON FRIENDS MEETING—WORSHIP 10:30 A.M. SUNDAY—ALL WELCOME."

"Sure," muttered Fujita, far from convinced. "You say that now."

Behind the meetinghouse lay the tiniest cemetery he had ever seen. A cluster of some fifty knee-high markers stood within twenty yards of a swing set and seesaw; these rounded white stones lay so close together, and were so unassuming, that the place looked more like a flower bed than a graveyard. Propped against one chipped stone in the center, some visitor had left a sheet of notepaper reading, "A very small amount of light can dispel an awful lot of darkness."

"A very small amount of light," Fujita whispered to himself, weighing the prospects. "An awful lot of darkness." The meetinghouse was locked and empty, but he walked around to the front porch and pressed his face to the window. The heat of his breath made the pane steam up, and he had to swab away the frost continually to read the sign posted on the wall of the vestibule within. It read:

> The Juggeston Friends invite you to share the hospitality of our Meeting. We will not define for or impose upon you a form for the Meeting, but we do ask that you listen both to the harmonious silence of waiting and to the spoken word that may blossom from silence. We ask you to wait with patience and openness for an understanding of the Friends Meeting. We ask, too, that you arrive at the appointed hour; Meeting will begin only when we are all joined in the silent waiting upon God known among Friends as Centering Down. Speaking aloud is an expression of a deep religious experience that must be shared. Whether sensed as an upwelling of the spirit or as an insight, this is the result of an earnest seeking and is never casual or argumentative. Our silence is not an emptiness crying out to be filled, but a disciplined and contemplative openness to the spirit of God. Meeting is a special time away from our worldly concerns in which we seek together, often in silence, the strength to meet our problems and responsibilities. We welcome you.

Fujita allowed his breath to close the window into the meetinghouse. "Patience," he droned to himself. "Opennesssss." He tested each word as if in a foreign language requiring an inflection long atrophied in him. "Centering down." He glanced at the porch floorboards, white-painted and flaked, trailing away at ground level beneath the snow.

"This porch needs a railing. Too open," he said, tramping back to the main drive. "I'm not sure I'm ready," Fujita confided to the Civil War statue, whose cap spilled over with ice and broken twigs. From the arcade porch, where he pounded dust from the welcome mat with a dowel, Alf saw Fujita and they exchanged waves. "Maybe see you at meeting on Sunday?" he called. The shopkeeper didn't seem to hear him, only waved again and returned to his chore. Fujita headed back to his buried nojo on Widow's Peak.

❧ ❧ ❧

Garvin knew his orders were firm: "Leave him alone," his mother had said. "Don't bother him now." Bother him? Garvin just wanted to do what he'd always done on Boxing Day, which he agreed was the best part of the holidays. The Tuftellers' Christmases had always crackled with the tension of holiday bills, of too much eggnog, of a holiday—especially in those depression years—doomed to pale beside the Christmases his parents would loudly remember. Boxing Days, though, his father devoted only to him, to the assembly and maiden voyages of new playthings. While his mother cleared last night's dishes and swept up pine needles and balled-up wrapping paper for the trash, Pop, hungover, would wrestle with the bicycle or mini-tractor or model fortress. Working with a beer and a purpose, he grunted and cursed and squinted against smoke from a cigarette clamped in his lips, an untapped, two-inch ash drooping but miraculously intact. "It's a good thing you've got a mechanically minded pop," he'd say, finishing the assembly two hours later. "Other kids wouldn't be riding the damned thing until spring." These were among Garvin's warmest memories of his father, and Boxing Day found him feeling more bereft than ever.

"I'm a little down just now," Fujita said tiredly, when Garvin found him shaving in the garage office. "I think I need to hibernate for a while."

"Me, too."

Though unhappy, Garvin was not unfeeling. He only meant to commiserate, but Mr. Fujita sighed and said, "Okay, let's see it." For about twenty minutes, he watched Garvin breaking in his new Flexible Flyer sled. After dragging it back up the hill for the twenty-fourth time, Garvin offered to surrender it for a bit, but the Californian appeared confused.

"That's it? You just go down and come up again? The coming up seems a lot of work," he said, and he frowned. "The zooming down looks dangerous. You've got a daredevil in you, don't you?" Garvin grinned at this. With his face wrapped and a scarf flying behind, he dove onto the sled once again, gripping the steering slat like the handlebars of a motorcycle, and *tried* to hit all the most insidious bumps and pits, launching and plummeting through the newly tiered hillside boldly as the war-hero father he was emulating.

"Thanks, but I don't think sledding's for me," Fujita said. "It looks too cold. You look like a glazed donut. Let's get some cocoa instead. I've got a little story for you."

Though sitting and sipping together at the kitchen table, Garvin and Fujita were worlds apart, the boy still daredeviling alongside his father in Burma, and the man still at Gila, where he'd last told the story. Little Bobby Tanaka had been there, and Bobby's friend from outside on the surrounding Pima Indian reservation, Tom Fields. And Yoneko. That's what he remembered now, the telling and the audience, as much as the tale he began.

Six-year-old Bobby Tanaka, from Block 59, had been disconsolate about Tony's leaving. The wheeled, wooden toy bloodhound Bobby constantly tugged around clattered as he trailed along behind his Uncle Calvin, who had been in turn the occasional third wheel appended to his friends, Tony and Yoneko. The trio treated Bobby much better than most adults did, and they made a remarkable train rambling about camp together. Beside Tony's slouch walk and Yoneko's bouncy strut, Calvin walked with a determined gait, hands thrust into his front pockets, eyes fixed on some distant landmark, his chest pushing him forward to the target. To keep up, little Bobby had to quick-step, his bloodhound clacking exhaustedly at the end of its string leash. Bobby, Calvin, and Tony could spend hours in wordless admiration of Tony's awful zoo, as if watching a ballet.

When Fujita found him one afternoon a few weeks after Tony's departure, the child was crumpled in a heap in the middle of F Street, his face webbed with stringy mucus, as if traversed by a garden slug. "What's wrong with him?" Fujita asked his playmate, the frightened Pima boy named Tom Fields, since Bobby could only gasp and drool. They looked like twins, Fujita noticed. Though a year younger, Tom Fields also stood as high as Fujita's crotch; he had a similarly round, open face, a cap of black hair with bangs, wide trusting eyes, and rubbery little legs bowed like soft bamboo. His skin was only a shade darker than

Bobby's; at the end of a typically dusty day, both appeared to be made out of the Gila earth itself.

"He can't go home," Tom explained, crossing his legs to keep from peeing.

"We always play here," Bobby moaned, mopping at his face with a sleeve, which only redistributed the mucus and dirt from the right cheek to the left. Fujita picked him up then and carried him back toward Block 60. "We never go to his house," Bobby sobbed, pointing accusingly at his friend, who followed sheepishly. Tom said he liked coming to camp to visit the *rich* people, which both amused and appalled Fujita, the penniless yet comparatively privileged exile. When they stopped at the communal latrines, Tom watched in awe as the golden stream arced into the commode where, unlike his family's outhouse, it was swept away by actual running water. To the two wrinkled old Issei seated to either side, grunting and staring at the floor, he beamed as if to say: Look at that! The old poopers frowned, and he blushed, having missed some etiquette known naturally to those born in the lap of luxury. He stared admiringly as his pal Bobby hopped onto one of the holes as casually as a prince on a throne.

When they were done, Fujita had them wash their hands, then headed back with them toward his apartment. "It's not *fair*," Bobby said, calmer, but still simmering with indignation. With the boy hanging about his neck, Fujita spotted Yoneko across the street, which sparked a nagging and indecipherable sense of déjà vu. Though her back was turned, Yoneko suddenly spun around, her expression as curious as his own, as if feeling it, too. The sensation passed, though, as she crossed the road to ask what was wrong. "It's not fair," Bobby repeated. Why could Tony go outside, he wanted to know, but not him? "That's not fair, is it?" he demanded. Fujita admitted that it was not.

Meaning well, Yoneko said, "Tony's a big boy, though. Someday, you'll be a big boy, too. Then you can do anything you want. You can go anywhere, and have great, heroic adventures."

Fujita snorted, and Yoneko looked up at him quizzically. No use lying to the boy, he thought. But Bobby, reminded of how he missed his heroic friend, began sniffling anew.

Fujita knew that Bobby had come to think of Tony as a big brother—riding around on Tony's back or playing airplane with Tony and his Uncle Calvin throwing him up in the sky. "When's Tony coming home?" Bobby wanted to know. Put out that the leg he found himself seated on was old Mr. Fujita's, which was too hard and bony, Bobby glared at Tom Fields. The Pima boy had made a pillow of Yoneko's lap, where she sat on the stoop also waiting for Tony's father's promised "little story." A story of heroes. A story of homecomings.

A Japanese child would immediately peg Fujita for a liar; a thumb-sucker could flag his errors and inconsistencies. The story Fujita had so mangled and twisted for Tony, for Bobby and Tom, and later for Garvin, was that of his own earliest hero, Momotaro, the Peach Boy, the peach of his parents' eyes. However, Fujita's Momotaro was not the same sort of boy he had heard about during his own growing up. In his revision, the Peach Boy emerged as a hero precisely because he did *not* abandon his parents to seek war with the ogres. Sensibly, he bided his time, studied, grew into a fine young man, and then met the demons armed with generosity and wisdom and strength. This was out-and-out nonsense, so far as a Japanese folklorist would see it, but much closer to the truth of family, love, and *ōn*, to Fujita's mind.

With Bobby Tanaka sitting alert in his lap, Fujita took a deep, preparatory breath. From Bobby's shiny, bowl-cut hair wafted the scent of damp clay, but it didn't smell unclean—not to Fujita—no body odor, no fearful sweat, no hormonal emissions. To him, it smelled like life, like possibility, and to prevent himself from kissing that head before him, he began.

In a land to the far west lived an elderly couple who were, of course, farm people (not woodcutters). The wife went to the brook one morning, not to wash laundry but to reroute some of its life-giving water to an irrigation canal. That's when she spied an enormous peach, as large as her torso, floating downstream. Excitedly, the arthritic old woman dove in and nearly drowned, but she managed to retrieve it (in Fujita's world, one didn't linger on the bank, leaving something worthwhile for the capricious tides to abandon on the shore). Although hungry and poor, the couple was old and thus not seduced by the instant gratification the peach offered them (in Fujita's world, age and wisdom were twins). She took the great fruit home to her husband for planting, not for dinner. Harvesting a tree sprung from a pit of such proportions, they hoped, would make them rich at market. One fruit could feed a whole family for days! Choosing a spot with excellent drainage, they prepared the earth with the proper fertilizer; it lacked manganese, and they added ten pounds of seaweed, which is high in potash and many trace elements. Finally, the farmer's wife brought a hefty knife from the kitchen, and the farmer prepared to make a small incision (called "scarification") in the pit to facilitate quick germination.

Just then, a tiny, human voice sounded from inside the peach. "Wait! Don't cut me!" Suddenly, like an enormous egg, the peach split apart and out jumped a beautiful baby boy! "Have no fear!" the baby said. "The Universe knew of your great loneliness and hardship, so I have come to ease your burden as a son." (*This loses a lot in translation,* Yoneko sighed.)

The old couple cried for happiness. They named him Momotaro, Peach Boy, and he grew into an obedient, hardworking chap. Then, when he reached puberty, he told his parents: "Parents, you've been so kind to me, and now that I'm a big boy, I must serve my country. Across the wide sea lies Ogre Island, a great fortress home to the ogres whose warships harry our shores . . ." (*Harry?* asked Bobby. *Wait, who's Harry? What's pyoobiddy?* asked Tom Fields.)

"They terrorize our land," Momotaro forged on, "kidnapping and stealing. I'll go there and fight the ogres and recover all the treasures they have taken from us."

At this point, the real legend became most absurd, and Fujita's version pivoted 180 degrees. In at least a dozen editions of the tale, found in Little Tokyo bookshops, the senile old codger swells with pride, outfits a *fifteen-year-old* with armor and sword, and the wife prepares her restless peach teenager an *obento* box lunch. Even before Tony's induction, Fujita could no more allow this narrative to continue than he could grow a tree of man-sized peaches. In *his* version, the sensible farmer yanks on Momotaro's ear; his wife slaps the boy's peachy cheek. "You'll do no such thing!" she cried. "You're only a boy, and we're old and all alone. Who will work the farm? It will surely kill your father."

"Your mother will die of a broken heart!" protested the farmer. Instead, they gave Momotaro a hoe and sent him back to the fields, where he belonged. They gave him a stack of books to study at night and finally sent him away to Harvard College, where he learned great wisdom (he studied constitutional law). In the dorms there he met Dotty Dog and Monkey, two sad, rambunctious creatures who cherished argument and were both sad because they were about to be expelled from Harvard College; decent but undisciplined fellows, they chose to go out at night to drink and play cards instead of studying. Magnanimous Momotaro, who'd been raised properly, took pity and tutored them in the evenings. (*What's magnatemus?* Bobby Tanaka asked.) He told them he intended to restore peace to the land, recover from the ogres all they had stolen, then return home to care for his elderly parents. Out of gratitude, Monkey and Dotty Dog begged to help Momotaro in his quest. The day they set out for Ogre Island, they met Sparrow, who'd had his tongue cut out by a greedy, mean-spirited hag who burned with jealousy because her husband loved the sparrow so—(*Now wait!* Yoneko said. *That's a different fairy tale altogether! It's supposed to be a pheasant!* Fujita only replied: *Not in my story, it isn't. Oh brother,* huffed Yoneko.)

At first, Monkey and Dotty Dog teased Tongue-Cut Sparrow. They pranced around the speechless bird, sticking their tongues out and saying things like "Antidisestablishmentarianism," just to make him feel lousy. They acted superior because they went to Harvard College. "Stop teasing!" gentle Momotaro scolded. "He's one of us!" Tongue-Cut Sparrow, the smart bird, was a lawyer, too.

"How can *he* be a lawyer?" his companions cried. "He can't even talk!"

Ah, but, clever Momotaro knew, he could *write*. Journal articles, legal briefs, anything. When Momotaro invited Tongue-Cut Sparrow to join them, Monkey and Dotty Dog were disgruntled at first—(*Wait, don't say it,* Yoneko groaned. *Because the bird went to* Yale. *This isn't interesting anymore*, she said, but she quieted down to hear the rest. *Dartmouth,* Fujita said triumphantly. *He only went to Yale for undergraduate studies. Legal briefs?* asked Tom Fields. *Like underwear?*)

The point is, Momotaro showed them they all had the same *goal.* They just needed to learn to cooperate. So they walked harmoniously together until reaching the sea. There they argued over how to reach the island. Tongue-Cut Sparrow couldn't carry them all. Dotty Dog and Momotaro weighed too much. The quartet sat on the shoreline, absolutely baffled. (*After all those years of Ivy League education?* Yoneko snickered.)

Yes, that's what Momotaro thought, too. But it gave him an idea. Ivy! He remembered that his mother had given him three magic beans when he left for college; they were stinky, slimy natto beans, and Momotaro never liked them, so they had been germinating in his pocket all these years. (*Yuck!* cried Bobby. Without knowing what natto was, Tom nodded, too.) It took his comrades an hour to pull them out of his pocket, for they had grown into such a tangle of vines. Finally, Momotaro instructed Tongue-Cut Sparrow to fly the ends over to the island while he anchored the roots on the shore. Then the adventurers carefully crossed the sea using the vine like a tightrope. The fortress looked impenetrable, with its locked gates, its ogre guards, its cannons and fences. But Tongue-Cut Sparrow flew over the walls to distract the ogres; while they tried to skewer the quick, brave bird with their spears, Monkey climbed over to unlock the gate, and Momotaro and Dotty Dog rushed in.

And they killed *all the ogres?* Bobby sang out expectantly. *What did they do?*

Yes, what did *they do,* Yoneko asked. *They* sued *the ogres? They* orated?

No, Fujita said quietly, shaking his head. *They traded.*

They traded? Yoneko said, outrage boiling in her face.

Augh! cried Bobby Tanaka and Tom Fields.

That's right, insisted Fujita, who never claimed to be a natural storyteller. Still, a devotee of Homer, he knew he'd lose his audience without *some* pointless bashing, some loss.

He went on with his story. The ogres *tried* to kill Momotaro's companions. The chief ogre snuck up behind with a club the size of a telephone pole. Only Tongue-Cut Sparrow noticed, but of course, he couldn't shout out a warning, and he couldn't write fast enough. First, the chief ogre clobbered Monkey; luckily, the chief ogre had poor vision; he was too vain to wear his bifocals, even for such an important battle. Monkey survived, but his head throbbed from the blow. Monkey had a terrible, simian temper, and he grew so enraged that he took a running leap at the big ogre chief, but dizzy and off-balance, he ran into the wall, *whump!* and knocked himself unconscious. The ogre would have stomped him into the dirt, but Dotty Dog thought fast. "Wait!" he barked. "Don't kill him. Momotaro values his friends. He'll surrender if you take Monkey and me as hostages." The big, stupid ogre was easily convinced to put Monkey in a cage and bind Dotty Dog in a leash and muzzle.

Fujita paused in his tale, crossed his arms, and beamed. Yoneko huffed, unsure she wanted to hear the rest, though he meant to sit there until begged to finish. *Yes,* she said unenthusiastically. *And then?*

What about Tongue-Cut Sparrow? Tom Fields asked.

Ah! Glad you asked.

The big, noisy ogres had forgotten all about the silent little bird. Big noisy ogres always do. Usually they do. Anyway, Tongue-Cut Sparrow thought the time had come for retreat. Knowing there were times to fight and times to reconsider your strategy, he flew back over the wall, took up the ends of the beanstalks, then pulled the green ladder over to where Momotaro sat sensibly negotiating with a council of ogre elders. Before he could reach his captain, though, an ogre guard with a mace bashed his tiny head so hard that the bird sank a foot into the ground.

The big mace mushed him, like a train hitting a little boy who plays on railroad tracks. When Tongue-Cut Sparrow was bashed into the ground, a snip of vine still in his beak, Momotaro realized what had happened and wept for his friend's sacrifice. Then miraculously, watered by his peach-juice tears, the cutting from the vine began to sprout, right into the sky. It rained beans. The ogres had never seen such a fabulous plant! Everywhere, ogres dropped their weapons, scooped up handfuls and began chewing on them. You see, they were hungry and poor, too, like the farmer and his wife. Hunger made them cranky, but they weren't really all evil—not beyond help. They bowed low before Momotaro, released all the hostages, and promised never to do wicked things again. Then they brought out all the treasures they had stolen. Gold, silver, jewels! A coat of shadow and a hat of invisibility. A spade that when thrust into the soil made a gold coin appear. And a magic rock that healed wounds. With these, Momotaro's company returned to enrich and heal his country. Families were reunited. How happy the farmer and his wife were to see Momotaro safely back from Ogre Island. Momotaro never left home again; instead, he farmed their land and they lived happily all together for a lifetime of peace.

In the long pause that followed, Bobby and Tom said nothing; they sat stony-faced, still expecting a real ending. Yoneko clenched her teeth in fury. "So, so," she sputtered, "Momotaro *appeases* the ogres, goes home rich, and gives up his law practice to be a farmer again?"

"Well, yes," Fujita replied, honestly surprised by her anger. "That's right. He's a born farmer."

"So Momotaro's not the hero of the story?" Yoneko said sadly.

"God, no! He's just a farmer. There's no hero. It's just a story."

"But what about the goddamned sparrow?!" she demanded miserably.

Fujita looked at her, uncomprehending. "Oh, they forgot all about him."

"Who did?" The girl looked on the verge of spitting at him.

"Everyone," Fujita confessed. "Things were pretty hectic." A battle and miracle was a lot for one day—no one noticed that the quiet little sparrow was missing (except for the ogre who'd clubbed the poor bird, but he never mentioned it). "See, the hungry ogres were too busy stuffing themselves," Fujita explained. "Relieved to avoid further violence, Momotaro wanted only to see his parents again. Everyone just sort of *forgot* about Tongue-Cut Sparrow."

"Oh God," said Yoneko. "I feel sick."

Tom Fields nodded his agreement. "That's the worst adventure story in the world. Is this a Japanese story?" he asked in a way that implied he felt less than thrilled at the idea of ever enduring another one.

"No, it's definitely not," said Yoneko, nearly crying. "It's a . . . it's a defeatist crock of . . . manure."

"No," Fujita agreed. "It's an American story. It used to be a Japanese story, but it's changed."

It was the only kind of story Fujita could tell. Fools, he believed, struggled against things that nothing could be done about. Fools expected the hail of bullets to dance around them, or a frozen lake top to not crack, or a fruit boy and three pets to survive fighting a hundred armed ogres. Heroes, Fujita thought, were people who tried to do things that could be done, however unlikely their accomplishment, however painful. And heroes came home.

"Which one is supposed to be *you,* Mr. F. ?" asked the spiteful girl who had once mistaken his nurseryman's hands for those of a hero. "Momotaro or the sparrow?"

"No, no, no," Fujita said. "I'm just the old farmer."

Two years later, the tale's conclusion would remain unsatisfying as ever, though after Tony's death its significance would change in evil ways. Still, withdrawing from the frustrated Garvin into his hibernation of remembrance, Fujita would remain unapologetic. For, both times, he knew, he had really told the story for himself.

Like Halloween, Juggeston Elementary's Winter Wonderland Arts Fair and Parent's Day had been Sig's responsibility, and his widow dreaded it. The only thing wondrous about "Teacher's Revenge Day," as Livvie called it, was how insipid and untalented other people's kids could be.

"Well, why don't we all go to share the load," Margaret suggested. "It would be nice for Mr. Fujita to get out and relax a bit, and to mingle."

"No," Livvie replied—too defensively, she thought. "I won't have Garvin traipsing in there with our little circus. Not in front of all those midget monsters and their nosy-body parents. Forget it." She rolled her eyes scornfully. "No, I'm his mother. I'll go."

As she and Garvin tromped across the school playing fields, hopscotching among frozen patches and ankle-breaking drifts, Garvin also wondered, "Can't Mr. F. come, too?" Sadly, he looked at the new wooden airplane; he practically slept with the gift now.

"No, honey," she said evenly. "You have to leave him alone." He nodded, but she could tell Fujita's withdrawal had hurt him. "We'll have fun, though, just you and me. Huh?" She meant it, too. She would enjoy herself like a model mom, coo and crow at his paintings, and she would brag about his artistic nature, and smile and nod as other parents bragged even if it killed her. Sick to death of her isolation, and grateful to be alone with her son, she bent to hug him.

"I guess so," Garvin mumbled, pulling away. Raising his model airplane, he dashed ahead of her up the stairs to the entrance, bombing invisible enemies.

"Honey, wait," Livvie called, rushing after him. Following him inside, she lost him at a fork in the hall. A right led to the music room and snack table, a left to the bathrooms and art studio. Disoriented, Livvie slipped into the bustling current of bodies flowing to the right and damming up by the punchbowl. A secret society had developed around these events—a cabal of haunted-looking parents who gathered to share spiked punch and toast the teachers' sainthood. From the music room, she heard what sounded like a live goose being plucked. Towering above her, the ragged, flushed-faced Pete Pedicott winced.

"Livvie," said the unhappy patron to the Pedicott String Quartet. "I'm sorry to see you made it." They both laughed. "I hope the new baby is a painter like your Garvin." Drawing his jacket open, he revealed a hidden flask and nodded in offering.

"Thanks," she said, patting her purse. "I've got my own."

"So, where's the rest of your gang?" Potent Pete asked, looking about the hall. Fortunately, they were interrupted by Garvin's homeroom and art teacher.

"Livvie," cried Moira Hardy, "how grand to see you. What do

you think of our exhibit so far?" Draped by a long, tasseled scarf and wearing mannish trousers, she gave what she had cultivated into a sparkling, continental sort of smile rarely seen in Juggeston. She clapped her hands above her narrow chest, then swung wide her arms and closed onto Livvie with a two-handed grip—a greeting better suited to a gallery opening on the Seine than a Parents' Day on the North Shore. This usually meek, moon-eyed schoolmistress endured each year in anticipation of this one annual event, so Livvie tried to appear gratified to attend.

"The Museum of Fine Arts would be proud to have it," Livvie said.

"It is magical, isn't it?" the teacher crowed, beaming. "Children have such a direct line to their creativity, to . . . to the soul. I think so, don't you?" Scanning some of the doodles, Livvie nodded neutrally. "Of course," Miss Hardy continued, "they haven't the technique; it's not merely splashing paint on paper, as *some* very successful people seem to do these days. No, someone must teach them technique."

An amateur painter, Miss Hardy sometimes sold watercolors in Gloucester on weekends. She was widely known to have a busy but empty life in Juggeston, and her great pleasure was to bus to the wharves, have a glass of wine, erect her easel, and paint the sea, the rigs, the lobster pots and nets, the gulls. She ate Sicilian food there, spicy and oily. Sometimes she went to restaurants and smoked and ate bar nuts. Not that it was anyone's business, but sometimes, went the rumor, the morning bus that picked her up in Juggeston returned without her in the evening. Livvie envied her this alternate life, though her admiration was tempered by a strong but unproven suspicion that Moira had been among Sig's many mistresses.

"I've been meaning to speak with you about Garvin," the teacher said, suddenly serious. "Did he show you his painting?"

"He disappeared the second we arrived," Livvie said, wishing she could disappear also as Miss Hardy dragged her by the hand through a bewildering maze of crayon sunflowers, charcoal beagles, blotchy clay ashtrays, and American-flag chalk doodles. Hearing the other parents cooing, she prepared her dutiful praise.

"I begged him to find a better title, but he insisted on calling it *My Picture*. Just being lazy, I suppose. Well, you know how children are." They passed a sobbing little girl drowned in a sack of green felt, apparently an alligator costume. "Its technique is so much more thoughtful than the others'. I think he shows promise, such promise. But I'm sure you know this. Well, here we are."

Displayed with distinction at the front entrance, Garvin's stark watercolor, clearly a painting of Widow's Peak, did stand out, and not only for its commanding size, wide as an open newspaper. He did not outline first, as did most other children. Rather, the muted colors bled into one another, soaking into the paper with edges like crystallized frost. "Such a difficult medium," sighed Miss Hardy. While mostly washed in gray tones, his landscape showed a gold cross shape on the Peak's crest; the trees ringing the hill rose in sharp spikes of orange, and the air surrounding it glowed red, as if afire. Antlike figures with mustard-yellow hands and faces seemed to be invading the Peak; a train of them streamed in from off the edge of the canvas. Above wheeled a squadron of small, black V shapes. "Birds?" Livvie asked, but Miss Hardy interpreted these as angels. "A devotional painting," she suggested.

In the center of the hill, a green teepee abutted a big blue square—the greenhouse and the Kelly house; beside them, a smaller white square marked the Tufteller house ("Perspective is so hard to master at such a young age," said Miss Hardy). The inhabitants stood below, in the foreground, just above the paper's bottom edge. The smallest figure on the left—presumably Garvin, with its spiky yellow hair—flexed its biceps, holding up what appeared to be a bush. The largest figure on the right, with a wide, brown face, also held aloft what was plainly a tree. ("The eye travels from left to right, and the composition has a sort of thrilling upward swish, don't you think?" remarked Miss Hardy.) In between stood the middle figure—a woman, judging by the sharp bell of her skirt, like an inverted martini glass. Livvie's heart sank. The woman had red—Irish—hair.

Squinting, she desperately searched the expansive *My Picture* until she located the fourth, disproportionately small figure—herself. It was barely visible in the window of the white square house so far away in the painting's background. Its cone of black hair melded into a black dress like a nun's habit.

The assignment, Miss Hardy explained, concern creeping into her voice, was to "paint from memory something important to you, something from your everyday life."

"It's something else," Livvie said, crushed. She turned her face away.

Perturbed, Miss Hardy leaned close and whispered, "There's a darker side, too." Glancing about them as if under surveillance, she gingerly lifted *My Picture* away from its hook. "It's *very* unusual for a young child to be able to conceive of a canvas in three dimensions, but, well, he's a very creative child. Look, here, in the back."

Livvie had to press her face against the wall to do it. On the underside of the canvas stood a frowning, broad-shouldered man, topped with spiky yellow, holding a kind of bag, and wielding a sword or a machete. A whirlwind of airplanes buzzed around him, spotted with orange-and-black rocket bursts. She didn't need to read the caption: "Pop." She saw, too, that the line of mustard-headed antlike people continued, or rather originated, there on the back side. Japanese figures, she was sure.

Moira Hardy was right: Garvin did show promise. How vividly he had managed to represent Livvie's own unexpressed anxieties, jealousies, fears—and her isolation. How vividly had he painted the life of a grass widow. Livvie set *My Picture* back against the wall and turned to bury her tearful face into the tasseled scarf draped on the art teacher's shoulder.

After a respectful pause, Moira Hardy asked, "Would you . . . would you like to talk?"

In the weeks of his hibernation, Fujita's arctic dreams worsened, each more paralyzing than the night before, until that landscape of frost surrounded him even in waking. Unwilling to inflict his company on others, he banished himself to the garage or greenhouse and fell into semicatatonia. One afternoon Margaret found him sitting slumped in the hothouse, his hands hanging slack between his knees, just staring dully at the warm flats as if expecting to see the seeds germinate.

Although he felt the lowest of men at the pit bottom of a pointless life, it appalled the widower to find he could not bear even to glance at the family photo taped by his bed. Disgracefully, he feared to recall them at all, as a man who never learned to swim fears the ocean and its tides. Easier to be a rock in the ocean—*oki ni ishi*, as his mother recited over Ichiro's deathbed, Lady Sanuki's poetic expression for a broken heart. In his heart was where he resolved to intern his sorrow; yes, better isolated in that central organ than loosed to spread via the eyes to the brain stem and nerves, muscle fiber and bone, the extremities. Nurse Kelly would deem it unhealthy, to strain that coronary muscle so. "I think one has to recall the *happiest* moments, too, if he wants to heal," she told him. However, Fujita feared that remembering would only exacerbate the sensation of his uselessness. *Oki ni ishi*—the lonely promontory. He gingerly placed the photo in his suitcase.

One shouldn't avoid remembrance, divert grief; that wasn't right. But could he just sit alone moping until finally going mad? What sort of memorial would that be? As his nights grew longer, he raided Margaret's vast library, figuring he might appropriately devote his grief to self-improvement, at least; he might convert that dead time into useful hours. Poetry suited grief, he supposed. Or better than gardening manuals or the *Bereavement* newsletter, anyway. He withdrew from his suitcases his mother's old waka-form poetry cards. Kept in the same red box, bound with a rubber band, limp and dog-eared, they still struck Fujita as something strange and new. Over the course of that sleepless, haunted week, he tried to distract himself by learning those verses he had only memorized before. It eased him, but it numbed him, too, until one snowy morning a sensation of gaping emptiness filled him—a lack and loneliness so vast, like shouting into the Grand Canyon and waiting for the echo that never returns. Scattering the cards across the carpet of his room, he thought, I have to do something!

As surely as a thundercloud, that lack rumbled outside after him when he wrenched the door open armed with a shovel. He could barely open the garage door for the snowdrifts. Fording through the swirls of ice whipping, he again wondered that New

Englanders could endure *this*. Even celebrate it, even *dream* of it, he thought, recalling Big Jim crooning "White Christmas."

After an hour excavating a meager path from the office to the house, and then to Ellsworth Place, Fujita trudged back up and was appalled by how little one man with a shovel could accomplish. In a certain light, the encrusted slope did admit of the tiered gardens they had carved in the ground, but the farmer looked to the mound now unrecognizable as a scarecrow and doubted he'd ever see the earth again. How optimistically he and the boy had set that coin of promise in the straw woman a few months earlier, ignorant of winter's horrors. Beneath them, all of Widow's Peak lay obliterated by the white. Like the buried Pompeii. He thought of some Little Tokyo funerals he'd attended; in the place he'd left behind, white—not black—was the color of death. He thought of the white stone in Gila River. Winter killed everywhere. At Gila, the desert floor lay strewn with skeletons, dried brush and tufts blown from the stripped cotton fields nearby. In the desert, things ran wild, naked. Civilization hid decay, he noted. It gave the illusion of peace.

For no clear reason, he needed to free the scarecrow. He tore at her snowy shroud as if his life depended on it. Scooping away, his hands numbed. His gloves grew weighty as if from brushing King Midas. His chapped lips burned. For this immediate gratification of an action he could control and finish, however, he would go on until he collapsed happily in the snow, his body slowed, and his soul fertilized the earth.

His satisfaction at seeing her liberated died quickly enough, as the first cottony dust of renewed flurrying drifted past his face. "Will it never end?" he demanded, supplicant arms stretched to the scarecrow.

The breathy, spirited whistle that responded Fujita knew to be a wind piping through the reeds of her body. Sounding eerily human, what this atmospheric accident said was: *It will.* Preposterous, of course—hallucinations, hypothermia. Yet the Nisei skeptic felt oddly reassured. Garvin would buy it: His world included Shazam and Mandrake the Magician. So would Margaret, who believed in both guardian and garden angels.. After all, Nurse Kelly had created the straw woman in her image—with a vengeance. What the scarecrow said to the lost gardener was: *Seimei, ōn, girí.*

Life, debt, obligation. These were the fragments that came to Fujita then—distinct, separate. In what the scarecrow said, whether elements of an equation, a directive in multiple nouns, or mere gibberish—she did not provide the syntax—she spoke through a veil. Like him, she was not fluent. Why can't you speak in plain English? he wanted to ask her, but even in that lowest of weeks, he hadn't quite sunken *that* low. And he also sensed that this scarecrow, with her knowing, spectacled stare, her physician's sensibility, was capable of making fine distinctions—more so than Fujita, at that moment.

Struggling with translation, he wondered: *Girí* and *ōn*? *Girí,* he recalled as a duty, obligation, something social—something one must do. And *ōn*—a debt of gratitude, debt of love, of family. *Girí* and *ōn*: distinct but intertwined. *Girí*: Tony had answered to the call of his country—it was his duty to America. *Ōn*: Hadn't he betrayed his debt of love, betrayed his parents? And Mari: Had she finally only answered the call of despair—or also a kind of debt of love? And if Fujita did not know for certain, what the hell did a scarecrow know about it anyway?

Or was what the scarecrow said—like the Momotaro story—really, ultimately about Fujita himself? Barely managing translation, he could catch hold of any interpretation no more firmly than he could catch one of the snowflakes swirling about him. Were these just instructions: *To have life, add debt, stir in obligation, and cook?* Or bleak commiserating: *Life* is *debt and obligation?* Fujita could easily believe this—he thought about *his* debts and obligations constantly. Didn't he have an obligation to find Yoneko, a debt to his late wife and son? And, he wondered then, which of these different kinds of responsibility did Margaret hold him to?

No, he just didn't get it. And so, at the dusk of that mercilessly short last day of 1944, as the snow settled on him and the scarecrow with renewed flurrying, he inexplicably found himself weeping.

Laying down his shovel, Fujita lurched into the main house without even shaking off his boots. Finding Margaret seated in the kitchen with her checkbook, he took her hand and blurted, "I want to go see Bob Ito."

Margaret caught her breath and stared at him, not kindly. She tugged off the gloves welded to his hands. Rubbing his frozen fingers between her palms, she shook her head. No. Too late.

"I need your help," he began, perhaps for the first time in his life. "Can we talk?"

TEN

Machigai/Mistake

Tony's zoo remained. The beasts served as reminders of Fujita's one-sided bargain with Tony: that he bore some responsibility not only for Lucy the snake and Nudie, but for Yoneko. The barrack that had seemed so small now felt unimaginably cavernous. Like a monsoon, leave clearance had swept the young away to Europe and Asia, to temp jobs or to college, anywhere but the West Coast. As in other home-front cities, Gila's neighborhoods grew older and younger. Darker, too, when some of the Pima sought residency in luxurious, vacated internee apartments. Not even the emptying Casa Grande Valley put enough distance between Mrs. Fujita and Miss Yamaguchi, whom Mari blamed for Tony's battle lust, so Fujita never suggested that the Yamaguchis fill in the vacuum left by Tony. He'd keep an eye on them from across the street. That hole was filled instead by one of Mari's elderly shut-ins, one Mrs. Sano, who required routine supervision. Though he first resented the intrusion, he could hardly criticize his wife's charity, which was her own busywork. Returning from the fields one afternoon, he found the ladies having tea and biscuits as contentedly as royalty in some ritzy restaurant after a hard day's shopping. Not only was Mari smiling again, but a red film like ground cayenne pepper sat unmolested on the front steps.

"Bill," Mari said, rising, accidentally jouncing the tea tray.

"WHAT?" yowled the old widow. Blind in the right eye and very nearly deaf, she communicated in a language of violent shrieks, peeks, and thumps. She was hobble-stepped, arthritic, toothless, and suffered from an inner-ear problem that kept her at a steady wobble and frequently sent her tumbling. The resulting bruises might convince a stranger she was a battered wife—or a boxer. And this symptomology counted only those maladies noticeable during the day.

"Ohayo, Sano-san!" Fujita yelled back. Searching that shriveled body, he could find no inch that wasn't damaged, except her voice, which bellowed, "WHAT? SPEAK UP!"

As a mechanic will keep a broken-down junker in the yard for weekend tinkering, this twisted car wreck of a woman provided Mari with an excellent "diversion," as Miyake and Tamie Fujita would put it. A "distraction" is more what Fujita would call that bumping, hollering presence, primarily referring to the nights, made long by her constant sinus congestion. The first night, the Fujitas were amazed by the seismic snoring that erupted from the woman's dry old throat. Holding their breaths and each other, they counted twenty minutes after shouting "GOOD NIGHT, SANO-SAN!" and still the plain wood walls rumbled. "It's an *earthquake*," Fujita whispered. Mari dug her nails into his back. "It's the cavalry arriving," she said. "It's the charge of the Light Brigade." They laughed then, and for the moment, it released them. Even Mrs. Sano's mighty grunts and snorts felt like perfect privacy, accustomed as they were to none. Banking on the spinster's infirmities, they made love for the second time in over a year, as vigorously as if on their desert island. Their noises terrified Jesse Owens the jumping mouse. Four feet away, their irritated new roommate shut her good left eye, rolled away, and pretended to snore.

Fujita took his paternal duties to his calabash family seriously, solemnly, and kept faith in his secret pact with Tony. He made a point to speak the Yamaguchis daily (and with civility), usually over a meal at the mess hall. He doled out small portions of Tony's paycheck to Yoneko—paid for her daily needs with his own scrip, the camp currency. The remainder he held for a college fund kept in a tin box under the floorboards beneath his bed. If he resented the manner in which she took the money without thanks—as if it were her due—it never occurred to him that *she* resented *him* for presuming to define her daily needs. Besides sharing this contact with the girl, he made certain to fetch her whenever a letter from Tony arrived. "That's all I ask," she told him once, as serious as he thought she could ever be. "The money isn't so important, but if you *hear* anything about him—anything at all—I want to hear it, too," she insisted. "Don't keep that from me, Mr. F. Just don't."

Letters detailing Tony's life on the front were often opened before delivery and sometimes arrived with whole paragraphs snipped out, but no longer were they stamped "Enemy Alien." That, to Fujita, was a kind of progress. Usually, their tone was jolly, full of bravado. Never very explicit, they indicated only that his job entailed interpretation. What did that mean? Surveillance? Propaganda? Espionage? With such phrases as, "We finally saw some action today," Tony immediately set his parents to fearing the worst.

"What *kind* of action?" Fujita would rage, but Tony or the censors didn't care to say. The photo Tony sent helped Fujita imagine: in uniform, grinning, darkly tanned, a Camel clamped below the beginnings of a mustache, and suspended from a cross pinned to his chest dangled metal proficiency bars engraved with RIFLE and PISTOL.

"How dashing!" Yoneko said.

"Ignorant girl!" said Mari, reveling in her freedom to be hateful as she liked.

Tony wrote to Jim that he had fought four times at H.Q. and was undefeated in the welterweight division. "White fellas?" Jim wondered. "Or Japanese?"

Then, in autumn, a monthlong silence from Tony kept everyone on edge. Fujita exorcised his fears by taking on extra shifts in the fields and collecting notes on desert flora. Mari took on extra work at the YW and helped Mrs. Sano get about on visits.

Yoneko's camouflage-net group had won a trophy for producing the most nets. She participated in the honor, though not in all of the actual work. For, on the last morning of heated competition, she became nauseated interweaving the ribbons of drab green, pea green, army green, baby-poop green, pond-muck green, and crabgrass green. She told her coworkers she felt faint and then removed herself to vomit. After seeing the doctor, she rested in the apartment for the rest of the afternoon but returned refreshed and in time to receive the trophy for her group as proudly as if accepting an Academy Award.

When Tony's next telegram arrived, Yoneko was sitting by Fujita outside as he read his book on Pima agriculture. She had coated her hair with lemon, eggs, mayonnaise, and peroxide and under the baking noon sun smelled rotten and tart. Chattering with Rose, she irritated Fujita no more than usual, but enough that he was contemplating escaping to the latrines to read in peace when he heard his wife's voice down the block. "Telegram!" Mari shouted, hurrying up to them with Big Jim, Bobby Tanaka's Uncle Calvin, and Mrs. Sano in tow, parroting in Japanese, *"Dempo! Dempo!"* Every miserable day of Tony's silence, the families listened for and dreaded that word—whatever the language. Yoneko burst into tears.

"What's wrong with you?" Mari asked, thrusting the paper at her. "Crying before you even read it? Stupid girl!" Grimacing, she sniffed over Yoneko's chair. "What's that stench?" Her expression, Fujita noted, held the same loathing that she usually reserved for her longtime enemy, the omnipresent red Rivers dust. It chilled Fujita how mean-tempered his wife had become, but Yoneko didn't seem to notice. Sniffling, she only scanned the paper in a blink, sighed, then frowned hard. "Read it aloud," he commanded. Writing from an Army hospital in Hawaii, Tony apologized for not writing sooner, then explained that his unit had been sent south and he'd "taken one in the arm."

"Oh!" Yoneko gasped. "Does that mean they'll send him home?"

"Humph," Jim snorted, "so much for his fighting career."

"HIS WHAT?" shouted Mrs. Sano.

"'The bad news,'" Yoneko read, then stopped. "Getting shot

isn't the bad news? Oh, you read it, Mr. F. My nerves won't take it!" she said, surrendering the paper.

The bad news, according to Tony, was that he'd been exiled from his unit for a month's recuperation. "That sounds like good news to me," Fujita said, reading on. "'Good news that Commander awarded me Purple Heart. Infected wound cleared up. Fit enough to rejoin unit in a week.' Now *that's* bad news," Fujita interpreted.

"Wow," said Yoneko, putting her hand over her mouth, then recoiling at the egg smell.

Tony concluded by writing that he didn't much like Hawaii. "Too many Japs," he wrote. "J-Hawaiians a different breed, hillbillyish. Have been island hopping. Will search all until find prettiest one for us to vacation after Victory. Stop."

Watching Yoneko bite into her thick, waxy-red lips, Fujita noted that his son did not specify who "us" included. Then the wannabe blonde, the aspiring movie starlet loosed a deep-bellied *brawwp*, a lumberjack's burp. Involuntary, surely, but Fujita found himself hating her. Despite himself, the devoted critic of rikutsuppoi in all its forms, the stiff-upper-lip and feelings-are-a-luxury man blamed the girl. Hypocritically, he blamed her for her heritage—for her suspect parents, "the real traitors," locked away in the Justice Department camp in Crystal City, Texas. He blamed her for being sexy and wanting to marry a "hero." His disdain for her paled beside Mari's powerful feelings, which even he knew to be irrational. But the girl was so stupid. And the ever-ballooning "whole thing" had convinced him that stupidity's potential destructiveness should not be underestimated. Unfettered stupidity, Fujita thought, might be even more dangerous than calculated evil. And she was an actress. Her lamentation for Tony's injury sounded false, overdramatic, like Tallulah Bankhead. Sure, the girl must worry, but she acted as if she'd *only then* realized that a war might possibly be hazardous to its participants, that those "dashing" uniforms were merely cloth and that bullets were metal.

"Tony'll be okay. The infection's the thing to worry about, but they've got these antibiotics now," Bobby's Uncle Calvin, the shy hospital assistant, reassured them, though with a detachment Fujita resented. Tony's friend whispered something in Yoneko's ear and then gave an oddly formal little nod. "If you'll all excuse us, please." They stepped aside to speak privately. Mari liked Calvin, also a Montanan—they could spend hours bitching about California together. Fujita distrusted him, though. At their first meeting in Tulare, Calvin declared, "I'm not staying here," and Fujita thought it a funny sort of thing to say. Kind of cocky. He watched Calvin now, stiff and polite even by his own standards, speaking so close and secretively to Yoneko, who stood nodding. Although he wouldn't mind if someone took the girl off Tony's hands, he couldn't help recalling his mother's term for Yoneko: *demimondaine*. However, when Yoneko began weeping and hugged herself instead of Calvin, Fujita scolded himself. Let's be fair, he thought. I suppose they're worried about Tony in their own way. It's good that they have each other. By that evening, he noticed, Yoneko had fashioned the white silk flag with a blue star displayed by families of living servicemen, though increasingly, those adorning the windows of Gila's barracks were turning to gold.

On the overcast night of January 4, they received the next and last communiqué from the Pacific announcing the presumed combat death of Toshio "Tony" Fujita. In the end, Tony did his part to prove he was no enemy alien; he received a commendation for valor in combat and had even been photographed for *Stars & Stripes*, though the picture was suppressed due to the sensitive nature of his intelligence work. At the same time, Intelligence in the Pacific routinely assigned a few regular soldiers to guard the Nisei there—partly for protection, but partly from distrust. Protection. Apparently, the buddy system was difficult to maintain in combat.

It would be two weeks and three days before Fujita learned more precisely the circumstances of Tony's service, and his death, when the man who last saw his son alive came to Gila. Alone in the apartment, feeling a numbness he could not even call grief, Fujita had been rereading Tony's letter regarding Hawaii's prettiest islands when the soldier arrived.

"F-f-fujita?" The voice floated into the barrack on the tail end of a Jeep's squealing brakes, then crunching gears, and the high whir of the vehicle backing up. He heard a child respond but couldn't make out the words. Little Bobby Tanaka, he guessed, for he heard the sick-duck noises of the wooden bloodhound toy.

Setting down the letter, he stepped to the doorway and saw Bobby pacing circles around the Jeep's driver, admiring the sidearm, aping the stern pout of the GI squinting at the number on the shingle. The soldier squatted to question the boy, who responded by pointing in Fujita's direction. A gangly, sandy-haired man of twenty with a limp and a distracting nervous tic, the soldier introduced himself stutteringly as Private Johnny Salisbury, "like the st-st-steak." By then, Mari was having her own health problems, with pneumonia and some soul sickness much graver, and was safely settled in the hospital. Just as well, for one glance told Fujita that this section-eight GI's already shattered nerves could not have withstood her loathing. While Fujita gradually grew able to endure hearing how brave and well-liked, et cetera, Tony was, Mari still could not hear "poor Tony, good old Tony," without whirling into a rage of curses and coughing.

As it was, Johnny Salisbury had difficulty enough relating the story. His progress through the block—teeming with the wide faces registering "The Enemy" to his shell-shocked mind—so unhinged him that he kept his thick-lensed eyeglasses fixed constantly out the window as he explained that his unit—about thirty boys, all told—had been puddle-jumping among several supposedly secure islands in the South Pacific, places so small that many had no names, or none known to Americans. "T-tony and some technicians spent the day looking for the b-best place to set up some fan-fan-fancy new surveillance thingy," the soldier told Fujita, his protruding Adam's apple gulping up and down his neck. "They were bushed, sleeping it off, and I was up in the gun t-tower on lookout. That's when the bom-bom-bombing started and things went crazy. Reconnaissance showed no carriers nearby, and we thought the island was free of-of-of . . ."

Private Salisbury was obviously having trouble spitting it out, so Fujita helped him. "Japanese," he offered.

Behind him, Bobby Tanaka's cheery voice sang out, "Japs!"

Intent on Private Salisbury, Fujita hadn't even noticed the boy standing in the doorway all this time. Instinctively, he thought to chase the child away, then thought better of it. Let him hear the whole sorry story, he thought. Let him listen and learn. Sitting on Mrs. Sano's cot, he placed Bobby in his lap. The child's hair smelled of soap and dust.

"Go on, Private," he instructed.

"Yes sir," the soldier said, blinking, then looking to the window again. "So, it was real c-c-confusion. I mean, it was . . . it was like hell, you understand . . ."

"I can imagine," Fujita said, in a soft but forceful tone. "Go on."

A common joke of the day held that "military intelligence is an oxymoron," and when Salisbury continued his tale, Fujita was baffled by more than his sputtering delivery. Intelligence had gotten it half right that day: There weren't any Japanese carriers nearby. It seemed the aircraft harrying the tiny, no-name island were Allied planes who were supposed to drop their loads on another tiny, no-name island fifty miles south. Tony's island was too small for an airstrip and too far from everything else to be of strategic value for much besides communications. The part Intelligence got wrong, then, was that there were a few dozen Japanese foot soldiers hidden in the island's coral caves, who—hearing the explosions and thinking the air raid was meant for them—probably figured their time was up and attacked Tony's encampment. A last hurrah.

Tamie forever urged her family not to forget their heritage. One could be in the Boy Scouts, play baseball, renounce his dual citizenship (which Fujita did), even live, marry, and die here, but he would always be American *and* Japanese. For Tamie, the two were not mutually exclusive. But apparently Tony did forget, dashing from his cot in only his olive undershorts and an unstrapped helmet, fleeing the actual Japanese then pouring out of the forest.

"The f-first wave of strafing, it . . ." young Salisbury winced to remember, "it caw-c-caw-caught me in the foot. I fell to the floor, and I suppose Tony must've seen the unmanned gun since he started scaling the tower. Like a c-c-cat."

Fujita nodded, closed his eyes, and filled in the details the stuttering soldier left sketchy. Tony would be a climber, agile enough to elude both Jap and Yank bullets and clamber up the bamboo legs of the forty-foot lookout tower. But, he imagined, a modern soldier doesn't box and parry his way through a fire-fight. Tony was not quick enough to identify himself to young Salisbury, then still tic-free and steely-nerved. Unfortunately, Salisbury's vision was not as strong as his survival instinct at that moment—he had lost his eyeglasses when shot. Tony saw this and tried to defend himself, releasing his right-hand grip, but as Big Jim Little predicted, he swung too wide, too slowly. Private Salisbury, taking fuzzy aim only on the dish-round face and eyelid folds, like those so exaggerated on the Nip bayoneting targets in boot camp, jabbed straight from the shoulder and KO'ed Fujita's son forty feet above the earth.

"It was a m-m-mistake," Salisbury moaned. "It was a horrible, horrible mistake."

Mistake was the word Fujita used when he wrote to his mother, concluding, "Oki no ishi," but he lied to Mari—he told his wife that Tony died quickly, killed in his sleep, but she didn't believe him. To old Mrs. Sano, he had to shout it over and over in Japanese, "*MACHIGAI! MACHIGAI!*" When he told Big Jim, he again called it "a mistake." Tony himself would have called it *snafu*.

Undone by his breathless confession, Private Salisbury stumbled on his way to the door. His business there was unofficial—he'd chosen to come see Tony's parents—but now that it was done, he seemed lost. Fujita had to help him limp outside, and he knew he could not take Salisbury to see Mari in the hospital. Like a fish tossed back into water, the GI gulped desperately at the wintry desert air. "D-do you mind if I j-just sit here a while?" he asked, and promptly crumpled on the stoop, hands over his bowed head. Little Bobby Tanaka took the opportunity to glue himself to the fascinating, uniformed outsider, chattering away about school, war, siblings.

"You have a sister?" Bobby wanted to know. "I have a stupid sister. You have a dog?" Perhaps any distraction would do, but the child's prattle appeared to soothe Salisbury's nerves. He demonstratively admired Bobby's wooden pet, tousled his hair, even tickled the boy, who emitted gleeful, ducklike noises of protest but did not run away. Then, warming with intimacy, Bobby Tanaka met the soldier's tic-racked eyes, blushed, and in a voice heavy with innocence and earnestness, he pounded the man with another question. "Do I look like a rat to you?"

Salisbury's response floundered in a wide-mouthed stutter: "Wha-wha-wha . . . ?"

Bobby was thinking of the Army recruitment posters, Fujita knew; the boy possessed a gift for hammering adults with queries from left field. Yet in the child's curiosity was an absolute absence of irony or wile that had often dumbfounded Fujita. *Do you have a dog?* and, *Do we look like rats to you?* In Bobby's world, Fujita understood, these facts had a certain symmetry. He could have intervened, but why? "Oh God, oh God!" Salisbury moaned, but if the soldier ever managed to spit out a reply, Tony's father did not linger to hear it. For him, there could be no distraction. He backed away into his haunted shack, full of his own questions and alone.

Immediately following the dreaded telegram, Mari had also fallen ill. Again, Fujita had been caught unprepared, sleeping. With the telegram still in his hand, he had clenched Mari sobbing against him on one narrow cot. He thought he should tell Yoneko, but in consoling his inconsolable wife, he had fallen into a black, troubled sleep.

Mari! Mari! Even beneath the pillow covering his face, he heard Mrs. Sano shouting his wife's name. Swimming up from sleep, he realized that the cot was wet beneath him but had no idea where he was or where he had been. He opened his eyes. The apartment was pitch dark and silent except for a droning like a stream of pebbles on the shingles overhead. He momentarily imagined he was back in the nursery, having snoozed on the daybed on the kitchen porch, lulled by the patter of sprinklers raining on the tin roof. But the rainfall he heard was punctuated by metallic thunderclaps, and the telegram, still trapped beneath his palm on his chest, was drenched from a small leak in the roof above him.

Mari! Mari! Wrapping the damp blanket about himself, he sat upright, the floorboards cold even through his socks. Still clutching the telegram, he stepped to the doorway and peered out through the rain; a gust of wind ripped his misty breath from the air before his face. His first groggy thought was neither of his wife nor the news in the telegram but of the crop beds on the northern perimeter of camp. He ought to have covered them—they might frost over in this chill. By Southern California standards, the rainfall was hardly more than a tease, the kind of one-day wetting that fell in bullets, stirred puffs of dust, and then vanished into the spongy earth. By first light of morning, the ground would be pockmarked, frosted, crunchy beneath the foot, but unsatiated. This sprinkle was no balm for the thirsty crops, Fujita knew. He scraped the clotted sleep-salt from his eyes and ran a hand through his hair. Little of the first-quarter moon could be seen that night behind the clouds, but he was guided by frequent explosions of forked lightning to the west, a few bare bulbs suspended above the common areas, and the floodlamps of the guard towers. Again came the call, "Mari!" and he hurried in that direction. He made his way past the latrines, the laundry room, stopped. Mingled with the echo of Mari's name was a sound of metal clanking on metal that reminded him of the wharf where his father had worked, the sheets of small sailing yachts slapping against the masts. Through a hazy curtain of rain like isinglass, he saw Mrs. Sano hobbling hunchbacked toward him, breathless, her ankles streaked with mud.

"Mariko's so sad," the old woman sputtered in Japanese. "I think she wants to die." She tugged him down past the chapel, past the end of Block 58, into the square where the flag and fountain stood. He could not see Mari until close enough to almost trample her, for the area was unlit and she was caked top to toe with dirt, her blue nightgown now plastered brown against her. On her knees, she wrapped her arms around the thick steel flagpole like a child hanging about a parent's legs, like a supplicant begging for her life. In the roaring wind, the flag's pulley rope and hook smacked the pole. Spindles of lightning unfurled all about them, close by, dwarfing the guards' floodlamps.

"You shouldn't have let him go, Bill," she moaned, as he tried to grip her slippery arm. "It's all wrong. He shouldn't have gone." He lifted her off the ground, squirming and weakly striking at him, to carry her to the hospital. And so it was, under this barrage—tramping through the mud, pushing against the chill rain and wind, deafened by thunder and his wife's curses—that Yoneko found him. Dashing out from the shadows, a screaming figure in brown descended upon him from behind, claws outstretched, like a harpy. With the hospital entrance a long four blocks away, he felt a fist pulling him backward by the collar and his bare toes slipping in the mud.

"When were you going to tell me?" Yoneko shouted, her usually piercing voice muffled by mucus from long sobbing. "Why didn't you tell me?"

Had Fujita not been blinded by the sudden glare of the guard-tower searchlight, he might have seen a nineteen-year-old girl, pretty, ambitious, trapped, who in her showy, overwhelming way had also dearly loved his son. Had he more than a split second to think, he might have swallowed his panic, recalled his promise to Tony, turned to embrace the girl, and made good on that promise. As it was, he only hugged his slippery wife closer, trying not to drop her, and stepped back from the headlights of a fast-approaching Jeep splashing toward them.

"What have I ever done to you?" Yoneko hissed in his ear, maintaining her furious grip on him. Losing his balance, he reflexively shrugged back against her warm body with an elbow, though not forcefully. He heard her cry out, felt a pain in his shoulder as she bit into him, then shrugged her away again. Mari moaned as he spun around to where the girl lay drenched and crumpled like a broken animal, streaks of black running from her long eyelashes and puffy eyes. He had only brushed her away, but she clutched one breast as if he had pounded her.

"What have I done to you?" she demanded again. Even in such a miserable state, he saw how appealing she was.

He would come to regret his response later. But with his wife's accusation still ringing in his ears, he faced what seemed to be a whirlpool waiting to engulf him. Without concerning himself with what was rational, right, or true, he said, "You killed my boy. That's enough," and even as he spoke the words, he sensed he was making another mistake. The nearby sound of brakes and the guards' warnings seemed miles away.

"I know what you think," Yoneko said, looking up at him, her eyes curtained by a dripping sheet of hair. "But you're wrong. You think he was just a hotheaded kid, wouldn't listen to anyone." Still massaging her breast, she rose before him, spitting in his face. "He'd listen to you. He'd go to jail with the No-No Boys if you said to. He'd only go with your blessing. He wanted *you* to tell him what to do. The big *hero*." Then, to his amazement, she sent a blow across his cheek, not an actress's slap but a boxer's fist. And to his greater surprise, he returned the blow—just one, for a guard swatted at him from behind even as Mari clung to his leg, and he toppled forward onto the girl, a forearm grinding into her stomach. Her terrible yowl echoed down the block—-in this desert, sounding like a coyote's cry. He struggled to extricate himself from the mass, but the ground or Yoneko heaved beneath him. The harder he tried to raise himself up, the more slippery the foundation became. All elbows and wrists and pressing palms, he ground deeper and deeper into the fleshy floor until he was exhausted. Then the guard's truncheon crashed upon his shoulder and clavicle. He felt himself yanked away from the crumpled pile—Mari lying prone and motionless, Yoneko curled over on her side, hands clutching her belly. That's when he knew: He would be a grandfather.

He awoke the next morning in the hospital to the frown of a gruff, silvery-haired doctor who reprimanded him for his behavior, saying Gila was peaceful, not like those other camps. After a guard warned him not to go near the Yamaguchis, he was sent home. They kept Mari a couple of weeks; that was when Private Salisbury visited. Even after she was released, Fujita did not voice his suspicion of Yoneko's pregnancy. Perhaps a woman would have guessed it already? Mari remained in bed with a violent cold that did not seem to improve during the week following. When he tried to speak to her, she merely waved him away, and he mistook her illness for grief. She said nothing for two days; on the third day, she ordered him to go to work, and reluctantly he left her alone with Mrs. Sano. The Issei was an attentive (if loud) nurse—she wouldn't have left Mari's side until she absolutely had to, until her bowels left her no choice but to run over to the latrines. In her condition, though, running over took a half hour minimum, and often twice as long, since the embarrassment of using the wide-open public toilets tended to constipate her, even when Mari accompanied her and shielded her with a blanket. Thus, Mari knew that she'd have time.

She breathed with difficulty, not only from the fluid filling her lungs but from a coat of red dust encaking her long-bedridden body, drying her throat and nasal passages. Rising made her dizzy, and it was a struggle just to open the rickety door to the apartment on Block 60. First, she liberated the Baileys, Tony's beetle family, then freed the black, brown, and red ants from their respective farms, to be immediately devoured by Humphrey the gecko and his terrarium-mate, Nudie. Oh, she hadn't counted on the stupid creatures turning on one another. They were desperate with hunger, though; no one had fed them for a week now. She sweat wildly, and a salty droplet rolled from her brow onto the jar from which a surprised Harry Tarantula plopped onto the floor, his eight eyes filled with confusion. He began to pogo about aimlessly, as if he suffered the disorder European folklore attributed to him. Put off by Tony's hobby, Mari had paid little attention to his lecture on tarantism, though the root of her soul-sickness lay in a world that considered "an uncontrollable urge to dance" a *disorder*. Off his ten powerful legs (she mistook his feelers for another pair) that would put Nijinsky to shame, he took one mighty hop and disappeared beneath her cot.

Increasingly breathless, Mari dropped the jar holding the scorpion named Karl, and she felt a sting in her ankle, though this was only a shard of glass. "I'll sweep the whole place when I'm done," she told herself. Jesse Owens the jumping mouse launched out of his cage like a jack-in-the-box, not about to wait around for her to release Lucy the snake. Mari had to sit a moment on her cot before freeing Brenda the black widow, who preferred to remain in the silken home she had fashioned for herself. "Come on," Mari said, overturning the jar and shaking it. "What's wrong with you?" She slapped the glass bottom, but Brenda held fast. Angrily poking inside with a lacquered, ebony chopstick, she broke a nail on the glass rim. "Ow," she cried, sucking the finger, tasting metal. She had such lovely hands, Mari Fujita—small and narrow, but womanly, not like a child's—they slid so easily down the jar's throat. "Come on, you sorry bitch . . ."

Later, when Mari died in hospital, after Mrs. Sano discovered her, Fujita would confront the silver-haired doctor, demanding an explanation. Could medication have an adverse effect? Might her pneumonia have produced hallucinations? Gila River had provided the doctor with plentiful experience in venomous bites and stings, but he shared with the husband a softened version of the symptomatology he imagined for Mari Fujita. The fiery red swelling, the nausea, muscle and stomach cramps. He doubted Mari would have noticed the further constriction in her chest, the high fever and increased sweating, symptoms also associated with her preexisting pneumonia, which added to the venoms' lethality. But that's not what Fujita wanted to know. Regarding him somewhat scornfully, the doctor would remind Fujita that people are not plants—as often as not, human blights came from within. From the peculiar collocation of so many various bites, the doctor "would not discount the possibility that Mrs. Fujita intended to end her life. It's not altogether uncommon here," he mumbled, with some distaste; it was common knowledge that the Japanese had an inborn, a genetic penchant for suicide, and he'd seen many in that desert colony. But, he hastened to add, "I'm sorry, truly, but I can't tell you for sure. I can only *guess*."

Then *guess*, Fujita's furious silence demanded, and the doctor nodded.

"Breakdown," sniffed the crusty man of science. "Heartbreak."

What surprised Mari about the sting, when it came, was its apparent kindness. To the nurserywoman, the slight discomfort felt like the familiar prick of a baby rose thorn; at first, it hurt less than the glass sliver in her ankle. She tossed Brenda and the jar onto the floor, and gasping, she lifted Lucy's glass habitat onto the cot beside her. Mari liked Lucy, the way she slept coiled up like a soba noodle, her sharp head slipped through a fold in her looped body, her little tongue flapping lazily. So content, Mari thought, unlatching the wire lid. Mari wished she could sleep like that, her legs up over her head—silly, but somehow it seemed so much more comfortable. It seemed so safe.

When he could bear to think about his family in the days after Mari's death, Fujita felt a mental loosening in him, just at the edge of his peripheral inner vision, like a preying vulture barely camouflaged in the belly of a cloud. Alone at night, listening to old Mrs. Sano's violent snores, he caught himself juggling terrible what-ifs, mentally rearranging his family's destruction in a macabre jigsaw puzzle. What if he'd not left Mari to work in the fields? What if he'd forbidden Tony's enlistment, endorsed his romance with Yoneko? Would wedding the girl have prevented his meeting up with Private S-s-salisbury—his life prolonged, if not safer, and his mother's heart left intact? Fujita weighed the tragedies: Sometimes he felt he could not live without his wife; sometimes it was his son's loss he couldn't bear. It was the vileness of this sick scale of his that most made him feel mad; it made him wish he could pray, or kill himself, or at least sleep.

Yet at the time he could do none of these, and one night, or morning, really, he defied curfew and crept out at 3:00 A.M. to sit atop the butte, as he had done with Tony. The butte was a freezer. Shivering, he heard across the flat miles two coyotes barking and a late-night door slamming. All night, he sat listening, until the moon browned over, until the rooster screeched its reveille. The Arizona dawn seeped in, its colors never resting long enough for him to recognize them as anything more specific than regal. He thought he understood why so many internees seemed to have found some comforting god or other at Gila; from another vantage point, this lighting of the nothingness would be considered among nature's greatest, most mysterious wonders. It could make people who had been close to the earth look upward. But not Fujita, who at that time had had it with Christians *and* Buddhists, with "It's God's will" and "Shikata ga nai." In his attitude toward gods and wonder, he felt closer to the Indian approach—they at least knew that gods could be tricksters, and they were watchful.

The night frost thawed from him, the sun's heat began to thicken, and around him the white nocturnal blooms of Cereus greggii, the night-blooming cacti, closed their spearhead bulbs imperceptibly with the sunrise—to him they seemed to snap shut. The first truck pulled into camp; people gradually spilled out of the barracks and teemed down the blocks to mess or the latrines, and he had to be astounded by the life in this unnatural colony sprung from the wasteland. "Oh, shit," he called out to the desert spirits. "What will I do?"

In his grief, still more a swoon than a focused sorrow, the world felt nightmarish. It looked uglier, its people fragile, crippled, its joys and meannesses and conflicts petty, insignificant. And so, anchored freezing and sizzling above Rivers, it seemed at first perfectly natural, as *right* as breathing, when the brittle, foot-high tumbleweed before him matter-of-factly burst into flames.

Tumbleweed burns curiously, emitting slim, hot tendrils; it appears to melt more than burn. He looked about guiltily, as if his staring had set the blaze, but no one else saw. "Crap," he said defiantly. Lowering his gaze to the ground, he sought the cause of the fire—wind velocity, minimal humidity, the perfect angle of sunlight on a flake of quartz or glass. Even people could explode, so he'd heard, for no reason at all. It was possible. Accidents happened.

If the fiery brush inspired him to any lasting religious reflection, it was only this: Patience, forbearance, cooperation, appeasement, turning a cheek . . . these so-called virtues had betrayed him. Had been mistakes. And there was a difference, he decided then, however difficult to discern, between mistakes and accidents. Was the nervous Private Salisbury's m-m-m-mistake just that, or was it really an awful but inevitable accident? Tony's conception: He and Mari hadn't planned it; that was a happy accident. Yet somehow Fujita had believed that *Yoneko's* accidental pregnancy out of wedlock sat firmly in the mistake category. That he'd fallen on Yoneko and hurt her must objectively be deemed an accident; however, that he'd alienated her, that he'd meant to hurt her in other ways . . .

The difference, Fujita decided, from his perch above Gila River Internment Center, lay not only in intention. Mistakes, he hoped, could more possibly be atoned for, corrected. He slapped his knee hard, infuriated to have sat so long feeling sorry for himself. Rising painfully and stretching his arms, the widower felt as stiff as a scarecrow, as brittle as tumbleweed. He cracked his neck and crushed the still-flaming bush under his boot, but the movement dizzied him; he was dehydrated and had to squat back down. He licked the dried salt from his arms and hands. Weakly, he rose and took the first, cautious steps of his descent and in his search for Yoneko.

After eating and washing, the widower walked down to Block 61 feeling clearer, and bearing more sympathy for the girl than he thought himself capable of mustering. Before the war, before he'd suffered it himself, he'd believed in the notion of heartbreak no more than in insanity, which seemed in many cases but a lazy unraveling of the mind. However, in the hateful glare Aunt Rose gave him from the doorway, Fujita thought he detected a symptom of both. She barred him from entering, but through the narrow opening, he could see her nose quivering like a rabbit's, her head shaking back and forth in an eerily mechanical fashion, and her eyes fixed on Fox Butte. "She's gone," Aunt Rose said, her tone mean and triumphant. "And you'll never catch her."

"I don't want to catch her, Rose," Fujita said gently. "I just want to talk to her. Do you know where she is?"

"Gone," Rose repeated. "Where you can't hurt her anymore. "You . . . you . . . ack!" She paused. Her expression became constipated. Even more than most Nisei, the son of a rabid vocabularist was accustomed to halting conversations in second languages. He waited patiently while Rose fished for the English term to convey the precise nature of her contempt. "You bad man," was all she could manage, but it was enough.

"I just want to talk," he repeated. "Where is she?"

Aunt Rose's eyes continued staring beyond him, but they shifted north beyond the gates. Fujita turned. Far off in the anonymous brown foothills, he saw a familiar plume of dust. Probably just a Pima tractor or some delivery truck.

"Outside? Rose, she left camp?"

"You'll never find her," Aunt Rose vowed again, then slammed her door.

A lazy pace ruled the administration building—the quiet, soulless feel of a school principal's office during summer vacation. A coffee percolator lay cold and unwashed on a tin file cabinet—and here it was two in the afternoon. A silly soap opera sighed on the radio. Fujita's inquisitors, a sleepy quartet of administrators, looked like matrons manning a ticket booth at a Sunday church event. Hanging limp and musty behind them, Old Glory was dusted red, brown, and blue. Wrought of only slightly better materials than the rest of camp, the examination room lacked the lived-in feel of most internee apartments. There was a gas stove, a cot, and a pedestal with a typewriter and a sheaf of paper. An enormous bookcase of green tin guarded the doorway. The furnishings sat in tidy order, officious-looking, but phony too, more like a Hollywood prop office than one inhabited by real people.

"You want out," said Mr. Johnson, presiding over the inquisition.

"Out," echoed the internee, trying to imagine it. "Yes."

They regarded each other sullenly for a long moment, schoolmaster and student, doomed by each other to share their vacation in detention. Once so buttoned-down, Mr. Johnson now harbored a spiky blemish on his throat where he'd missed a spot shaving. Either his trousers fell too short or his socks rose too low, for the straps of his garters appeared clearly where he crossed his ankles beneath the table. Dark rings cupped his eyes. It vaguely occurred to Fujita that the years spent getting to know their captives might have dulled these men's passion for the work, that indeed, some might have found their roles as jailers unpalatable from the start. He could possibly even imagine that a man, after freely heading to the white folks' compound out behind the administration building, might yell at his family over dinner and lie beside his wife sleepless, constructing and destroying one rationalization after another, racked by doubt, by conscience, and vaguely fearful for his soul.

But then, would someone in Fujita's position really have cared?

The administrator yawned, then excused himself, but Fujita's native distaste for civil servants and government employees snapped awake. Sit up straight! he wanted to shout at them. Why can't you at least be men at your jobs? But set on getting out, he bit his tongue.

"You want out?" the official repeated. Beneath his jacket, his hand massaged his right breast in small circles. Heartburn. "Okay, that's what we all want. Really, it is. But there's a little problem. I refer to this Application for Leave Clearance." He held up the stapled sheets. "This is your signature, yes? You filled this out?"

"That's my loyalty review, yes," Fujita said, staring hatefully at the paper he'd once hoped would save Tony. "So am I a patriot or a public menace?"

"We don't call them loyalty reviews, as we're in no position really to make such judgments. Nonetheless, we have certain criteria—no, guidelines for determining whether arrangements can be made to get you people out of here. That's our charge, you see—it's our job. So, this application . . ." He waved the offending papers. "Frankly, I'm too busy to fart around with you. There're questions here, simple yes or no, but you write *War and Peace* for me. So here's an opportunity for you to reconsider your answers. Okay?"

"But you see," Fujita explained, "I had questions of my own. These are not yes-or-no questions."

The man rolled his eyes to his comrades, hacked, and rubbed his chest harder. "No, no. What I'm saying is, these *are* one-word answers. Trust me. Look, from what you tell me of your situation, you need out. We want you out. We don't want you here. Why the hell can't you people just get that part right?"

"Maybe it has something to do with being shot if we try to walk out of the gate," Fujita said. This sounded right but felt weak. "I didn't understand the questions," he said.

"Good Christ, man! What's to understand?" Fujita was serious, but Johnson leaned back in his chair and laughed. Lit a cigar and laughed! "Your problem is, you don't know what you want. If I were you, I'd want to leave this hole—vamoose!—not understand it. You know how much it costs us to keep you people here?"

"Do *you* know, sir," Fujita said grimly, not missing a beat, "how much it costs us?" One of Johnson's colleagues snorted and dramatically dropped his head to the table.

Sighing, the official sat back, puffing on his stogie and rubbing his heart more vigorously, as if to knead the correct wording from that organ, and Fujita sensed he was gaining some advantage. He knew that the WRA had recently learned some hard lessons in public relations and semantics. Hired to oversee a controversial enemy concentration camp built of "military necessity," Johnson found himself pressed into a career change; no sooner had he requisitioned materials to ease life at the more agreeably renamed "relocation center for evacuees' protection" (that salon of coddled Japs), than he had to cancel the order. The WRA's stated raison d'être shifted from temporary relocation to "dissemination and distribution"—the president's term for dispersing Japanese America away from the West Coast. To Fujita, the "new policy" was old hat: He'd watched the Grower Shippers Association and other western "grass-roots" groups agitate for the same thing for a half-century now. Yet there in the office, measuring his adversary's resolve, Fujita saw that "distribution" was new to Mr. Johnson, and the man choked on it. Were he a synonym buff like Tamie, he might choose *scatter*, *dispel*, *break*, *disassemble*, *sunder*, *divide*, *disband*. Like Fujita's greengrocer neighbor in the Los Angeles market, the WRA didn't want him locked up—it now just wanted him *gone*.

Watching Johnson's difficulty, Fujita saw that he could get out—but at an enormous cost.

Mr. Johnson changed his tack. "Come now, you and I are not soldiers; we're not politicians or lawyers; we're essentially businessmen." Fujita winced at the buddy-buddy tone, the false camaraderie of someone uncomfortable holding all the cards. With a conspiratorial smile, Johnson continued, "Let's be practical, not political. Look, it says right in our charter we gotta make you a reasonable place to live as much like home as we can. An *equitable substitute*, it says, a place you'd *want* to live. *Now* they tell us that at the same time, we must find you jobs and places to go and incentive for going. Take my advice, Fujita, and don't try to understand that 'cause it doesn't make sense. Hell, we're starting to pay people to leave—we'll give you bus fare to wherever you want. Throw in a box lunch for good measure. Someday we'll kick you out, so you might as well go while the going's good." Johnson looked as if he could not remain awake a minute longer. "You want out, those are the terms. If you stay in here another year, two, three, no one else is to blame. It's all your fault."

"It's all my fault," Fujita echoed. Envisioning outside, he could yoke together only blurred images. His greenhouses just jagged frames stoned to death by the mob. A slab at the foot of the butte, viewed through the meshed diamonds of storm fencing. Then a drugged sensation, his face sweating, his throat clinching tight. "Yes," he croaked, sounding miles away from himself. "I'll take bus fare." Feeling claustrophobic, he tried to stand up.

"That's right," Johnson said. "Smartest move, brother. The best way. So you'll just fix this . . ." He pushed the application across the table.

"Bus fare," Fujita repeated. "East. I guess I have to go east." Already visualizing it, jouncing across the mesas, the window shades up, reading a real newspaper. He felt nauseated. "Far," he said. "A train? Maybe train fare."

"We can maybe swing a train, sure. Depends where you go," Johnson said. He slid a pen from his shirt pocket, unscrewed the top, shook the ink into the gold nub, and scribbled a few lines and circles on the document. "A few pen strokes and bone voyajee. Here."

Still Fujita did not accept the papers. Through the window, he saw a dust devil dance up to the gate. He felt on the verge of collapsing, but he refused to do it.

After watching Fujita remain stock-still for a moment, Mr. Johnson ordered his colleagues to leave the room. When they were alone, he continued softly, "I got a problem with my ticker, see, so I don't need any unnecessary upset. Look, I figure the country owes you, so I've been looking the other way, but I can only do that so long. What you've been through, don't get too hung up on being rational. Grieve. Get mad. Don't think too much. You lose your wife, your boy, a house—of course, thinking about it will make you crazy. But *don't be crazy.* Sign this fucking thing, Fujita. Lie, cross your fingers behind your back, but sign it, then go start your life again."

What was left to want? Only Yoneko, who had a week's head start. Limping over to the table, he took the fountain pen. "You win," he said, signing.

"*You* do," Johnson said, taking the revised application. "Now, that other thing you asked about," he continued more officiously, delving into a valise set on the table. "The Yamaguchi girl." From the case, he extracted a stuffed manila folder and pried the folds apart, exposing a stippled, wide-ruled notebook. "I'm sorry, but I can't tell you where she went." Setting it flat open, he turned to look out the window. "What a day! Not too cool, not too hot. Quiet. Days like this, you think there are worse places to spend a war."

"Yoneko (Yvonne) Yamaguchi," Fujita had the opportunity to read. Yvonne! He could just hear her: *I prefer Yvonne; it's so much more* continental, *don't you think?* More important information followed; it read: "Billings, Montana, Sheriff's Office: reported scheduled check-in, WRA Station, Boston, Mass."

"No," Johnson repeated, turning around, shutting the file, rising, and resuming his Napoleon pose, "I'm sorry, but I can't tell you that." He accompanied Fujita into the front office. With a firm handshake, he said, "Well, good luck. And I'm sorry."

"Right," Fujita said, crossing to the door, temporarily satisfied. Then he stopped at the threshold. Johnson had turned away and stood on tiptoe, reaching up to replace the folder atop a file cabinet. To the man's back, Fujita said, "You're just doing your job. Um, take care of your heart."

Did the skies and heat over Gila River truly hang clearer and warmer during his last weeks as an internee? Or was it only anticipation, the lightening of guilt, that made it seem that way? Although the fair weather made his good-bye visits more bearable, he had hoped, upon leaving, to remember at the last Gila's other aspect, as the armpit of hell. Fujita grasped at Mr. Johnson's offer like a shipwrecked sailor groping at slick flotsam for any fingerhold. Each second between him and that resurrection seemed eternity, until unfortunate bureaucratic details prolonged his stay by a week, then two. His California bank, unwilling to part with his savings funds, had refused to answer two communications from him; finally, it replied to a call from Mr. Johnson, insisting that it required Mari's signature to release amounts over five hundred dollars. A letter to Harv Clemens, the potter (supposedly, *hopefully*) caring for the nursery, met with a similar, unsettling silence.

The waiting affected Fujita like an eerie narcotic. "I don't feel like I'm here, with these people anymore," he told Big Jim at their last meeting. He waved his hand toward the red-capped white rows, his artificial community for almost two years, then pointing beyond the fence. "And I'm not out there with those people, either."

The enforced delay had other effects, too. In the empty hours alone—aimlessly wandering camp, or packing and repacking his luggage—visualizing what might await him "out there," the loyalty-review business still pained him. Johnson was a fool! Only a fool, a *free* fool, could confuse freedom with starting over, conscience with politics, or dishonesty with expedience; only a fool could mistake their symbiotic roles as jailer and jailed for any mere business transaction. He felt like an inu. Tending Mari's gravesite those weeks forced him to reconsider his former life, its priorities, its overtime and business trips and unrealized plans for that family vacation cruise. He certainly had time to brood. Considering how few possessions the Fujitas had brought with them, ordering the meager estate took a surprisingly long while. In Rivers, each tattered sweater, each worn sock was an asset of value. Keeping the ceremonial tea set and her wedding gown, he donated Mari's articles to various women or to the YW. One sleepless night he sat up trying to unearth from her bumper crop of romances a book he could bear to read on the train. Guiltily appalled by his wife's literary tastes, which were primarily medical, he found that she had mail-ordered a virtual pulp hospital. In addition to the plainly titled *Nurses* and its sequels, *Nurses, Nurses, Nurses* and *Nurses and Doctors*, the provocative *Medics Amour* made Fujita shiver; he had always hated and feared physicians ever since his vigils over his father's deathbed.

"Good God, Mari," muttered Fujita, who could imagine no

profession *less* romantic than medicine, except perhaps *field* medicine. Apparently, the war had cast its shadow over love, like everything else in those years, and the newer additions to Mari's library took an odd, warlike twist. The cover of *Kisses and Bullets* promised "Doomed Love!" while *Fighting Nightingales* recounted the tale of "Brave she-heroes in white" who "find danger and passion in the trenches of darkest Sahara!" Scanning a copy of *Battle Surgeon* by the appropriately named Frank G. Slaughter, he grimaced to read the plot summary: "Doctor and nurse—their urgent, hasty love was born of war!" A devout Slaughter enthusiast, Mari had also devoured *Air Surgeon* and *Buccaneer Surgeon* and *Sword and Scalpel.* But *Battle Surgeon* was the last book Mari Fujita ever read, and the dog-ear on page 42, where she presumably had stopped to fetch the telegram notifying them of Tony's death, showed that she never finished it. Overwhelmed by what Fujita supposed was an unknowable feminine mystery, he dumped every last book into a pile marked with chalk, YWCA.

One morning, as he sat trying to crush his suitcase closed, the letter arrived. Without the delay in his departure, he would have missed it, and so would later have cause to appreciate those troublesome two weeks. Sent from an address in Philadelphia, from the American Friends Service Committee, it offered a job interview in garden supply in Boston and provided a listing of free AFSC hostels to stay at in the interim. He wouldn't have to wait for the bank mess to sort out.

Boston? he thought. Tea party. Baked beans. Massacre. Cream pie.

His last day in camp, Fujita crossed F Street to see Yoneko's Aunt Rose. After he'd avoided her so long, she seemed even shorter in stature than he recalled, and much frailer. Once a champion door-slammer, the aging Issei's reflexes or spirit had waned; her right hand, a talon of arthritic pain, moved too slowly to prevent him from inserting his foot in the crack. "Rose," Fujita said, "I've brought you some things." The bitter woman still refused to admit him. He just nodded and laid the heap on the stoop—a warm shawl, Big Jim's necklace, and assorted toiletries.

"I don't need your handouts," Rose insisted. "And I'm still

not telling you where she is, so turn around and go." In fact, she looked pained not to admit him, so lonely now, with Yoneko gone. The Gila sun did not like Rose; her already wrinkled skin now looked like tortured leather. Fujita did not fail to remember that Tony had asked him to look after Aunt Rose, too. But with no time to waste, he grabbed her stiff hand, pried the fingers open, and pressed most of his camp scrip into her palm, along with the AFSC office address.

"This is yours, Rose. Use it to write to her, and to me. I'll send my address and what money I can, and you send it to her." The wizened old hand shook in his. "If you can get out, call me and I'll help you."

"Where am I going to go?" Rose said distantly.

Unable to look at her, he scuffed his toe across the step, cutting a yellow line through the dust. "If you can see your way clear . . ." he began. "If you can forget about . . ."

The woman's eyes became gashes. In a falsely haughty tone, Yoneko's aunt said, "I'll ask her. She may want to talk to you, but I'll advise her against it. She's a good girl, innocent, but I'm not. Maybe you fooled her, but not me," she repeated. Like a pawnshop buyer appraising a worthless trinket, she swatted his arm, raising a red cloud. "You're not so great. You're not such a great man."

Fujita did not bother to shrug or nod. The old woman began to cry then, and though he had meant to ask if she would care for Mari's grave, what could he say now? He only released his grip on her hand, bent to kiss her between the eyes, and left her.

Then he fetched Mari's Bible—the one she would take to a desert island—and the mountain of pulp novels to carry over to the YW. The slim, lively organizer, Janet Hara, cried over the gift, pushed it away even as her fingers tightened on it. It clearly meant more to her than to Fujita. "I don't need it," he insisted, pressing the hefty tome back on her. "Maybe someone here can find a real use for it."

Miss Hara's face was a whirlpool of appreciation and resentment and pity and concern for him, but she nodded, and without his asking, she assured him that Mari's grave would be well kept. "We all need comfort sometimes," she said. "We all need help."

The grateful widower knew then that she was going into her wind-up, preparing to make her curveball pitch for Jesus. Fujita bunted. He wanted to stay grateful, so he abruptly excused himself and tithed some of his remaining scrip to the church. The exchange also upset his internal scale, his community conscience; thinking there should be some equilibrium in his hypocrisy, he decided to leave the Buddhist priest precisely the same amount.

For no clear purpose, his last visit was to the WRA office. Finding Mr. Johnson out, he waited for twenty minutes where the secretary placed him in the office. When a banging of file cabinets and mild oaths told Fujita the secretary was busily occupied in the other room, he ventured the quick, soft steps to Johnson's desk. On the short pedestal behind it, the typewriter and paper sat alongside the notebook containing Yoneko's address. He did not *need* to steal the book, of course—could he ever forget the address of the Boston WRA check-in station? Best to be prepared, though. What other details might it contain? When he left the office, the rigid cover pressed into his hip and lower ribs, forcing him to walk with a slight stoop. His billowy shirt did not betray him; Fujita had lost much weight at Gila. If the secretary noticed his altered gait as he walked out that door for the last time, what of it. Wasn't she accustomed to seeing people leave bowed with defeat? How many internees had *skipped* out of a visit to that office?

"I'll tell Mr. Johnson you were here," the woman said over her shoulder, still struggling with her filing cabinet. "What's your name again?"

"Please don't bother him," he said. "I'll find him another time."

An hour later he fastidiously repacked and retaped his suitcase with the notebook hidden inside and vowed he would not unpack until he was home, wherever *home* would be. He was still barred from California; and wasn't home buried here, in the hot red sands of Gila River?

"Good-bye!" he shouted to Mrs. Sano, who appeared to be

snoring, though she sat upright on her cot, her hands folded, her eyes slightly opened into thin, wet lines. "Good-bye!!" he shouted again, to Gila River itself.

Smuggled in his suitcase, the notebook felt heavy as a cannonball. It didn't help that little Bobby Tanaka had also latched on to his coat, with his wooden bloodhound in tow. "Where you going?" Bobby wanted to know. "Going east? Going to see New York? I never been there. You taking a train? I saw *King Kong*. You ever been to New York?"

At the checkpoint by the north gate of the internment camp, documents were shown, signed, countersigned. A few friends, coworkers, and well-wishers gathered to see him off, but he barely felt the hands patting his shoulder, his arm, or the kisses brushing his cheek. He would remember none of the messages he was asked to pass on to friends and relatives of those left behind. Only the stone-faced, armed gatekeepers—those bland young men, he'd remember—as they laced their clawed fingers through the wire and parted the gate. The Jeep that was to transport him surged beneath him, and he felt a rush as if swept off the ground, and passing the shadow of the gun tower, he was afraid. Then as suddenly the car halted. They changed their minds! They know about the notebook! he thought, but the pause was only momentary. Waiting for the relocking of the gate, Fujita looked back to the butte and to the patch where two years' gravestones squatted at its base. That *other* side already seemed distant as a past life—as distant as Mount Fuji in the Tokyo mayor's wall hanging that so eased his mother as the two of them passed into America. A few hours later, on the train, Fujita would realize exactly what the camp looked like: Though the rising sun flag above it was Arizona's, Gila looked like another country—it looked like a nightmare Japan. He envisioned himself a phantasm still seated there atop the butte, legs folded, the tumbleweed burning. In the absence of any real resolution to this life, it comforted him to think that some part of him, if only a shadow, remained in this city of dust.

He envisioned a later day when this city would return to dust, the Pima sitting on Sacaton Butte, shielding their eyes, watching government contractors level this plain again. Smoke, smoke, dynamite, and great pillars of dust. It would sparkle for a moment, he imagined, and the dark-skinned onlookers would chuckle, maybe drink a beer in the heat, finally shrug. In a few days, they'd recover their sliver of rocky nowhere. Left to wonder over traces of two lost peoples, two Hohokam, the Pima would see their land carpeted with concrete slabs and white boards and tar paper, some old tires, a porcelain commode bleached bone-white like a dinosaur's skull, perhaps some dresses, a crucifix. Headstones. Across camp, where Fujita's crops now cut verdant stripes through the desert floor, he pictured desiccated mounds of quartz and clay, the empty water tower standing above like the husk of a dead spider. After days of searching, a devastated Pima father might think to seek his missing daughter at the bottom of one of the cisterns left hidden and gaping under decades of brush. Too many of them to cover. After the irrigation ditches had been rerouted back toward the city, Gila would again shrivel into nothing. And Fujita, now midway through his life, would have left behind nothing.

What he really meant was, he had saved, created, or *contributed* nothing, but this was not entirely true. He forgot that he had given Bobby Tanaka's Pima friend, Tom Fields, some cuttings from his splendid garden in Block 60. Little Tom, who had always thought those Japs a "rich" people, took the exotic gifts home to his mother (some from seeds that had traveled across the Pacific), who tended and planted them. Those alien flowers would grace the earth long after Fujita, or Mrs. Fields, or even little Tom, who would one day cross the Pacific himself for the Korean War, but only in one direction. It would be Tom's sister, not yet born at their planting, who would recall the source of her inherited garden one day when she found a bewildered and dehydrated young "Jap," a Sansei named Freddie Tanaka, pushing a fuelless moped about the reservation, unable to find his way out. After filling Freddie and his moped with the necessary fluids, Ms. Fields would show him the garden and relate her dead brother's story. And, as she expected, Freddie would appear envious and angry and grateful to the hear the tale from a distant Native American, from a stranger.

Freddie's type is familiar to the Pima, the type who occasionally stops at the tribal office to ask permission to see "The Camps," which are endowed with a nearly biblical importance and spoken of in hushed tones. The Pima understand Freddie's type: They appreciate respect for ancestors, which others mistake for ancestor worship; and they know that beyond rediscovering family "roots," the Japs' children share with Pima very real questions about American politics and justice, values and tolerance. When they drove through the unhappy, forgotten town of Sacaton to get gas for his moped, it would embarrass Freddie to pass the drug-rehab center and signs for the new casino. Ellen Fields knew that if she remembered the Japs, in her way, the Japs had mostly forgotten the Pima. She would point this out but see that Freddie was too awestruck by the garden and ruins from "Back Then," and by all the history his parents had decided to keep from him. *Mukashi no hanashi.* For the most part, the slim remaining connection between the sister of Tom Fields and the son of Bobby Tanaka were Fujita's flowers, from across decades and oceans, and Freddie would only be able to nod and say, "Wow."

Of course, sitting in the back of the idling Jeep, Fujita could not see that far into tomorrow. At the very threshold of liberty, he was still looking backward, not forward. *To undo mistakes is always harder than not to create them originally,* Mrs. Roosevelt had observed after visiting Rivers, *but we seldom have foresight. Therefore we have no choice but to try to correct our past mistakes.* Her advice—delivered to her husband, then written in an unpublished *Collier's* article—seemed doomed to fall on deaf ears. But now Fujita willed himself to look ahead, hoping that the "whole thing" was almost over, fearing it was only just beginning. There before him was little Bobby Tanaka, on the other side of the fence, but as strenuously as he tried, he could not press himself through the latticed wires. Fujita could not bear to look at the boy. He looked up again only when he heard the child turned away by the soldier's heavy hand, followed by his crippled wooden pet—*clack, click, clack.* The Jeep's engine revved again. Then Fujita was free.

ELEVEN

Accounting

The snowbound New Year's Eve Fujita unrolled his tale to Margaret, he watched the fireplace glimmers play over her where she sat on the floor, enwrapped in a crocheted yellow quilt, and was astonished at how *full* she looked, and how empty he felt. His story seemed to him clinical and remote, as if it had all happened to some other sorry fellow. It was the only way he could tell it.

"I'll tell you, a person could freeze to death out there when he wasn't boiling to death," he said, and he felt drunk.

They had scotch and water, cheddar and crackers. Woozily, he stretched on the floor beside Margaret, propping his feet on the brick lip of the hearth, liking the rare sensation of having dry socks. It all seemed inexorably New Englandish, this hearthside scene. In Southern California this fireplace would be an ornamental luxury, a privilege only of such men as the King of Cleats. In Juggeston, it was the house heart, its bubble of greenhouse warmth fending off a season that still felt colder than Fujita's arctic dreams. (Last night he'd stood bound to a stake while a tribe of hostile snowmen circled him waving icicle spears like jungle-movie headhunters.) Fascinated by the blazing fir and oak logs, he pushed aside the brass mail curtain; embers hopped like crickets onto the stone lip, and with a thumb he flicked them back into the masonry mouth. The sporadic distractions let him feel careless, distanced from the story he pushed out.

"Mari and Tony and I would huddle around this tin pail full of coal embers with holes poked in it. Handy, because you could carry it around camp with you, take it to the latrines, or when they'd show films sometimes. Am I boring you?" he kept asking. Margaret frowned and tsked him. "You're sure?" Her foot would emerge from the quilt to prod him on.

He downplayed Eleanor Roosevelt, mimicked the legendary snoring of old Mrs. Sano, seethed over the Tulare yokels with their pipes and twenty-twos. And, of course, the bush that had ignited so ominously before him in his early grief. "Just *poof*."

"Poof?" Margaret echoed, watching him. "A miracle. You saw a miracle."

"No, a fluke phenomenon. An accident of reflected light. Those things happen."

"A miracle," she repeated. "I wonder what it means."

"I think *I* caused it," Fujita said, staring blankly toward the hearth, conscious of an expanding sensation that everything had been his fault. "Nothing very interesting has happened to me, I suppose," he said, feeling exhausted, embarrassed, spent. With a look of infuriating benevolence, Margaret inched closer. Fujita began perspiring. She slid closer. "I'm no Homer, I guess." Heat emitting from her quilt, from the fireplace. Desire. "I'll understand if you want to go upstairs—"

The fireplace.

"To bed—"

The *fireplace!*

The sentence concluded with a rocketing yowl, but Fujita was still lost in desire and the past, as far off from himself as the shrub that flared on Sacaton Butte. It took a moment to realize that it was in fact his sock and cuff being engulfed in flames. He tumbled away from the fireplace kicking the woolen torch aloft, away from Margaret, the rug, or any furniture. He groped at his calf, wishing perhaps to remove the foot altogether, fleetingly thinking: Margaret, I've done my part, I haven't set the house on fire, so *do something*. Struggling with his sign language, Margaret just wavered before the foot like a snake charmer, and the words erupted much less orderly and cool-headed.

"AAAAAAAGGGHHHHHH!" Fujita said.

Meaning to extinguish the flames, Margaret groped for the seltzer but in her panic, grabbed and dumped the fifth of scotch, inspiring a much lustier conflagration. Crying out in dismay, she manned the correct bottle and attacked the blaze. After dousing it, she removed the charred, dripping sock and helped him into the brightly lit kitchen to examine the damage.

Unable to decide which was more agonizing, the second-degree burns or the embarrassment, Fujita hissed, "Ow, I *really* don't manage very well—ow—when I have to talk about myself, ow."

"Be quiet now." Margaret set him down at the table. She tenderly probed the pads of his sole, frowned, then stood. "I'll be right back," she promised, and hurried out the porch door.

"Wear a coat!" Fujita tried to call, but his lips wouldn't move. Slumping back wet and overdone, he watched her disappear into the flurrying night. He could just make out the scarecrow, though his vision blurred and his eyes kept closing. Like smelling salts, the slam of the garage office door jolted him back to clarity. Not that he had anything to hide up there—only baggage, a few garments and odds and ends—but the regular intrusions after Pearl Harbor had left him sensitive to such violations. It is *her* garage, after all, he reminded himself, and this pained him.

The lower he sank in this relationship, admitting his dreary secrets and displaying his family's dirty laundry, the more it energized her, the more it unraveled him. Now Margaret knew more about him than anyone in this whole half of the country save for Yoneko. How had that happened? He recalled his mother telling him, when he'd been wrongfully accused of copying a school chum's history essay, "Hakujin love confession—they love to shout confessions at each other. Tell them you did what they say you did, and you're sorry, and they'll raise your marks for your honesty." Was that what was happening here?

Staring at the scarecrow, Margaret's snowy facsimile, he brooded, suspecting he was being pitied—or *treated, healed*—when he had wanted, had imagined . . .

What was the shock or the booze or the scarecrow or his conscience telling him—or warning him—he wanted? *Danger, thin ice! Go back, Bill Fujita. Go back.*

Awaiting his dreaded anniversaries, just what could he possibly want of Margaret? Maybe just to accompany her upstairs—to show her the resuscitated radio, find some Bing Crosby to hum along with. She'd like the cards with the waka poems written in kanji and hiragana—no point not showing them to her, now. But he'd crippled himself, couldn't move. Thinking he'd *really* like some of that wasted scotch now, he had a moment of sudden, crystalline insight into his father's boozy life. The Ichi-Bomb could make walls crumble, doors open, armor shuffle off with a clang. It could inspire courage and romance. It could bridge oceans.

He lurched to standing, and a searing pain tore through his foot. He remembered hearing that lard soothed burns, and finding a jar in the icebox, he scooped out a greater handful than intended and smeared the goop on. Immediately, his foot sizzled anew, and he launched himself out onto the porch and into the searing snow. He collapsed then—he just released his knees and let himself topple backward in such relief, it was as if he'd walked all the way from Mr. Johnson's office that day and had only just arrived. Sunken into the snow, he was amazed, even delighted to realize that for the first time since moving to Juggeston, he did not feel cold. In the swish-swish of his bare foot kicking, plunging in and out of the cool powder, he thought he heard something.

"Margaret, is that you?" he asked of the white-coated figure with her arms outspread, growing fainter and fainter. "Mari?"

When no answer came, he sighed and lay himself down on his back and began to make his first-ever snow angel.

Nurse Kelly would have known the "lard cure" for what it was—an old wives' tale—and she could have accomplished what she most wanted then: to *save* the widower, if only from further frying his foot. But an old wife herself, she was distracted in her late husband's office, where she hadn't been alone for a long while. It felt more like home to her than the big house. She thought of an exchange, moving Mr. Fujita over to the house, quickly dropped the idea, then imagined just moving herself over to the garage and dropped the idea even faster. She had then a sensation unfamiliar to her—it was guilt. During his story, she had fixated on what *her* people did to his people, as she thought of it, and she couldn't help feeling a little guilty by association. But there was something else, something more, too. She sensed that confiding in her that way had been for him an act more intimate than any imaginable—more vulnerable, more taboo even than making love. She feared he was, in some essential way, in real danger.

No longer certain what to call this upstairs space, Margaret searched the dark for traces of the two men who had lingered there. Like tagged exhibits in a courtroom, suitcases sat open-mouthed on the examination table, with clothing in neat checkers of muted color, pressed and folded, only dotted with balls of sock here, curled-up leather belts there, an occasional bland necktie. If the last few months had changed Jack's room at all, it looked only sparer, less lived-in. The medicine cabinets sparkled, the floorboards glimmered with thorough waxing. His, Fujita's, only other footwear—a pair of battered work shoes—waited straight-toed and spit-shined on the mat by the stairwell. The excess laces sat carefully tucked in the cavities, propping their barely creased tongues erect as soldiers during inspection. The skeleton, which he had decked out as a sinister, quadruped effigy of himself, toasty in his scarf, gloves, overcoat, and knit cap, grinned cleanly in the dark.

Inside her swept a wave of discontent. To fill the early absence of Jack, she had sat on this floor for a week talking to him while sorting through his papers, tossing out old pharmaceutical samples, boxing his records to ship to Dr. Swenson; she had *loved* its messy clutter. She hadn't thought to vacuum up the splinters of tongue depressors Jack had so voraciously chewed when he wasn't smoking; lodged in the fibers of the rug, these had made the place comfortable as a pub lined with sawdust and peanut husks. She envisioned Fujita spending nights upon nights on his knees extracting each wooden sliver—with tweezers, if need be—innocently assuming that it was a service to his landlady.

"Well, it *is* his room, after all." Massaging at a rising lump in her throat, she sat on his cot. Shadows of Jack still shuffled about the room, now more echoes than presences. Notably, the olfactory memories were extinguished; cigarettes, rubbing alcohol, disinfectant soaps had been replaced by wood polish and the warm bouquets rising from the garage and greenhouse below. Except for a diffuse immaculateness, only the photo from Gila River, the Tokyo mayor's scroll, and the ragged radio indicated Fujita's ever passing through there.

"Well, it's no wonder," she berated herself, falling back onto the thick, wool blankets made up taut as a drum skin. As she tried to look at the ceiling through Fujita's eyes, the room began spinning to the left. "You've got him surrounded by ghosts. There's no *room* for him in here," she said aloud. "What do *you* think, Jack? We can make the poor man comfortable, at least?" The absurdity of the decor flooded over her. The dull steel instruments lining the cabinets. Speculums like mandibles of some aquatic dinosaur in a museum. Forceps, syringes, the cyclops-eye reflector, the telescoping steel stirrups. Why, it must seem like a torture chamber to him!

"For God's sake, Maggie," she scolded herself. "Give the poor man a lampshade."

When she noticed the diary's dappled cover, she recognized the moment for what it was: a test of her character. She knew that much. She tried to tell herself she understood the apparent comfort that battered notebook, playing dress-up with the skeleton, and the isolation of this space could provide him. She tried to respect his deep need for privacy, tried not to resent that he preferred the company of ghosts to her own presence beside him on the loveseat or over tea. And for all her obsessional helpfulness (rationalized as altruism, not intrusion; concern, not curiosity) she would never have considered prying into his secret letters to himself—even though the nosy nurse within insisted that healing patients rarely need what they *think* they need. A testimony to her essential honesty, Margaret Kelly realized all this, argued on his behalf, and hesitated.

Yet, staring with new wonderment at the ragged Christmas photo, she felt she finally had a grasp on Fujita and "the whole thing." He needed help, not just healing; and she knew she needed his help, too. And now his suitcases were packed.

Forgetting her purpose for coming there, she nimbly lifted the diary without leaving any prints on the burnished instrument tray. The book was the wide-ruled sort used in schoolrooms, its edges yellowed, thumbed-through, and its cover marked with the owner's name, Johnson. Setting it on the pillow made by the lap of her skirt, she said, "Well, I just have to, don't I?" The first page was stippled with water marks—tears, she imagined. On page 2, written in a spiky print, were several Japanese names, addresses, and phone numbers. Among them, she now knew the name Yoneko (Yvonne) Yamaguchi, and her destination, "WRA Station, Boston, Mass." Turning the page, she found a draft of a letter. "I oughtn't to read this," she said, reading, "Dear Mother, I am finally" followed by some disruption, then concluding, "on the train to." The scripted letters lurched above and below the lines in mimicry of the tracks themselves.

"This is not right," Margaret whispered to herself, peeling open the next page.

"My Dearest Mari," Fujita wrote, "I'll find her. I can't say how I will manage. You'll think I am gone, but I'm not really. I'm still there, really. I'm in this hotel in Chicago, but not really. The others staying here talk to me sometimes as if they can see me, but they really can't." And, "My son," began pages 4 and 5. Page 6 was addressed to "You manipulative, rotten-to-the-core, sniveling little bitch! You whore vampire *actress!*" Her pulse quickening, Margaret fanned through his yearlong correspondences with family and antagonists alike. He valued clarity in spelling, grammar, style, and penmanship. On and on, the pages flickered, black dancing on white like a flip-book cartoon. Miles of grumbling, months of unvoiced complaint filled Margaret with a guilty exhilaration—he *did* get angry, swear, and have petty thoughts; he *wasn't* some rock of Oriental manners and denial. He had wounds, loves, needs. "Dear Mari," she read.

"Margaret is good. You would like her, if you came here. And Livvie and Garvin, too. And the Wellingtons, even Lil—she's had her tough times. I even like that silly scarecrow, and even the snow, sometimes. I'm sorry, Mari, but I do. I suppose that's why I'm still here, stuck, in Massachusetts."

Elsewhere, he confessed: "I DID IT: I KILLED MY OWN SON." Then below, as an afterthought, he added: "I think I killed my grandchild, too." He didn't confess to murdering his wife exactly, but he did write, "I could have killed them all and maybe saved her!"

The following page chilled Margaret even more. A spreadsheet of rigid, orderly columns in obsessively neat lettering listed in dollar amounts the debits and credits of Fujita's daily life from Pasadena to that day on the Peak. Included was the largeish COLLEGE FUND he'd socked away for Tony—and now Yoneko. LEGAL FUNDS, PRIVATE INVESTIGATOR, and TOILETRIES were earmarked. He'd recorded TRANSPORTATION costs: a train ticket to Boston and another to a place known only by **?**—someplace far, for he budgeted himself a dollar a day, meals and travel expenses, for five days. He'd figured taxi fare, an apartment deposit, first month's rent, "Gerber's?", and "Diaper Service?", "Repmt. to M.K." and the cost of filling up the Dodge. She understood his self-flagellation and thought it pretty normal. Jumping off a bridge was not unfathomable. But this morbid . . . accounting?

On her lips sat something along the lines of her usual, "Oh, you poor man," but then, on the next page, ASSETS?, more substantial figures caught her eye. His joint business accounts with Tamie, still frozen; and one with Mari, still inaccessible. "Oh, my," she gasped. Other columns estimated the values of his California properties—whether leased, lost, destroyed, or stored—that remained out of his control: his greenhouses, stock, business machines, furnishings, cars and trucks, house, and the land itself—no mere Juggeston real estate. "Oh, *my.*" Thousands, that might pay for his new life. Tens of thousands . . .

"'Give the *poor man* a lampshade,'" she spat at herself, slamming the book shut. "Oh, Margaret," she said, shaking her head, feeling queasy. "Oh, Margaret . . ."

"Margaret?" she heard from somewhere outside, as though echoed by the winter wind. Quickly replacing the notebook, she ran to the window and saw it was the handyman, "Margaret's refugee Japanese," the internment poster child; it was grumpy old, utilitarian Farmer Fujita of the Kelly nojo, her project, her busywork, the poor widower who needed to have some fun. It was Mrs. Kelly's charity case greeting the scarecrow, lying on his back in the snow and trying to fly.

"Oh, Margaret, Margaret, Margaret . . ." she chanted. "Oh, Bill . . ."

I need you to wake up now, came a voice. Creeping his way back to consciousness, Fujita became dimly aware of Margaret and her warm body whispering against him—on top of him, actually. He fleetingly noticed that his shirt had been removed. For a moment he thought he could stand being frozen a little longer, but that notion was soon dispelled as he felt his eyelids being forcefully opened. Hovering there, Margaret's face was full of concern, frowning at him as she checked his pupils for dilation. He tried to struggle, but her body had him pinned to the floor.

"You can breathe?" she asked.

Fujita tried to say, Of course I can breathe, but no sound emerged from his now stinging lips. She pressed her hands to his face and rubbed it hard until some feeling began to return. It hurt, but he couldn't protest, couldn't move. For the longest time he lay weighted down beneath the good nurse's warmer body and a great heap of blankets, feeling like a mummy—or like Bob Ito, he thought. But slowly, her gentle attempts at rousing him had the unfortunate result of arousing him, too. Though groggy, he felt himself growing as rigid as an icicle.

Margaret hurriedly decided his torso was warm enough and sat upright to begin probing at his toes. He winced. "That's a good sign," she mumbled to herself, approvingly.

Prying his toes apart, she separated them with gauze squares, then plunged the foot into broken glass—or actually, a lobster pot of tepid water, as he could see when he jackknifed upward to howl his inexpert second opinion: He did *not* agree that the pain roaring back down his leg was "a good sign." Gradually, he could feel his other extremities again, too. Though his protruding ears burned like hell, his nose was okay; wide and flat, laying close to the face, perhaps the Japanese nose was better adapted to extreme cold?

When she at last spoke to him, he thought he detected a hint of detachment, maybe even disapproval, in her voice. "How do you feel?" she asked, plopping the medical bag down beside his ear. Mechanically, she unsnapped its clasps, rummaged within, extracted various sterile-smelling utensils. She withdrew a half-rolled metal tube of salve and set to anointing his burn.

"I've been running sort of hot and c-c-cold lately," he said, shivering.

"Why, Mr. Fujita, I do believe you just told a joke," Margaret said lightly, but her chest heaved with each breath—from anger? Or just the stench of his seared skin? "What on earth were you doing out there?"

"Playing in the snow," he admitted, and he had to smile. "Well, waiting for you, I guess." Her hair fell prettily as she bent over his foot; it danced with brilliant reds and oranges from the hearth light, a little unruly around the temples. Propping the foot up on her thigh, she didn't even seem to mind that she sullied her skirt. From the bag, she removed a pair of safety shears, sleek as mercury. Fujita gulped. "A penny for your thoughts?"

Margaret swatted that ball back into his court. "No," she said aggressively, "*you* first." She clacked the shears open and shut, open and shut, her pale, oval face neutral and inscrutable.

He strangled back a cry because he didn't know what words would come out. He tried sitting upright, but it took too much out of him. "I'm lucky to work for a nurse," he finally said, hating himself.

The shears fell quiet, and she stared at him as intently as if deciding how to begin dissecting him. He didn't dare say anything else. Then, just as her silence became unbearable to him, she crossed her arms. "Give me a dollar," she said testily. "Well, come on. Do you have one?"

She seemed serious. Fishing in his pocket, he came up with enough change. "I only have coins," he said apologetically.

Margaret huffed. "Okay, that will do."

"That will do what?" he asked, handing her the money.

"Congratulations," she said. "You're now an official sharecropper. Half my portion of the cultivated property on Widow's Peak is yours. That's our lease. No, not a word: I suspect you're good for it. Now, be quiet and let me work." The tension in her escaped through her agile hands as she swiftly sliced his trouser leg from hem to waist, then parted the fabric like a banana peel. "Hold still. Trust me. I am a *nurse*," she said dangerously. More gently, she snipped bits of dead skin where they adhered to the cloth.

"G-g-good thing, too," he said, trying not to cry out, "because you're a lousy fireman." The man who claimed he never told jokes was just full of good humor that night.

"No, that's right," Margaret said. "Just a nurse."

"And a good one, too," Fujita whispered, biting his lip for the pain that never really abated until he awoke on the couch the next morning, in 1945.

"It's not his fault, Moira," Livvie sobbed, and to be heard over the din of the Wellingtons' New Year's Eve party, she spoke too loudly. Moira Hardy glanced around them, watchful for eavesdroppers. "It's not her fault, either," Livvie added. "It's lonely on the hill. I know that. It's good that they have each other," she burbled miserably. "She's lost Jack, and he's lost his wife, Mari, and—"

"Shhh, shhhh," Moira urged, both in consolation and in warning. "You must all be so very lonely," Garvin's art and homeroom teacher said.

Nodding, sobbing even more vigorously, Livvie managed also to assume a big, cartoon smile for Alf Wellington, who waved at her from across the overfull lounge; swaddled in a diaper-toga ensemble, he made an absolutely terrifying Baby New Year. "I work all the time now," she said, catching her breath, "with the stupid holidays, and Garvin always wants to go over there to the greenhouse and now he can't, and he's just gloomy all the time and he doesn't want to be with me, and I want to go over, too, but I *can't*." When she paused for a gulp of air, Moira took the opportunity to pour them another round, and they toasted 1944 into oblivion.

"Thanks, Moira. You really are a lifesaver," Livvie said, exhausted. "Again." Arriving that night with Garvin, Livvie had been so upset that the usual queries—*Where's the rest of your gang? Are Maggie and the new man coming?*—nearly drove her to violence. Moira swooped to the rescue, yanking them into a line of dancers doing a bunny hop. Leaving Garvin to play darts with other kids, they planted themselves at the card table to talk, intimately and more or less alone. They had dined together after the Winter Wonderland Art Festival, and Livvie found Moira remarkably easy to talk to despite—or because of?—her suspicions that Moira had had an affair with Sig. In her gratitude for a sympathetic ear, Livvie had to fight to keep from saying too much to her new confidante and drinking buddy.

"But I'm spoiling the party for you," Livvie said, wiping her teary eyes. "Don't let me keep you here all night. Go dance, go dance." She waved toward the overflowing dance floor.

"I don't dance anyway," Moira said, smiling. She stuffed a cigarette into her six-inch lacquered, rhinestone-studded holder, lit it, and passed it to Livvie. With a moist drink napkin she blotted at Livvie's running mascara.

"You don't?" For some reason this struck Livvie as just about the saddest thing she'd ever heard. "I *love* to dance," she crowed. Weeping anew, she confessed her girlhood dream of being a dancer. "Not a ballerina, but ballroom-style, with corsages and thick heels, gowns and long scarves." On the air, she painted the dancer with swirls of smoke, using the cigarette holder as a brush.

Perhaps the eavesdropping Frank Childs meant well in his silly attempt at chivalry; approaching Livvie and giving a funny little bow, he said, "It looks like your dance card's kind of empty. What do you say I twirl you around a bit?"

"How's your finger, Frank?" Livvie sneered, rolling her eyes. His grin melting, he turned on his heels and stomped around to the other side of the table. He began whispering to Lil Wellington.

"Asshole," she muttered. Then. Suddenly. Soberly earnest,

she said, "I'm not really like this, Moira. I'm not. Not usually."

"Yes, I know that—we *all* know that." Moira pointedly looked around the table, since it had become ludicrous to pretend that the half-dozen folks sitting nearby weren't straining to hear. "You've been through so much," Moira declared. Paulette, Lil, Frank, and Dolly Doe all hastily looked away. "You *all* have on that hill, and thank God you have each other to help and understand. With so many big changes, losing your spouses—"

Livvie hissed and shook her head violently so that her dark sheet of hair completely hid her face. "Oh no," she said, choking. "You can't compare, you can't compare!"

Moira stiffened. "Livvie, I don't mean to diminish your loss in any—"

"*He* lost his *son,* too. I mean, this may sound absolutely evil to you, but I do know: You lose a husband, you may or may not be ruined. But if your *kid* dies, you *never* recover," she said, her voice spiking with fury. "Never." Looking out through her curtain of hair, she pointed to where Garvin was playing darts with Franklin Bunkinson. "If anything happened to Garvin . . ."

Across the table, Paulette Pedicott traded a quick, sympathetic glance with Livvie over Moira's shoulder, summoning one of her superior frowns at the childless schoolmistress, who shook her head sadly. "I'm sure you don't really mean that," she said. "I mean, they're apples and oranges, but *both* experiences are awful. Losing Sig—"

"Did you screw my husband?" The shift was so abrupt, Moira just sat bolt upright and blinked helplessly. Suddenly, the party seemed much less noisy. "Oh, forget it," Livvie said, waving it away. "It doesn't matter. The point is, I was a grass widow before I was a war widow," she said, almost jauntily. She became sidetracked for a moment delivering her lecture on grass widows and the dearth of terms for "used" men, and so forth. "Anyway, it was less awful than you think. For me. I don't know if it's the same for fathers," she admitted, "but I'll bet it is for him. And he's lost everything—no home or money or friends. And if Margaret has all those things and is such a wonderful, generous, giving, do-goody, goddamned saint, can I *complain* about that? Can I *begrudge* anybody a stupid little shred of comfort? Can I *blame* anybody just because he's a man and Garvin likes having a man around?" Livvie felt on the verge of collapsing. "But who do I have, Moira? I'm all alone up on that hill!"

Then, without knowing how she got there, Livvie was out in the snow, leaning against the Union soldier statue with a coat draped over her head, gasping for breath. She could hear faint laughter and music, and Moira nearby calling, "It's okay, dear. Your mom got a little dizzy, but she's feeling better now. Go back inside so you don't catch cold." Then a hand caressed the small of Livvie's back, and her body slackened in relief. "You are okay?" Moira asked. "You needed some air." Under her veil, Livvie nodded. "And some things are better said outdoors, if you take my meaning." Again, Livvie nodded, but in the viciously sobering winter air, she realized some things were better not said at all.

She could not tell her new friend what had so upset her. How she and Margaret had planned to attend the Wellington's fest together, leaving Mr. Fujita in peace—no New Year's, no birthday party. And how she had looked forward to some "girl time" alone with Margaret, and even to New Year's Eve. After surviving Christmas, she thought things were really looking up and had resolved to face 1945 on the Peak with optimism and energy, and so she'd refused to be put out when Margaret neglected to call her back that night. When she and Garvin went to fetch the nurse, arriving at the rear entrance to the living room, she peered through the steamy window that was too high for Garvin to reach and saw an empty fifth and decimated cheeseboard and the fireplace, by whose glow she could see everything: the two of them lying together on the floor. The man on his back, his cheeks fiery red as Margaret held them in her hands and stared into his fleshy, squinted eyes. His bare foot and calf and chest peeked out from beneath Margaret's body and the heap of blankets draped over them. And how all of Livvie's newfound hopefulness fell shattering about her like icicles.

It was cold, and late. Removing the coat from her head, she stood upright to face her shivering friend, kissed her, thanked her, and reassured her: "I'm okay, it's nothing, really."

"I'm relieved and glad it's nothing," Moira said. "Although, as a painter, I can tell you that nothing looks very different to different eyes. And *some* people these days are getting very rich painting nothing. Endless interpretations of nothing are possible, you know."

Livvie knew. Wishing her friend a happy new year, she excused herself to go find Garvin, whom she'd left alone for too long. She wanted him with her when they gave this crappy year the boot, believing that whatever came to pass, 1945 couldn't possibly be worse. Right?

Inside, the countdown began.

What would come to pass became, after long germination, the first truly joint effort of the Tufteller-Kelly-Fujita nojo. Livvie had provided the seed long ago: If he couldn't return to California, couldn't he bring California to him? That had been the idea behind the greenhouse. Sown along with the coin in the scarecrow, that kernel of an idea had lain fertilized by Bob Ito, the Quincy Market Nikkei, Lil Wellington, and Officer Gunnison; it had warmed under Yoneko's heat. Sometimes, slow-germinating seeds require scarification—a cut in the hard outer casing; revisiting Gila in his fireside stories and the gift photo had certainly scarified Fujita (not to mention the scarecrow's cryptic pep talk). And Margaret, in her loveseat invitation to him, in their dollar "lease," had given Fujita the growing medium. But amidst all this cultivation, the boy was the greenhouse itself. It was finally in Garvin where the idea's contours and colors and shape could be seen.

Defying his mother's stern warnings, Garvin snuck away on the second day of the new year to seek Mr. Fujita and found him back at work. Holding the tube behind his back, he entered through the garage, carefully as always; despite the massive loads of snow on the greenhouse roof, he suspected the glass structure was more fragile than it appeared. He loved everything about the hothouse—the light and tables and electrical systems he had helped install with his own hands. Most of all, he loved the air: Warm, moist, rich—it always felt like he'd walked out of a refrigerator and into a huge mug of hot chocolate.

"Um, Mr. F.?" he said softly. Interrupting the man's hibernation, Garvin was prepared for a cranky greeting, but Mr. Fujita seemed glad to see him.

"Hey, happy new year, pal," he said, wiping his wet hands on his pants. He'd been unclogging one of the misting tubes. "It's good to see you. It's been a while."

"Mom said I'm not allowed to come over," Garvin replied, somewhat peevishly.

"Oh," Mr. Fujita said. "I see. Well, it's our secret. So, you've come to work?"

"Not really." From behind his back, he produced the gift, rolled into a tube. "Happy birthday," Garvin said tentatively. He'd found it tough to swallow that Mr. F. didn't *want* to have a birthday, but he wasn't sure. "It's called *My Picture*. I made it."

"Well, thanks," Mr. Fujita said, patting Garvin's head. He removed the outer wrapping and unrolled the watercolor. After long staring at the armed, besieged figure marked "Pop," he whistled admiringly. "Wow, you did this, pal?"

Garvin nodded. "For the art fair. It was in the best place. Right up front so everybody saw it when they came in. Um, turn it around. There's stuff on both sides," he explained.

Flipping the huge page over, Mr. Fujita followed the marching line of yellow-skinned antlike Japanese creatures around to the front, past his own stick-figure image, and up onto Widow's Peak. His face contorted first in amusement, then puzzlement.

"It's like that peach-man story," Garvin explained. "When all those people were stuck on the island. See?"

"Oh," said Mr. Fujita, reexamining both sides, then, more loudly, "*Oh*." He pointed to the train of Japanese. "They're not invading—they're coming home? Your pop's like Momotaro, sending them here to Juggeston? He's sending them home from Ogre Island, right?" Garvin nodded, delighted that Mr. F. got it. Mom hadn't gotten it at all. The man laughed and placed his moist hand around Garvin's shoulder. "Garvin, my friend," he said, "this is a masterpiece."

Garvin's *My Picture* struck Fujita as more than just a painting. Recalling what the scarecrow said—*seimei, ōn, girí*—it seemed a blueprint to how he might satisfy all obligations—to the farm, his family, his community, and himself. Together, the four farmers settled on the plan: They would wage their own campaign to liberate Ogre Island. They would sponsor the release of other Gilan internees, and they would begin with Yoneko's Aunt Rose.

It would be necessary to prove that the old woman had a place to go, away from the West Coast, and a means of support: a job in Juggeston as a farmhand. Naturally, Margaret was thrilled. "Well, if that's really all it takes—just any old *job*—why stop there? Maybe others can come stay with us as well?"

"Yes, we'll need hands if we're really going to run a *farm*, right?" Livvie asked with a curious tension in her voice. Coming out of her own wintry isolation, Livvie agreed that helping the relocated internees might be a good, even exciting thing to do, but in discussing the particulars of the plan, she acted cautious, sometimes even suspicious.

But surpassing the farm, Fujita had one priority: Instead of aimlessly looking for Yoneko, he hoped to lure the girl *to him*. "Let's just see how it works with Rose first. Let's not get carried away," he urged.

Apparently, the cranky old Issei lost no time forwarding his invitation to its true, ultimate target. A week later, it was Yoneko who fired back from New Haven: "Give your stupid job to someone who needs it! I have too many jobs already! Auntie and I don't need your charity." In a postscript, she added, "Those women up there sound very nice, at least. You're lucky. It's high time you thought about helping people instead of hounding me. It almost makes me think better of you."

"Gosh, she's *really* mad," Margaret said, sounding impressed. Fujita, who had sent the usual check with Rose's letter, snorted.

"What do you expect?" Livvie said. Her alliance with him on this and many points was much less wholehearted than Margaret's. "It's entrapment! You want to take her aunt hostage."

"Really?" said Garvin, intrigued.

"No, not really," Mr. Fujita said. "I just. . . . Sure, I'd like to help Rose out, but . . . well. All right, that's it, then."

"What's it?" Livvie demanded. "So, you're going to *leave* her there?"

"Of course not," he said, and begrudgingly he wrote Rose

that he'd try to get her out but that she could go . . . wherever. He knew this was the right thing to do.

"It's a smart thing to do, too," Livvie said. "I think I know a bit what this Yoneko is about. Be careful. There's a big difference between helping and controlling someone."

Careful Fujita had never planned anything so carefully as his revised-to-death letter to Mr. Johnson of the War Relocation Authority, in which he flexed every persuasive muscle he possessed. He paved the way with flattery: *How did you know that Massachusetts would be so receptive to providing Japanese Americans with opportunities to be constructive citizens again?* He lied: *What a happy set of coincidences brought me to this town. I've almost forgotten California.* He reasoned: *Our needs are complementary: You've been charged with our relocation away from the Coast. My employer's growing agricultural enterprise requires open, easy access to a worker pool that can be tapped as labor needs increase without delays that impede production.* His final warning he couched as a confidence—hakujin loved confidences: *I'm in a real pickle. We workers are treated well, but Management rules with an iron fist and is impatient to get production up to speed. By suggesting the farms contract internees, I hoped to repay your favor of pushing me into a rewarding new life in Massachusetts. Management agreed to consider Japanese-American workers but reluctantly. As you've said, sir, you and I are businessmen, not politicians or soldiers, so you'll see that I can only prop open this window of opportunity so long before Management seeks laborers elsewhere, rather than abide bureaucratic hoops. Thus, your immediate response is appreciated. I hope and trust that we can make arrangements to our mutual benefit.*

Indulging himself, he showed his handiwork to Margaret, who said, "My goodness. Next time I'm late paying bills, I'll have *you* write the letter. You're quite good at this, aren't you?"

At lying, you mean? he thought, embarrassed.

Livvie insisted on signing the letter. "If we're in this together, then we do everything together," she said.

"Oh, I don't know about that," Fujita muttered. As preparations sent him into town again, he had vaguely noticed that

Juggeston had grown cooler toward him, even as he thawed. Childs's gas station always seemed "closed for lunch" just as Fujita pulled up. Even chummy Alf Wellington limited his greetings to a curt nod. Curiously, Lil Wellington alone seemed to have a smile for the Nisei those days. Dreading what prickly trouble might lay ahead, Fujita powerfully desired to keep his friends all at a safe distance. He veiled his concerns in a lesson in cacti and spurges. Though he'd studied them and carried common varieties at the nursery, he told Livvie, he had never "been with" these marvels of adaptation and self-reliance before Gila. By "been with," he meant having the long-term, hands-on experience a good nurseryman needed to know a plant. ("He sounded positively carnal about it," Livvie told Margaret.) He came to identify with the Jumping Cholla, a fruit-bearing desert plant that grew to fifteen feet with white flowers. Its loosely jointed, hairlike protective spines tended to "jump" at the slightest breeze or vibration, painfully and doggedly attaching themselves to a body. "My troubles jump," he warned Livvie, "and they have sticking power."

He believed his new friends had all done their part—especially Margaret, whose enthusiasm for the project bordered on impatience. But did a greater patience exist, a greater trust than she had invested in him? If their roles were reversed, would he give away his time and money, allowing a stranger to import nonalien enemy prisoners into his home? Am I patient enough for that? Fujita wondered. Frankly, he doubted it. He had a personal stake in this home-brewed plot. Beyond snaring the girl or even some friends who knew her whereabouts, he knew he most needed to relearn to value his own skin. He knew he had an obligation, too. He would never let himself forget how he could have comforted Bob Ito just a little, but didn't. He also recalled the Quincy Market Nikkei who had spurned him. Mostly, he had a nagging sense of *ōn*—and it was the only possible tribute to Tony and Mari. But what was in it for his new friends? He had lost so much on his trek from California to Widow's Peak, not least of which was his faith in acts of conscience.

"You can't have all the fun," Livvie said firmly. "I've spent the whole winter in solitary confinement, and I'm not about to be left out again. We're all in this together," she repeated. "Got it?"

"Fun?" Fujita echoed tiredly. "Right."

Of course, Garvin and Margaret wanted to sign, too.

The replacement panel Fujita had almost mounted on the exterior whistled like a guillotine blade and then shattered on the walkway, spraying his feet with a rain of diamonds. When Margaret's cry reached him he'd only just finished sweeping up the first shards, scattered when some nocturnal attacker hurled a softball-sized rock at the outer pane.

"Telegram!" Margaret called again, from inside the greenhouse.

The most loathed word in Fujita's vocabulary sent a tangible jolt through him, sparking the first macabre thought: *Who's dead? Who's* left? he thought, hardening himself. Mom? Yoneko?

"It seems we'll be having company!" Margaret cried, opening the door. "And so soon!"

"Having what?" He ripped the paper from her hand. They went back inside the greenhouse, and Fujita tried to decipher the shorthand message. "Igawa? Who . . . ?" Envisioning a soft-focused form, young, stocky, with a sharp chin and wide face. "Oh. *Calvin* Igawa."

So, the first internee to seek refuge on the Peak had found them, and not vice versa. His recollection of Bobby Tanaka's uncle was fuzzy but basically favorable. "Calvin's a forgettable sort. Kind of stiff and quiet," he explained. Margaret grinned. "No, he's *really* quiet. A nice boy. Med student, I think." Handsome fellow: His hair sported a dashing natural wave—it always looked whipped. But Igawa hadn't started out in California—one heard in his voice a tinge of something backwoodish. Montana. Like Mari. That was it: As a camp hospital assistant, Igawa had comforted Mrs. Fujita in her final illness. His memory blurred because Tony and Yoneko's friend had tended to hover about on the periphery of life in Block 60, in the background, always smiling but always distant, watchful, soft-spoken, whispering.

The telegram offered no more information than that Igawa had been released to go to college, but "things didn't work out," that he'd found this address "from the grapevine" and he planned to "be in the neighborhood." Flipping the paper over, Fujita scowled. "That's it? It doesn't tell me *anything*."

"What do you want, a resume? A biographical essay?" Margaret said, assuming it was a response to their offer to Mr. Johnson. "I'm so excited!"

Certain that their letter had not yet even reached the Rivers post office, Fujita held his tongue; for, *excited* understated Nurse Kelly's manner—one could plug a lamp into her and the bulb would work. Worriedly regarding the vandalism, which Margaret hardly seemed to notice at all, Fujita felt a nervous energy run through himself, too. Bowing over a worktable to examine a sieve full of clay-coated tamotsu seeds, Margaret hummed "Anything Goes" as she stirred the clay balls with a finger, adjusting her eyeglasses and marking her face with gray. Perhaps only a man of Fujita's botanical bent would find appealing a woman with a stripe of mud down her nose, yet he thought her especially radiant this morning. "Rodent-proofing," he said. "Clay protects the seeds."

She examined an armored seedling. "This one is already sprouting. I wonder. Do you think we could shape things from this, like pottery, and fire it without hurting the seeds?" Fujita cocked his head questioningly. "We could sell little plant sculptures, you know, shaped like the *Pieta* or something. Or no, like hair—you could do animals. Sheep and poodles and such. It's like . . . what's it called in Japanese, when you arrange the flowers? Or those little trees."

"Ikebana? Bonsai? No, but those are different." He thought of the Civil War statue in the square, bound in ivy, greened over with moss—an eyesore. "Who would *want* a hairy-looking sheep plant? Nobody would buy it."

"Oh, use your imagination! Housewives would buy it—a pretty winter kitchen garden. The army could put fresh herbs in field kits."

Mr. Fujita would bet his very life that the army would *not* outfit their KP with herbal poodles. Yet now that their plan was bearing such unexpected fruit, he dreaded anything that would disturb or harm her or ever prevent her from having those blessed, Margaret notions, those fantasies that let her discount determined vandalism as a "harmless child's prank." Fujita looked at the wrecked, double-paned window, where the interior panel had held but was webbed with cracks. The attack had been *barely* harmless, he knew. "So," he said anxiously. "We're going to have company."

He took Garvin along to the train depot for a private talk before Calvin's arrival in mid-January. Wiping the windshield made opaque with their breaths, he said, "So, pal. What do you think? It'll be neat having some other guys around, huh?"

"I guess so," the boy said, wiping his side of the glass. They had already talked about this.

"You take some ribbing at school," Fujita said. "That right?" Garvin said nothing. "About me, I mean. They tease you about me?" He swabbed again at the windshield. Garvin shrugged. "I was teased all the time. Other kids thought I was weird." Garvin nodded. Fujita chuckled. "I guess I thought something was wrong with me. But you know, if people tease you, it doesn't mean there's anything wrong with *you*—only with them. And a little teasing can be good for you," he said philosophically. "I really want you to understand: Calvin's only coming to help out a while. He's a good fellow. He's in school, too. His nephew, Bobby, is about your age—we were pals in Arizona, like you and me. You know?"

"I understand," Garvin said. "I don't care about being teased. I can take it."

"Good," Fujita said as they arrived. He let Garvin pull up the parking brake.

Fujita barely recognized Calvin Igawa, limping along with his suitcase on the train platform. Gone was his chesty, purposeful stride; his jet hair was matted down, his trousers and jacket were crumpled, his shoes a mass of scars. "Mr. Fujita," he said, and even that effort seemed to exhaust him. "Oh. Hi," he said, noticing Garvin.

"Welcome. Good to see you," Fujita said, and this felt mostly true. After half-dragging Igawa and his bags to the Dodge, he'd just hit the ignition when Calvin dozed off in the back.

Garvin sat on his knees, facing the rear seat and staring at the *new* new man. "Yeah," he whispered. "He's not too talkative, is he?"

On the way home, they pulled into Childs's Filling Station to gas up the Dodge. As a rule, Fujita now did this only while out on some other errand, and usually when someone other than Childs was working. The long snowy drive, however, left them running on fumes as he pulled up to the pump just before suppertime. When the smirking Frank Childs loped toward them, Fujita groaned and rolled down the window. "Good evening," he said. "Fill her up, please."

Ignoring him, Childs stuck his face into the Dodge; his skin was ravaged by the harsh winter. The mechanic spoke only to Garvin, who was fishing in the glove compartment for gas coupons. "Hey there, kid. Long time. How's your mom? Sure cried up a storm at the New Year's party," he added, with a hateful glance at Fujita, who was confused.

"Hi, Frank," Garvin mumbled. He handed the coupon to Fujita, who held it to the mechanic, who blinked at it and sneered. In the back of the truck, Calvin released a powerful snore. Childs craned his neck to see. "Hey, who you got back there?" he shouted, rousing the sleeper. Fujita gagged at the boy's breath, rank with stale coffee and chewing tobacco.

Disoriented, Calvin sat up and squinted at Childs. "Oh. Hello," he said, but Childs jerked away from the car as if he'd seen a snake.

"Shit Christ! There's *two* of you!"

Fujita only nodded. "Fill her up, please."

Childs crossed his arms. "I'm closed," he said. "Six o' clock. Says so right there on the sign. There's a war on, you know."

Fujita checked his watch unnecessarily—the sun would be down by six. "Five twenty-two," he read. He held up his wrist in evidence.

Childs shrugged and said, "Your watch is wrong."

Perhaps Fujita felt the newcomer in the back somehow stood in for Tony, making it a point of honor; or else he realized that with two of them in town and more coming, he could no longer remain invisible; or perhaps it was something as simple as there now being two against one. In any case, deciding he'd make Childs do his job if it was the last thing he ever did in this town, Fujita began leaning on the horn. At first Childs laughed, but the bellowing did not stop. Then he scowled, and still it went on. Faces began appearing in the windows of Wellington's and Town Hall across the road. Fujita settled in comfortably and pressed his palm more firmly into the horn. People emerged from the arcade and walked toward them.

"Um, maybe we shouldn't call attention to ourselves," said Calvin nervously.

"I've been trying not to call attention my whole life, Calvin," Fujita yelled gravely over the blare. On and on, the horn screamed. Neighboring dogs started barking. An icicle broke from the sideview. The curious townsfolk surrounded the car, peering in. Gripping a windshield squeegee like a sword, Childs kicked at the tire and growled, "Are you nuts?"

Nodding, Calvin checked the lock on the truck's rear door. Both mortified and thrilled, Garvin sat rigid until Fujita said, "Hey, pal. My hand's getting tired. Can you take over for a bit?" The boy slid over to replace him, both little hands on the horn, when Fujita shoved the door open and slipped outside.

"Why, hello, Pete. How are the little ones?" he said in a tone of warm surprise, to Pedicott, first among the wary and curious crowd. Fujita smiled but never wholly took his eyes off of Childs. Walking around to the back, he unscrewed the gasoline cap. "Oh. Afternoon, Alf."

"Afternoon," the puzzled shopkeeper called over the horn's blare. "A little car trouble?"

"Hm? No, I don't *think* so. Just stopped by to fill up the ol' Dodge. Oh, it seems my watch is broken. Have you got the time?"

"Er," Alf said, looking at Garvin, still dutifully honking away. He checked his watch. "I got five and half."

"Ah, thanks." Mr. Fujita and all the others turned their attention to Frank Childs, limply holding his squeegee and trying to make himself very small between the two gas pumps. Sulkily, the mechanic took up the nozzle and slipped it into the tank. Fujita winked at Garvin, who let up on the horn. In the sudden quiet, the dinging pump bell sounded loud as a gong. Only then did Fujita act as if he at all noticed that a crowd had gathered. "Hey. What's everybody doing out on a cold day like this? Well, since you're all here." Yanking the rear door open, he revealed the discomfited Igawa. "This is Calvin. A good fellow, come to help us out on the Peak. Calvin's going to be a doctor," he bragged paternally. "Say, Alf. How's Lil? You know, I *still* think about that terrific banana split she made for me. A stop at her counter would be a real Juggeston welcome for Calvin, eh?"

He could not wholly mask the tension in his voice as he instructed Childs to check the oil and see to the windows, which had accumulated a healthy layer of road salt, but Juggestonians always knew what was and wasn't their business. Fujita introduced Calvin all around and was pleased that despite his bewilderment, the newcomer was rather personable. By the time Childs had completed his work and Fujita was fishing out a few cents' tip, Igawa was easily chatting with Alf about the shopkeeper's piano playing. Good boy, Fujita thought. Keep that up and we're on our way.

"Natives a bit restless, huh?" Calvin said, once they'd moved on and turned up the drive.

"I don't know." Fujita tried to laugh. "Let's keep this just among us three for a while. Okay?"

At the house, Livvie and Margaret had prepared roast chicken and potatoes for their new guest. Greetings flew around, but Igawa fairly collapsed into a kitchen chair, barely strong enough to cut the meat, unable to stomach the potatoes. "It was some trip," he explained apologetically. "Almost nonstop from Chicago, via New York and Boston. I'll be more presentable tomorrow. Promise." Margaret ordered him to go right up to the office for some sleep.

"Hey," Garvin said, following the men outside bearing Calvin's meal on a tray. "Can I sleep over?"

Fujita shushed him. Trailing behind up the stairs, he forgot to warn Calvin about the skeleton, but the weary med student made a beeline from the stairwell to the cot without even blinking. Stripping to his boxers, he fell asleep immediately.

"The poor boy," Margaret said later. "We've got to put him back together. Vitamin shots?" she mused. Now that her ward was filling up, Nurse Kelly was all business.

"A good night's sleep will help," Fujita said. "Then I'll take him into town—"

"Don't even think it," Margaret said. "Tomorrow he sleeps—all day, if that's what it takes. Three square meals and nothing strenuous."

True to his word, Calvin awoke infinitely more "presentable." "I sleep fast and hard," he told Fujita, springing out of bed. "At the hospital, I can get by on three hours' sleep, but those three hours I'm deader than dead." Striding about the office brushing his teeth, Calvin examined every piece of medical equipment and every drug vial as if studying for an exam. After he'd shaved and rewhipped his wavy hair, the men descended for an excessive breakfast where the women subjected Igawa to a grilling even more strenuous than Fujita himself had undergone at their hands. Fujita planned to do his own grilling, too.

Everyone noticed it immediately—even Garvin, even Fujita himself: The two Nisei unbundling their snowy selves by the kitchen door could be confused for father and son. Both were round-faced with impossibly high cheekbones; both were onyx-eyed, bowlegged, slim, and broad-shouldered; stiff and aloof and run through with nervous energy. Setting to the meal, both men placed their forearms on the table while their hands nimbly danced through three hasty helpings of flapjacks. Simultaneously, they dabbed their lips with napkins they had strangled into feathery pulps, and the women could no longer restrain their chuckles.

"Oh, boy!" Livvie laughed, shaking her head.

"Two peas in a pod!" cried Margaret, shaking hers.

However, it didn't take long for their serious, subsurface differences and tensions to reveal themselves—also those of father and son. Certainly, young Calvin proved to be more forthcoming about his odyssey from Gila River. Like steam from a pressure cooker, an intense anger escaped from him as he began.

It was the Californians. The small-minded, bigoted, isolationist Californians—the Fresno raisin brains, the Gilroy garlic breaths, the mealymouthed farmers of Orange County and fisherfolk of Terminal Island. It was the so-called Native Sons and Daughters of the Golden West, the white supremacist spawn of the gold rush. These, Calvin Igawa believed, were responsible for "the whole thing," but to the Montanan, Little Tokyo itself was to blame. "All those Japs bunched together, just sitting ducks."

Born a child of the railroad frontier, Kazuo "Calvin" had only minimal contact with other Japanese families in Butte, where his father was a rep for a Seattle Oriental trading company. Ambition for a career beyond the bottom rung at the roundhouse took Calvin to live with his older sister in California, where the first two years of college were an inexpensive extension of the public schools. "I went from having all Caucasian friends to having none," he said. "That's okay. People get on my nerves, actually. That's why I never wanted to be a clinician," he said, mostly to Margaret. "I started out as a lab rat." As a research assistant, Calvin worked under a renowned neurologist whose research in public health would one day earn him a Nobel Prize. Fujita knew of the great scientist and had to be impressed, though he couldn't help resenting how that "essential" work also earned Calvin a draft deferment. "My prof was really nice to us after Pearl Harbor," Calvin recalled. "He's a bit of a rebel. Likes to buck the system. When we had to go away in '42, he wrote all sorts of letters trying to spring me. We devised an independent study by correspondence, though I had to let it go once I got that stupid job at the hospital. They kept me hopping with all these chores." He paused, realizing the painful associations Fujita had with that hospital. "Well, I mean, I learned a lot, I guess. Nutrition, dermatology, obstetrics, a bit of everything. Baptism by fire." The neurologist never forgot his student in those years and finally secured a research fellowship for Calvin far from the Forbidden Coast, in Wisconsin. At this, the young man halted, looking pained.

"It got pretty sticky, me leaving camp. My sister was *really* ticked off, my niece and nephew didn't understand. And, well, I've kind of got a girl waiting for me, too," he confessed. His paper napkin was now a lump of confetti. "But truthfully, I couldn't get out of there fast enough. The plan was I'd go out, find a place, start classes, get my first fellowship check, and bring them out, too. I took a train by way of Salt Lake up to Montana, to head east from there. My mistake was stopping in Butte a few days to see my folks and my younger sister, Peggy."

"Seeing your family isn't a *mistake*," Fujita said sourly.

Calvin shook his head and frowned. "You know, I think they'd have done better in camp. Pop had just gotten a little dry-goods store up and running—only thing he ever did right—when the boycotts started. They trashed it, beat him up. We used to have a house, too; that's gone now. I found them in a shack a Scottish friend had leased to us, trying to farm just for food on the corner of this lousy land. Mom was real sick when I got there. Iron-deficient anemia," he told Margaret. She nodded. "So unnecessary. Their diet was awful, and they couldn't afford a doctor. I stayed a few days to work in the field and take care of Mom, put her on a diet of apples and liver for iron and left her all my meat coupons. And Peggy. . . ." His voice lowered. "She used to be such a pretty girl, you know? Had this real fine skin, and a tiny nose, and eyes the size of silver dollars. Always had fellows around. One of her teeth was black, just rotten. She was getting cross-eyed because her eyeglasses were a wreck. One of the lenses was all cracked, and a temple had broken off. I felt so bad. I took her out to buy a new pair, but heck, what more could I do? I didn't have much money. My folks were keen for me to get off to school, so I went on and stopped in Minneapolis. Where Tony was trained," he said. Fujita nodded and gently urged him to go on.

"I caught the 500 Line down to Madison and met a friend who'd transferred there, stayed at his boardinghouse for international graduate students. They were really nice to me. Took me for a beer, showed me around. It's a pretty campus, on an isthmus. That's a strip of land between two lakes," he told Garvin, careful to include him. "Nice student union right on the water with a little yacht club. I was sitting watching the sailboats and drinking this beer, you know, and I really thought I'd arrived somewhere. I could have sat there all day and all night, but I was hot to get started, so I went to meet with my new department chairman. I present my papers and say, 'I'm ready to start!' But he just shakes his head at me and says, 'Sorry, you can't matriculate here. University's off-limits to anyone of Japanese ancestry.' A new military program had started up the day before. 'But stick around,' he says. 'Maybe something can be found for you to do.' I stuck around about two weeks. *Nothing*. Nobody would *touch* me. So what can I do now? I call up a fellow I know from Altadena living in Chicago. A lot of Japanese are going there, so I head down to look for work. I washed dishes at night and worked for a rich woman processing poultry during the day. Plucking and gutting them. Beheading them."

Imagining it, Garvin whistled. Calvin laughed. "This lady was a real operator! Bought all these peepers, see—about three *thousand* of them—and put them in her three-car garage. Mind you, this is in Chicago. I'd help her feed them until they were fryers. At harvest, we'd use a sharp knife: Stick it right in here." He demonstrated with a thumb against his throat. "Clip the jugular, dunk them in boiling water, then throw them in this rotating drum with pieces of rubber hose that would rip the feathers when you spun it. Then we had to gut them: put the hearts in one place, gizzards in another, livers in another. You're supposed to put the innards back in the chicken and sell them as chicken with parts. But she had us put only one of the livers back in; she'd sell the others separately, make an extra buck. She was really something. Knew how to make money, that's for sure."

"Thirty-six percent!" Margaret sang. Calvin was confused, and when she explained the women's labor statistic to him, he seemed unimpressed. As in Fujita's family, the Igawa women had always worked—sometimes two or three jobs at a time. "Soon," he continued, "the city health authorities got wind she was raising all these chickens in her garage in a residential area and closed her down, so I lost my job. Then I heard about you . . ." Again he left his conclusion up to the tabletop.

"Through the grapevine?" Fujita asked suspiciously. "From Yoneko, right?"

Igawa crushed his handful of napkin confetti as if he wouldn't be satisfied until it completely disintegrated. "We talk sometimes," he said cautiously. Then, to them all, "But hey, I can't tell you how incredible this is, you having me here. It's rare these days. I'd still like to get back in school, but until then, I'll do my very best for you. I mean it. I can't thank you enough."

"Of course you're going to school!" Margaret cried, placing her hand on Calvin's.

"Sure you are!" Livvie said, but she sounded far less convinced.

In the following weeks, Calvin Igawa certainly earned his keep, though Margaret thought his mere presence an adrenaline injection in that unhappy season. On the dark anniversary of Mari's death in late January, Calvin very adeptly ran interference for Fujita when Margaret's nursing became unbearable. "Maybe it's better if I talk to him," Calvin suggested. "Only because I knew her, you see." Knowing just what to say and do, he declared the greenhouse off-limits that day while he and Fujita worked alone. "I want to tell you something," he said, as they experimented with grafts between two strains of sweet Japanese eggplant. "In the hospital, I saw her a lot toward the end, and I don't think it was suicide." He braced himself for a punch, but Fujita just paused in his work, keeping his eyes on the fragile stem before him. "I think it was a willing accident. Like after Tony and everything, she thought some accident was bound to happen, so any one would do. Hand me that twine there." Sensibly, he said this only once, finished his work, and left a grateful Fujita in peace.

In the next day's mail, the harried WRA administrator, Mr. Johnson, sent this brief note: "Yes, of course I remember you. Just tell me how many, and we'll get on it right away." Fujita was puzzled. "That's it?" he asked distrustfully, reading it aloud to the others in the greenhouse. "Something's fishy here, I think."

"No, there's a lot of inside pressure on him now. Mostly it's the old Issei left, and they're nervous about being sent home." At Fujita's dumbfounded expression, Calvin said, "You *do* know about it? Don't you follow the news at all?" Stunned, Fujita just shrugged. "Well, the Supreme Court finally decided it's probably a wee tad unconstitutional to keep people locked up for no good reason. Us *loyal* types," he sneered. It surprised

Fujita to see such ferocious cynicism in a man so young. "They say they plan to open up the Coast again this year. Isn't that swell of them?"

"Home?" Fujita found himself murmuring. Placing the letter on the worktable, he rose to look out the steamy glass wall at the ice-glazed back of the scarecrow.

"Oh, my," said Margaret. She seemed almost disappointed by the news. "Well, I suppose you'll be our first and last guest, Calvin."

He shook his head fiercely. "Oh, they'll come in *droves* if you let them. You'll have your own Little Tokyo right here if you like. I can tell you that I'll never set foot in that state as long as I live. If it drops into the Pacific tomorrow, it's not soon enough for me."

While assisting Fujita, Igawa also helped Garvin with his science homework (as a Montanan, he also enjoyed playing daredevil on that treacherous sled) and fixed one of Livvie's sewing machines. He spent hours talking with Margaret about her hospital work and even volunteered with her. Driving home one night, she asked him to fill in her mental picture of Yoneko. Normally straightforward, Calvin was guarded. "Oh, she's a great girl—sweet, you know. Very attractive. Remember, she and Tony met in school—they were seventeen or something, before the war. I know she really wanted more than anything for the Fujitas to like her, but the thing is, she can be . . . pretty overwhelming, and she somehow started on the wrong foot with Tony's folks. Mrs. Fujita never cared for her."

"Is that so? Why, do you suppose?"

"Oh, I'm not sure I can say. You can ask him." Squirming, he quickly let his glance flit to Margaret and then back onto the road ahead. "You *should* ask him," he added.

Whether his innate character or as a result of the war, Calvin possessed an extraordinary sense of purpose for a man of twenty-two. Working tirelessly on the Peak in no way dulled his determination to return to school. Several rejections only added gas to the fire beneath him. Shooting down his application, a scholar at Penn State wrote: "You don't have it so bad. Just think of all our boys who have to go fight overseas in Germany," perhaps not realizing that Nisei could be drafted, as were two of Calvin's brothers and his brother-in-law, Shigeki Tanaka.

"How beastly!" Margaret said.

"That pompous S.O.B.! His research stinks anyway. He manipulates his results," Calvin railed. Without his medical-student status, however, he might be drafted. But as a hospital volunteer, he so impressed Dr. Masters that he added another recommendation letter to those from the one-day Nobel Laureate in California and the chief physician at Gila River. Finally, he won a fellowship at a reputable medical college Fujita hadn't heard of. "It's more than reputable," Margaret told him.

"You really want to go back to school?" asked Garvin, finding it hard to believe.

Little more than a month after he arrived, Calvin prepared to leave. There were signs of a spring thaw coming, and they had driven to the coastal town of Gloucester for a load of piping to build an overhead irrigation system.

"Do you know where she is, Calvin?" Fujita finally asked. Igawa said nothing. "Look. You were Tony's friend, and she was his, well, whatever. And I'm his father." Calvin nodded at these certainties. "I admit, Mari and I weren't too sympathetic back then. We all make mistakes. *But*, just acknowledging mistakes doesn't absolve us of our responsibilities. We all have obligations and debts, too. You see?"

"Yes, I do," Calvin said, pointedly made aware of his own debts.

"You worked in the hospital at Gila," Fujita said, but it wasn't a change of topic. "Among other things, you learned obstetrics."

"Right," said the trapped medical student.

"I'm no doctor, of course. I'm just a plant man."

Calvin looked to the Dodge's roof and sighed. "Okay, yes, I saw the sample. I processed it, actually. It was positive. It was his—no question. I talked to her about it. We talked about ways of stopping it, too. No, I don't think that's a family matter, either. Especially there. But that's really all I can tell you that you don't already know."

They drove the rest of the way to Juggeston in icy silence.

Only as they unloaded the pipes did Igawa say, "I understand. If I hear from her, I'll see if I can't . . . represent your position. That's all I can promise you. I've got a lot of things of my own going on just now."

"I know you do, Calvin," Fujita said. "And I know you'll do your best for me."

When the time came for Calvin to depart, Margaret gushed, Livvie took him aside for a secretive good-bye, and Garvin followed him around all morning until he was loaded into the Dodge. For his part, Fujita could not drive Igawa to the train station fast enough. He did at least realize that his annoyance with Calvin was self-reflective; in the young man Fujita saw his own nagging impulse to blame and forsake his own past life, skin, and community. With the hour of departure upon them, Fujita forgave Calvin for mirroring his own bad qualities. They stopped and tanked up at Childs's Filling Station—Frank was almost mockingly courteous to them, but Fujita decided that was an improvement and made sure to tip the mechanic—and then had coffee and sandwiches across the street from the depot. "You don't need more coffee," Fujita said, grinning. "You're like me. You don't travel well."

"Does it show?" Out of his utensils and the salt and pepper shakers, Calvin had constructed a train on the tablecloth. His feet tapped on the floor while with his hands he subjected his napkin to cruel and unusual contortions.

"Only a little," Fujita reassured him, meaning, it showed only a little that Calvin was a lot like him. With a pang, he caught himself wishing Tony had been more like his careful, nervous friend. That is, he wished Tony had stayed alive. He thought Calvin might have a shot at carving out the safe, disciplined life for himself that Tony never achieved. A *doctor*, he thought. The war made things easier on Igawa, in a way; before the war, Japanese-American doctors did not specialize, but now specialists were needed. He also realized that some things would be harder for Calvin. Laborers of Ichiro Fujita's generation who were invited, used, then cast out knew how a society could insist on a minority's industry but also resent a minority's success. Calvin had few friends in California, where he would never live again. "Someone in camp had the nerve to call me inu. Why? Because I had friends, knew the ropes, knew how to get supplies I needed—because I *got along*, working in the hospital for nineteen bucks an hour. To hell with them. To hell with the stupid Japs. I worked for us, you know? Where do they get off?"

But watching the boy now performing a twitchy jitterbug in his seat, Fujita suspected that whatever obstacles lay ahead, Calvin would probably not stop to notice them. "You're a fine young man," he said by the idling train—a rather empty sort of thing to say, but Fujita wasn't a gusher. "You'll keep in touch," he said.

"Yes," Calvin said. "If I speak to her, I'll do my best."

When the train became a tiny puff of smoke on the horizon, Fujita turned back to his nojo in relief.

Others came, as Calvin promised. First there was Jingo Yamashita, a scrawny beach boy who had worked (if one could call it that—he moved so slowly) in the crops at Gila. The past year had not improved his work habits, but he was off again after a week anyway, to join his brother at New Jersey's Seabrook Farms. "Hate to eat and run," Jingo quipped to Margaret and Fujita at the train station after only four days in Juggeston. "You've been swell. I'll never forget you."

"I've already forgotten *him*," Fujita grumped to Margaret in the car. "It took me all this time just to get him up to speed on a task, and then he ups and leaves!"

Beside him, Margaret merely sighed. Other internees relocated from Rivers, Arizona, would tell her their stories over coffee, wolf down her miserable lunches as if she were a top-notch chef, and indulge her in sing-alongs, but with her unhappy penchant for developing too close, too quick attachments, Nurse Kelly would never again let herself be as fond of any who followed the medically minded young Nisei, Calvin Igawa. She viewed Jingo as something of a transition and in a way was thankful for his hasty departure. "They can't all stay, I suppose," she said to Fujita with feigned heartiness.

"None of them can stay," Fujita pointed out. "They're not supposed to. Remember?"

"I know that," Margaret snapped, being terribly emotional.

Of course, they were both aware that Fujita himself wasn't *supposed* to stay, either.

Then came Ernest Tanji, an aspiring Gene Kelly who whistled and soft-shoed through his chores. At night he and Livvie drank together and jitterbugged in Margaret's kitchen; as winter inched to an end, he sat with Garvin on the swing and played harmonica; he danced a mean, one-sided rumba with the scarecrow. His second day in town, he ran down to the arcade, chatted up eight people in as many minutes, then sang a bubbly round of "Don't Fence Me In" with Alf Wellington on piano. In Fujita's opinion, Ernie had the brains of a marshmallow, though he was a fine gopher and was terrific at charming the townies. Drafted in late March, he would spend the rest of the war singing in an Army band. "It may be my big break," Ernie said, and his bosses cringed at this echo of Bob Ito—whose big break was to jump out of planes into battlefields. It was just as well that Yosh Masai, doomed to follow the beloved Tanji, barely unpacked his duffel bag before heading off to an engineering school in Maine.

"They zoom through so fast, I can't keep up!" Fujita complained. Things weren't getting done. "It's a diminishing-returns proposition. How can I run a farm like this?"

"Oh, to heck with farming," Margaret scolded him. "We're trading in people now, which is much better."

Fujita bristled visibly at this, but Margaret believed it. For all her fantasies of being a gentlewoman farmer, she knew she was still just a nurse—and in those long winter months, she felt she'd become a truer, better, and more needed nurse than ever before. If they harvested only a single pea pod, it wouldn't break her heart.

Yet Fujita felt very differently. They both also knew that all along, he wasn't only looking for people to help out—and to help him work—but also for someone who could *replace* him when he located Yoneko.

After Yosh came an Issei farmer in his fifties, Hideo Okamoto, who had only recently forgiven Fujita for sabotaging his chance to meet the first lady. Hideo brought his thirty years' farm experience to Widow's Peak and little else. He had three outfits—two overalls and a khaki suit. He only wore boots or straw *waraji* sandals, and he kept an unlit pipe in his mouth at all times (Garvin thought he bathed with it, too). He waved away Fujita's suggestion that he avoid wearing waraji into town. "Nonsense. They're my shoes." Speaking poor English, he socialized little; for the first time, a Japanese-English pidgin was spoken on the hill. He only descended from the Peak on chores, such as accompanying Fujita to Annisquam to load the Dodge with kelp for fertilizer. Having lost his own twenty-year farm lease, he worked with purpose, helping more than all his precursors combined. He could not have been a more able replacement, nor more unlike Fujita.

At the end of March, although Widow's Peak remained subject to snowstorms, there were intimations of winter's weakening resolve. It was not quite spring, but the same force that fractured ice sheets in the flat arms of the firs—an assurance of better days to come—filled the coworkers' bodies through invisible entrances. A smell they could not name, or sunlight of wavelengths too fast to see as it infiltrated the cloud cover and broke loose in weak threads but great numbers. At last, they all could look out at that land and think, Yes, we might actually have a real farm.

One day, in anticipation of a thaw and the season's final frost, Fujita went out to pick up a leased rototiller and other machinery. While he was out, this note arrived: "She's in Philadelphia. I can try to make arrangements for you to see her. Let me know. Best to L, M, and G. Calvin." Poring over it together at the kitchen table, Livvie and Margaret argued.

"Calvin, you *angel*," Margaret whispered to the paper. Livvie frowned, though, and bought herself some thinking time, fishing for and lighting an Old Gold.

"It's not fair to stick Calvin in the middle of it," she said. "And really, don't you find it odd? Chasing her around like that? Private-eye stuff? It's a bit creepy."

"It's his grandchild!" Margaret cried. "The only family he has left!"

"We don't know there is a grandchild," Livvie reminded her. "Even if there is, it's *her* child, and this girl is not his *wife*, after all. Strictly speaking, she's not even a Fujita, but he acts so . . . proprietary. He's so obsessed, it's like he's planning to kidnap it."

"Oh, Livvie," Margaret said, but she fell into a dark brooding. Looking out the window at the thawing hillside, she whispered, "You know, it almost looks like a little farm out there."

"Well, isn't that why he's here?" Livvie asked—again. She pressed this point when she tried to dissuade him from racing down to Philadelphia. "At least don't go off half-cocked," she said. "Stay here, get the workers set up, take time to mull it over, and let her prepare herself, too. You can hate me for saying it, but I imagine she's got plenty of obstacles without you . . ." Mr. Fujita gripped the letter so tightly it tore halfway down the middle. "Look," she said more gently, "I'm just saying, I sort of understand her position."

"I know you do, Livvie," he said, unable to look at her. "I know that."

"You want to take blame for everything, but in a way, that's sort of conceited, isn't it? So you want to use this girl to alleviate your guilt, but I have to tell you: After Sig, the last thing I want is some man hanging around trying to run my life. If you go after her too hard, you may very well make her run away again, and she'll feel justified in it. She'll never get her life together."

To Margaret, recalling his never-unpacked suitcases and Tamie's scroll, it seemed as if he were still aboard the *Pacific Angel* waiting to reach his final port. She feared he could never lay anchor himself until he and the girl reached some resolution. If there was a chance that he'd ever come back to stay, she knew he had to go away. And though she hadn't quite understood all of that *ōn* and *girí* business, she knew how his obligations and duties were at odds, and that she had to make his leaving possible. Making herself open her purse, she withdrew a dollar and hesitantly placed it in his palm. "I hope it works out the way you planned," she said weakly.

"I'm not sure I have a plan," Fujita realized, now that the moment had arrived. "I just *need* to go down there."

"Yes, you do," Margaret agreed. "I hope you'll come back soon."

He stared at the dollar in his hand, then nodded and pocketed it. "I won't spend this," he said. "But it's good to have spare cash when traveling."

"Yes, just in case," Margaret said.

So focused on making plans of some kind that week, Fujita barely took notice when he heard the radio report that the president had died of a cerebral hemorrhage. "He had a lot on his mind, I guess," he muttered, but in private he grieved a little.

Speaking to Garvin was hardest of all. Excited by the thaw, he came over so that they could break in the model airplane Fujita had given him at Christmas but found the man preparing to leave. "That's the lady you been looking for, right?" he asked gloomily. "So, you're gonna stay there? What about the farm?"

"The lady?" Fujita said, thinking of the young girl he'd abandoned, who'd abandoned him. "Yes, that's the lady. I need to go see her, pal. For a while," he said ambiguously. "I'm counting on you to hold down the fort for me, okay? See that everything runs smoothly."

When the time came for them to drive to the train station, Garvin hid himself in the elm tree and did not come down until Mugsie's Dodge had carried "the new man" away.

TWELVE

The Freedom Trail

As the locomotive caterpillared out onto the flimsy suspension bridge, Fujita saw a racing skiff below crawl across the Schuylkill River like an insect on a greening pond. Along the east bank sat a miniature neoclassical city, a complex of antique waterworks, all sandy-hued triangles and columns of an older, alien world—the Homeric world he had so thoroughly navigated in his high school readings—not modern Philadelphia. Rising squat and sturdy above the riverbed flora, they reminded him of bears caught resting by a watering hole. Darkening these shelters, from the hilltop beyond, loomed the palatial art museum. With its massive Corinthian columns sprouting bouquets of rock, the building seemed so impervious that even a California earthquake could not upset it. Its crown of sharp-billed gryphons could shrug off a barrage of buzz bombs, he thought. The two wings of its *U* stretched toward Center City, meaning to impress, to dominate. No Philadelphian had ever dared to erect a modern skyscraper to challenge its command of the parkway that unfurled like a carpet down to the very steps of City Hall. This, Fujita thought, was a city.

When the train rattled off the bridge, he saw the zoological park pass surprisingly close by. Looking down over a low wall, he saw a muscular, uniformed woman, sleeves rolled to her elbows, leading a leashed baby elephant across a dirt lot.

"Effant, Mama!" a girl seated behind him squealed delightedly, and, "Gamul! Gamul!" Outside, he spotted two pig-tailed kids jouncing atop a ragged dromedary hump. "Ostrich! *Funny* ostrich!" The child's mother cooed appreciatively, but a pinch of nostalgia made Fujita sink lower in his seat. South Pasadena boasted a "world-class ostrich farm," Tony's favorite childhood haunt, where the beasts were put to ingenious use. Attached to buggies, Cawston Farm's tragic birds made splendid kiddy rides; plucked, their feathers produced desirable women's hats; "harvesting" of a young ostrich reaped about fifteen feet of leather and ninety pounds of meat. *Funny ostrich*. How Tony had reveled in the simple act of naming, and how the father had envied what the boy saw, or didn't see. On wildlife excursions to San Diego, or to the deer park up north, Tony could point above the concrete moat and confidently dub the hulking figure: "Buffalo!" He never seemed to sense the inadequacy of it—of a name. Just as he never noticed that the blind, old beast wore an encrusted gash on its haunch, probably gouged on barbed wire or the rusty lip of a watering trough; nor see the shamed resignation in its fist-sized, soulless eyes when a pesky bird settled to dine from its throw rug of a shoulder.

Trying to recall his own childhood, a time when all that could be known about a thing was contained in what he could devise to call it, Fujita found he could not. Was it his mother's influence, that buffalo must also necessarily be *suigyu?* By comparison, *suigyu* resonated with such buffaloness, its flavor intensified with the spice of secret language, secret knowledge.

"Giraffe! Giraffe!" the girl now informed the train, as they chugged past the last wall of the Fairmount Zoo. Fujita turned to stare until even those mottled, stalk-like necks faded away.

Yet, admittedly he was not immune to the spell of names. He believed it mattered what name you gave . . . a child, for example. When he imagined her—Yoneko—when he hoped, he wondered: *Tony, Jr.? Mari? Billy?* He imagined a boy, penance and forgiveness, and the remnants of his shattered family culminating in the peachy infant, William Tony Fujita, packed like so many odds and ends into a suitcase. Of course, Tony never even married the girl, never made her a Fujita, he thought, keenly aware of his own participation in that little oversight. But did a name truly matter? Hadn't the world shown it was too big to care if "Fujita" ended with him?

The Pennsylvania Railroad Station at Thirtieth Street still showed aspirations to the era of Parthenons and Athenaeums. Roofing the landing platform, green-shaded glass windows bathed waiting passengers in emerald light. The platform steps emptied onto a concourse so spacious that all sunlight soaked ineffectually into its pale stonework. He rolled his head to grind the travel knots from his neck, then crumpled onto a wooden bench to ground himself in this city. People of all colors hurried about. Newspaper and pretzel vendors shouted. Porters rumbled past with baggage carts. He counted more sailors in navy whites than he'd ever seen in one place. Spotting him, a portly cabby yelled, "Taxi?" then spied other prey and disappeared into the mob.

"Paper, mister?" a boy shouted.

Don't fall asleep, he warned himself, laying his head back against the bench. How very high up the ceiling hung, ornamented with rose-pink diamonds bordered in gold. The gray and black shapes of pigeons flitted about windowsills where their roosts sat too high to knock down, or alit to wander unselfconsciously between bustling feet. One disheveled bird hopped on one wrinkled leg below the bench to peck at a soft pretzel. Its other leg had been chopped down to a stub, pale and waxy, like a softened birthday candle.

Losing no time getting to Philadelphia, he was half-following Livvie's advice: He allotted himself thinking time by arriving three days earlier than planned. While Calvin had insisted on hosting him, Fujita wrote that he'd check into the Friends hostel temporarily. "Don't bother meeting me at the station—don't miss your morning classes on my account. We can meet later." Reviving himself with a cup of coffee, Fujita went outside and on the fourth try found a cabby willing to take him. The ride to the hostel offered glimpses of Philadelphia's other face: the smokestacks and steel plants, cable cars and pushcart markets. On the banks of the Schuylkill, sooty warehouses with their hundreds of blackened windows tumbled toward the river, their cranes and lifts and docks reaching into the green artery like nerve endings. From anywhere in the city, a traveler could see the dark statue of its founder, William Penn, still presiding over his "Holy Experiment" from the top of City Hall; no other building stood so high, and the resulting sun-lined streets eased Fujita as the cab pulled up to the address. Erected in less hectic days on a wider boulevard, the hostel had seen its property chipped away by the city's expansion. Fujita liked the neighborhood, though, its proximity to new factories and sweatshops, its apparent industry. While counting out the fare, he saw the hostel buzzed with activity. Hanging out a second-floor window, a pretty Nikkei girl screwed up her face, held an oval rug at arm's length, and shook it into the breeze. A flurry of silver dust particles fell onto the shoulders of a hefty, broad-backed Nisei boy sweeping the stoop below.

"Now, cut that out!" he shouted, shaking a yellow-handled broom at her. "I'll have to do this all over again!" He whisked dust clouds back into the air toward the street, then saw the newcomer stepping onto the curb and waved. "Howdy!" The girl in the window waved, too.

"Don't stop on my account!" Fujita called back, resting his bags on the pavement. Descending to help, the boy lifted the full suitcase as carelessly as if it were empty. He could be a wrestler, but for his awkward, taped-together eyeglasses. Fujita imagined he saw Bob Ito.

"Chad Suzuki!" the boy declared. He tucked the broom under his armpit, and they shook hands.

"Bill Fujita. Thanks. I've been traveling and appreciate a bit of muscle."

The boy beamed, his cheeks round as a chipmunk's. "I keep fit," he said, eyeing his thick arm lovingly. "Fujita? Not the one with the fishing boat off Terminal Island?"

"Pasadena."

"Oh, Pasa*dena* . . ." From this springboard, Suzuki launched into a list of possible common acquaintances. There were many, as it turned out. He remembered driving by the nursery, and knew Yoneko, whom he'd seen in Philadelphia less than a month ago, though he'd lost track of her. "People come and go here," he explained. "It's a good city for us. Mostly tolerant, with things to do. There's some fun historical stuff, like this Cradle of Liberty Walking Tour that leaves from Independence Hall a couple times a day. And these Freedom Trail rides, you know, on horse buggies. You should check them out. I know, it sounds boring, but it's kind of interesting to see the real McCoy. They showed us where they signed the Declaration of Independence; saw the Liberty Bell and this little naval museum with models of old warships and stuff." He shrugged. "There are worse ways to spend a few hours."

Three days passed before Fujita had a few hours to spare. The Society of Friends was not exactly known for its recreational activities; its hostel came rent-free, but transient guests were expected to earn their keep. When boarders weren't on job or school interviews, checking in at the WRA, or slogging from apartment to apartment that inevitably had been rented moments before their arrival, there were plenty of chores. But with a lemming's instinct, Fujita the believer felt drawn to the "Cradle of Liberty," from which stemmed so many questions he had struggled with these years. Also, he missed his Juggeston friends more than he'd expected and wanted to buy them all gifts—proof that he was thinking of them.

In Olde City, a cornucopia of pushcarts and gift shops selling colonial-type knickknacks, Fujita browsed a cart of "Independence Figurines"—a Lilliputian army in tricorn caps and long-tailed coats, some with bandaged feet, others with eye patches or arm slings. Did a fatherless boy need such reminders? Were there no Minutemen free of disfigurement? He opted against the "Marksman," a cheery fellow, squinting down his rifle sights, and chose instead "The Young Defender." Such detail the artist had given to his expression, his jaws etched with the highest purpose. Free of scars or hate, the gray metal teenager plunged a ramrod into the barrel of his musket—alert but innocent. He also bought a palm-sized replica of the Liberty Bell for his mother and could not resist getting one for Garvin, too.

Weaving through lines of tourists, he caught sight of a felt tricorn cap rimmed with gold, set above two crossed poles on which were draped the trappings of a colonial soldier; the shaky cross reminded Fujita of the scarecrow. Red-on-white-on-blue ribbons formed a blossom on the cap's left side. Frivolous as it seemed, he envisioned it on Livvie, her dark hair spreading from beneath it like a cape, and the image was fetching. Running out of hands, he wore this around town for the rest of the day; he felt compelled to buy a small one for Garvin, too. At a bookseller by Independence Hall he purchased a biography of Betsy Ross for Margaret, a Pennsylvania Dutch cookbook for the DiPassios, and for himself, fake parchment copies of the Declaration of Independence and the Constitution. He also bought copies for Garvin.

When he decided to return to the hostel, his route took him by the same courtyards and sculptured gardens, cemeteries and carriage houses that Jefferson and Hancock passed on the way to work. He saw an old guard stand, like a six-sided outhouse, and imagined Benjamin Franklin tipping his hat to a cranky, underpaid guard named Richard. *"How's business, Dick?" "Humph. A penny saved is a penny earned."* And there, on that stoop, he imagined Washington scraping manure from his boot before entering the Man Full of Trouble Tavern to tie one on after a hard day at the office. Chad Suzuki was right: The real McCoy was interesting. Fujita felt momentarily transported to the older, saner, freer, more innocent America of his imagination. Land grants! he thought dreamily. How much space they must have had. Then he thought guiltily of the Pima and let this fantasy pass.

In the throng of tourists glutting the Assembly Room of Independence Hall, many stood taller than Fujita. On tiptoe, he caught a glimpse of what an unseen tour guide claimed was "the actual silver inkstand used by the delegates at *the* signing."

"Gee," said Fujita. Wishing he had a camera, he pressed forward for a closer look. The City of Brotherly Love had a history of tolerance and goodwill; like Juggeston, it was built by Friends. There was nothing friendly, however, about the gray-haired gentlewoman who turned on Fujita. She looked, for all the world, like Ben Franklin in a dress, with her great gut and flat breasts, her tiny, round-spectacled eyes set in a long, oval face beneath a receding hairline. Jostling her tour-group companions like a clipper ship coming about in a harbor full of dinghies, she twisted her bulk around and sniffed audibly at the Nisei dressed as a Minuteman.

Fujita let himself be lured away by another lecture to a less crowded part of the hall, where he immediately recognized the great, broken hunk cast by the metalsmiths Pass and Stow. The model for those bells tinkling in his shopping bag, America's most beloved goof hung from what looked like a discarded railroad tie. In textbook pictures and replicas, the famed crack—its third—appeared to stop at about the midpoint, but he was interested to see that it extended several inches higher. The balding tour guide delivered only the most uninformative patchwork hurrah, sounding like a forgetful drunk trying to memorize catchphrases for a multiple-choice history exam. "Proclaim *Liberty* throughout all the Land unto all the Inhabitants Thereof!" he roared—the inscription around the bell's top. "Life, Liberty, and the Pursuit of Happiness!" he declaimed, switching gears. "We, the People!" he sang, mixing documents.

Raising a hand, Fujita asked softly, "Um, excuse me. Did they ever, er, think to fix it or maybe get a new bell?"

"What?" The guide blinked at the philistine Jap in the tricorn hat. "I think they sent it back to the forge a couple of times," he muttered.

"I see," said the Nisei, whose work ethic and intolerance for botched jobs would make the more humorless, eighteenth-century Puritans and Quakers blush. Symbols were all well and good, but he hoped the revolutionary Congress had thought to get a warranty.

Inevitably, the self-congratulatory tone of the Independence Mall forced Fujita to reconsider the value of his American liberty. He had once imagined that internment, stripping people of inalienable, individual liberties, was the cruelest blow. But then, in a highly organized fashion, the nation had broken up his community, jailed its leaders, separated families, and willfully dispersed them—"distributed" them—throughout the country. *That* was the cruelest blow: to deprive people of those they loved and depended on; the cruelest blow was to destroy a family, he knew.

"Let freedom *clunk*," he muttered, leaving that most famous of town halls where the call to community had so often failed.

He decided then it was high time that he and Yoneko stopped trading blows; it was time to call Calvin. He bought a hot dog, then returned to the hostel, where two letters awaited him. One, from Garvin, remained unread because the second, scribbled in lipstick on a napkin promoting Classy's Stage Door Island Taxi Stand, read only: "6 PM — Y."

"Who wants her?"

That, friend, is an excellent question, Fujita thought. "I'm Yoneko, er, Yvonne's father . . ." He meant to say "father-in-law," which seemed wiser than saying, I'm the wandering, lunatic ex-prisoner who she's spent the last year fleeing because she fears and hates me. But the host, convinced of a family resemblance, clapped his hand in warm greeting. "Oh, her pop! Hey, Stick's a swell girl, really the best. Hold on a sec. She'll be so excited!"

"I'll say," mumbled Fujita. He parted with a few precious cents to buy a tin of mints from a cigarette girl done up like Carmen Miranda. Checking his coat and hat, he scornfully examined a phony floral arrangement on a pedestal; of course, the nurseryman was at war with fake flowers. Wrought of what appeared to be construction paper drenched in wax, the cobwebbed monstrosity bore as much resemblance to real daylilies as this dingy establishment bore to its model, the real Stage Door Canteen. As its name implied, the dance hall called Classy's Stage Door Island Taxi Stand was a hodgepodge of disparate genres, as if co-owners had haggled over several thematic decors and decided to implement them all, so that the result looked like a brothel used to store grade-school theater-crafts projects. Above the main floor, a mirrored globe spun stars across a vaguely South Seas decor—coconut mobiles, cardboard palm trees, prints of dark women in grass skirts. Rather than dance cards, men carried loops of cinema-admission tickets reading, TAXI STAND—1 PASSENGER FARE. Camouflage nets like those Yoneko made in Gila billowed from the ceiling to suggest "army."

He stood there some fifteen minutes, perhaps seeming in need of a dance partner. Across the darkened dance floor, a curvaceous, Caucasian taxi dancer with curly reddish hair sniffed new prey and began strolling swishily his way. Standing rigid and stiff-necked as a prisoner being fitted with a noose, he urged himself to retreat. As she neared, he saw she wore a slinky brown dress of cheap material that wrapped around at her waist, a silk flower in her hair, and miles of costume jewelry. When she reached the midway point—and it became unquestionably rude for him to turn away—he detected a tanness about her. Filipina, perhaps? Or no, lighter. And in her curls, a tint of red mahogany, a Mexican tint, like the hair of his adolescent "Helen," the maid of the King of Cleats. Then the approaching girl's features again shifted. Without greeting or any sound but the ice clinking in her unnaturally pink cocktail, she halted a yard short of him—a familiar starlet wannabe and an absolute stranger.

Yoneko made an exceptionally alluring taxi-dance girl. Not the theatrically smoky siren he'd met at the Union Church, nor the silly teenager who had bleached her egg-and-lemon coated hair in the Arizona sun, this "Yvonne" Yamaguchi frowning at him wore a hardened confidence he had not noticed before. His eyes searched her body's slopes and chutes for some trace of motherhood until she impatiently whipped her drink with an American-flag stirrer. Glancing up to her face, he could think of no apology suitable for all the things he felt sorry for. "You look well," he said. "Fit." In fact, he thought she looked unhealthy, almost ghostly—perhaps just from seeing him.

She shrugged. "I don't care. I'm used to being looked at." She tossed her head toward the dance floor and pivoted on her heels. Fearing that she meant to make him dance with her, Fujita popped a mint and followed. Instead, she led him to a booth, and they flopped down onto the overstuffed seats. "You look like hell."

And you look so different, he thought, but he nodded. "I've waited a long time," he said.

Yoneko misunderstood. "I came over when I could. I work, you know." Leaning back over the booth, she waved to the bartender and performed a series of hand signals like a baseball catcher.

The burly man called back, "Okay, Stick," and saluted her.

To Fujita's questioning look, she said, "I was the most flat-chested girl who auditioned here, so they called me Stick, and it stuck. I have the best legs, though," she added matter-of-factly.

"Well, here we are," he tried with a poor attempt at casualness. He wondered how he'd have fared with a daughter. Were parents like magnetic poles, naturally suited to one child or another? In Japan, certain boy children enjoyed some privileges: His father's brother, the *chonan*, the eldest son, inherited the entire estate. Only Ichiro was free to work, live, and die half a world away—the family had *a son to spare*. Would Fujita have been more protective of a daughter? At least, the army would not have taken her. But if he could keep her safe, would he know how to talk to her, or just adore the girl from afar, leaving everything to Mari, until one day shocked to see his child transformed into . . . a taxi dancer, for example? In a year, Yoneko had changed into something else entirely, and he didn't know how to begin with her. Sounding unsettlingly like Margaret Kelly, he found himself saying, "Start over: I want to hear all about what you've been up to."

Her laugh, superior and bitter, made him wince. "Okay," she said. "Let's see. In the morning I wake up, have coffee, eat, and go through my regimen. Some days I see friends at the hostel or around town, or go to the employment agency. A couple hours a week I clean house for a Quaker family in Haverford, outside the city, where I was this morning. Sometimes I go to the theater or films. Then I come here at eight o'clock every night, excluding Tuesdays and Sundays. That's what you really want to know, right?"

"I want to know—" Fujita began.

"I know what you want to know," she said. "But I'm telling you what you need to know. As you see, it's not the Stage Door Canteen, but it serves a purpose—you know, nice guys who are lonely, missing their girlfriends, or just out for a fine time on furlough or something, maybe after ending a shift at a factory. I like to dance; I'm very musical; I can jitterbug and swing and generally cut the rug better than most girls here. Oh, I'm very popular. Does that surprise you? No? It surprised me, at first. I took the long way out east. I was used to people spitting on me, you know, but this isn't the West."

"No, it sure isn't," Fujita agreed, nodding.

"Especially the military types. That surprised me. Some are really nice, and some . . ." She laughed, and it was a clear, honest sound. "I think some boys have a funny idea in their heads. Sort of Tokyo Rose. I'm Philadelphia Rose. Race Street Rose, maybe. One fellow told me that Tokyo Rose was bigger with the boys than Betty Grable. I don't believe it. Anyway, I'm the first Japanese taxi dancer in Classy's, probably in all Philadelphia, possibly the whole coast. Well, maybe it's not much to you, but it means a lot to me."

Feeling he had been invited to congratulate her on the dubious honor, Fujita was relieved when the barkeep interrupted with her order—a shot and a glass of water. The obligatory paternal figure Fujita imagined all such places must retain, the stocky, graying gentleman was about his age; he sported a biceps snake tattoo, and his manner indicated that he tended more than just the bar. Placing the drink on a doily, he slapped a heavy beef patty of a hand on Fujita's shoulder.

"Having a good time?" he boomed, and without awaiting an answer, he roared, "Good, good!" His breath carried a surprising, alert mintiness. As the protector hovered, beaming at them both, Fujita thought he was expected to tip on Yoneko's behalf and dug hesitantly in his pocket. "Nah!" the man protested. "I just wanted to meet Stick's pop and tell you she's a great girl, respectable and hardworking. We all think she's tops."

The actress that was Yoneko instantly turned on an adoring, Shirley Temple smile, and Fujita shook the man's hand. Squinting at her, the barkeep gave her the drinks and said, "Looking a tad ruddy there, Stick. You're spitting, right?"

"I'm spitting, I'm spitting," Yoneko said. When the man returned to his bar, her smile disintegrated. "We're supposed to spit the booze into the chaser," she said, swishing the shot around. She shook her head. "My pop, huh? I should have said you were a suitor."

"A *suitor?*" Fujita demanded, flushing.

Yoneko giggled. "Oh, I have lots. The bouncers keep an eye on them, just in case. Suitors have to behave themselves, or they can be thrown out with a wink."

"A suitor. I see."

"You're a country suitor. You can always tell country boys from city because they blush a lot and act like you're doing more than just dancing. I suppose farm types don't dance so much. City boys are different; they're rougher on the outside, and call you "baby" and "doll," but are warmer on the inside. They like to have fun." She paused for a moment, then mused, "You country boys seem guilty about having fun."

Fujita stewed. He had assumed that when they met, he, the elder, Tony's father, would take control of the meeting, but Yoneko's voice had turned mean and authoritative. Eyeing the muscular bartender, he bit the insides of his mouth and curled his toes in his shoes. He didn't want to spook her now; she seemed on the verge of either attacking him or bolting. He raised a palm to her. "You don't have to tell me this."

Yoneko rose to round the table and slid onto the seat beside him, her perfume filling the booth. "That's true. Still, you're almost like family. I don't mind telling you," she said, her manner indicating that she *meant* to tell him no matter what. Before she could begin, however, another taxi girl wobbled up and made a most extraordinary face at Fujita, a contortion intended as a smile, he supposed. Crunching her eyes, lips, and all features as if facing a powerful electric fan, she had the sort of cutesy, squint-eyed smiley visage one put on when playing with a baby or a puppy. "Hey, Mr. Yamaguchi!" the girl said. "How great!" Absolutely golden, from her hair to her gold-apple cheeks to the pendulous earrings like bunches of gold grapes, the dancer tossed herself backward onto the seat and lifted a meaty leg to unstrap a shoe. With a moan, she massaged the purplish dent ringing her ankle. Fujita understood then why coworkers called Yoneko "Stick."

"He's not my father," Yoneko said. Fujita sensed that the girls didn't care for each other. "He's my father-in-*law*," she said. He looked to the ceiling, dancing with stars cast off from the revolving mirrored ball.

"You're someone's wife?" The big golden girl pulled back frowning as if Yoneko had admitted to having a communicable disease.

"I'm someone's widow," Yoneko corrected. Her look to Fujita said: If you want to act like dear old Dad, I can play it that way, too. "We're just catching up," she said to the gold one. "I was telling him about farm boys, like those two from Chester we went out with last week."

"Oh boy," said the other taxi dancer. Although she carried no purse that Fujita could see, it intrigued him that a cigarette had somehow managed to materialize in her hand.

"It's so very important to these guys that a girl have a good time. They keep asking, Do you like it here? Is the management nice? Things like that."

"And you have to say, 'Sure, why not?' and 'Oh, they're swell to me and the girls—just like family,'" laughed Goldie. "And 'I luuuv guys drooling at me, trying to cop feels!' They get all bent out of shape if you don't."

Fujita bit the sides of his mouth so hard he felt they would spout blood. Not unused to imagining conspiracies against him, he sensed the barkeep's owl-eyes watching them; Yoneko had probably asked the gold-apple girl not to leave her alone with him. She meant to gag him, to wield her sordid life like a club, to bludgeon an apology from him. "I don't see what this has to do with me."

"Sure you do," Yoneko said deliberately. "They think of you as dirt and feel guilty or shamed for wanting to be with you, but they come after you anyway because you've got a spark, because you're alive, see. It's cowardly, you ask me." Seeking agreement, she looked to Goldie, who seemed to be dozing off, her flytrap eyelashes fluttering spastically, her chin bobbing on her huge gold chest.

"You're implying that I see you that way," Fujita said tensely. "Or is it that *I* somehow pushed you to . . . come here? You think I should feel responsible." He *did* feel responsible—for everything. Uncomprehending, Yoneko studied his face, which drooped with guilt. Then something dawned on her, and she laughed.

"No one makes *me* do anything," said the haughty Yvonne. "See, there's nothing *wrong* with being looked at, if it's on your own terms. You're Nisei, but really you're like an Issei, a fuddy-duddy, with your fucking Japanese *propriety*." He found her swearing repellent, but just the sort of thing he imagined one picked up in the company of sailors, like the clap. "So this place is a dive—we don't have to measure up to the Stage Door Canteen. The only measuring stick is if fellows want to dance with you and think you're beautiful, and they *do*, with me. Do you know what that means to me? Maybe you had your own troubles coming east, but you're a man. You don't know what it was like for a Japanese girl, a teenager, to travel alone cross-country. When people aren't looking at you like you're a spy, or like you're just crud, they act like they don't even see you. In Salt Lake, I had this big, fat ox *sit* on me one day in a bus—like I was invisible."

For a moment, Fujita sensed he was hearing the real Yoneko and not Yvonne, the last link to his old life, a woman he might speak to as he spoke to Margaret. Yet, in the time he hesitated, the simmering Yvonne snapped back to life. She downed the shot she was supposed to spit out into the water chaser and began fishing for something under the table.

"Here you get so much attention," she continued, "it's addictive. When you get to the real world and your beau doesn't shower you with his admiration, doesn't pay attention to you, it can be pretty confusing." Sitting back upright with a cigarette in her hand, she turned to look at him dead on. "It can be devastating, actually."

"You, um, have someone?" Fujita asked. It should have occurred to him, but it hadn't.

Yoneko tossed back her head and let forth such a piercing, shrill laugh that Goldie snorted in her near sleep and Fujita cringed. *That* was Yoneko. That was Tony's girl, whom he had so imprecisely observed as she sat beside him just like this at their first meeting in the Far East Café, a seeming lifetime ago.

The overwhelming demimondaine who drove the Chinese waiters batty, killed Tamie's appetite, and made Tony drop his silverware—the girl who was wholly unlike a Fujita. Such a deafening clarion call to sound from that slender throat, now thrust back in laughter. That dark, girlish throat, thought the man who had been intimate with so few women and knew nothing of cosmetic arts. Even now he did not immediately recognize the edge of the pale, powdery foundation mask beneath her jaw, which he had mistaken for the mask of illness, or shock, or merely an actress's expression. The longer she laughed and the longer Fujita stared at the whitened makeup line, the more startlingly it contrasted with her throat—as sharp as the line between visibility and invisibility, between being a grotesque and a ghost. If the girl had seemed from a distance to blend in well at Classy's, she now began to appear to him as a figure of kabuki theater. She was so lovely, he thought, and yet so desperately wanted not to be who she was—even more than the Quincy Market Nikkei, or Calvin Igawa, or Fujita himself. How was it that he'd never noticed this? How this girl, in making herself so extraordinarily and determinedly noticeable, all along only meant to erase herself? Tamie and Mari had noticed, he realized then, recalling how small and quiet they had appeared beside the girl. They knew. They knew.

"Listen," Yoneko finally said, catching her breath, and there was nothing small or quiet about her manner. "I don't sleep around. I'm not one of those cuddle bunnies after uniforms. I'm no bobby-soxer. Guys come to *me*. You did," she added. "Lots of women support themselves this way. I'll bet lots more will take it up now that a lot more of us are widows. It's not a bad living. A woman can bust her nuts at some dead-end job all day and not get the same pay as the asshole who left the job to go and get shot and leave her with a kid in the first place—like that neighbor of yours, just for one example. So why not do it? Because fuddy-duddies like you think it's improper that I'm not standing around with my head in the sand trying not to be seen? I'm making myself noticed. I'm taking control. And you . . ." She reached for her shot glass, which was empty. "I bet you hate looking in the mirror, right? Up there with your hakujin harem in New England. Well, I think you need to get your head out of the sand. You need to take your clothes off and jitterbug a bit. It would loosen you up. It would warm your heart."

Fujita sighed. "I'm sorry," he said evenly.

Yoneko rolled her eyes. "For what?"

Fujita opened his arms wide—a posture of helpless acceptance, hugging "the whole thing." But he said, "It was an-an-an accident." He had meant the accident in camp. I'm sorry for falling on you, for hurting you. And I think you were pregnant, and I am mortally afraid I hurt the baby you would have, too. He said none of this. At that moment, a towering, hairy man in navy whites approached the booth and held a dance ticket out to Yoneko. She waved him away.

"Sorry. Off duty, handsome," she said. "Try her." All three looked at Goldie, snoring open-mouthed. The sailor's olive face soured; he shook his head.

"I want you, doll," he said, smirking, but he was looking at Fujita when he said this. He made the mistake of grabbing Yoneko's hand. Taking up Goldie's shoe from the table, she hammered the heel down on the man's knuckles. He drew back, yelping, "Fucking slant cunt!"

"Fucking Wop prick," Yoneko said, matching his pitch exactly. He retreated. Seeming satisfied with herself, she shrugged to Fujita, who was tensed and alert. "Some guys forget we're a classy place. Come on. I'm taking off tonight. Let's get out of here."

"Where?" Again, she shrugged. He looked at the snoozing Goldie, then checked his watch. "I should call Calvin. I'm staying with him tonight."

"I know," she said. "But we've got time. There are some people you should meet first."

Hazy with humidity, the night air turned the lampposts into dandelions of light. Yoneko marched ahead at a driven pace. Fujita thrust an arm in front of her as she stepped off a curb, just in time to prevent her being run over. "My hero," she smirked. "I *saw* the car." Fujita looked down at his roughened, callous hands that Yoneko, he now remembered, had once described as "strong."

"There's something I've wanted to ask," he said, though there were quite a number of things he wished to ask. "You once said we'd . . . met before the church. You'd said . . ."

Yoneko, or Yvonne, or Stick, or whoever she now was, turned to him. "Oh, that. You still don't remember?" she said, and Fujita thought she sounded sad. "No, you wouldn't. I was young. I remember crying so hard I couldn't talk. And, of course, my skirt was up over my head at the time."

"Your *skirt*?" he demanded, stopping short. But then, out of his muddy memory, the kernel of an image began to sprout.

"I thought Tony was so brave, but you were braver. And definitely much bigger."

"Wait a minute." Fujita's understanding tried to catch up with a sensation in his arms—of weight, warmth. "You said you were young? You were a *child* . . ."

Yoneko nodded. "I told you, it was a long time ago."

The newest addition to Tony's elementary-school class in Pasadena, Yoneko Yamaguchi was a bright, willful little girl who wore pigtails and short frilly dresses and always had scrapes on her knees. Though pretty, she had a penchant for rock candy and gummy rice candies—free from her parents' Oriental-goods shop in Los Angeles—that gnarled her baby teeth. Having more money than time for parenting, the Yamaguchis sent Yoneko to the civilizing influence of Auntie Rose and Pasadena. Saturdays, instead of going to the gakuen, she went home.

On the day Fujita couldn't remember and Yoneko could never forget, Miss Yamaguchi was a six-year-old, her legs too short to reach the ground as she sat on her favorite leather-and-chain swing in the schoolyard. Usually the swings were lower, but older boys often whipped them up to wrap around the crossbar, elevating the seat. That day little Yoneko had to jump and pull herself up, but she liked that view from the heights, and she loved to fly. She had a good arc going when a ruffian boy who "liked her" snuck up and pushed her from behind. Sliding forward, she found her dress snagged in the chain along with the skin beneath her arms. Dangling, she hadn't the strength to pull herself back up onto the swing. The hem of her dress caught tightly beneath her throat, the belted waist slipped up to her chest, exposing her from the top of her ribs down except for her tiny bloomers, socks, and saddle shoes.

Like a pack of adolescent wolves, the boys gathered from around the playground. When the momentum of her swing slowed, they took turns starting her up again. Swishing like a clock pendulum, she felt a sharp pinch as the chains tightened their bite on her arms. It was a good dress—sturdy and well-stitched, from her own parents' store—and it did not tear. Kicking out, she managed to catch one boy on the nose with her heel, but the movement intensified the hem's grip on her windpipe, and she dizzily let her legs hang to rest. The boy whose nose she had smashed, reddening with rage as well as blood, took the opportunity to punch his unmoving target in her soft, flat belly. Even as she jackknifed midair, it pleased young Yoneko to see how the brute bled and cried. She determined she would not cry herself, and though blind with tears, she bit her lip and made no sound. The only girl she could see, in the periphery, stood at a safe distance from the whirlwind of jeering boys, placing her fingers to the corners of her eyes, stretching the skin back over her temples, and grinning with buck teeth. Yoneko felt rough fingers scratching at her midriff, felt her panties being yanked down, heard laughter.

Tony Fujita had stood by watching for some time, at once nauseated and thrilled to witness her humiliation. He didn't push Yoneko, but he didn't help her, either, perhaps because like most of the Japanese kids, he was accustomed to teasing, and one could be glad to *not* be the butt of it for once. When Yoneko's flailing shoes found Tommy Tompkins's nose, Tony had to grin. He didn't see Tommy retaliate, at first, because his attention was on the other girl—on Millie—drawing back the folds of her eyelids, which enraged him more than anything. Tony recognized what the besieged Yoneko could not, though he couldn't have given a name to it—to a sense of irony, an older boy's insight creeping up on him: Millie was Millie *Chu*, and apparently ignorant of her own Asian features. In her enthusiastic exaggeration of Yoneko's epicanthic folds, she so forcefully yanked her own that her eyes became slits of happy meanness. Tony saw mirrored in her elation his own relief—*Thank God it's not* me—and he sickened. Then he saw Tommy pound Yoneko, and saw the girl's panties yanked down. Stomping toward the circle, he shoved Millie from behind onto the blacktop, kicked her—sugar, spice, and everything nice—and punched everything he could until he was beaten to the ground himself.

Mr. Fujita, summoned to a conference with Mrs. Malison, had arrived at the time of day when the teacher was likely to be least harried. From across the playground, he immediately spotted a swarm of tiny bodies hopping and squawking like carrion birds, darting aimlessly (he thought) around the swing set. Such a *mass* of them. Wandering closer, he saw that the little mob was not without aim—it was trained on his son, curled on the ground, and on the half-stripped girl suspended from two chains like a discarded rag doll. Wading into the swarm of fists and feet and faces glossy with startling cruelty, he sent the boys flying and hauled Tony up.

Tony bled from the mouth and had difficulty catching his breath but shrugged his father away and started to bolt after one of his assailants. Holding him back with one hand, Fujita lifted the girl with his other arm, inspiring a salvo of hard-capped saddle shoes. Fortunately, Yoneko's squirming at last unsnagged her hem without tearing her favorite dress. Collapsing against his chest, she shook with weeping. He could see her tonsils down in her wide-stretched mouth, a quivering string of saliva, but it was as if someone had clipped the child's vocal cords. She made no sound at all. Fearing that she was choking, he squatted down and shook her violently by the arm, but she fought her way back into his chest and held fast. Tony, seething, flopped down cross-legged on the dirt, caught his breath, and gasped, "I'm gonna kill Tommy." It seemed to soothe the girl; she drew her face away and nodded emphatically.

It had surprised Fujita. Not children's cruelty, but how quickly they became attached; the girl's relief, adoration, and gratitude startled him as much as the strength of her interlocked fingers and her arms looped around his neck. He would soon forget about this day of petty meanness, forget utterly. How could he know that that child would never forget how she had been lifted up in the arms of a hero at the direst of moments—a sensation she would feel she could not live without for the rest of her life? With Tony grumbling behind, Fujita had carried the girl into the school feeling fused to her; and this carrying a child only seemed the simplest, the most basic of human actions, like sleeping, or dying.

Transported back to Pasadena, Fujita had barely noticed how Philadelphia grew ever dingier during their walk. Darker, too, both the pedestrians and the actual sidewalks, which yellowed under inadequate street light. The single working lamppost revealed that not an inch of space separated the facades lining the canyon of row houses. "Believe it or not," Yoneko said, slowing her walk, "that's when I knew I wanted to marry Tony." She turned up a stoop onto a covered porch, so dark that Fujita bumped into the railing shared with the next building. A chuckle sounded in the darkness.

"Evening, Yvonne," a raspy man's voice said. Fujita heard Yoneko's keys tinkling.

"Hey, Moses. How's tricks?" Another chuckle.

"Oh," the man said, "getting trickier all the time."

Then they were inside a dark hallway reminiscent of Fujita's childhood home in the L.A. Nihonmachi. The darkness enhanced an evil chemical smell. His heart thudded and thudded. "That's when I knew I wanted be a Fujita," she concluded. "Oh, well."

How could her fantasy of him be stretched so vastly out of proportion? It had no logic to it at all. "So, so, that's *it*? *Any* parent would intercede like that."

"I know that now," Yoneko retorted. "My mistake."

The key latch clinked open. The residual odor of a DDT pesticide bomb rushed out, but no light. Then, in the darkness, he heard it.

The baby's cries.

What happened then, he could not be sure. Stumbling at the threshold, he felt Yoneko's hands catch him under the elbow. Breaking away, he blindly waded toward the sound. "Wait a minute," she called after him. "There's something else I—"

Beset by objects at his shins at every turn, he ordered, "Light!" Something squeaked and gave way beneath his shoe.

The overhead bulb flashed on. In the doorway to the apartment's only other room stood Calvin Igawa, looking extraordinarily disheveled, sleepy-eyed and messy-haired, in a tank top and khakis, several cloth strips over his shoulder, four open safety pins bristling in his mouth. Fujita saw, in the bough of one arm, the bundle he'd hunted after for so, so long.

"Um, hi," Calvin said, jangling his pocket change. "I mean, welcome. Would you like anything . . ." he began clumsily, but Yoneko walked between them. With ritualistic solemnity, she took the papoose and placed the baby in his grandfather's quivering hands.

"It's a boy," she said simply. Staring at the infant as if into a crystal ball, Fujita teetered so much that the young pair guided him to a tattered sofa and sat him down.

Recovering from his initial nervousness, Calvin Igawa, who was so like Fujita, whispered, "Might as well put you to work. I did the messy bit, but he needs to be powdered and diapered," and surrendered the gear. Never taking his eyes from the round, pouting face, the grandfather gave his stiff-necked nod. With this necessary focus, he snapped out of his trance and laid the child out on the sofa beside him. His fingers had not forgotten, and nimbly he undid the wrapping and set to powdering the tiny rump no bigger than his palm. To either side of the sacrum, the bluish marks like thumbprints, the so-called Mongolian spots characteristic of Asian infants, had not yet wholly faded. He kissed both of these and finally wept.

Respectfully, Yoneko and Calvin retreated to the bedroom and closed the door.

Seimei, ōn, girí: What the scarecrow said became Fujita's mantra to himself in the two weeks he stayed with Yoneko, Calvin, and baby David Toshio. It took him that long to forgive Igawa. Not merely for being there, for moving in on, or with, the girl who considered herself Tony's widow. He assumed they made love, but he wasn't certain—if they did, they abstained during his stay. They had twin beds, but these could be pushed together. Also, though Calvin tended to hover protectively, he did so with Fujita's own stiff, rather paternal formality. He wouldn't blame

Calvin for loving the girl, but he was less generous in forgiving deception. "I sort of have a girl waiting for me," Igawa had said that first day on Widow's Peak, trying to juggle debts of gratitude along with debts of love.

"He didn't say *what* girl!" Fujita fumed in the belated birth announcement he sent to Widow's Peak. "He didn't say *the* girl!"

"Leave Calvin alone," Yoneko said. "If it wasn't for him, you wouldn't be here. He sold me on the idea of having you come down after you helped him. And I was a *hard* sell. You really hurt me, you know. Especially in Gila. It could have been okay, it could have been bearable—"

"It was an accident," Fujita said again. "That night, with Mari, I just couldn't—"

"Not that. I mean, for Tony and me. Oh, sure, I'm just the dirty kid from a family of *real* Jap traitors. And you Fujitas are so together, so superior. The great nursery family. Well, to hell with your judging. So my father never met the first lady—all my folks did was have a Japanese import store—a big security risk." Although he'd never thought of it before, it was true that Fujita the believer and fellow WRA prisoners did feel superior to the Justice Department prisoners at places such as Crystal City, though no case of Japanese-American sabotage had been proved. He refused to buy her story that Crystal City housed Japanese Peruvians "kidnapped" for use in hostage trades, but he began to sympathize with the "real traitors," just a little.

Efficient as ever, the man who would try to improve any barren place took over the custodial chores Calvin and Yoneko had negotiated to undertake for a reduction in rent. He also paid the remaining balance that month. With what money he had left, he bought a camera and film and devoted himself to spoiling his grandson, buying cases of formula and bottles, diapers, baby clothes, toys, and even books. When David cried at 1:00 A.M., it was always Grandpa who gave him his bottle. It vaguely alarmed the new grandfather how swiftly and completely he'd become attached to this child. Holding David against his chest with one hand, burping him with the other, Fujita could feel the hollow taps vibrating right through the infant's body into his own heart, and it was as if the boy had been sutured there.

As the April nights grew warmer, he liked to administer the feedings on the porch, chatting with the neighbor called Moses. "You're gonna grow tits pretty soon, the way you're always feeding that child," he told Fujita one night, chuckling. With hair of gray steel wool, Moses could sit from sundown to sunup on that porch in his rattan chair, watchful and unmoving as Margaret's scarecrow. Also a widower, he wore a quilt over his legs "like President Roosevelt," he said. Moses seemed protective of Yoneko and adoring of her infant. "You know," he told Fujita, "Negro babies have those spots, too."

"Really? Mongolian spots?"

"Sometimes," Moses said, nodding. "Sometimes there's just one, but if there's two, you catch them at the right angle, they look like bowling-ball holes." They both laughed.

Many relocated Nikkei resented that their evacuated Little Tokyos had become "Bronzevilles" during the war, but Fujita felt comfortable in a colored neighborhood. Within two weeks, he'd spoken with half the block while he pushed David around in a pram. Several neighbors were charmed by the novelty of the Japanese baby and were accepting, if not always warm, toward the Nisei. Easterners had often not heard about "the whole thing," but his new Negro neighbors had less trouble believing it than most people. Moses was sympathetic but cautious about drawing too close parallels. "It's that *distribution* part gets me," he mused, shaking his head thoughtfully. "Nobody tells Negroes to go out and mingle."

"No, I guess not," Fujita said.

"Someday," Moses told him, "you'll have to decide if you're black or you're white." Fujita thought this preposterous, but Moses quizzed him aggressively. "I've only ever been as far west as Detroit, but here in the East, you'll see—there's no yellow here. Now that they sprung you, say you go south. Which water cooler do you drink from? Where do you sit at the movies?" Carefully, Fujita readjusted David's bottle and explained that he never went to movies. "All right then. Picture this: You're getting on the bus. You look around. You're sitting down. Where are you?"

"I'm right here," the Maybe-Maybe Man said, pointing at the

stoop and sighing. "I'm hanging from a strap, standing right here in the middle in my own yellow section." Moses snorted. "Okay, then: Where would *you* be if you were me?" Fujita asked.

After some thought, Moses shook his head. "I'd *walk,*" he said, and they both laughed. More seriously, he said, "Not David, though. With Calvin and Yvonne pushing him, I bet he'll own the bus one day. I've watched those kids. She's good at momming, and *he's* even better. They're good neighbors, too," he said, almost proudly.

In his generous mood, Fujita tried not to bicker with either of the "kids," but by nature, his giving took a controlling form. "I'll change his diaper," Fujita always said when the unpleasant chore presented itself. "I'm good at it." This was true: Spurred by guilt for not having helped Mari with Tony enough, he took to changings with relish, and by the second week he could perform one as handily as rolling a cigarette. "*I'm* good at it, too," Yoneko would say. One midnight, when she insisted that he go back to sleep and let her feed David, he became defensive. "I can't sleep anyway," he said crankily.

"Uh-huh. Maybe that's why you're so cranky, Ojiisan. You'd better try harder."

All three adults had their cranky moments. The apartment, only slightly larger than those at Gila, did not easily accommodate a live-in nanny. Fujita's presence made Yoneko and Calvin argue, and one night they both emerged from the bedroom fuming. With Calvin standing behind her, as if holding her at gunpoint, Yoneko said, "I guess, with everything that's happened, I never gave my condolences. About Mrs. Fujita, I mean. I'm sorry." She looked as if she would say something else, but then didn't or couldn't. Fujita nodded and thanked her. Then she went back to bed. Calvin looked reluctant to follow her, so Fujita went outside to sit watch with Moses.

"I'm overstaying my welcome, but what can I do?" he demanded of his friend. "Can I just pack up and go home?" After he said it, it struck him powerfully that he'd meant Widow's Peak. A bad, bad sign. Trying to hide his consternation, he droned on about the cramped spaces of the Nihonmachi and

Gila River, and how big his nursery and Margaret's house were. That led him to how he and Margaret and Livvie and Garvin had carved a farm out of the raw hill in Juggeston.

"That sounds nice," Moses said, and Fujita agreed, it was—that the work may have saved his life. "I guess it's good for the boy, too," Moses urged, and Fujita nodded wholeheartedly and recalled how Garvin especially loved the greenhouse. "And I'll bet it takes a real load off his poor, widowed mother," said Moses, and Fujita said he hoped the little farm would turn a profit at market, easing Livvie's financial load, too. "And that nurse sounds like the kind of woman the world could use a lot more of," Moses said, and Fujita bobbed his head emphatically. "I guess it's easier living than it was in California," Moses said, and Fujita sat bolt upright to stare at him.

Moses adjusted his lap blanket, clucked his tongue and shook his head. "Except, like I keep saying: Here, there's just white and off-white. And in that town, I'll bet you're way off," he said, grinning. "You've got to choose."

"I'm not going to make that choice, Moses," Fujita said, frowning. "I refuse."

Their talk made Fujita feel guilty for not calling or writing more to the Peak since arriving here, and that reminded him that he'd utterly forgotten to read Garvin's letter, which had arrived with Yoneko's first note at the hostel. He realized he not only missed them but also worried about them, how they'd get on with old Hideo. And was Hideo getting on with the town, he wondered, thinking of the shattered greenhouse glass. He returned to hunt for Garvin's letter in the hopelessly messy front room of the apartment. "I can't find a thing in here," he grumbled.

He finally found the letter crumpled in some trousers pocket the next morning. Sent nearly the same time Fujita left Juggeston, the letter asked when he would return—and to please bring a musket with him when he did. "Just a toy one is okay," Garvin assured him. "My school is having a spring fair on May 5. Will you be home by then?" the boy wrote hopefully. Cursing himself, Fujita intended to go out and find a public phone to call the Peak straightaway, but then David awoke with a hearty shriek, and the apartment was a flurry of activity as Yoneko prepared for her housecleaning job and Calvin for going to classes. With his day full of David, he never got to call, but later that afternoon he received a telegram from Livvie.

SORRY FOR BOTHERING YOU STOP, she began, and Fujita felt miserable that she should be sorry about that. He had just finished feeding David when he set himself on the sofa to read. SOME TROUBLE WITH TOWNIES BUT I THINK I KNOW WHY AND M AND I CAN HANDLE IT SO DON'T WORRY STOP.

"Trouble?" Fujita asked. "Handle it? What's 'it'?" He readjusted the baby on his chest.

I KNOW WHAT YOU'RE DOING DOWN THERE IS VERY IMPORTANT TO YOU. At that moment Fujita managed to burp David, who released a fine stream of spittle onto his shoulder, and yes, it was important to him—and so was Widow's Peak. Why was Livvie paying for all this preamble in a telegram? What the hell was wrong up there?

I NEED TO KNOW ARE YOU COMING BACK HERE AND ARE WE GOING TO HAVE A FARM OR NOT? STOP. Fujita tried and tried to divine some inflection in the cold document. David released a sniffle preliminary to a good bout of crying. M WOULD KILL ME FOR WRITING SO DON'T TELL HER STOP.

"She would?" Fujita asked, frowning.

WE'RE ALL HAPPY TO HEAR YOUR GREAT NEWS STOP DON'T BE TOO HARD ON CALVIN WHO'S DONE HIS BEST IN A LOUSY SITUATION STOP I WAS WRONG ABOUT THE GIRL HUH I'M GLAD END.

"No, Livvie," Fujita told the paper, "even when you're wrong in certain ways, you're mostly very right." He bundled up the baby and went out to call from a pay phone but failed to reach anyone. He thought of sending a telegram himself but then realized he didn't know what he could say in it. Just: HEM STOP HAW END.

That evening, when Yoneko returned from Haverford and Calvin from school, Fujita proposed that they move into a bigger apartment. "It's not good for a child to live in such a crowded, messy little space," he said with authority. Yoneko bit her lip to refrain from pointing out what Fujita already knew: that the space had been considerably less crowded before he arrived. "Three bedrooms," he prescribed, and Yoneko stepped on Calvin's foot.

"Don't worry," Fujita said, ignoring her obviousness, "I'll wire my bank in California and try to get some money for the balance." Calvin stepped on Yoneko's foot. "You're busy, so I can even do the searching. Maybe people will be more willing to rent to an older—"

"That's it!" Yoneko wailed, slapping her hips. In his makeshift crib in the bedroom, David began wailing, too. "No, Calvin, no—I've been on my best behavior. I've been so good it makes me sick. Boy, are you a piece of work," she said, pointing at Fujita. "Why are you here? Huh? See, you never even thought it out, but I've thought about it every day for a year now."

"I . . . I want to help," he said.

"Maybe you haven't figured it out yet, but I invited you down to meet David, not to *buy* him. It was the right thing to do, and I promised Tony to make peace with you, so if you want to be dear, old Ojiisan or Uncle Bill or whatever, fine. But look around this room," she said, throwing her arms out wide. "There are *no Fujitas* here except you." She looked so miserable then that Fujita thought only that he should hug her—comfort her like the hero of her childhood fantasies—but of course he couldn't. He was one of only two people in this strange city she knew well, and who knew her. Knew of her weighty remorse. He so deeply disappointed her, it seemed to physically hurt her.

"Yoneko, you're being—" Calvin began.

"Oh, stop it, Calvin," she yelled. "This is my fight."

"There doesn't have to be a fight," Igawa protested, but her mind was made up. He went to check on the crying baby.

To Fujita, she continued, "This is *our* home. If you want to get a place in the neighborhood and baby-sit and such, fine. You can visit, and that will be appreciated. If not, fine. Send Christmas cards. I'm trying really, really hard to be kind about this, but you have to get it straight: I'm David's mother. We have a life here now—us and Calvin—and I don't need you chasing me and hanging around and fussing and trying to buy us anymore. You're not going to move in here and take us over like your stupid plants. You need to find yourself a new hobby."

"A hobby? I only mean to live up to my—"

"Too late. I could've used a hand before, but we're doing okay *now*. Maybe better than you. *And*"—she furiously dug into her purse—"I make my own money now. Here." She pried open his fingers and deposited a pile of bills into his hand. "Thanks for the loan, but I don't like the strings that come with it."

"Your own money," Fujita echoed after the taxi dancer. He looked to the bills, then to Calvin, who was highly agitated, looking to the window as if preparing to jump out of it. Then Fujita decided to mention the college fund he'd saved from Tony's army paychecks. "Hell, I forgot. There's a lot of money, actually. I've been saving it—"

"Damn it. I told you. No thanks. No deal. Keep your charity."

"Not charity. It's for education, see, it's—"

Calvin broke in. "I think I need to say something at this juncture—"

"No, you don't," said Yoneko.

"But the thing is—" he sputtered.

"Not now, Calvin," Fujita said.

"Oh," Igawa said. "Okay. I'll just check on . . ." Their glares chased him back into the bedroom.

"Listen," Yoneko said. "I don't like talking about this, so I'll only say it once. I loved Tony, and he loved me. We had plans. Or do you suppose I got knocked up on purpose?" From his expression, she understood he did not discount the possibility. "Jesus. I mean, you didn't exactly find Mrs. Fujita on your own; my folks didn't even *meet* before they married. But *we* found and chose each other, and he would have married me. So the way I see it, I've inherited the right to tell you that you're off the hook. Forget about that duty stuff. You're paid up."

"How dare you—"

"I feel responsible, too, every single day, but I've moved along with my life. And from what I hear, that's what you should be doing, too. Don't you get it? You've come down here to take over our lives, but *we don't need you*."

Fujita slumped onto the sofa, which was blotched with various baby stains. Outside the one apartment window, a blooming maple tree scratched at the pane. Philadelphia's spring had a sizable head start on Juggeston's, he thought. Perhaps Yoneko realized it, too. Sighing, she mushed in beside him on the small sofa, crossed her arms, and pointed to the budding branches.

"Shouldn't you be up there with your harem about now?" she said. "Aren't you supposed to be working with them and that kid, doing whatever it is that you do?"

"Margaret," he corrected her. "Livvie and Garvin Tufteller. Yes, I should," he said, worriedly. Scratching, scratching at the pane, the revivified maple flared with its new life. There would be rain in Juggeston—still cool, still possible frosts. The tulips he'd planted—freebies from Bud—would be ready to break out about now. He thought of the radishes, which, planted in the fall, acted as biennials, like carrots and turnips and beets; they'd produce flowers and set seed in their second year. Sowing them, he'd wondered, Was it too optimistic, forcing an annual to become a biennial? "I'm looking forward to it," Fujita said, amazed to realize it. Time for peace. For "house peace," as Margaret put it. Maybe David's family had a chance to be okay. Maybe not happy, but okay. Better prospects than some people's. Many minutes later, he said, "All right, Yoneko. You win."

Neither of them was sure who'd "won," though, for neither quite understood the contest in the first place. In the following days, Yoneko didn't feel like a winner. After all, who sends her earliest hero packing and considers it a victory? A stalemate, perhaps? She confessed that she too *partially* blamed herself for Tony's fate. She echoed Fujita's opinion that "It would have killed Tony not to serve. You know, like he thought he needed to go or he wasn't American enough somehow. I thought I agreed with him," mused the girl whose parents remained imprisoned as "real traitors." "Now . . . my thinking's changed on a lot of things."

Regarding Fujita as someone on his deathbed who would painfully hang on until assured that he'd left his affairs in order, Yoneko and Calvin devoted themselves to proving they didn't need him. In the last week, she kept the apartment clean, labored to make barely edible dinners, kept up with the shopping. In addition to his studies and custodial duties, Igawa took the lion's share of the messier baby chores. "See, we can be responsible," Yoneko chuckled. "And taxi dances can provide for a baby pretty darned well." Both Fujita and Calvin visibly bit down on their lips, and Yoneko flooded the apartment with her dreadful, shrill laughter. She mussed Igawa's whipped black hair. "Oh, don't worry," she told Fujita. "Calvin's going to make an honest woman of me someday."

Poor Calvin. Like Margaret, the med student knew that healing processes were rarely painless, and with grace and forbearance, he undertook a thankless middleman's role to promote a rapprochement between Fujita and Yoneko. In an urgent, instinctual last-minute attempt to bond, the two Californians ganged up to try the Montanan's fiercely assimilationist views and his distaste for things "too Jap."

"Little Italy, Germantown, Welsh Valley," Yoneko scowled—all neighboring areas. "They're okay, they're American, but not Nihonmachi? Is that it?"

"What about Saint Patty's Day?" Fujita asked. "The D.A.R.!"

"I'm not saying it's right," Igawa grumbled. "It's just the way it is."

"He won't even eat with hashi anymore." Yoneko laughed. "Chopsticks are subversive."

"I'll just go check on the baby now," sighed the doctor-to-be.

"Calvin's a very, very nice man," Yoneko said when he was gone. "He's a great friend. He's unique."

"Yes, he is," Fujita said. And he's *here*, thought Tony's father, who would never be able to wholly suppress his bitterness at the fact.

On his penultimate day in Philadelphia, they all went to Independence Mall so Fujita could buy Garvin's toy musket. His imminent departure allowed their outing to be fun. They took a side trip down to the Swedish American Center to see a dance recital, but David howled so inconsolably they had to leave. They had ice cream and hot, soft pretzels and took a Freedom Trail buggy ride. Nestled in Grandpa's arms, David liked the jouncing motion of the carriage and burbled profusely. When Fujita updated them on what had happened at the Peak—the arrivals of lazy Jingo Yamashita, happy-footed Tanji, and cranky Hideo Okamoto—Yoneko regarded him, just for a moment, with that six-year-old's adoration again. "It's great that you're helping all those people," she said. "I guess those women you live with are pretty nice, too."

"Yes, they are," Fujita sighed, watching the horse's tail whisking at flies. But watching Calvin, remembering Bob Ito, debating "distribution and dissemination" with Moses, he was no longer sure how "great" their pit stop from Gila River was. Many of those people who had cast the Nikkei out of the West Coast were now determined and happy to *keep* them out, he knew; by facilitating further eastward "dissemination," now that internees were at least allowed to fight their way back home again, he'd begun to feel like an accomplice, like an inu. At the end of the Freedom Trail, he shifted topics, preferring to talk about Garvin's artistic interests and how Livvie's attire had appeared to grow less frumpy for her dances with Ernie Tanji.

That night Fujita telephoned the Peak, receiving no answer. "Where is everybody?" he barked, already nervous about traveling. "What's going on up there?" To soothe himself, he went out to say good-bye to Moses.

"Those kids will be okay," his friend reassured him. "How about you? Going back to California?"

"I suppose so," Fujita said glumly. "No reason not to, now. I was so concentrated on coming . . . here, I hadn't really thought about what would happen next. I just thought, I'd get here and . . . and find David, and the whole thing would just be over."

"The whole thing?" Moses said. "Maybe you've only seen *half* the thing yet. Like I say, my friend: I don't think you can keep hanging on to that strap. That's part of the whole thing, too."

In the morning Fujita unsuccessfully called the Peak from a pay phone three times. Calvin said he'd try to call once they'd put him on the train. As was his habit, Fujita made them deliver him an hour before the scheduled departure. The first train, 6:00 A.M. As they waited tensely together on a long bench in the concourse, Fujita said, "When I arrived, I saw a one-legged pigeon under that bench there. I hope you'll keep in touch," he said, as if these two thoughts flowed together naturally. He said a postcard would be nice, despite his unhappy associations with Yoneko and postcards.

"Maybe we'll call," Yoneko began, then let it drop. "Yes," she said. If they needed anything . . . "Yes, yes." If he could help out—a loan, for a bigger apartment—or maybe baby-sitting sometime . . . "I don't know. We'll see," she said, leaving to change David in the ladies' room.

"You keep holding on to that college fund," Calvin said when she'd left. "And don't worry. She'll call. It may take a while, but she'll call."

He held David all the way onto the first step of the train and even there handed the child back only reluctantly, as if considering shanghaiing him. To keep from snatching him back, Fujita thrust his hands into his pockets and began jiggling his change. Calvin stopped the jangling in his own pocket and laughed.

Yoneko would have kissed him good-bye. Ever an actress, she had an instinctive respect for the drama of partings. Any partings. She was by nature a gusher to equal Margaret Kelly. And the recently bereft know that partings between people—whether loved ones or not—are always leaps of faith. Any separation could be an opportunity missed, any handshake the last, any ticket open-ended until you were home. But Yoneko, who had traveled so far herself, was learning. She subjected him to no final teary apologies or interminable embraces. She spoke no heartfelt regrets or knee-jerk promises. "Have a safe trip," she said, and kissed David instead.

"Yes, thank you," said Fujita, as the floor slid forward beneath him and the train began pulling him away—back to Juggeston, back to his nojo.

THIRTEEN

Yellow Is the Color of Love

Widow's Peak remained prey to chilling influences that April—to frosts and cold rains, to an anonymous snowball assault on Hideo driving the Dodge, to a cooler-than-usual reception when Margaret called Lil Wellington to check on a space reservation at the farmer's market. Yet there were always more hopeful glimmers. The sunny news of little David in Fujita's letter from Philadelphia filled the Peak farmers with tentative optimism and set them to their on-again-off-again farm labors with renewed vigor.

Margaret's appreciation for Mr. Okamoto deepened. Hideo made an able replacement for Fujita, if not always a congenial one. He was excruciatingly polite—and respectful, since Fujita had warned him that the women were the bosses here—but their intercourse was limited to smiles and bows and nods. Lumbering oxlike across the hill, he labored steadily, but without joy. This depressed Nurse Kelly, who nonetheless rolled up her sleeves to assist him along with Livvie, digging trenches, turning fertilizer, mixing "manure tea" for the sprayers, maintaining the hotbed boxes—all just sweat and seeds and dirt and offal.

"What did you expect?" Livvie asked one tired, rainy night when they sat together in the living room watching Hideo teaching Garvin to play goh. The Issei had tried to teach it to Margaret, but she hadn't the concentration for the game. "It's worse than chess!" she had cried in frustration, surrendering her seat to Garvin, who picked it up immediately and could soon compete with Okamoto like an old fellow Issei. "That's what farming is, right?" Livvie said. "Sweat and dirt."

Margaret said she supposed so, but surrounded by silent people and by rain, she found herself beset by uncharacteristic doubts. Since Fujita's letter about David, she had begun to wonder: If he'd set his own life aside in pursuit of the baby and this Yoneko, hadn't her life also stalled? No longer Jack Kelly's nurse, was she only playing at the gentlewoman farmer to avoid having to find something else to do? "Maybe I don't really like farming," she admitted to Livvie. But she did like it—its tidy always-something-to-do-ness, even the smell of dirt. With Fujita as guide, the everyday garden had been revealed for a vibrant, pulsating shadow world full of ritual and war and hunger and rebirth.

"You liked it with *him*," Livvie muttered. She raised her face, which went from flush to pale. When her eyes found Margaret's, they were glistening wet and hard—half afraid, half belligerent.

Fierce as a hailstorm, it occurred to Margaret what Livvie had been feeling in those last cold months—like a child left out of her parents' private conversations. Livvie thought she and Fujita were somehow a couple. How could I have not seen this before? Margaret wondered. "You think we were . . . intimate," she said carefully.

Livvie nodded. Under Margaret's delicate questioning, she went on to confess in whispers her jealousy, suspicions, profound loneliness, and what she thought she had seen on New Year's Eve. Wide-eyed, Margaret shook and shook and shook her head. Livvie said it had relieved her to learn that she'd been mistaken that New Year's Eve, because although it was no one else's business, the idea that Margaret and Fujita were together in *that way* had hurt her. "Together?" Margaret asked. The idea had lingered in her like a jewel too precious to bring out and wear. That Livvie had somehow witnessed her desire made it seem at once unbearable and possible.

And dangerous, too. Livvie then realized that *she* had inadvertently let loose those rumors that now had Juggeston chilled over. Aghast, she drew her hands over her mouth. "I mean, yes, I thought you two were—were making love," she stuttered. "But I *swear* I would never tell anybody about *that.* All I said was I was alone while you two had each other, and they just inferred. . . . And now that I know you weren't. . . . Oh Margaret, I am so, so sorry."

Margaret placed her hand on Livvie's knee and squeezed it, hard, to keep her voice down. She kept shaking her head, not in anger or disbelief, but for the way this joke, if that's what it was, folded in on itself. "Livvie, the problem is," she whispered slowly, "I think I *would.*"

"Oh," said Livvie—the only word to pass between them during the next two whole games of goh.

Although Margaret didn't want to force Livvie into the confidante's role, she finally said, "Is that mad, silly, wrong? Hypothetically speaking."

The remorse left Livvie's face, replaced by earnest consideration. She set a cigarette burning in the ashtray, closed her eyes, and mused on it for so long it almost seemed to Margaret that she'd fallen asleep. At last she said, "Hypothetically speaking, it would be *hard*, Margaret. And I think much more so for him, and especially in public. Oh, I don't doubt you could make him stay here—"

"Livvie, that's not what I want. That's the problem. He's so . . . *grateful.*"

"When he comes back from Philly," Livvie said, then halted while both of them considered that "when." "He doesn't *belong* here. He's still got a home and business in California, remember? When the war's over, Margaret, what then?"

"Then I'll have radishes," Nurse Kelly said gloomily. With considerable guilt, she caught herself thinking she wouldn't mind the war lasting a little longer. "I'll have lots of *peas.* Oh, I wish I knew what the heck was going on down there!"

Livvie suggested that she call Fujita, but Margaret firmly

refused. "No—not a word. He's got plenty to worry about with . . . with his family," she said. As for Juggeston's mistaken notion of a Widow's Peak romance, Margaret and Livvie decided to take corrective measures. "I don't much like people talking about me until *I* give them something to talk about," Margaret said, trying to recover her humor.

"It was my mistake," Livvie said so sharply that Garvin and Hideo looked up from their game. "I'll fix it. Wait until I get my hands on Frank." Margaret smiled, and Livvie seemed suddenly encouraged, her bearing more straightforward, more adult.

In the next two weeks, however, the women took care not to protest overmuch as they set themselves to dispelling the gossip—chopping away at people's suspicions with a mocking laugh here, a roll of the eyes there. Paulette Pedicott had pitied Margaret as the prey of a fortune-hunting wolf (if only she had *children* to stand by her in her widowhood), but learning of the widower's ennobling quest for the lost little child, David, reduced her to penitential tears.

Confronting Frank Childs at his garage, Livvie decided to keep her hands off the mechanic, who kept his own hands safely in his pockets. The unrepentant Childs grumbled against the "Japs pillaging our women" and so forth. "*Our* women?" Livvie scoffed. "*You* don't have any women to pillage, Frankie." She laughed, her tone modulating between flirtation and scorn. "That's why you've got to imagine illicit affairs where there are none. Just because you're always hard up doesn't mean everybody else is."

Most stubborn and surprising, to Margaret, was Alf Wellington, who would only say, "I'm a friend, Maggie—I don't judge you. You're brave and good-hearted, covering like this, and I don't say anything, but *everyone* knows you gave him money and he disappeared." Despite her firm insistence, she couldn't snap him out of it. "I don't judge you, Maggie," he kept saying. "Not you." But he stood rigid, another hurt child, behind the barrier of his countertop.

This effort, combined with the capricious weather and the intense planting preparations with Hideo, finally left Margaret exhausted, overwhelmed, and victim of a fierce flu for three days. Stuck in bed, she brooded on everything, her own inactivity most of all. I could afford to live without ever finding something else to do, she thought, and die of boredom. She tried returning to *Pride and Prejudice*, thinking it would lift her spirits, but again found that something had spoiled it for her. What? Elizabeth Bennet remained a delightful creature—smart and feisty and willful—a *doer* after her own heart; it was Darcy who'd changed. Before, she had privately fancied that she saw some of that stiff, aloof gentleman in Fujita. But alone with her favorite romance, in her sickbed upstairs in the big house, rereading the same old lines, she found the picture had changed. Now, it was the saucer-wide, dark-hued, flat-nosed face that superimposed itself over the long-beaked, jowly, horsy face of the patrician Darcy in the waistcoat and top hat—and the effect was startling to her.

"He was looked at with great admiration for about half the evening till his manners gave a disgust which turned the tide of his popularity," she read with an inward groan. "For he was discovered to be proud, to be above his company, and above being pleased; and not all his large estate in Derbyshire could then save him from having a most forbidding, disagreeable countenance." And what strange new light was cast on the fantasy as she absently fanned the worn pages to find Mr. Bennet's prenuptial warning to his daughter, "My child, let me not have the grief of seeing *you* unable to respect your partner in life."

"But it's just a book, Maggie," she said, and this time she tossed Jane Austen onto the floor. "Just a stupid book, really." Looking to the window encrusted with remnants of last night's violent, late-season hailstorm, she rose from bed and announced to the seasonal gods: "That's it. I need photosynthesis. No more frosts, no more rain." As proof, she spent the morning designing for the scarecrow a new spring wardrobe—an airy yellow sundress with orange flowers, a sheer neck scarf, and one-button day gloves of white mesh—but even these preparations gave Margaret no pleasure. Glumly, she dressed herself and took the new outfit down to the kitchen. Having her coffee, she stared at the telephone and sighed. He could at least call, she thought.

Scooping up the scarecrow's new outfit, she kicked at the

kitchen door. It opened with a soft swish. Stepping out onto the porch, she was just about to embark on an inner tirade about Fujita's infernal fixing things when she lurched to a halt and cried out. Amid the patches of fading ice and mats of decayed leaves, Widow's Peak sparkled with what appeared to be a hundred dancing gold butterflies. Rising even through the gray-brown slush around the porch, the path to the garage and the gravel drive, scores of infant crocuses and daffodils had arisen so abruptly that it seemed like an act of vandalism. The Peak had never looked like this in Aprils previous. Had Fujita left a gift?

Gripping the railing weakly, she made her way down for a closer look and bent to sniff a patch just beside the stoop. Not much fragrance yet—the nurseryman had a fastidiously light touch in that regard. He had often voiced his deep distaste for "overstinking" a garden and his prejudice against its most unabashed culprit, the so-called English gardening style. He preferred to lace the more subtle daffodils with a stronger-scented variety of narcissus—just a sprinkling—whose white and yellow blooms blended in nicely and added just a hint of perfume. White and yellow. Margaret being Margaret, she couldn't resist adding an interpretative spin. As with his Thanksgiving puttanesca, he had poured real love into liberating these lion-headed flowers from the frosty earth. And why not? He was a nurseryman, albeit one *without* a nursery, she reminded herself, and she knew she *had* to help him get it back. He had to have his own ground, his own home. Even if it pains me, she thought, shaking her head to those vain and lovely new blooms that he'd planted in secret.

"Telegram for W. Fujita," the deliveryman puffed, out of breath from climbing the swampy Peak. Sweat varnished the unruly curls around his ears and temples. No one had answered at the big house. "That's curious," Livvie said. They had planned to have lunch together if Margaret felt well enough—perhaps she was still sick, sleeping. "Well, I'll take it." Though reluctant to surrender the telegram to Livvie, the deliveryman was clearly even more reluctant to climb the hill twice in one day. He released the note and slid back down the gravel drive.

Like Fujita, Livvie Tufteller the war widow was unable to imagine that a telegram might carry glad tidings. Maybe it's his mother? she thought. Maybe she's ill? Or, if it was just farm business—a query from Gila River—Livvie might handle it herself and not bother him. Before reading it, she ritualistically prepared herself, arranging ashtray, cigarette case, lighter, and shot like a tabletop altar around the paper. By now, she knew the name of the Pasadenan Herb Nicholson, who wrote: BAD NEWS CLEMENS GONE STOP NURSERY NEW OWNERS STOP TRYING TO VERIFY WILL WRITE SOON STOP FIND LAWYER END.

"New owners? How can they do that?" Livvie asked, but neither Nicholson nor Garvin knew the answer. "They can't do that," she decided. "There's been a mistake." Her proximity to Mr. Fujita, though, had taught her how unchecked mistakes had a way of snowballing. "I have to let him know," she said.

"How ya gonna reach him?" Garvin asked, looking down at his toy plane, which was becoming his constant accessory, like Bobby Tanaka's wooden bloodhound on wheels.

"Oh, Christ, Garvin, I don't know! I'll have to go find an open telegram office," she snapped, recalling that Mr. Fujita had no phone and that he hadn't responded to her previous telegram. Whether from brandy, nerves, or hurry, she stumbled twice as she whirled about collecting keys, wallet, cigarettes. Squatting on the floor, she half-tugged on one shoe and paused. "I'm sorry," she said. She took his shrug as a sign that things were back to a simmer, then finished dressing herself. Sitting back on the floor, one shoe on, she stared blankly at him. "How *will* I find him?" she asked, checking her watch. "Where did I put his address?" She ransacked the kitchen drawers, the desk, her purse until she found it, then shook her head violently, trying to clear it. "Okay, got it," she said to herself. Then, to Garvin: "I don't know how long I'll be gone, honey. Go over to Margaret's. If she's still sick, help Hideo get her something to eat, okay?" She rose and pulled herself into a light jacket.

"Mmm," Garvin said, noncommittally. Biting his tongue tip in concentration, he carefully wound and latched the rubber band attached to the propeller of his wooden flyer.

"I'll be back soon. Don't get into trouble," Livvie said, less a command than a parental tic. She stirred the contents of her handbag, which sounded like a sack of broken clockwork gears. "And try to get some fresh air, won't you?" She forgot to kiss him good-bye.

When Garvin left the house ten minutes later, he hadn't meant to seek out trouble. However, the boy had been cooped up too long that morning. And his mother had ordered him to get some air, after all. Across the hill, he found neither Mugsie nor Hideo at home, which was fine with him and his airplane. Though he had intended to delay the flyer's christening until Mr. Fujita's return, who knew when that might ever come? Weeks had passed, and still Garvin's letter had received no response. In a pensive mood, he stepped outside and blinked against the sun. All around him the Peak buzzed, a newborn orchestra tuning instruments—transparent chicks and humming katydids, and cicadas, bees, horseflies. He imagined he could hear the moist soil separating with new growth, each blade of grass; but no wind, not the slightest puff. How could Mr. F. miss this? He breathed in a chestful of warm, pollen-filled air. A perfect, perfect day—the kind of spring morning to be airborne.

He strummed the airplane's taut rubber band. *Boing!* Its low hum begged him for release. A vibration ran up his fingertips, as if the pilot buried within the closed wood cockpit had set the engine idling. The hum snaked across the surface of his arms, followed by a wake of goose prickles. In the sunlight the plane's shellac took on an unexpected sheen. Freckling its nose cone, each of the sixteen red "kill" circles showed flawless definition; these were Garvin's additions, painted with the head of a pin, using his mother's magnifying glass; dotting a sharpened pencil eraser with authentic exhaust soot from his mom's car, he'd smudged streaks on the plane's engine. Though shrunken, down to the last detail his plane looked like the real thing. Hummm, it begged. Fly me.

Of all people to share in the maiden voyage of this miniature wonder, why the mean-spirited Fatty Franklin Bunkinson? The day's slow heat made Garvin lazy, but more than mere convenience compelled him to seek out his closest neighboring schoolmate; he imagined the boy's fat face exploding with envy.

Mrs. Bunkinson greeted Garvin coolly. "Your new man seems to have vanished, Garvin," she said, while Franklin finished taking out the trash before going to play.

"He's just on a trip," Garvin replied. "He'll be back," he said, because it gratified him to lie to the unlikeable woman.

The boy did not believe it, though, or he would not have found himself at the crest of Widow's Peak, in a moment both proud and bittersweet, locking the taut rubber band for launching. He could see all of Juggeston—all that existed in his world to be seen by human eyes. He willed the remote height to be anywhere else. His imagination laid another map over the tiny Massachusetts town, light and perfect as a shaken linen spread.

Captain Tufteller flew fearlessly and tirelessly—from feverish to freezing in the extreme altitudes of the treacherous Hump over the Burma Road. His mission: Deliver payloads of munitions to the besieged allies of Kunming on the far side of Widow's Peak. He must brave determined resistance. He could hear the scrambling of talons on the overhanging branches, the great black-raven squadrons idling, waiting to attack. Squirrels lurked within every bramble, garter snakes in their trenches. Such dicey conditions called for careful strategizing, and Corporal Bunkinson's men cleared the way, firing barrage after barrage of pebbles to dissuade all challengers. In a flurry of black alarm, the ravens skittered on their perches, and the good captain's rubber engines roared to life again and again, each takeoff potentially the last. So deeply devoted was he to his loyal Chinese allies, he continued to fly well after his ground support had exhausted itself.

"Come on, Franklin," Garvin shouted in his scratchy, radio-transmitter voice. "The place is crawling with the Enemy. This is no time to go yellow on me!"

Garvin was deeply gratified to see Franklin red-faced with jealousy, rubbing his sore elbow and picking crusts of mud off his palms. He had given up pleading, "Let me try. Come on, I want to try." Instead, he sulked, following the warplane with his eyes as it arced just inches above the shoulder of the scarecrow. Then a mischievous expression came over his face. Scooping up a handful of stones, he let the pebble pile cascade from his left palm into his right, then cocked his arm. Garvin began his run too late. Franklin, releasing the volley with a grunt, raked the scarecrow top to toe with flak. The pebbles thudded, crackled. There was a glassy shattering. Her yellow bonnet slid backward at a precarious angle.

"Yes!" the marksman shouted triumphantly. He bent to reload and extracted a damp mound of earth. Squinting, he raised his leg in a baseball wind-up and had just begun throwing all his weight into his swing when Garvin slammed him face-first onto the ground. "Hey!" The word erupted with a spray of soot.

"Not her," Garvin hissed, knees bent, ready to knock his opponent down again.

"Are you some kind of kook?" Franklin whined, pushing himself up. "Uh-oh," he said, looking sorrowfully down at his dirty clothing.

"Just don't do that." Shaking, Garvin stepped back, allowing the boy to rise. Embarrassed, he picked a twig out of Franklin's hair—the light brown strands on his forehead were also stiff with soil.

Fingering the airplane, Garvin looked into the sky. In the time they had been playing, the shadows of the trees had pivoted to face the opposite direction; his campaign to liberate Burma had lasted hours. Regarding his sad playmate, Garvin strummed the rubber band thoughtfully, like a musician testing his lyre, reveling in its vibrations.

"Come on," Franklin pleaded again. "Let me try it, can't ya? It's the least you can do . . . just look at me! Or maybe I'll go home."

Garvin grinned, ready to refuse. Franklin's covetous hands were planted in his pockets, maybe to keep him from grabbing the toy. Garvin's eyes began to twitch, reminding him of their brawl eons ago. Sizing up the pudgy boy, he said in a low, matter-of-fact voice, "I could pulverize you."

Sheepish, Franklin discovered some sooty point of fascination on his shoes. The spring air held them like still bathwater. Garvin nodded in his own affirmation: not a threat, just a simple truth. With a shrug, he surrendered the toy. Sometimes there was nothing for it but to placate the natives, throw them a bone. "But be careful with it," he ordered, "or else."

Boredom. An hour later the boys sat in the lengthening shade of the garage comparing their swollen elbows, absentmindedly scraping the driveway gravel into mounds. The day seemed to have too much life, to draw on forever. By now accustomed to the steady buzz of spring, Garvin wondered at the human silence of the Peak. What a hullabaloo adults could make, he realized. The slope was strung with twine and markers and buckets and hoses and early vegetation. He tried to teach Franklin the game of goh, but the bonehead couldn't even get past the explanation of the rules. Then Franklin taught Garvin how to make birdcalls by clamping a grass blade between the sides of both stiff thumbs, splaying the fingers like legs of a crab, and blowing into the slit below the first knuckles. When Franklin did it, a piercing whistle sounded, reaching even to the ravens in the highest treetops. After a few toots, the blade would split or grow soggy, producing a sheeplike bleat. Garvin kept blowing too forcefully and only managed a splatting noise. As he practiced blade after blade, Franklin took a walk around the garage and attached greenhouse. Returning, he asked, "This is where he lives?"

"Hm? Oh, yeah," Garvin blubbered into his hands. Flecks of green like shards of a broken Coca-Cola bottle ringed him.

"What's all this junk around the garage?" Still fortified with the bundled straw of winter, the garage resembled an enormous compost heap.

"Just insulation," said Garvin. "The furnace in there heats the greenhouse. He says you gotta keep the plants warm. The germinating seedlings."

"German-ating? It's weird. It's not even cold out. It's spring."

"Not when he left," Garvin said, realizing it.

"Let's take a look," said Franklin, already trying the latch.

"It was still cold then," Garvin mumbled. Although he knew they shouldn't be playing around the greenhouse, he had to follow Franklin inside. He rationalized the excursion as just a looksee, just to make sure everything's okay. I'll just check the furnace, he told himself, and then we'll leave. Curious Franklin poked about inside like a bloodhound sniffing after crime clues.

He squatted beneath the coal beds, examined the lethal-looking shelf of garden chemicals. Garvin was looking for clues of another kind. Above the barely warm coal beds, the great flats of seedlings had been lovingly but mistakenly overwatered—probably by his mother. Hideo knew his business, but he was only one man and couldn't watch over *everything.* The peas looked spindly and limp; the Japanese eggplant stalks were beginning to brown over. The evidence of neglect astounded Garvin. If nothing else, the man who'd come and befriended him a half year ago was attentive—he might either abandon the project or he would care for it, but he neglected or forgot nothing. Or almost.

They passed down the long aisle into the garage. They snooped around for a long while in that treasure trove of mechanical devices and workbenches and gardening supplies, but Franklin grew restless again. He discovered the coal-burning furnace in the corner and smacked its side with his stick, reveling in the thick, metallic clanks. Unlatching the sooty door released a flurry of fine ashes. Igniting the tip of a stick, he branded a leg of the wooden workbench.

"Cut that out!" Garvin shouted. The stick issued choking tails of smoke—Mr. F. had said that was bad for the plants. "Let's go! We're done here." When he shoved Franklin toward the garage-door exit, it surprised him to see dusk awaiting them outside. How long had they lingered in there? And where was everybody? Where were all the adults? Where's *Mom?* Garvin wondered, as he pushed against Franklin's pudgy back, which stopped short at the doorway and pushed back with more heft.

The harder Tufteller pressed him, the heavier Franklin grew until both boys fell backward into the dark garage with a crash. Empty terra-cotta pots crashed all around them; those pots filled with earth exploded in loud pops. The one that landed silently on Franklin's stomach made him jackknife and roll off of Garvin, who screamed in a panic, "You stupid *jerk*!"

Determined to pulverize his neighbor, every force within Garvin quickened: the beating in his temples, the pounding of his heart. His palms turned into fists. Though heftier, Franklin was a slow, awkward coward, and large enough to be an easy target even though a speck of dirt blinded Garvin's left eye.

For a time, Garvin held a controlled distance from his adversary, jabbing at the freckled cheeks. For a time, he fought with an agility uncommon to very young boys, and it might have been safe—as safe as bloody noses, safe as bruises. Then eventually, perhaps inevitably, they fell into a clench, both boys slippery with exertion and the misty heat. The garage floor seemed to buckle beneath them, followed by more thuds and an enormous crashing of pottery and glass. And still it might have been safe. Squirming, shoving, heaving himself to a seat above Franklin, he pinned the squealing boy's arms under his knees. Whipped on by guilt, nothing could hold him back now—not even the vague realization of the door opening behind him or the shriveled shadow figure entering—an old woman, hobbling, dropping a basket, waving her arms. With a queasy exhilaration he sought Bunkinson's swollen eye socket, fired home, and felt the other boy's legs convulse beneath him.

He heard first the thud—Franklin's foot hollowly echoing on iron—the furnace doors. Then the smashing of pottery, a shriek in some queer, alien tongue, and a crash as the furnace's face toppled forward. A hiss of steam surrounded him, and then the dragon's breath consumed him. Did he really see her, the Annisquam Witch? Or feel the grinding secret path through the abandoned quarry? At the last, he felt his flesh seared from him as he sank into the churning broth of her cauldron. And then there was nothing.

Six months after he'd first arrived in Juggeston, the weary Fujita again ascended the drive up to the nojo he'd neglected too long. In the fading light, the stalks of the tulips he'd scattered at the base looked like tiny sticks of unlit incense. Passing on, his eyes found a portion of the terraced vegetable beds, where his sculpting had changed the very contours of the hill. But toward what harvest? Even by Juggeston's standards, it was late in the season, he thought, sniffing at the air.

With the warm ocean wind at his back, he didn't smell the ash until he'd almost reached the garage. The light switch was out, and his first careful steps inside met with a crunching of pottery that immediately recalled his vandalized nursery. Bending down, he felt the moist floor and soggy clumps of potting soil and coal. The garage felt unusually cool; he could barely make out the furnace and the broken steam pipe. "Goddam it," he muttered. Certain of vandalism, he dropped his heavy suitcase, checked the greenhouse—it was okay—then headed for the kitchen, the only lit room in the house. He was winded. To manage the hike up the hill, he'd strapped Garvin's toy musket onto his back, and he wore Livvie's tricorn cap so it wouldn't be crushed in his bag, but the other Philadelphia gifts, especially the pewter, made his climb rough going. Calvin must have failed to get through by phone, or someone would have picked him up in the car. He knocked before letting himself in, then counted to ten before opening the door. From the gasp inside, it sounded as if he'd startled Margaret anyway. "Sorry," he called. "It's just me."

The old woman held so still that he didn't notice her at first. Her tattered brown shawl and boots and skirt all blended with the shadows in the crook behind the porch door, where she quivered in fright. The rustling of the notepaper gripped to her chest alerted Fujita to her presence, and when he swung on her, the woman gave a little hop.

"Oh. Hello," he said softly, doubting that she could have been the vandal. She appeared to be made out of earth, and about a hundred years old. "Who are you?" he asked. Perhaps she was a friend of Margaret's. But wasn't he really an outsider here, too? "Sorry. Bill Fujita," he said, extending his hand. "I live next door. I've been out of town for a while," he added. When he backed away, she relaxed enough to pull the note away from her heart. Inching around the half-open door, she held the paper out to him, pointed to the table, and said something indecipherable. What Garvin took for a witch's incantation sounded to Fujita like and unlike Spanish—he'd grown up in Los Angeles, after all. Portuguese, he guessed. He waited for her to say more; as an immigrant's son, he knew one could decipher a great deal from non-English-speaking people if only one listened patiently and concentrated on body language. Also, he knew the erasing effect of nerves on one's vocabulary in a second language. He dug around his mind's attic for some Spanish phrases she might halfway make out.

"Enfermeira," she said, pointing to the table. She seemed guilty. "The boy."

"Nurse," he strained to interpret. He went to scratch his head and remembered the tricorn cap. "A note," he said, doffing the hat, unslinging the musket from his back. "You were leaving Margaret a note."

"A note!" the woman cried, excited and terrified, and she dropped the paper onto the floor. When he bent for it, she scuttled out onto the porch.

"Boys to hospital. Burned bad," he read. "What boys?" he asked, but with a hissed farewell to the scarecrow, the Annisquam Witch had disappeared into the darkening Walpurgisnacht, Witches' Night, exactly six months since she had last haunted Widow's Peak, and since Fujita himself had first arrived.

"Relationship?" asked the hospital's desk nurse, in a tone of annoyed boredom. A wiry, unkempt woman with an impatient pout, she continued holding a phone receiver to her ear with one hand while extracting Garvin's file from a drawer with the other.

Here we go again, Fujita thought. "I'm his, um, guardian," he said. "One of them." The nurse's lip curled up on one side when she finally glanced up at him, but scanning Garvin's chart, she announced that the patient was sedated and critical and couldn't have visitors. "You can speak with his physician." Scribbling the doctor's name and office number on a slip of scrap paper, she returned to her phone call.

From the start, Fujita's hurried tour through the hospital did not inspire confidence. Almost no directions were posted anywhere, and he became soundly lost in the mazelike corridors strewn with abandoned gurneys, laundry carts, IV racks, crutches, and wheelchairs. The building stank, too. Not of disinfectant—Fujita wouldn't mind that. Sterility is good, he thought. Rather, it smelled filthy and positively rife with germs. Disinfectant was in short supply; the medical industry had devoted much of its resources, including skilled personnel, to the war efforts abroad.

Racing about looking for the office, it unsettled Fujita to note that this hospital's clientele appeared to be mostly military. Popping his head into one suite, he saw a child-sized figure swathed in white. Halting, it took only two heartbeats to realize that he faced not a boy—not Garvin—but the half-body of a quadriplegic soldier. It took only that long to register the terror in his bandage-masked eyes. Perhaps any stranger would have frightened the infantryman in his utter vulnerability, but recalling the twitchy, paranoid shell shock of Johnny Salisbury, Fujita became self-conscious of his likeness to the Enemy. Although he had little love for soldiers in general, he had much sympathy for these men and bore them enough respect to avoid stumbling broadly upon them while hunting around the hospital for office 17-2B.

Overwhelmed as any food cannery, any appliance factory or steel forge, and direly understaffed, the hospital had come to depend on med students, nurses, orderlies, midwives, volunteers like Margaret and Calvin. Overwrought interns and residents tested themselves against the limits of their experience. Such a young man was Garvin's Dr. Small, whose appearance only exacerbated Fujita's already considerable dread of doctors. Certainly not yet thirty, the first-year resident bore an older man's wrinkles around his eyes, which were bloodshot and cupped with bruise-colored half-moons. A shocking white stripe cut through his chestnut hair. Seeing Fujita, he snapped out of his trance, shot up behind his desk, extended his hand with the alert quickness of guiding a scalpel through the air, and became all business.

"Here's the short version," he said, and as he led Fujita to the Critical Care section, he rattled off the facts. Having suffered severe burns on his back, legs, arms, and neck, Garvin required skin-graft surgery to prevent fluid loss and infection. Both of these could be fatal. The hospital's reserves for everything were at an all-time low. A live donor must be located. "Decisions must be made now," Small said, more to himself than to Fujita. They halted by a window into the ward. Fujita gasped. Inside, Garvin lay on his stomach, bandaged from ankle to jaw. "Are there parents, do you know?" Small asked.

"A mother, yes. I haven't been able to reach her, but I've left messages." And where the hell is everybody? he wondered. The nurse had said an ambulance brought the boys in.

"We can wait, then," Dr. Small said, clearly reluctant. Not only was a delay worse for Garvin, he told Fujita, but since the Allied push from Leipzig to Munich, a bumper crop of casualties was due within seventy-two hours. "But we can't wait long." Small's attention faded then, and Fujita grew impatient—unwilling to wait at all.

"Goddam it," he said to his own face, reflected in the window. "Okay. Let's do it right away, then." He anticipated resistance. At Small's delayed response, he said, "The sooner, the better—that's what you're saying, right? You *can* use me for a donor, right? Use my skin? My *yellow* skin. If you're not willing, tell me right now—we'll save Garvin a lot of time and I'll find another doctor. Can you use me? Yes or no?"

The physician's expression betrayed only his weariness. Then he nodded and smiled sympathetically, as if this would have been his own decision, their roles reversed. "You should think it over," he suggested. "There are serious risks."

"Yes. Let's do it right away," Fujita repeated, his patience exhausted. "What needs to be done now?"

The doctor hesitated. "Let's get some air," he sighed, leading Fujita by the elbow down the hall to an outside courtyard.

The North Shore coast on April 30, 1945, was cool, cloudless, and comfortable after a week's rain. It calmed both men. If the surgeon-in-training doubted his ability in any way, only his body revealed it. His hand quivered as he lit a cigarette and sucked as wolfishly as Lil Wellington. He's young and fatigued and doesn't look too clean, either, Fujita decided. As if reading his mind, Dr. Small drew a deep whiff of himself. "Goddam, I *stink*," he said, grinning. When he shook his head, his unwashed hair remained perfectly motionless, cemented by multiple applications of tonic. "I haven't been home in a couple of days," he explained.

"You look like you've earned a break," Fujita agreed.

Small shrugged. "Don't worry," he said. "I'm more alert than I look. I *will be*," he amended, "in surgery. Normally, we'd consult about this. Normally . . ." Using up precious energy, he explained that *normally* he'd consult with the senior surgeon about techniques; they'd weigh the benefits to the recipient against the costs to the donor and, frankly, to hospital resources. Fujita wondered, How can you weigh the fates of a healthy child, accidentally burned over some 60 percent of his little body, or an eighteen-year-old soldier—also essentially a child—burned very purposefully on 45 percent of his larger body? Normally, Small would show photographs, explain the risks and cosmetic effects. Full-thickness grafts extending to the dermis could, under optimal conditions and if they "took" to the wound, minimize abnormal skin appearance and function. Yet, with a large, thermal burn such as Garvin's—so susceptible to infection, and covering too much area—the doctor would opt for a split-thickness graft. The wisdom of Dr. Small's training held that these should be thin as possible—through the epithelium only. Normally, only the most skilled surgeons were entrusted with the task—essentially, shearing lubricated strips of skin with a freehand knife similar to a straight-edge razor. Conditions at that hospital, however, were far from normal. And was there ever an *optimal* war?

Fortunately, the war provided such budding professionals with much practice in skin-graft techniques and its perils. "It can be long and unpredictable and exceedingly painful," he warned, meaning the surgery and recuperation, though he might have been referring to the war, too. Facing eastward, they could not see the ocean from that courtyard, but the breeze was coastal; it revivified the doctor. Fujita, too, had a nose for the sea, which he associated with his tough-willed parents, and with hope. And could these men also have detected in that air a hint of the war's end? The trace of gasoline and hair and burning flesh, so appropriate to Witches' Night? It wafted in not from Juggeston but from a pyre in Berlin, where Walpurgisnacht was already well under way at the *führerbunker*. Where that night the German führer, having first poisoned his dog, Blondi, then his newlywed bride, Eva, with his own destruction heralded the way toward V-E Day.

"No, I don't suppose it will be easy," Fujita said. "Um, can I have a cigarette?" Only the third cigarette of his life, how much more smoothly did it fill him than on Sacaton Butte above Gila River with Tony. The nurseryman and healer regarded each other as two green paratroopers about to take their first jump together.

"I could use some . . . I could stand to spend some time alone with my wife," young Dr. Small suddenly announced with a confessional smile. Fujita nodded and said, "Yes, yes. I'm sure." Having grafted plants himself, and knowing the care, the needed dexterity, the possible complications and infections of that far less delicate operation, he decided he could not do enough to bolster this tired man's peace of mind—if it eased the fellow to wear a dress beneath his scrubs, that would suit the patient just perfectly. "But other than that," the resident said, "I'm holding up just fine. Don't you worry." Then, stamping out the second cigarette he'd only just lit, he said, "Okay. It's show time."

As Fujita was prepped for surgery, Dr. Small said that another reason for haste was that split-thickness skin grafts, meant to cover large areas, were best "harvested" from the thigh, thin enough to allow rapid healing of the donor site. This accommodated further harvests in the not-unlikely case the first attempt failed. Fujita noted that the doctor avoided the word *cut*. Still, he stiffened on the operating table. Garvin was small for his age, but not *that* small. He glanced down while a nurse busily painted his legs with disinfectant, and wondered and worried about his favorite nurse and Livvie. Where were they? He asked an assistant to call Alf Wellington, that the shopkeeper might spread the news and locate the women. To steady his nerves, he envisioned his Pasadena greenhouses, their cool luminescence just before dusk. His favorite hour: when the sun pooled in the pouty lips of the cattleya orchids and the wide cups of the mountain laurel blooms; when Mari emerged from the shop to drag him in for supper, Tamie returned from her constitutional, and he and Tony drew the sliding doors of the storage shed closed. Then the anesthesia settled in like the end of a busy day, and Fujita slept in peace.

The pain in his legs and rump roared like battlefield trumpets. Unable to focus on the figure in the doorway, his first waking thought was: medication! "Is that the nurse?" he asked hoarsely.

"Yes and no," returned a familiar voice. In dungarees and a

man's work shirt, her red hair falling loosely from the familiar pinned bun, Margaret Balford Kelly looked positively proletariat.

"So," she said, and to Fujita, her grin had an analgesic effect. "How was Philadelphia?"

He tried to laugh but emitted instead a wet-lipped, toady sound. She swept across the room to his bed, drew the curtain closed, and took his hand. "Garvin's okay for now. Livvie's with him. Well, I won't bother asking how you feel," she said. Then she frowned, perhaps recalling that it was the phrase she'd used to describe the body-cast boys. Fujita nodded. He felt as if he'd been flayed from his belt line down and half submerged in a pool of salt. An accurate sensation: It was the burn of saline that sizzled up through him from his stripped lower limbs. How did he expect to feel afterward?

Unfortunately, he did not awake to such stinging *afterward*, but during. Joining them, Dr. Small explained that the inflammation in Garvin's wounds had precluded immediate surgery, so they had to wait. Once incised, the grafting tissue must be "stored"—lacking certain technology, this was often done by replacing it on the donor site. It could stay there as long as five days, but after twenty-four hours, the donor's bleeding and pain increased. Dr. Small hoped it wouldn't take twenty-four hours but did not sound confident.

"If it does," Fujita managed to say, "I hope you won't take *these* twenty-four hours to go spend time with your wife." Margaret raised an eyebrow, and the physician blushed.

Small explained to them that he would use a meshed skin graft; passed through a mechanical device, the skin strip emerged pierced with rows of incisions; it expanded under pressure and was altogether more flexible in matching the body's landscape. Fujita wondered, Would the impression of this lattice of teardrop holes remain fixed in the boy's skin? Though no dermatologist, the Nisei knew something about skin, about blood and pigmentation, and he feared for the boy's disfigurement. Would his own sallow skin, once removed, lighten? Would it transform—would it *revert*—to white? Fujita recalled the much publicized home-front hoopla in which protesters attacked field medics for giving white soldiers "Negro blood" transfusions.

Was there ever a dying teenager who really cared, who chose to expire rather than alter, dilute, poison those superior fluids within him? Who feared darkening more than death?

"Good riddance," Dr. Small opined, shrugging. "There are lots of other men who could use that blood." Then he left them alone.

It concerned Fujita, though. Did the protests have any scientific basis at all? he wanted to know. Scars lightened—they didn't tan like normal skin. Or would Garvin be forever branded, scarred . . . yellow? Enmeshed by yellow diamonds? Overcome by the yellow?

"For God's sake, it's just cosmetics," Margaret said, her voice tinged with frustration. "It's just pigment, just *skin*."

"No," Fujita retorted, shaking his head firmly. "No, it's not."

"I think it's fair to say you saved Garvin's life," Margaret reassured him, brushing the hair away from his dark, heavy-lidded eyes. "He's lucky to have you."

"I just don't know," Fujita whispered, but then he closed his eyes at her touch. "That's good," he murmured, dozing off again. "That's good."

In fact, it took Dr. Small and his assistants nearly seventy-two watchful hours to prime Garvin's wounds for surgery. Fujita could not walk (they forbade him even to stand upright), and no one would convey him to Critical Care to see the boy, not even on a gurney. He tried writing a note, but managed only, "I got you a musket, but I forgot it at home," then gave up, his energy spent from fighting—denying—the booming pain in his legs. While the staff prepped Garvin for the operation, Livvie tore herself away to sit with Fujita for the first time.

Before anything else, he noticed that her attire had reverted to a formless brown sweater slumped over her shoulders and a long, nondescript dress with deep pockets. She looked like that strange old Portuguese woman lurking behind Margaret's kitchen door. For a time, during Ernie Tanji's tenure at the nojo, when they were all working together, Fujita had hoped she'd sworn off for good her frumpy, body-masking style. Take off that damned sweater! he wanted to say. This was not out of any prurient impulse—though admittedly, she had a lovely figure, and a relatively youthful one at that. Rather, he had thought her *behavior* was becoming more youthful, too; when he saw her in a sundress dancing with Ernie, he had recalled that she was only thirty. The age distance between them had bothered him a little—for example, how she so easily sympathized with Yoneko—but how wonderful to see her liking her own appearance. Now she looked older again. She looked not only haggard and disheveled—that was to be expected—but haunted.

"Hi," she said, sitting next to him, hugging herself. Though her eyes glowed red, she didn't cry—not right away. Instead, she seemed angry, clenching her jaw as she measured what to say to him. "I should have come before," she began. "I'm sorry."

Fujita, drugged, waved away her apology. "I know how you feel," he said. "It would be a kind of relief to take blame for everything, but like you said, it's conceited. Nothing's your fault. Some things can't be helped. Maybe you resent me for this, or think it should be you lying here. It's selfish of people to do you favors without permission. I'll understand if you don't want Garvin . . . if you want another donor. But it's a favor to me, too, Livvie. I'm sorry. I'm sorry."

Then Livvie really cried, on and on, as she tried to explain her real anger—how she had taken the car to the next town where she could send a telegram. She would not tell him which telegram until after the operation. "Well, I ran out of gas," she said guiltily. Nodding, Fujita began to say that she must have been in some hurry, but he stopped himself. She'd broken down on an empty rural route, and it took forever to find a phone. She had no choice but to call Childs—the only mechanic around. "I didn't expect him to be thrilled about it, but . . . but . . ." It seemed she would choke for sobbing; Fujita raised a hand but failed to stop her. "*Three hours!*" she wailed. "Three hours that monster made me wait, when I should have been . . ."

"I know," Fujita said softly. He did, too. He knew her anger, born of the revelation that fate could easily overturn her young life *twice*. When she'd calmed down, he asked, "Hey. Are you still 'Convinced'?" She frowned but then shrugged. It was the right thing for him to say.

The operation took place over two days. Fujita did not get to see Garvin until a week after they had first arrived at the hospital. That day, May 7, a Nikkei stranger in dirty overalls and boots and a hat of battered brown felt woke the recuperating Fujita from a nap. Presenting a wrapped tin of manju, he self-consciously introduced himself as Charlie Plotnik. "It's an adopted name. I was an orphan," he blurted, though Fujita hadn't asked. Unable to speak but ravenous, the patient gratefully bit into the doughy rice cake and, discovering a milk-chocolate core, nearly spit it out. "Melted Hershey bars," Charlie said. Pulling up a chair, he gabbed away for twenty minutes about his expectant wife, Olive—who was responsible for the mutant manju—Juggeston's weather, and rumors of ex-internees who had braved the return trek to the West Coast. A real talker, he had lots of energy. A good thing, since Fujita would be crippled for some time and Hideo was no spring chicken.

Still disoriented, Fujita waved for Charlie to slow down. "Plotnik? What block were you in? Were you in Butte or Canal?" he asked, unable to place the face or name.

The boy appeared confused. "No. Me and Olive were at Heart Mountain camp."

Fujita didn't understand. "In Wyoming?" Charlie nodded. "So, how did you find your way to Margaret's place? Do you have people in Gila?"

Again, the boy seemed lost. "Oh. I just met Mrs. Kelly at the arcade yesterday. I went there with Mr. Pedicott, you know. I just started working on his farm, see, and Olive helps Mrs. Pedicott with the kids. And boy, does she need help," he added with a snicker.

"So, so, you don't work on the Peak?" Fujita lay still, considering it.

According to Charlie, a few of the local Friends had followed the Peak's example and invited some dozen Japanese Americans to work in Juggeston. "I guess me and Olive are the first," he said. "Haven't seen any others, anyway, but that's okay. Maybe it's better to just sort of spread out for a while. Stir up the mix a bit. You know?" Fujita regarded his sheared legs. He recalled Calvin's first meeting with Frank Childs—*Shit Christ! There's two of you!*—and grinned. As farmer Pedicott himself had observed the day Fujita became Juggeston's first Nikkei: The meetinghouse is tiny—things echo.

He suspected he might be hallucinating the Nisei named Plotnik when four patients, racing neck-and-neck in their wheelchairs and whooping, zoomed past the door. Rolling up from the rear, behind by several lengths, one young man was struggling under the added weight of the candy striper sitting in his lap. Like water from a crumbling dike, a din of clanging bedpans and hurled breakfast trays and drumming crutches and some loud weeping poured down the corridors. They transferred me to the mental ward, Fujita thought. He heard a shrill woman's voice—"It's over! It's over!"—and the squeal of radios tuning in.

Fujita and Charlie Plotnik shook hands to commemorate the end of what had begun five years ago as the War in Europe. For a moment, they even forgot about the other war. "Go to your Olive," Fujita ordered. "But do me one favor first." At Fujita's behest, Charlie swiped a wheeled gurney to "sneak" him toward the critical ward. They rolled into the throng about as sneakily as an elephant wading through a crowded Bombay bazaar, but in the swelling pandemonium, no one seemed to notice or care. Fujita sat upright, hands protectively above his outstretched thighs. To his left, a one-eyed soldier, who hadn't forgotten the other war, pointed at him and shouted, "One down, one to go!" To his right, a more robust, uniformed GI bent over a nurse in a passionate smooch—Fujita could only see her shapely, white-stockinged legs. When they broke apart, the nurse kissed Fujita's cheek. The stubble-jawed GI kissed him, too. Every bump and nudge to the gurney sent a fire through his legs. "Get me out of here!" he cried to Charlie, who made honking noises like a truck's horn.

Once they'd pierced the heavy double doors leading to Critical Care, the halls fell so quiet they wondered if the news had yet made it to the ward. It had, judging from the terribly emotional way Margaret ran toward them. Fujita feared for his thighs—it appeared that she might be unable to brake on the slippery floor, or might launch herself on top of him. Instead, halting before him and cupping his head in a hand, she gently laid him down on his back. "Thank you, Mr. Plotnik, but I think

I'll drive now," she said, relieving him of the gurney.

Warning Fujita to "hold on tight," she steered her patient to Garvin's curtain-enclosed cubicle. A clear tent hung above the bed to fend off contamination. There Livvie held Garvin's hand and cried and cried over him, and they parked his gurney beside the sleeping child-mummy in the hospital bed. What little could be seen of the boy beneath the wrappings was salmon-colored, and Fujita had to look away. Two beds down, a nurse was drawing a sheet over a patient's face; Fujita hoped the soldier had heard the news before expiring. Closing his eyes, he placed a hand against the sterile tent plastic, precisely two and a half inches above Garvin's swaddled paw, and fell back asleep, too.

For a time, the staff allowed Fujita to remain in Garvin's ward, in the bed where the dead man had lain. Waking, the boy could barely talk or hear under his bandage mask. They whispered to each other via Livvie and Margaret or, occasionally, the Negro man from Detroit named Clyde who lay between them. Fujita would say something, Garvin would ask, "What?" and Clyde would relate, "Man says, 'Hey pal, don't go getting any infection 'cause'. . . Say that last part again. Oh, yeah. 'Cause his legs hurt like the dickens and he doesn't want to do this again." Garvin would respond, via Clyde. "Kid says, 'Okay,' he'll try."

Back on the nojo, Hideo Okamoto was proving to be among the best decisions Fujita had made after Gila. He visited the hospital only once, bringing an extraordinary bouquet of daffodils, white narcissus, and a sprinkling of orange-pink tulips. "Why do you waste time visiting me?" Fujita barked. He whipped a tulip against his bed railing, accidentally clipping his thigh as with a riding crop. They'd stopped medicating him the day before, and he bit his lip until he bled. Livvie scolded him; he glared at her, growling like a sick bear.

"Sumimasen," he said to Hideo when the pain passed. *Sumimasen*, or, "It—this guilt I feel—is without end," is a common "I'm sorry" for minor transgressions, but his tone was less than sincere. "Yurushite kudasai," he begged, but old Okamoto had already forgiven him, understanding that in those orange blooms, Fujita saw how far along the season had progressed since he'd been away. The Nisei could have wept for his frustration. "You've been invaluable, Okamoto-kun," he admitted, "but you need help. And I have this little problem . . ." He indicated his useless legs. "Call Mr. Johnson to get some more fellows out here right away." Hideo, who had already anticipated and worked this out with Margaret, said only, "Yes, an excellent idea." The Issei delivered a two-hour progress report, then remembered to deliver the latest telegram from the Nicholsons.

"Uh-oh," Livvie said, reaching too slowly to intercept it. "Before you read that, there's something we've been waiting to . . ." She fished in her handbag for the first message, folded there since that fateful Walpurgisnacht. By the time she found it, Fujita was pale as a fish, reading:

NEW OWNER CONGLOMERATE BUYING UP NISEI PROPERTIES FOR DISCOUNT NURSERY CHAIN STOP POSSIBLE HIGHWAY ROUTE AND MUCH PROFITS STOP BILL I THINK THE LORD MAY HAVE GIVEN YOU A REAL LEGAL CASE TO CHALLENGE THE WHOLE THING STOP MADELINE AND I CAN HELP STOP PLEASE ADVISE STOP HERBERT END.

The trio sat as still as if suddenly locked within a glacier. Respectfully, Hideo turned away. Livvie froze with a hand in her purse—in its mouth, Fujita could see the cap of a silver flask and the corner of the first note: NURSERY NEW OWNERS STOP. He reached out to withdraw both items, ignored Livvie's "Do you think you should?" and then gulped at her brandy desperately, anticipating in the telegram a discomfort more severe than having his skin sheared off. He passed the remnants to Livvie; she waved the flask on to Hideo, who, though no drinker, would not let his boss drink alone. He rose as if for a toast, quaffed, bowed, and left the room.

"We wanted to wait until you were well," Livvie mumbled, but the telegram had deafened Fujita to explanations or sympathy, and she followed Okamoto out.

"Until I was well," the embittered patient echoed. "Yes."

At the base of the Peak, the tulips glowed like blown sticks of incense in the purpling evening light. Farmer Fujita did not love them, though; these scrappy orphans had to fend for themselves;

a few might be adopted by people in passing cars. "I just tossed them there. They're merely ornamental, merely for color," he told Margaret, who resented the "merely" and said so. But returning to the nojo so late in the season, the wounded farmer had eyes only for the scarecrow, keeper of that token of promise he and Garvin shared.

Assured that the transplant had succeeded, Dr. Small released Fujita to the custody and home care of Nurse Kelly. Eventually, he would regard his wounds as a mixed blessing, in the spirit that Calvin Igawa considered the dissolution of the Japanese-American community a fortunate, if painful, by-product of the war. Recuperation gave him time to wrestle his fury at Clemens into submission, when he might have charged back out west as blindly as he had pursued Yoneko. He had time to visit with Garvin, still in the earliest stages of his long healing process; they usually played goh, which Garvin could manage well enough while lying on his stomach, like a turtle with its shell ripped off. And Fujita had time to rest, and to envision and reenvision his California homecoming. He had time to talk with Margaret about it, and about David, old Moses, farming—a lot. And he had time to replant himself in the work that nourished him.

The arrival of the brothers Akira and Benny Sato stretched the capacity of the office-cum-dormitory, and Margaret moved Fujita into the unused sitting room on the first floor of the big house. There he could come and go without climbing steps, and she could keep an eye on him. Sometimes he slept in the greenhouse. His first few days home he nearly drove the Satos right back to Gila River. Every inch as irritating as old Miyake, he orchestrated their labor from his wheelchair, waving his arms, shaking his fists, and even accidentally setting himself wheeling down the uneven slope. The Satos had to drop everything to extricate him from a bush.

"You're being a real nuisance," Margaret said. Over his protests, she tethered his chair to the scarecrow, where he was a useful appendage. A scarecrow's effectiveness is always short-lived. Crows and blue jays wise up quickly; within mere weeks they are found in a coffee klatch on the effigy's shoulder. In late spring, with the seedlings particularly vulnerable, the birds were capable of wiping out 75 percent or more of a small farm's crops. Scarecrows should be moved about, dressed up, and appear animate—the clang and flash of attached metal pie plates or a clapping wind sock always helped. A top-notch scarecrow, Fujita knew, was a dynamic being—boisterous, loud, never content to rest. Circling about on his leash, the disgruntled overseer made an excellent scarecrow for a while. He could walk with a cane by the second week, but his thighs and rump still felt tender and tight; with his ever-stiff neck, he strode about rather like a toy soldier. He'd taken to wearing old zoot-suit pants Livvie had found, but often the cloth brushed him the wrong way and he'd freeze up midstride rigidly as the old scarecrow or, as Margaret jokingly called him, "a wood nymph."

There was also time for Margaret to convince the attorney Randolph Hessing to lend them legal assistance. A friend of a friend of Jack's, the Harvard professor had the lean elegance of a whippet, with silvering hair and piercing gray eyes. Why should Fujita trust lawyers or laws? Having followed the internment more closely than most easterners, Mr. Hessing opined that "the law needs some spackle. Martial law always makes a mess of common law. Military necessity is one thing—even if it's bogus—but property's another thing." Like Moses, the lawyer was certain that "the whole thing" had only just begun: "This is some wacky, meaty stuff. Courts and scholars could chew on this bone for decades. I think you'd have a case," he advised, "and if you're the first, you might just make some history books, too."

Fujita shook his head firmly. He'd been reading the Ben Franklin pamphlet he'd bought for Tamie on the Freedom Trail and quoted one of his favorites among Poor Richard's wisdoms: "Historians relate, not so much what is done, as what they would have believed." The only "fascinating" aspect of the whole thing, he declared, "is its dreary stupidity. When it's all in the past, it should stay there. Nobody will want to read about it." He was less sure, though, when Hessing cited among his "homework" readings the soon-to-be-published work of one Lincoln Osawa, Ph.D., which he'd seen in galley form. Apparently, only at that final stage did Osawa recall his promise to use pseudonyms—on Hessing's copy, a red pencil had belatedly transformed William, Mari, and Tony Fujita into Wally, Martha, and Tommy Fuchida. When he first heard about Fujita, he'd made the connection instantly. Hessing said he'd returned his copy to a sociologist colleague, but he'd try to dig it up again. From the disgust in Fujita's "Oh, *screw* Lincoln Osawa," Mr. Hessing supposed he shouldn't dig too strenuously.

"I'll work on him," Margaret reassured Hessing. "He just needs some time to choose a course of action." She turned to Fujita. "I don't think there is a choice. I think you *must* sue."

Livvie concurred. Returning one night from the hospital, where Garvin would remain under observation for two months, she said simply, "Criminals must be made to pay for crimes."

"Yes," Margaret agreed. "It's your duty, I think. As a decent, law-abiding citizen and a sane man of conscience, you have no choice. It's become bigger than just your life now."

"I don't know. I'd pay a lot to have my own small life back," said the nurseryman. "The thing is, I'm not sure I can find it in California anymore." As the words emerged, he was surprised he said them, but they did feel true. After a few days of brooding, he called Hessing at his office in Cambridge. "Can you keep me out of it?" he asked.

"Well, not entirely, no," the lawyer admitted. "But I'll do my best."

Fujita insisted that they wait. He had no desire to make legal history. "I don't know. It feels treasonous, somehow. I mean, while we're at war." Hessing argued it would be treasonous not to sue *when the war was over.* No one knew just how soon that would be. "You have an opportunity and a responsibility to spackle some holes here. You want to be American, that's what it's about: Every good citizen's an ombudsman."

"That's easy for you to say, Randy," Fujita retorted. "And I don't want to *be* American—I *am* American. Don't forget that, or I'll call it all off."

Immediately after hanging up, he expressed his ambivalence in a letter to his mother, who was, legally, still his business partner. "I suspect I'm really going after Clemens, not the nursery," he confessed. "All along I've been thinking (if you can call it thinking) of finding Yoneko and David, and getting you out, then going back." Having to write it out, he realized then how preposterous the idea was—Tamie and Yoneko and himself and a baby living out there. Just imagining the two women sharing a bathroom together made him shudder. And now I have to add Calvin, he thought. And why not Bobby Tanaka and Tom Fields? Astounded, he felt he had to go outside to bully the Sato brothers for a while. When he came back inside, he'd decided, "It's the *right* thing to do, but even if I win, I'm just not sure I belong there anymore. But do I really *belong* anywhere?" he asked Tamie. "I've become very fond of my new friends here." Then he thought, Yes, and . . . ? He let the letter trail off into details of farming and Garvin's recuperation. He enclosed a photograph of David.

Tamie lost no time in firing back her response: "You torture yourself about all the wrong things! Leaving California is such a big step? Look how far I have traveled. I am a pioneer. If I don't like a place, I move on. So you don't like California: Hitch up the wagon and go east, young man." The aging Issei prisoner had been swapping dime-store westerns with a German prisoner of war all that spring. "I was never crazy for plants anyway. However, this lawyer must get *our* money back. And while he is at it, I think I am almost ready for him to spring me from the joint." Tamie had traded gangster novels with an Italian inmate, too. "I told them I am getting bored, but now they like me and don't want me to leave. Maybe I will go to Chicago."

Fujita looked up, exasperated. To Margaret, reading over his shoulder, he warned, "If you say 'Thirty-six percent,' I'll scream." He continued reading: "Of course the demimondaine doesn't *want* you. Still, it is an elder's prerogative to impose himself on anyone he chooses. I would like to see my great-grandson, but I will *not* live with that annoying girl." Fujita rolled his eyes. Tamie in no way acknowledged his role in Garvin's recovery from the accident; only, "How is that boy?"

Margaret chuckled. "Oh, I'd say your mother's running at about *ninety-six* percent!"

Yoneko, too, was swept up by the idea of a lawsuit. "Dear Mr. F.," she wrote. "That's your nursery. It was Tony's home. Get it back. I don't think you can do this quietly," she warned, underscoring what Fujita already feared. "Calvin says good riddance, but I don't know. I think I'll want to go back west someday. To Hollywood," she added. His spirits flew higher than they had in months when he read, "I have to admit that David misses you. He cries a lot now, or maybe me and Calvin just hear him. I think Moses misses you more. When I told him your news, he said to tell you, You've got to either sit down somewhere or walk, but you can't keep hanging from that strap. What's that mean? Anyway, you know what's best to do. If you want, I'll help. A lawsuit. Wow. If you go into court, can I come see?" She concluded, "P.S. David's proud of you. P.P.S. Remember when you mangled the Momotaro story? Can't you maybe be the hero and the old farmer too?"

"I don't know," Fujita replied. Pocketing her note, he hobble-stepped among the freshly transplanted seedling beds with a bucket of manure tea. He'd left for Philadelphia at a critical time, and even the skilled Okamoto could not compensate for his absence. Vital suckering had been ignored or done hastily and belatedly. Livvie and Margaret had unknowingly distressed several plants with improper foliar feeding—watering the leaves in direct sunlight and searing them with underdiluted fertilizers. Some beds fell prey to the intermittent frosts and storms. To a Nisei who was just relearning to walk, it was hard enough just being an old farmer.

Fujita wanted to see Garvin, to make sure that the boy understood his decision to sue, and one night Margaret drove him terrified to the hospital. In the passenger seat, he gripped the dashboard with whitened knuckles and could not help stomping on an imaginary brake despite the pain it inspired in his legs. She made an illegal U-turn, missed two stop signs, and drove for a block on the wrong side of the street. Walking through the hospital corridors, now as familiar to him as a second home, Fujita was so rattled and he perspired so, he felt he needed a bath. He'd made friends and enemies of some of the long-term patients there; his reception was always a crapshoot. Nisei had some champions among these patients from the European theater, some of whom had never seen a Nikkei before the war, and they had heard of the widely touted "success" of the all-Nisei 442nd and the 100th Battalion. Such successes included campaigns in France to liberate Bruyères, Biffontaine, and Belmont, and the assault of the Gothic Line and Nazi holdings in Italy. The most notable "success" was the rescue of the trapped 141st Infantry's "Lost Battalion," which hailed from Texas, where the elder Yamaguchis were still held. After two other battalions' failed attempts, the "Little Iron Men" were sent in, and the "Go for Broke Regiment" saved the 211 Texans at a cost of 800 casualties. The army calls that success, the nurseryman thought bitterly. With management like that, any other business really would go broke. But gradually, reluctantly, he had begun to see that for young men like Tony, success lay in their postwar legacy. For its size and lifespan, the 442nd would be credited with the dubious (to Fujita) honor of having suffered the highest casualty rate and garnered the most decorations in American military history. Its sacrifices would be part of "the whole thing," too.

One such sympathetic GI at the hospital was Eric, a dairy farmer's son from Waunakee, Wisconsin, and himself a victim of severe burns. He always greeted Fujita fondly and inquired about the nojo. Much less sympathetic was his bed neighbor, Jesse, whose left calf had been fed to a land mine and his knee to gangrene. Jesse had actually vomited into a bedpan upon learning of the Tufteller kid's "disfigurement," by which he meant the graft, not the life-threatening burns. He scowled or cursed whenever he saw Fujita; once, he announced plainly, "I don't like you." That night the soldier only mumbled, "Disgusting," as the Nisei limped past his bed supporting himself with his arm around Margaret's waist. But Fujita now noticed these petty offenses no more than the buzz of mosquitoes. He just smiled and said, "How's the leg today, Jesse? Keep a stiff upper lip," as if the man had only saluted him.

They found Garvin wearing his tricorn cap, with his toy musket slung from the bed railing. He seemed to be made entirely of raw skin and scab and still had a pained grogginess about him. They played goh while Fujita explained about the lawsuit. "There might be some flak, pal," he said. "Can you handle it?" Finding speech a strain, Garvin only nodded. "The rabbits and mice are having a field day while you're in here. You think you can get back to the front soon?"

The little Minuteman nodded again and placed his black stone onto the board. Then, with enormous effort, he said, "I'm sorry." Fujita eyed the boy curiously. Sprouting from the bandages, his light hair needed a cut and a thorough washing. "About letting Franklin in the garage, I mean. Boy, was that a mistake."

Squelching an impulse to pat the boy's shoulder—which could be painful—Fujita shook his head and placed his white stone down in a defensive position. "No, Garvin. It's okay. It was just an accident," said that scholar of mistakes and accidents. He was learning more and more about them and their power to endure every day.

Changing the nursery's name to Clemens Nursery—what a mistake that had been! Of course, sacrificing his name had just seemed sound business given the anti-Japanese sentiment of those years. But as he had decided on the train to Philadelphia, names mattered. For example, the longer a man called something his own—even if it was borrowed—the more strongly he came to believe it. Witness Harvey Clemens, who, amidst a divorce and serious financial woes, ran the business as if it were his own—that is, right into the ground. It shocked Fujita to learn that Harv had been a gambler; as a rule, Ichiro's son was good at sniffing out certain addictions on people. When a potential buyer came by to rescue the ruined potter, a glance at the sign above Clemens Nursery was good enough for him. It was the most insidious kind of deal, the kind built on cash and a handshake. No, it hadn't really been the Fujita Family Nursery for years now.

In a way, he was able to restore his name in Juggeston. A week later, when the farmer's market started, their enterprise had to have a name. Tufteller/Kelly/Fujita Farms was too unwieldy. Garvin suggested, "Let's mush our names. Tuffujelly," he tried. "Futelly. Fuffkeller."

"Nojo Farms," chuckled the subversive Nurse Kelly. Acutely conscious of the war still raging to the far west, Fujita saw nothing funny about it.

"Not only is it unnecessarily provocative," he said, "it's redundant. Farm Farms?"

Margaret wanted a name that captured the Peak's "unique aspect"—she supposed that aspect was Mr. Fujita. It came to her one morning when she went up to the office to change the men's linens. The creative Sato brothers, too, had taken a shine to the skeleton; it sat behind Jack's desk smoking a cigarette and reading a copy of the *New England Journal of Medicine*. While she made up the cots, she glanced to the Tokyo mayor's scroll, the graduation gift to Tamie. Like the Issei pioneer, Margaret could not help staring at that lone, bell-shaped figure atop the peak and associating it with Fujita himself. Reentering the kitchen, where the crew gabbed on a coffee break, she announced: "Hiro Farms."

It came from his middle name—Hiro was short for Hiroshi—but she meant Hero, too. They had to admit, it had a nice ring, so they painted it on the Dodge truck that had once been Juggeston's ambulance, and on the farmer's market booth. At first the placement of their booth was so poor they feared no one would see the sign anyway. Twice Lil Wellington insisted that Fujita move the Hiro Farms booth, claiming first that it obstructed access to the store (it did) and then that it drew flies just beneath the grocery-shop window, inviting customers to complain (no one did). Upon Lil's third attempt to move them, Margaret Kelly stormed into Wellington's to do the negotiating. Fujita thought he'd never seen her look so angry. She emerged two minutes later. They did not move again.

Manning the Saturday booth provided Fujita's only truly guilt-free recreation. Occasionally, jugglers wobbled amongst the farmer's market shoppers, or some livestock exhibit brought cattle or swine. Pie-baking contests were followed by pie-eating contests (then "gagging and vomiting contests," as Akira Sato put it). The high school band played patriotic tunes badly, but with feeling. In this almost casual context, Fujita renewed his efforts to "melt" into the town he'd discovered—or had discovered him—eight months ago. He spoke with the neighbors he'd avoided for months and reintroduced himself to the nickel-and-dime gamblers of his first excursion to Wellington's lounge.

Collegial relationships grew out of small favors: making change for bills, watching things while a neighbor went to the can, trading seed.

Fujita found Pete Pedicott, who ran the next booth, a particularly likable fellow, but for his height and his habit of bemoaning his potency. Fujita had little patience for those who sniffed at the great fortune of having healthy children—even five, soon to be six children—but the farmer's generosity toward the Plotniks supremely impressed him. When he said so, Pete just arched his willowy body back and laughed good-naturedly. "With my brood, what's a couple more mouths to feed anyway? Those kids pay for themselves."

A congenial rivalry arose between the men—both primarily in the "vegetable racket" (though Fujita also brought his Pasadenan's passion for cut flowers to the market). "Your eggplants don't look too robust, there," Pedicott suggested, curious about the greenhouse-started tamotsu. "Look kind of stunted. Like purple hot dogs."

"It's an Asian variety. They're supposed to be like that—long and thin. Very sweet."

"Oh. Kind of small, though. Funny color," Pete observed, a bit defensively because a woman from Pigeon Cove bought a dozen for a picnic. "Kind of pale."

Fujita laughed. "I'll tell you what, Pete. One day, we'll hold a picnic of our own, and you'll see for yourself."

Pedicott was visibly shocked at this unprecedented overture: Was it possible that Fujita might *invite* someone to the Peak? (No one counted Christmas Eve, when the carolers had really invited themselves.) "That would be nice," Pete said, with an alarming urgency. "Not that it's my business, but I think it would be nice for *everybody*, if you take my meaning." With a mixture of annoyance and amusement, Fujita understood that his no-longer-new neighbors considered him standoffish. Not that anyone had exactly thrown any welcoming parties for him, either—only eggs and rocks. "I'll tell you, I had my doubts about you," Pete confessed. "When Margaret came to talk to me and Paulette—sort of told us your story a bit—and then we heard about little Garvin, and . . ." He had some trouble.

"That's when you hired the Plotniks?" Fujita asked.

"Well, what you've done up there on that hill—it's really something. We'd *all* like to see it."

To that end, the Hiro Farmers devised to hold the promised picnic on Independence Day, celebrating Garvin's release from the hospital. Fujita sat for hours with Garvin when he came home. It took him that long to muster the stomach to take a good look at his own, shed skin. When Margaret changed the dressings, he broke into a sweat and had to leave, but he saw enough. On the whole, the grafts would always retain a different hue and texture than the original skin. Margaret tried to reassure him: "That would be true even of grafts harvested from a patient's own body." Fujita resisted an impulse to touch a patch of raised, swollen tissue that looked a bit like cake icing. Garvin's arm was purpled with bruises from banging on the bed railing; normal sensation wouldn't return until he reached junior high. The meshed, teardrop marks were clearly visible—as if he'd been branded with a heated wire net—though these would mostly fade in time.

"My, someone's being terribly emotional today!" Margaret teasingly called after the retreating Fujita. Garvin would have giggled if he wasn't biting his lip.

"Sorry about that, pal," Fujita said, returning when the procedure was done. "No offense."

"I look weird," Garvin agreed, nodding. "No offense, either."

"You look beautiful, honey," Margaret insisted. She kissed his unburned scalp, and Livvie kissed his unburned nose. Fujita did not kiss Garvin, but it hardly mattered—in a way, a part of Fujita would be kissing the boy for his whole life. Instead, they played a quiet game of goh together before it was time to get ready for the picnic, and that was almost as good.

For the nation's birthday, the scarecrow put away her stethoscope and wore a fresh, festive dress. Benny and Akira Sato rigged a tent for Garvin, who would remain under strict orders to avoid direct sun for years to come. Though the North Shore's general blackout had gone the way of Adolf Hitler, they lit no fireworks out of respect for those soldiers still facing the real thing. It took much planning and daring improvisation, but the

Hiro Farms crew assembled a banquet to introduce their more unusual garden-stuffs to the locals. "A publicity event," Livvie suggested, though even P. T. Barnum would have been hard put to promote Japanese-style cuisine in the summer of 1945. Mostly, Fujita intended the picnic to be by and for the Juggeston Nikkei, for Garvin, and for himself.

Olive Plotnik made mochi in broth and sweet bean manju cakes. They had salty meboshi—a pickled plum, eaten with rice—and tsukemono, a pickled cabbage. There was tea. In the shabu shabu nabe main course, guests prepared their own food at table, dipping meat and vegetables and noodles into pots of boiling broth. This method made Garvin nervous, so Livvie and Moira Hardy took turns cooking for him. Like gladiators, Fujita and Pedicott squared off at the grill over the contested tamotsu. "This is the real test," Fujita said, brushing the eggplants with oil and plopping them onto the flame. "No farting around with sauce or spices," he said. When the skins faded to a dull green-brown, he nimbly rotated the vegetables with chopsticks. "No gussying up with frills. Just you and the vegetable, mano a mano." The plump purple sheath split. Pedicott raised a spoonful of its steaming, yellow innards to his lips, tasted them, and frowned. "Okay, okay. Not bad," he admitted. "Sweet. But it's not so special or anything." Fujita caught him taking two more a few minutes later.

Margaret beamed at this friendly exchange. Watching the guests gossiping and mingling, she noticed that the Nikkei mustered less enthusiasm than the hakujin for Fujita's pending lawsuit—a conversation topic he quickly squelched. The newcomers as a whole rarely talked about what they'd left behind. She wondered if this was a quality inbred in the culture, or if she was witnessing some wordless pact being made. Fujita might have told her it was both, but she didn't feel comfortable voicing the observation to him; like the return of Garvin's sense of touch, or like forgiveness, that would take time. And yet, could anyone blame Nurse Kelly for the prideful gratification she felt, overseeing Widow's Peak's first celebration in more than a year? She, who had charmed guests, made matches, and introduced intellects to one another as hostess to so many gatherings in her married life. She, who was no less a romantic than Mari Fujita, no less willful than Tamie, no less ambitious than Yoneko Yamaguchi, and no less stubborn than the Little Bull. Could anyone blame her that she looked on her old and new neighbors, and fervently hoped that "the whole thing" was over—that they'd all wrestled with war and prejudice and finally prevailed?

That idea, to Fujita, was pure rikutsuppoi. Unlike Margaret, he knew that food was just food, neighbors just neighbors. Were there two hundred Nikkei working in Juggeston and not two dozen, what could dispel panic of the Yellow Peril? Certainly not the novelty of an exotic eggplant. Unlike Margaret, he never for a second imagined that Lil Wellington's pleased nibbles at the sweet manju would change what she thought of him. Or that Frank Childs, then weeding the alien radish strips out of his dish, wouldn't withhold his precious gasoline again. Guilt over his inadvertent participation in Garvin's accident had momentarily humbled Childs, but what was guilt but a transitory state of being sorry? Its usefulness, like a scarecrow's, was short-lived. He was sure that Harvey Clemens suffered guilt, but not enough by half—not enough to matter. Guilt was no replacement for shame, which clung, which insisted on action; to abandon shame, one had to *act* to eradicate its source. Guilt was a game you played with yourself; shame was your bargain with the world. What use in being guilty about your mistakes? the Nisei asked, and he directed this to no one more strongly than himself. Just correct them.

To solidify this promise that Independence Day, he gave Margaret a crisp dollar bill.

Among his many mistakes, he thought, had been avoiding meeting. This point was driven home by the round, rough-skinned Dolly Doe. Cornering him at the tail end of the picnic, she introduced herself as the wife of Harrold Doe, the man whom Lil so intimidated and who was recuperating at home from a stroke he'd suffered that winter. "It's so nice to meet you, finally," she said. "You really have to try joining us at meeting, at least once. See, it's not that folks aren't willing to accept you. It's just that they got to get to know you. Get me?" In a more logical world, Dolly would be a perfectly suited spouse for Alf

Wellington. She spoke to Fujita like a charm-school instructor teaching him how to socialize at a cocktail party, shooing him in and urging, *Go on—mingle, mingle.*

"Right, Dolly. Got you."

"What I'm saying is, people will let you fit in, but you got to fit in. See?" In Dolly's view, Hideo was a square peg. He hardly ever said a word, and what was with those funny shoes, anyway? "When in Rome . . ."

Rome? Fujita thought, but he held his tongue. Being "Friendly," as he put it, he tried to practice tolerance, which was all he felt he could ask for himself—and had a right to expect. Not acceptance—he no longer concerned himself about that. Though grateful that the Juggestonians offered to accept him and the other Nikkei, he also suspected it was *easy* to be accepting. In a town of conscience, conditional acceptance could be pro forma—just toe the line and *melt*. Tolerance, however, took work, imaginative energy, and empathetic courage. How many people had that sort of energy or courage? Margaret Kelly did, by the bucketful. Garvin did: Children have lots of energy. Livvie had enough.

Fujita had been thinking about tolerance a lot that spring, and wondering if he was "ready." Potent Pete's aid to the Plotniks had inspired him to read some Quaker histories and accounts of the sect's persecution across centuries and continents. Branded yellow as pacifists, or browned as abolitionists, the Friends themselves were often deemed intolerable. Indeed, a handful of Juggeston's young Quaker men had themselves spent that war in a sort of segregated camp, doing compulsory forestry work and the like as conscientious objectors. It puzzled him that Friends had been stigmatized as "mystical," despite practices that seemed, in his unforgiving view of religions, the most practical and least gaudy going—no lights, smoke, and hocus-pocus; no gongs, incense, and robes; no gargoyles and winged babies. After the picnic, he told Margaret that, ready or not, it was time to attend meeting. "When in Rome!" he trilled in mimicry of the gung-ho Mrs. Doe.

"Oh, don't," Margaret said. "Don't be bitter." An unfortunate phrase, since this too had been the stout Dolly's advice: "I admire your grace. You have so much cause to be bitter, but you're not. A lot of folks could learn a lesson from you." Mrs. Doe had meant it as the highest of compliments, but Fujita fairly reeled at her presumption. What in hell gave her *that* idea? he wondered. It would take him some years to answer, You did, Fujita. You did.

Well, wasn't it a sad fact of the world that tolerance was confused with weakness, forbearance mistaken for defeat, and forgiveness taken as a return to normalcy? "Forgive and forget"—what a phrase that was! Until his death, the nurseryman knew he'd never lose the virulent bitterness he bore for his old pal, Harvey Clemens. He would never be *that* forgiving or forgetful. He had fought to hide it throughout that spring, but the resulting strain rendered him moderately insane—or at least noticeably eccentric. Once or twice, Hideo spotted him clenching his fists and talking to the scarecrow. Margaret saw him hobble-chasing a rabbit, maniacally swinging his cane in the air. Though he could walk without the cane, he'd become attached to it; sometimes he'd hook it in his belt loop like a rapier, its point tilling a path behind him.

But he wanted to forgive and forget. And so the next Sunday, or "First Day," after the picnic, he did try attending meeting with Livvie, but when he returned, he was more baffled than ever. Margaret asked what was wrong, but he scrunched up his face. "I think I missed something," he said, and they went into the living room to sit alone. "We just sat there, right. There was this candle in the middle of the room, and all these benches, and I kept waiting for someone to pray or sing or say something. Then, after a while all the kids just stood up and followed Paulette and her *dog* out of the room." He paused, and Margaret just grinned. "I mean, no one said, 'Okay, kids and dogs out of the room.' So, we just sat there some more, and after a *long* while, Pete stood up and said, 'While the war has taken so many of our friends away, it's a double blessing when it brings us some new ones.' Then he asked us to pray for the war's end and sat down again. It was really nice that he said it, but it was the *only* thing said the whole time." Wildly confused, he stopped short.

"It's just your speed!" Margaret cried, laughing.

"I suppose it is," said Fujita, and he blushed. He had to admit this sort of observance suited him very well—this indirect talking by not talking, this being-left-alone-without-being-alone, and even the utilitarian decor. "Damned if I know what it was all about, but the amazing thing is that for no good reason, I actually feel better. I'm not exactly *Convinced* yet," he hastened to add, and they stared at each other seemingly forever. "But maybe I can be an Attender for . . . however long it takes."

It was then that Margaret, out of sheer joy, threw her arms around his shoulders in an embrace. Her hip, radiating with warmth like a fresh-baked loaf of bread, rubbed his raw thigh. Unable to remember when he'd last been so close to someone else, he grimaced for the pain, but held on to her, too, for a long time. He fought and fought against it, but his fingertips themselves remembered exactly tracing the round little muscles of Mari's arm, the skin roughened by sun and rose thorns, the texture like a silk-wrapped lemon. And they noted that the skin of Margaret's arm, in her sleeveless summer dress, felt different—a bit like that on a grape. And he felt in his throat a burning like a sharp brandy, fermentation of the most forbidden of fruits. He hated making this sensory comparison, but he couldn't stop it—no more than he could stop the war.

With his face brushing Margaret's cheek, and feeling her shifting on the sofa cushion, Fujita opened his eyes—he wanted to tuck the memory away, he wanted to see Margaret. First, he watched the red golds of the hair dancing down her jawline and neck. It smelled moist—it smelled of greenhouse life. She pulled away, sitting back, and they watched each other—and perhaps they could have remained like that for . . . as long as it took. But Fujita was done waiting. He raised his hand to cup her fine, sharp chin, sat forward, and kissed her.

When she at last rose from the sofa and turned to walk toward the stairwell, the ex-nurse, Margaret Kelly, did not help him up, did not fetch his cane, did not ask what he needed or if there was any way she could make him feel better. She did not even look at him as he struggled to rise himself—she merely began to climb the long stairway toward the second floor of the big house that Fujita thought was growing smaller. *Shikata ga nai.* Lifting his raw, stiff legs that wouldn't be fully healed for a long time to come, Fujita took the first step up, then the second, and it hurt like hell, but he followed her anyway.

The advantages of a greenhouse to a small, family-run farm are often seen early in the season. What the limited crops lack in critical mass, they make up for in rapid growth—the smaller, transplanted crops may be more "pampered," as Fujita put it. If a farmer can maximize the use of a greenhouse, he might employ a sterile, artificial growing medium to prepare seeds for later planting and, with some planning, even manage two crops in a season. For example, he could help certain tomato crops get a second wind, harvesting in both spring and in late fall. This was Fujita's plan for Hiro Farms.

When he had built the greenhouse, he hadn't been sure just how necessary it would be. He'd have preferred to rely on the structure less, and to have ten more hands and a fleet of heavy machinery—to sow shotgun method earlier in the spring. Were this a strictly profit-making enterprise, he'd place his bets on quantity over quality. As it happened, June and July were lucrative months for Hiro Farms. They enjoyed a solid, early harvest—and even a bit of recreation time, with various itinerant workers continuing to help out en route from Gila to some (hopefully) happier place. Moira Hardy, no longer Garvin's homeroom teacher but still his art mentor, became a regular feature on the hill during the school's summer vacation. Though "not really the outdoorsy type," as she described herself, Livvie's friend thought Widow's Peak "wonderfully earthy." She was excellent at making Fujita cringe.

"What does that silly woman want up here, anyway?" Fujita grumbled once to Margaret, when Livvie and Moira were off somewhere across the hill doing something or other—but for sure that something wasn't *working*. "Does she want a job or what?"

"You can't just put everybody who happens by out into the field with a bushel basket," Margaret scolded him. "We're the farmers. Moira's an artist."

Fujita rolled his eyes. Sitting with Garvin under his protective tent by the scarecrow—or occasionally inside "the conservatory"—Moira would erect two easels, and they would paint portraits of the others as they labored. Fujita would frown at her as sourly as he had at Yoneko when she lounged out in the Gila sun bleaching her hair.

"She could at least *pretend* she's painting a tree or something," Fujita hissed, but it seemed to ease Livvie to have her lazy companion dallying about, so he mostly kept quiet. Just as Livvie was trying to cut back on the booze—with a bit of help from Moira—Fujita had sworn off trying to control everything. If he relapsed, he always had Nurse Kelly there to remind him that they'd had a fine early season, that they'd all earned some leisure, and that "work isn't its *only* own reward."

Yet Fujita knew that without the greenhouse, his trip to Philadelphia could have proven ruinous. And, he also knew, the later half of the season was still a challenge, a mystery. They still had work to do to reap that second crop. For no matter how your crops were "loved" (as Margaret put it), the universe possessed a ready armory of perils. Whether wielding a slingshot or a buzz bomb, it was never unarmed.

That hot August torrent blasted in like the tail of a comet. At 97 percent humidity, the very air seemed to sweat that morning, until a wet gale raked the Peak so furiously that the workers raced about all afternoon staking plants and buttressing trellises. An orange-carp wind sock tore free of its post and flew out of sight as if in the claws of an invisible kingfisher. "My God!" Fujita cried to Pete Pedicott, who came by to return a bypass lopping shears. "Is it a hurricane? Is this *normal?*"

"It gets pretty active up here," Potent Pete yelled back. "Usually in winter. I've never seen it like this!"

Jack Kelly's office slapped itself with a loose storm shutter and a shingle whizzed off the roof onto the greenhouse below, cracking a pane. A dislodged robin's nest plummeted to the grass. The most hysterical clapping came from the scarecrow, from her flowered yellow sundress whipping up over her face like a tangled, half-opened parachute—she'd lost her bonnet long ago. A wall of almost visible air, reminiscent of the Gila River dust devils, blindsided Fujita, nearly knocking him over.

Still the winds grew angrier, toppling even the birdbath where the Annisquam Witch had refreshed herself. In the manner of a weather vane, the scarecrow's sewing-dummy body pivoted on its sturdy spine post. All aswirl in trails of yellow, it spun and spun like a dervish. "My God!" Fujita cried again as his favorite, battered fedora launched skyward over Juggeston.

Only much later, and only for a flash, would he reflect on that gusty sixth day of August. Was it only a coincidence that he'd found himself that afternoon, melting from the heat, stiff from bending to save the collapsed tomato stalks, thinking of his old mentor, Miyake? Later that afternoon, Fujita stood with Garvin, looking southwestward out over the nojo they had built, assessing the damage. Garvin wore an oversized shirt to protect his tender hide from the sun, but the wind had blown the collar down to his right biceps. The farmer put his arm around the boy to cover the shoulder, and he let it stay there. For the longest time they stood like that, watching the sunset flood that horizon whence Fujita had come, and the Nisei recalled the day he'd met his own second father. Junichiro Miyake was out there somewhere, he thought, grumbling and smoking in his own garden in Hiroshima-ken. Somewhere out there.

They stood frozen and staring, as if given time enough, they could see everything. The saguaro atop Sacaton Butte. The banners above Tulare Fairgrounds. The swaying palms over Suicide Bridge. Ichiro's jutting rock by the L.A. fishing wharf. The smoke above Pearl Harbor. The engine steam of the *Pacific Angel* itself. The taillights tracing the Burma Hump. They might at least have had a chance to make out the world's largest mushroom—swelling high as some forty Empire State Buildings—above Hiroshima. In retrospect, they would imagine they'd witnessed in that storm the shock waves of Little Boy—the first atomic bomb—and the end of the war. But of course they could see these things no more than what they most sought on that horizon, asking, What on earth will happen to us next?

With its crystal eyes and stethoscope ears, here's what the scarecrow saw.

William Hiroshi Fujita was born "with a bang bang bang!" to Japanese immigrant parents on January 2, 1897, on the mainland United States of America. His mother, Tamie, née Asakawa, was nineteen years old. Upon her release from FBI custody in 1946, she would be sixty-eight in American reckoning, and still full of pioneer zeal, which would lead her to Chicago. There she lived among a close-knit group of Nikkei friends and taught English to recent immigrants, primarily Issei and European refugees; she could have taught it well enough to be employed by any public elementary school. She bought season tickets to Wrigley Field and learned that batters were allowed only three strikes, though many of the finer points of America's favorite pastime would forever elude her. Never a plant woman, she underwent a career change in the Midwest; she dabbled as a painter, and a rather good one, too. Under the patronage of her surprised son, who'd never known her to so much as lift an inkbrush, she became accomplished enough to have her first showing at a small gallery at seventy-one years of age.

Garvin Tufteller, aged thirteen, accompanied Fujita to the opening and much later credited Tamie with encouraging him to become an artist in his own right and his own medium. As an adult, he would be best known in New England for his kinetic sculptures, such as *Dis/Figure* and *Scarecrow III*, in which he set massive and dynamic objects in "improvisatory dances" with "elemental objects"—fire, water, wind, and terrain. Though proud of his work, his mother never really understood it. Ever since that Parent's Day art show, she had approached even his most abstract creations as if they contained some autobiographical narrative, a habit that infuriated her son. "God, Mom. It's just a moving *blob*!" he'd complain, then add, "Albeit a very well-wrought blob." For technical advice, Livvie relied on her close friend and companion, Ms. Moira Hardy, who observed that his technique betrayed "Eastern influences."

"That's such *bullshit*, Moira," Garvin would rail, but many shared his former art teacher's assessment. In 1967 one enterprising critic traced that influence back to an obscure, Japanese Midwestern painter of the late forties, whom he described to be "like a grandmother" to the sculptor. In an interview, Garvin admitted to a familial relationship but denied an artistic one. "I can't speak to her technique, which really was essentially Eastern, but for me, how Tamie shaped an image was nothing next to how she shaped the *world*. I learned one invaluable thing from Tamie Fujita: She taught me how to think *big*."

It was Tamie's lot in life that her personality inevitably overwhelmed anything she made—even very good things, like her paintings or her son. This eventually made her the reluctant role model for a set of degenerate young students and artists orbiting about the University of Chicago. These were the so-called Bohemians, though Tamie had not met one actual immigrant from the Bohemia region among them. Ever the socialite, she also visited gatherings of the Communist party a few times but soon stopped. As she told her concerned son, "Some party! So boring! You would have loved it."

Tamie would never live with her son again; she didn't want to. Reminding him of her enormous efforts at delaying his birth and making him American, she said she'd already held on to him longer than most mothers would. She never told him whether that story of the *Pacific Angel* was actually true, and she never "made his manju." As he grew older, he agreed that it didn't really matter (hadn't he designed one or two hefty deceptions of his own?), and he believed there would always be time to ask if it suddenly did matter. There was not. Tamie died early in 1952, the year the McCarran-Walter Act eliminated race as a bar to naturalization and assigned immigration quotas to all countries. Although she never got to become an American citizen, she certainly could have passed the test. She did manage to file the paperwork, spotting several spelling and punctuation mistakes, which she scornfully read down the phone in her last conversation with her son and Margaret.

Yoneko Yamaguchi and Calvin Igawa would "make it legal" by the time David was old enough to start asking questions. She and Tamie had reached the uneasiest of truces by the time Tamie died, but Fujita and Calvin negotiated enough "house peace" that David's family visited her in Chicago a few times. It would occur to Fujita then how shockingly and unfortunately similar the two women were—more than Mari and Tamie, or he and

Tony, or even he and Calvin. Despite her conversion to the artistic life, Tamie hypocritically continued to refer to "that actress, that demimondaine," though at least not within Yoneko's earshot.

"Yvonne" Yamaguchi, occasionally a.k.a. Yvonne Chan, made a fair living in bit parts, in live theater and as a generic, B-film yellow siren. Most prominently, she portrayed Tokyo Rose in one among a rash of self-congratulatory war-nostalgia films of the fifties, and she was credited as being, arguably, the first Nisei woman to appear—in a ballroom dance segment—on *The Ed Sullivan Show*.

Calvin Igawa would have a rough start in medical school. With no money, no eastern relations, and few friends, he would prove a Herculean studier. Of course, his experience at Rivers also gave him a head start in clinical work. *He* would never faint in a delivery room; *he* would never vomit at an autopsy (or make jokes about a cadaver). Ludicrously, a few envious classmates would posit that his early field experience was an "unfair advantage" denied them while they were occupied at *normal* pursuits. He eventually became assistant department head of a small teaching hospital in Philadelphia. True to his word, Calvin never set foot in California again—not even to attend professional conferences, not even when invited to speak at them.

Yoneko Yamaguchi had known since Gila River that America would never suffer a Nikkei movie starlet in her lifetime. She found something else to do in one Harvard law professor named Randolph Hessing. Noting her interest in Fujita's lawsuit, he steered her to a now-and-then career as a legal secretary, by which she "supported her acting habit." She would one day become a now-and-then civil rights activist, too (the actress's life is always now-and-then), and work on the National Committee for Redress on behalf of relocated Japanese Americans. She had great and many passions, but politics was not among them; her involvement in these movements had less to do with her own political convictions than with her son's.

David Igawa would grow up in the town of Haverford, where his mother once cleaned house for a Quaker family, on the affluent Main Line of Philadelphia. He would attend a private

Friends school and decide, like his Uncle Bill, "I'd be a Quaker, if I were to be anything." It concerned his family that he didn't care to be anything at all. He preferred television and pop records to books, but by 1963 he had studied well enough to attend Haverford College. (He'd wanted to go away to school, perhaps a California state school, something on the beach, but his overprotective parents nixed the idea.) In college he lacked direction. Asserting that agricultural work was character-building, his Uncle Bill offered him a summer job, but the freshman had recently discovered that he preferred smoking plants to growing them.

Then, one hungover and just-a-teeny-bit-stoned afternoon in a philosophy lecture, he stopped massaging his temples so he could catch that word again. The lecture, pretty boring so far as David could follow it, had meant to apply Heisenberg's Uncertainty Principle to the examination and recording of historical events. Both familiar and not, the name was "Gila River," appended to a long list of others: Manzanar, Heart Mountain, Crystal City, and so forth. From another fucking war, the name had the air of long history, though it had never appeared in his history books. The professor, his pale, drawn face reddening with indignation, glared at the class. David didn't realize how sourly he was glaring back at the prof, as a web of associations radiated from the name. "Camp": His parents' veiled references to it had once inspired visions of a recreational campgrounds—a canoe and bonfire and panty-raid sort of place. "Dumbshit Californians": Dad and Uncle's term. "9066": just numbers to David, not an executive order. "Evacuation": with a flavor of "rescue"—*They evacuated the burning building*. A story, intuited rather than heard, had germinated for years just in the periphery of his memory, and when it finally bloomed before him, it was as if it had always been there.

"Something to add to our discussion, Mr. Igawa?" the prof asked the gaping freshman.

"No," he said. "Not really."

Thus through a hakujin stranger, David Toshio Igawa, like so many young Nikkei, first learned of "the whole thing." Betrayal, curiosity, the climate surrounding civil rights, as well as the

Vietnam War—the "white man sending the black man to fight the yellow man"—sent David spiraling back to his elders full of questions and resentment. Dad was tight-lipped as ever—just, "Have you been smoking that crap again?"—but in 1960-something, when subversion was back in fashion, even he began eating with hashi again. Uncle Bill defended himself with a faulty memory: "It was a long time ago, David. There's a lot I don't remember. It was a busy time, and I wasn't exactly at leisure to keep a journal, you know."

David's mother scowled at this response: "Oh, he remembers all right. You're just asking the wrong questions." She would tell the story, but only piecemeal: With her short attention span and her actress's instinct for dramatic pauses, it would take four years before she and Calvin decided to tell him about Tony Fujita.

Like his biological grandfather, David was a late bloomer. They waited until he was mature enough to recall how much he'd been loved and was loved by them all—his Aunt Joan and cousin Bobby Tanaka, Aunt Peggy and the step-grandparents who had died in poverty in Montana shortly after the war, by Aunt Rose and Tamie and perhaps even the Arais—who, learning of Mari's and Tony's deaths only after the war, never returned to America. The calabash family was, after all, the Little Tokyo way. And especially "Uncle Bill": While the Nisei never once expressed his love in words, like the name Gila River it enveloped David like a blanket that he'd never noticed but had always been there.

In life, unlike art, such revelations may have limited usefulness beyond a slight shift in perception, and the artistic temperaments of Tamie and Yoneko had skipped over David entirely. Like his grandfather, he broke his mother's heart and went on to business school—at Harvard—to learn how to make money as a strategic consultant. It took him much longer—over a decade—to learn about on and giri, and to decide that he had inherited his own role in the ever-expanding "whole thing." As a "practical" man, David eventually joined the Japanese-American redress movement only when it appeared that the battle could be won—upon President Ford's "American Promise" proclamation that at last buried Executive Order 9066 in 1976. As with Dr. Hessing, an emeritus professor at Harvard when David had attended, it would take something like property to get him involved. Property was altogether more tangible than justice or liberty, and like so many young Americans of his time, David considered these synonyms. He helped by honing economic arguments for congressional hearings, and by enlisting his energetic mother and his more energetic wife, Elaine, a Jewish woman from Delaware whom he'd met at Harvard.

In Massachusetts, David grew closer to Garvin Tufteller. Though a mutual jealousy underscored their friendship, they felt they complemented each other well: David was handsome and thoughtless, and Garvin was "disfigured" and sensitive; David was a nattily dressed extrovert, while the soft-spoken Garvin swamped himself in oversized clothing to hide his scars; David was a financial whiz and Garvin a boob with money; David was practical but lacked direction, while Garvin had direction but was too impractical to get where he was going. Also, they shared "old Fujita," their worry for him, and his constant worry about them.

It was really Garvin who inspired David to "get involved" one night at David and Elaine's apartment on Brattle Street in Cambridge, drinking and watching *The Late Show*—the fare, James Whale's classic horror movie *Frankenstein*. "Fire! Ugh!" cried Karloff and Tufteller as one—Garvin knew the script by heart. "Fire *bad*!" observed Boris and Garvin. Mimicking the monster, Garvin growled and shielded himself with his arms; the sleeves of his billowing poet's shirt slid down to his misshapen elbows.

David winced and said, "You're really screwed up." Beside him on the sofa, the very pregnant Elaine chuckled and continued slathering her dry skin with moisturizer. Garvin stopped laughing, however, and pointed to the hulk on the screen.

"Hey," he said solemnly. "There's a piece of me in there." David gaped at his friend, now cast in an eerie, flickering TV light. The sort of flighty, hippie-dippie thing Garvin always said—was that meant to be funny? David found it gross and shook his head. "Whatsa matter?" Garvin asked, grinning.

"You're turning white." Suppressing her laugh, Elaine released a most indecorous sound.

"No, I'm a *banana*," David said, cracking a smile. "I'm just white on the *inside*."

"So *I'm* an egg," Garvin said. "Maybe a little scrambled," he added, and they all laughed.

Elaine was kneading the moisturizer into her fabulous, smooth-skinned belly—a beauty regimen that could always paralyze Garvin in a trance of longing. "And what's *she* going to be?" she wondered, splaying her hands on either side. They all thought about that for a moment.

"A banana custard," David suggested at last. "That's what *he'll* be."

But Garvin, intensely focused on that great swell of Elaine's unsullied skin, said, "It will be beautiful no matter what. It will be perfect whatever it is, because it will be made from love."

"Jesus, Garvin," David muttered, downing his beer. Though it pleased him, he could not begin to imagine how to respond to that hippie-dippie proclamation, so he let his wife do the emoting. Not comfortable with hugging those days, Elaine kissed Garvin; she considered him perfect, too—after all, despite the painful method, wasn't Garvin the egg also laid out of love?

They talked about Garvin's worry for the old man; at sixty-eight, Fujita was still at work, still trying to control everything. And he was still squabbling with Livvie, who had found something good to do, something better than seamstressing, and had largely taken over managing things on the hill. "Frankly, he's driving Mom *nuts*," Garvin said, grinning. Then he told them about first meeting old Fujita, whom he'd taken for a vampire. "Bela Lugosi, you know? That's *just* what he looked like, to me," he said, shaking his head. "Frankenstein and Dracula. Oh boy."

His friends knew he didn't want children himself, nor to be married—"not nohow, not ever," as he'd once vowed to Mugsie Kelly. As married parents will do when confronted with childless single people, the Igawas assumed this to be a hang-up rather than a conscientious preference. It was actually both. He'd be a terrific father and husband, they insisted. "My associations with matrimony aren't too pleasant," he reminded them. "If I had kids, I'd be so anxious I'd have to have *a lot* of them, and I can't afford it." Still, in the grand tradition of *shashin-kekkon*—as in the arranged joining of Tamie and Ichiro—these two yentas, as Elaine put it, routinely tried to make Garvin a match. He dated and even loved a few times, but like all of his own best role models, that other calabash family on Widow's Peak, he never felt compelled to "make it legal."

Of course, Garvin grew up in a family that had seen plentiful evidence that love—romantic or familial—survived only *despite* laws, taboos, executive orders. In 1945, the year of his yellowing, "miscegenation" was legally forbidden in much of the Union, and the last prohibition would not be struck down until 1967, the year David met Elaine in a coffee shop in Harvard Square. By then Margaret Kelly would be seventy-two, and as passionate as at sixteen, thirty-five, or fifty, though perhaps less immediately concerned with the sort of physical intimacy these prophylactic regulations meant to impede. "Be thankful for taboo," she told Garvin just before she died in the big house on the hill at the age of eighty-one, in 1976. "How boring life would be without it!"

In that bicentennial year, Felicity Igawa was born, and in four years remaining to him, her great-grandfather came to agree with Garvin—the *hapa* baby was "perfect."

Both only children and by their own admission "real brats," David and Elaine had always planned to give Felicity at least one sibling, but they waited too long. Some mistakes can't be corrected. In 1983, a few months after the bills authorizing reparation were introduced to Congress, David was killed on a consulting trip in Michigan. He'd been asked to consult on procedural and organizational alternatives to a planned downsizing at an automotive factory. He'd inherited his grandfather's no-nonsense professionalism but unfortunately not his patience. Rather than wait for the "fucking criminals at the fucking garage to fix the fucking Buick," he took Elaine's Toyota Tercel. The orange sedan, though small and quick, was loud enough to make a fair target for a large enough projectile—a cinder block hurtling down from an overpass. In Elaine Igawa's opinion,

David had followed in his dead father's footsteps: He was killed by friendly fire. Although no foul play was proven, she knew Michigan had no love for things Japanese—cars or faces—and was certain it had killed him. Had his grandfather survived to see the tragedy, he would have wondered: Maybe it was just an accident? A flaw in the construction? Or just another piece of "the whole thing"?

And what, finally, was the whole thing? Fujita would occasionally wonder throughout his life. Ever growing, shifting, was it all just about evacuation and internment? Relocation, deportation, "distribution," assimilation, miscegenation? Suppression of evidence, repression of grief? Martial law and the Constitution? Military necessity or public hysteria, Yellow Peril and racist policies evolving over centuries? Was it about Pearl Harbor and No-No Boys, inu and "Go for Broke"? Was it the sundering of a community from within or without—those who broke Little Tokyo, or those who then abandoned it, too? Which water cooler you drank from, where you stood on the bus, and the beauty of a hapa baby? And wasn't it also redressment, reparation, apology—and forgiveness? As his old friend Moses had predicted, Fujita would never really get to see the *whole* thing.

Since his carriage on the *Pacific Angel*, William Fujita had always been an older Nisei—the first among the second—whether in Little Tokyo, Gila River, or Juggeston. Like his grandson and more than half the Japanese Americans interned during World War II, he would not survive to see his countrymen offer any formal apology and reparation. Not that it much mattered: By the time the hearings commenced, reopening old wounds and old schisms in the Nikkei community, he was so old that it really *was* mukashi no hanashi. To the Nisei, it was all just long ago—an old, old story. In fact, while David's belated interest in his grandfather's tale thrilled Fujita, it baffled him, too. He would have appreciated a presidential apology, though. He had once suggested to Hessing that he'd consider settling with Harvey Clemens et al. for an apology and court costs. The lawyer went through the roof.

"Money talks and *only* money talks!" Hessing raged. "If you're peeling off bills, you can't keep your fingers crossed behind your back." The money was loquacious when, after a quick turnover, the nursery was liquidated, razed, and carpeted by a freeway, virtually overnight. "You want an apology, there's your apology. There's one goddam big fat stuck-in-the-mud *elephant-sized* apology just waiting to be bagged." Over the next five years until settlement, Fujita's suit became the favorite hobby of the lawyer, who referred to himself as the great white hunter. "Make room for the sons of bitches' heads above the mantle!" he said, but he thought, *What mantle?*

To his mind, Fujita wouldn't *need* the reparation money, anyway, though others would. Throughout his long life, Fujita did what he had to: He made do. He invested Tony's "blood money" wisely—most he placed in trust for David; some he borrowed to pay former internee workers and to support Tamie; some went to Randy Hessing's crusade. The rest he gambled on a long-term investment, with a very favorable rate of return, in the nojo that he, Margaret, Livvie, and Garvin had begun and would finish together, as a family, in Juggeston's Hiro Farms, on the hill once called Widow's Peak.

Yet in August of 1945, as he and Garvin watched the setting sun, trying to divine their futures in its exhausted rays, Fujita could foresee none of this. Unlike the grass woman who comforted them but had failed to protect their farm, they possessed only human ears and eyes and could see no farther than the ravages of the storm over Hiro Farms. "Will it never end?" the farmer asked.

It will, the scarecrow had said.

And what the straw watcher now said, and what Fujita had also learned, was, *But it will surely happen again.*

For what scarecrows know is that they can watch and sympathize but can protect nothing—their enduring power is always and only over people, never birds. Brass rooftop roosters and silken carp can only ever measure the winds; scarecrows are only and always fixed. Scarecrows, lawn jockeys, whirligigs, garden angels, and garden gnomes—these totems can only give the illusion that home is secure. From carrion birds and crows, dust devils and pit vipers. From stupidity and rikutsuppoi and accidents and mistakes. What the scarecrow said was: *In the end, we are all only Attenders here; but we can try to be ready, and hope to be Convinced.*

"Oh boy," young Tufteller whispered, frowning at the storm-wracked scarecrow to whom he had given that hopeful token but who he thought had not lived up to her end of the bargain. The weight of Fujita's hand on his raw shoulder hurt him. He liked it, though, so he distracted himself by counting the upended stalks and collapsed tree boughs. Even Garvin, at nine years old, knew it would be a break-even second harvest at best. "It looks like we've been bombed. What'll we do? Can you save it?"

"I don't know," Fujita said, frowning and shaking his head. "I don't think so." Though angry with himself for what he hadn't anticipated, he knew it couldn't be helped. Rattling the change in his pocket made him think back to their coin in the scarecrow, but he was looking backward less and less in those days. And though he wasn't Convinced, he still had faith: On the order of fixing things, a nurse, a seamstress, and a young artist were about the best allies one could hope for. "Pal, we can only learn from our mistakes and correct them. We'll just have to be more ready," the plant man said. "Next year."

Author's Note

The better historical novelists, like the better historians, have always understood that representing history is a dodgy business founded more upon selection and creation than on objective reportage. The best kinds of these two professionals also share a belief that what makes their historical quilts important is that they can be made useful today and tomorrow. This is the approach I have tried to emulate in this book, which seeks to authoritatively represent no fixed body of people or circumstances except for those contained within it. I plead the standard Hollywood disclaimer: All similarity to persons living or dead is coincidental—except where it's strictly purposeful.

So far as it's possible, I try to represent honestly the hallmark acts that directly affected these characters' lives, and most often I present these in chronological order. A novelist also must occasionally take license with dates and events; and inevitably, necessarily, one must omit more information than one can include. This is also true in writing author's notes. While I cannot begin to list all of the many sources to which I am indebted, I can recommend a few basic resources to anyone wishing to gain a fuller understanding of the histories of Japanese Americans. *Japanese American History: An A-to-Z Reference from 1868 to the Present,* edited by Brian Niiya (Japanese American National Museum/Facts on File), provides clear, quick reference to many key ideas, moments, and players in this history. Michi Weglyn's *Years of Infamy* is among the most influential works on internment history; Peter Irons's *Justice at War* provides a clear overview of the legal aspects of wartime internment of civilians; for more extensive treatments of Japanese-American history, the works of Ronald Takaki, Roger Daniels, Myron Ichioka, and Gary Okihiro are seminal.

pg. 48 Concentration Camps/Internment Camps: With the exception of reparation paid to former internees, the reference to concentration camps has been perhaps the most hotly debated issue related to the internment. Brian Niiya, editor of *Japanese American History,* has made the compelling argument that only those detention camps run by the Justice Department are properly considered internment camps. Niiya suggests that those camps run by the War Relocation Authority for incarcerating most Nikkei are most accurately described as concentration camps—as indeed they were considered and explicitly referred to by many of their earliest advocates and architects. The world's subsequent horrific associations with the term "concentration camp," as used to describe those in Nazi Germany notwithstanding, official media accounts and government literature of the period acknowledged that the WRA camps were conceptualized as concentration camps. That said, I most often use here the term "internment camp," as is consistent with what I have found to be the preference among Nisei I've interviewed.

pg. 63 Gentleman's Agreement: In an effort to pacify both the Japanese government and the California anti-Japanese movement, the U.S. government forged the Gentleman's Agreement (between 1907 and 1908), restricting immigration to Japanese who had been to America and were returning, and to those immigrants' immediate relatives. A loophole allowed the immigration of picture brides, resulting in increasing numbers of Nisei births and the domestication of what had previously been a primarily bachelor society. The change did not last long. With renewed exclusionist pressure, the Japanese government stopped issuing passports to picture brides in 1920. One authority estimates that 24,000 single Issei men remained in America with no prospects for ever building a family.

pg. 68 and throughout Nikkei: I use here the relatively recent term Nikkei in a particular sense to mean a person of Japanese ancestry living outside of Japan, especially in America. While its most popular use refers to American-born citizens, i.e., Nisei, Sansei, and later descendants of Issei pioneers, it also represents here any Issei who might become spiritually, emotionally, or culturally tied to this country, whether willingly or not, permanently or not, legally prohibited or not.

Thus, my use of a few context-sensitive terms in describing my characters are founded on one basic assumption: that there is a distinction to be made between Japanese and people of Japanese ancestry in America. Japanese are in Japan; "American Japanese" are Japanese citizens living in America; and Japanese Americans are a type of born, naturalized, or spiritual American, no matter where they are, and however great or small their contribution to America's daily life. I've altered my use of this last term from its common usage during the war, opting to use the current standard, Japanese American, wherein Japanese modifies American—an American possessing a quality related to Japaneseness, among other qualities. I use a hyphen only to create a compound adjective; for example, "He's a Japanese-American doctor." During the war, Japanese Americans and others regularly hyphenated the term rendering it a compound noun—a person other than an American, a third thing—in keeping with the popular perception of that group by other Americans and, unfortunately, by themselves.

Amid today's purported tyranny of so-called political correctness, my concern is with linguistic correctness—it is with accuracy—and this is the style standard I've applied to this novel. Of course, mere grammar does not comprise conscience, tolerance, equality, understanding, etc., today any more than it did in WWII.

Yesterday and today, use of the term "Japanese" by Japanese

Americans has been a convenient, shorthand way of differentiating themselves racially or culturally in America (as opposed to, say, Korean Americans); unfortunately, the term also continues to be used to racially discriminate against people of Japanese ancestry by anyone who doesn't care for Japanese (cars, people, etc.). The term is more unfortunate when used racially, violently, and inaccurately—for example, when used as the rationale for the beating death of Chinese American Michigander Vincent Chin by laid-off auto workers in 1982. When possible, I use Nikkei.

pg. 69 **Agriculture:** The relative success of Nikkei farmers in California is reported to fall between 10 and 40 percent of the state's total crop production at different times, and depending upon the reference source. Whether 10 percent or 40 percent, the admiration and resentment this conspicuous achievement earned the early California Nikkei was considerable.

pg. 69 **California Anti-Japanese Movement:** The history of organized, anti-Asian efforts in California have been documented by many scholars, and notably by Roger Daniels in the *Politics of Prejudice* (Berkeley, Calif.: University of California Press, 1977). Core to the anti-Japanese movement and influential in promoting the 1920 Land Law was the Japanese Exclusion League of California, whose roster included representatives of such organizations as the American Legion, the Native Sons and Daughters of the Golden West, and the American Federation of Labor.

pg. 73 **Alien Land Laws:** Collective name for a series of ever-tightening state and federal laws passed around the turn of the twentieth century that sought to limit immigrant rights to naturalization and to forbid any alien ineligible to citizenship from owning—and then leasing—land. Though nonspecific in their wording, these laws essentially applied only to Asian immigrants. These efforts were also bolstered by restrictive measures on the federal level such as the Gentleman's Agreement (1907–8), the Supreme Court's Ozawa case ruling (1922), the U.S. Immigration and Naturalization Act (the Asian Exclusion Act of 1924), and others.

pg. 170 **Herbert and Madeline Nicholson:** The real-life Nicholsons are local legends and heroes among many western

Nikkei. As a friend and occasional minister to the Japanese Union Church, the real Herbert, like the Herbert in this book, repeatedly proved a model of integrity, self-sacrifice, and friendship to the evacuees. Surviving Nisei recall him driving numerous cross-desert trips to various internment camps during the war, carrying their valuables out of storage, news from the outside world, and strong religious faith. Nicholson's exhortations to faith were not empty gestures; he also proved a man of action, whether personally arguing the Nikkei's case to military officials or being jailed in a small and small-minded Colorado town as a "spy" while on errands to friends in camp. Written accounts of the Nicholsons' admirable lives and works include *Treasure in Earthen Vessels* (Whittier, Calif.: Penn Lithographics, 1974) and *Valiant Odyssey: Herbert Nicholson In and Out of America's Concentration Camps,* by Michi Weglyn and Betty E. Mitson (Upland, Calif.: Brunk's, 1978).

pg. 244 **Eleanor Roosevelt:** "She could tell her husband a thing or two." She had, often. According to Roosevelt biographer Doris Kearns Goodwin in her Pulitzer Prize–winning *No Ordinary Time* (New York: Simon & Schuster, 1994), Mrs. Roosevelt from the beginning had argued against the evacuation, to no avail. She later visited Gila River at the request of her husband, but her subsequent report fell on deaf ears.

pg. 395 **Skin Grafts:** The method of obtaining skin grafts such as the one harvested from Mr. Fujita may be considerably less painful—or even painless—to a donor today. Harvesting from corpse donors is now a common method of procuring skin grafts (with improved methods of storage and preservation). Today, skin can also be grown in laboratories from a few cells on special media. However, the methods Dr. Small chose have not disappeared. Grafts may still be harvested from a patient or a donor using a freehand knife or a dermatome (albeit a more precise, electric version).

pg. 421 **The Atomic Bomb:** The precise measurements of the mushroom cloud arising from Little Boy's explosion seems to be a matter of dispute among historians. One source reported it to be 18,000 meters and another at 40,000 feet. (The Empire State Building is 1,250 feet tall; the mushroom cloud would have stood as high as 47 or 32 such buildings piled one atop the other.) Similarly, estimates of the carnage and later attributable deaths vary wildly. As I wrote this note in August 1995, the Hiroshima bombing's golden anniversary, I saw or heard nostalgic news reports on TV, radio, and in print estimating the toll to lie between 80,000 and 300,000. Well, what's 220,000 people, give or take?

pg. 430 The letter that accompanied the reparation payment—the one that Fujita unfortunately never lived to see—is printed on crisp, white half-sheet stationery. Controversial from the start, the movement for redress is considered to have its roots in a 1970 conference proposal by Edison Uno; through the work of several committees and individuals, the movement continued growing through a number of presidential administrations until culminating in a one-time $20,000 payment and an apology letter such as this one sent to my grandparents. It's not every day one gets a personal note from the president and with such a limited-target mailing, it is worth recording here for posterity.

THE WHITE HOUSE
WASHINGTON

A monetary sum and words alone cannot restore lost years or erase painful memories; neither can they fully convey our Nation's resolve to rectify injustice and to uphold the rights of individuals. We can never fully right the wrongs of the past. But we can take a clear stand for justice and recognize that serious injustices were done to Japanese Americans during World War II.

In enacting a law calling for restitution and offering a sincere apology, your fellow Americans have, in a very real sense, renewed their traditional commitment to the ideals of freedom, equality, and justice. You and your family have our best wishes for the future.

Sincerely,

GEORGE BUSH
PRESIDENT OF THE UNITED STATES

OCTOBER 1990

BUTTE CAMP NO. 2

Pima Butte

Hospital

Staff

Fluorine Filter Plant

Motor Pool

Lumber Yard

Transportation and Engineering

73

74

ADMIN

72

REC

ADMIN

WHSE

WHSE

WHSE

61

62

Church

Internal Security

60

Church

Store

Newspaper

Road to Canal Camp No. 1 4 Miles

Amphitheater

Sacaton Butte

Honor Roll Monument

Water Tower

Fire House

Sumo REC

Community Center

REC

Library

Judo

H.S.

Civic

School

REC

REC

REC

Baseball Field

INTERNMENT AND POW CAMPS

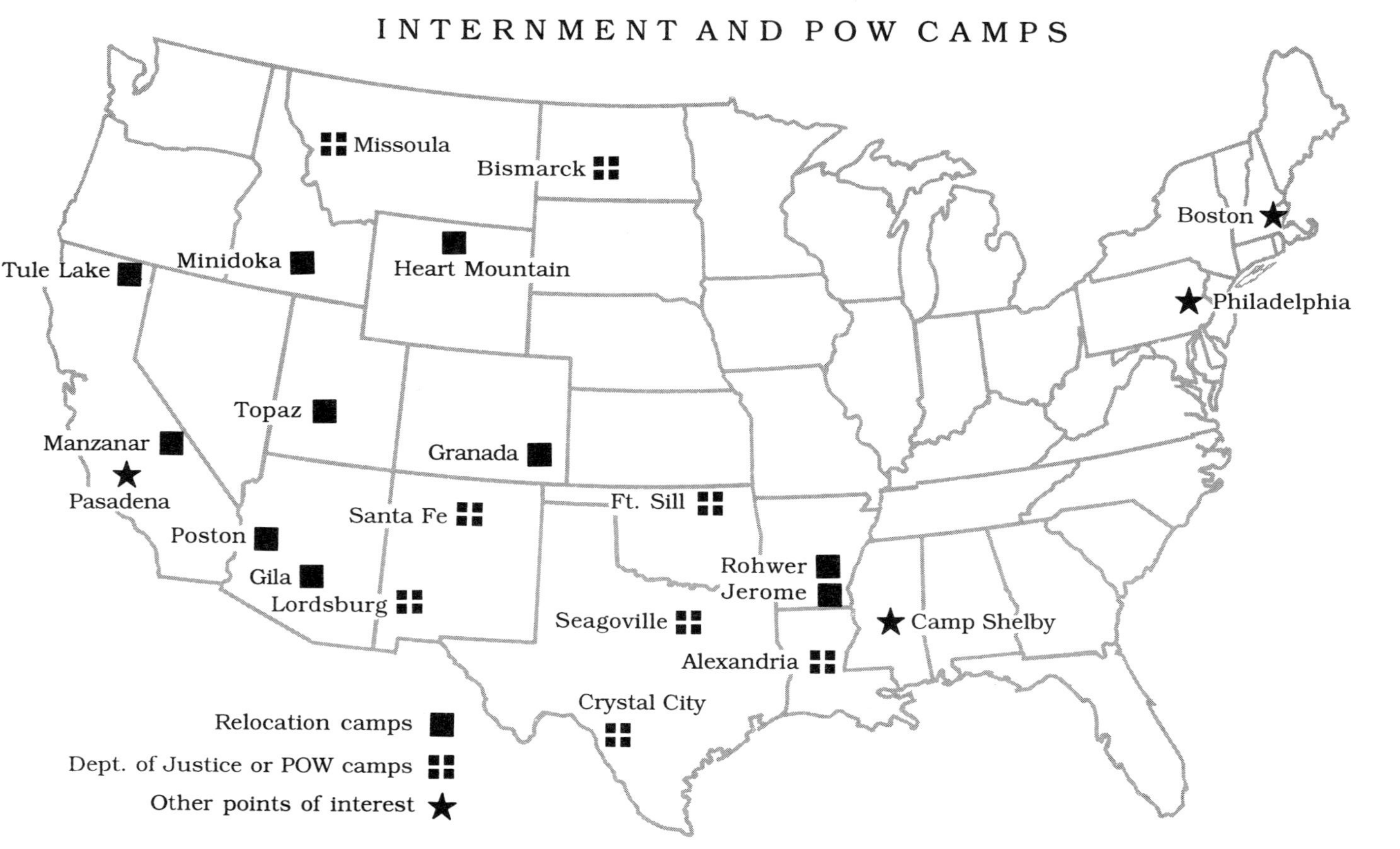

Glossary of Terms

Bakatare: Forcefully derogatory term, approximately, "Blithering idiot"

Gakuen: Japanese language school

Girí: Refers to contractual or moral obligations as a result of accepting favors—goods, services, etc.—though not between parents and children.

Goh: Strategy board game

Hakujin: "White person"

Hapa: Person with one Nikkei parent and one non-Nikkei parent, originally from the term hapa haole (half-white), once a pejorative term in Hawaiian pidgin

Hashi: Chopsticks

Inu: Literally, "dog." An outdated, context-sensitive term, *inu* metaphorically described those thought to be traitors or informants against supposedly suspicious individuals in the Nikkei community; later it referred to those perceived to be collaborators with internment camp authorities. Some observers—ignorant of the context of its wartime use—have incorrectly assumed it to mean "traitor to the Japanese emperor"; more precisely, *inu* carries connotations similar to those of "Uncle Tom" in the African-American community, and suspected camp inu were frequently at risk of violent assaults.

Issei: Literally, "the first": designation for immigrants to America—significantly, the first American generation, despite longstanding prohibitions on their naturalization

Koya: Hut

Manju: Japanese confection, often festively colored, often made of sweet rice or a sweet bean paste—doughy and heavy

Mochi: Cakes made of pounded rice

Nihonmachi: "Japan Town" name of Little Tokyo area

Nikkei: Person of Japanese ancestry

Nisei: Literally, "second": designation for the American citizens born to Issei parents

Nojo: Farm

(O)baasan: Grandmother (also, obaachan)

Ohayo: "Grand morning"

Ojiisan: Grandfather

Ōn: Refers to profound social, psychological, and emotional debts incurred from receiving a favor or gift of overwhelming proportion, so that one can never fully repay it—i.e., one receives *ōn* from one's parents, who bestow the gift of life.

Sansei: Literally, "third": children of Nisei

Seimei: Life

Sensei: Teacher

Shashin-kekkon: "picture marriage"

Shikata ga nai: "It cannot be helped" or "It must be done."

Sumimasen: "I'm sorry"; with *yurushite kudasai,* "Please forgive me."

Zurui: Sly, sneaky